Pra... the Bobby Girls se...

'Filled with richly drawn characters that leap from the page, and a plot that's so well researched and well written you will believe you are in the thick of wartime policing, *The Bobby Girls* is a must-read for all saga fans'

Fiona Ford, bestselling author of *Christmas at Liberty's*

'A lot of research has gone into this book and it's all the richer and more readable for it. An exciting new voice in women's fiction'

Kate Thompson, bestselling author of *Secrets of the Singer Girls*

'Johanna Bell has hit the jackpot with this striking WW1 story. . . a heartening central message conveyed with verve and empathy'

Jenny Holmes, author of *The Spitfire Girls*

'Written with warmth and compassion, *The Bobby Girls* gives fascinating insights into the lives of three courageous young women'

Margaret Kaine, RNA award-winning author of *Ring of Clay*

'As a former Special Constable, I love Johanna Bell from the bottom of my heart for giving a voice to the women who first made a way for me and countless others like me – to work as real police officers in the service of our communities. In their own small way, the first Bobby Girls changed the world for women everywhere'

Penny Thorpe, bestselling author of *The Quality Street Girls*

'A well-researched and interesting story giving a great insight into early women's policing'

Anna Jacobs, bestselling author of the Ellindale series

'A lovely story! The author has researched the era and the theme very well. The characters stood out on the page and through their eyes you are transported back to a different age'

AnneMarie Brear, author of *Beneath a Stormy Sky*

'I really did enjoy *The Bobby Girls*. It has a lovely warm feeling about it and ... Maureen Le... ... *the Dark*

Johanna Bell cut her teeth on local newspapers in Essex, eventually branching into magazine journalism with stints as a features writer and then commissioning editor at *Full House* magazine. She now has more than sixteen years' experience in print media. Her freelance life has seen her working on juicy real-life stories for the women's weekly magazine market, as well as hard-hitting news stories for national newspapers and prepping her case studies for TV interviews. When she's not writing, Johanna can be found walking her dog with her husband or playing with her two daughters.

To hear more from Johanna, follow her on Twitter @JoBellAuthor and on Facebook /johannabellauthor.

The Bobby Girls' War

Book Four in the Bobby Girls series

JOHANNA BELL

HODDER

First published in Great Britain in 2021 by Hodder & Stoughton
An Hachette UK company

1

A CIP catalogue record for this title is available from the British Library

Paperback ISBN 978 1 529 33425 8
eBook ISBN 978 1 529 33427 2

Typeset in Plantin Light by Palimpsest Book Production Limited,
Falkirk, Stirlingshire

Printed and bound in Great Britain by Clays Ltd, Elcograf S.p.A.

Hodder & Stoughton policy is to use papers that are natural, renewable
and recyclable products and made from wood grown in sustainable forests.
The logging and manufacturing processes are expected to conform to the
environmental regulations of the country of origin.

Hodder & Stoughton Ltd
Carmelite House
50 Victoria Embankment
London EC4Y 0DZ

www.hodder.co.uk

To Joan and Derrick Baker – and to Bobegon,
where all this started.

Dear reader,

First of all, I would like to apologise for making you wait a little longer than planned for *The Bobby Girls' War* – the fourth in my Bobby Girls series.

I wrote book three during the first lockdown and despite having a lively toddler at home with me 24/7 I seemed to steam through it. Everything felt a little tougher when we were locked down again, and I had a newborn and a relocation with my family to contend with, too, meaning my Bobby girls had to be put on hold. But delving back in to writing Poppy's story sparked me back into life and I was soon lost in all the fascinating research around Gretna and enjoying building storylines around what happened there. Once again, reading and writing about the incredible men and women who helped get our country through the First World War gave me a sense of perspective.

I hope what I created brings you a sense of escapism, and I really hope you enjoy my latest Bobby Girls book.

Johanna Bell, August 2021

The Bobby Girls' War

I

Brunswick Square Gardens, Holborn, London, September 1916

Walking through the gardens in the early autumn sunshine, Poppy Davis rubbed her hands together to warm them up. The mornings were getting chillier despite the sun and she wasn't looking forward to patrolling London's streets through another tough winter. As soon as the thought entered her head, she chastised herself. Poppy's mind quickly became filled with images of brave British troops on the front line suffering through icy cold conditions while fighting to stay alive and protect everyone at home – including herself. At least she had a cosy room to return to after her shift, and a kitchen where she could rustle up a tasty, comforting stew – even if she did share the cooking space with twenty policemen. Not that any of them ever seemed to bother making anything.

'Should we go and see if Sara's around?' Maggie asked as they approached the Foundling Hospital.

'Good idea,' Poppy replied. 'They'll be doing breakfast for the little ones about now so she should be free to talk.' The pair had just moved on a group of young boys they had caught throwing stones at cars, and Poppy quite fancied a hot cup of tea and the company of some well-behaved children.

Poppy had become firm friends with Maggie Smyth through their work for the Women's Police Service, or WPS, and they had been patrolling their Holborn patch together as a pair for the last six months. They often checked in with the staff at the Foundling Hospital to see if they'd heard about any young-sters they could help. The home for abandoned children and babies was always over capacity, and it broke Poppy's heart to think of youngsters in need being turned away.

As Poppy and Maggie approached the Foundling Hospital's main entrance, the door flew open and Sara bustled out.

'What's the rush?' Maggie giggled as Sara bounded past. She was so distracted that she hadn't even noticed the pair of them, despite their striking WPS uniforms and riding-style hats.

'Oh! Goodness!' Sara cried as she spun around, flustered. She tucked her wayward blonde hair behind her ears and rubbed her right temple. 'I was just on my way to the police station.'

'Well, here we are.' Poppy smiled. 'How can we help?'

'Yes, I couldn't remember when you were next on patrol . . .' Sara mused, rubbing her left temple.

'Why don't you give us the note?' Poppy asked with a friendly but firm tone, gesturing at the scrap of paper crum-pled up in Sara's hand. She was fond of Sara, but she found her to be rather scatty and prone to rambling on if she wasn't encouraged to get to the point quickly enough. Poppy wasn't quite sure how Sara managed to keep things in order at the Foundling, but it always seemed as if everything was under control when they visited.

'Yes, of course,' Sara replied, snapping to attention and handing over the scribbled note.

Baby left on doorstep. Is there space at Annie's?

Let me know,

Sara

Their friend and colleague Annie Beckett had paused her life on the beat with them to focus on setting up a WPS baby home, after discovering that she was pregnant last Christmas. She'd been almost six months gone when she'd realised she was in the family way. Having lost her fiancé in the War, she'd thrown herself into her police work, becoming embroiled in a secret mission to bring down a trafficking ring. She'd been so caught up in exposing the culprits and their well-known clients, as well in as her own grief, that she'd missed all the signs that she was pregnant with her late fiancé's baby. Now, her daughter, Charlotte, was six months old.

A WPS benefactor named Lady Wright had allowed Annie to use her home in Hampstead to temporarily house vulnerable pregnant women and new mothers, as well as abandoned babies, until a permanent building could be found. But when Lady Wright had died unexpectedly a few months later, she had left her home to the WPS in her will and Annie now had it up and running as a permanent retreat. With the Foundling Hospital frequently over-capacity, it had been a relief for Poppy and Maggie to finally have a safe place to send vulnerable pregnant women with nowhere else to go, as well as abandoned illegitimate babies they came across during their police work.

When Poppy had been sent to join Annie and Maggie on their London beat for the WPS the previous May, the three of them had quickly bonded. Poppy had been worried at first: both girls were in their early twenties, making them a good ten years younger than she was. Furthermore, she had replaced their colleague Irene Wilson – even moving into her old bedroom in their shared flat. It was immediately obvious to Poppy how close the three girls had been, before Irene had been transferred to a post in Grantham. They had even nicknamed themselves the Bobby Girls. Poppy had been anxious about fitting in with two women so much younger than herself, but they had welcomed her with open arms and, before she knew it, they had even started classing her as a fellow Bobby Girl. She had unintentionally slipped into a sort of mother-figure role with them both, but it seemed to work for everybody.

'Poor thing.' Poppy sighed after reading Sara's message. 'Was there a note or anything from the mother? Do you know if she's okay?' As hard as it was for her to accept women could give up their children in this way, Poppy knew the baby's mother must have been in a desperate fix to take such action. They had come across women who had been so anxious to keep their illegitimate babies secret they had lived in agony in corsets for the last few months of their pregnancy before scurrying off to a back alley to give birth away from prying eyes – and ears. One unfortunate soul had lost so much blood during the labour that she'd almost died. She would have done if Poppy and Maggie hadn't reached her in time.

'Nothing,' Sara replied. 'The little blighter didn't even have a blanket, but thankfully whoever left him knocked on the door before scarpering, so he wasn't out in the cold for very long. He's just the loveliest little thing.'

'We'll come and collect him at lunchtime when our shift is over and we'll take him to Annie,' Maggie offered. Poppy's heart skipped a beat. She was always glad of an excuse to drop into the baby home. She loved babies, but Charlotte had stolen her heart the very moment she had met her as a wrinkled, helpless little bundle of flesh, just hours after her birth.

Poppy had always longed to have a baby of her own, but since losing her husband John on the front line she had accepted it would never happen for her. At thirty-five, she was realistic about the fact that if the time ever came when she was ready to move on from John then it would surely be too late for her to start a family. Poppy was so close to

Annie that she felt like Charlotte was related to her. The same went for Maggie. The two of them were like extra aunties to the tot, who already had Annie's three sisters on hand to look out for her. But whenever Poppy spent time with Charlotte, her joy was tinged with sadness at the reminder that she would never have a daughter of her own.

Seeing how busy Sara was, Poppy and Maggie decided not to bother her for a cup of tea and continued on with their patrol. Maggie made her way to King's Cross Station while Poppy carried on patrolling the nearby gardens. King's Cross had become a regular spot on their beat following Annie's discovery that the leaders of the trafficking gang she had been investigating had been using it as a prime location to pick up their victims. The men had preyed on refugees fresh off the trains into London and so Poppy and Maggie had made sure they regularly met such trains once they'd started patrolling as a pair. They then escorted the women and children to the staff waiting to take them to dispersal centres before anyone could intercept them and coax them away.

Maggie had taken over the charge against the slavery ring on her own in recent months. It was such a big, time-consuming task that the girls found if they dedicated as much time to it as they needed to, in order to save as many women as possible, then the other areas on their patch became neglected. It was simply impossible for them to cover everything. So, for the last few months, Maggie had been spending a lot of time watching over the refugees at King's Cross on her own while Poppy patrolled the rest of their patch on the lookout for prostitutes and drunken soldiers to help or move on.

Poppy was happy with the set-up, but she was starting to feel as though she might enjoy a bit more of a challenge. Annie had the baby home to focus on and Maggie was pouring most of her energy into protecting refugees. Poppy was content patrolling solo when Maggie was at the train station, and she knew she'd helped a lot of women. The fact that prostitution was dwindling in the area was testament to what a good job she and her fellow Bobby Girls had done. But because of that, she couldn't help but feel in need of a bigger task. She had always enjoyed pushing herself to achieve, and life in Holborn was beginning to feel a little repetitive now things were relatively under control.

Back in April, when the WPS headquarters had been placed at the disposal of the Ministry of Munitions and the organisation had agreed to provide policewomen to patrol at factories and munitions areas, Poppy and Maggie had both been terrified at the prospect of being separated. But their sub-commandant Frosty – affectionately nicknamed by Maggie for her apparent icy demeanour – had recognised how well they were working together as a pair in Holborn and kept them where they were. But the more Poppy heard about the recruits sent to patrol at the munitions factories popping up all over the country, the more her feet itched to get involved herself.

'You'll be pleased to know you'll be seeing the back of me soon enough,' a voice bellowed out as Poppy walked through St Andrew's Gardens. Poppy recognised the voice immediately. It was Alice, a prostitute she had come to develop a love-hate relationship with over the last year. Alice was rough around the edges and she was forever giving Poppy and Maggie the runaround to try and get away with having illicit liaisons with soldiers from the nearby Gray's Inn Barracks. She had even dressed two of them up as women to smuggle them past the Bobby Girls, back when Annie had been patrolling with them. But despite Alice's determination to continue selling herself and her refusal to even try and find some honest work, she had a heart of gold and Poppy had a real soft spot for her.

'Oh, I would never be pleased to see the back of you,' Poppy called back caustically as she headed in Alice's direction with a slight spring in her step. Alice was standing at the entrance to the gardens with her mousey, scraggly hair blowing in the wind and her tatty green shawl wrapped tight around her body. Poppy knew exactly what she was doing there: she was waiting for a soldier to walk past who she could talk into dipping into a nearby alley with her for some 'fun' in exchange for a bit of money or even a few drinks in a local pub. The fact she had called Poppy over anyway demonstrated how brazen Alice was. Poppy laughed to herself. The conversation would be the same as always – Alice would be a little cheeky and then Poppy would move her on. It had become like a ritual they had to go through to get through every patrol.

'I'm off to do munitions work,' Alice boasted proudly. Poppy couldn't help but look shocked.

'You? A munitionette?' she asked, failing to hide the surprise in her voice. She immediately scolded herself for speaking before thinking. Thankfully, Alice wasn't one to easily take offence.

'I know, I know!' she laughed once Poppy was standing next to her. 'You girls have been trying to get me off the street for about a year now. Well, you've finally succeeded. Actually, not you, but my sister. She's been working at Woolwich Arsenal the last few months and her latest letter convinced me to join her. I might have to put up with looking a little yellow but there's some lovely-looking foremen there, according to her.' Poppy had to laugh. Of course the pull towards a better life had involved men. But she was happy for Alice. Prostitution was no way to make a living. Munitions work might have been highly dangerous, but at least the women were making an honest living and they were helping Britain win the war.

'I'm proud of you.' Poppy smiled. 'But I can't say I'll miss our daily run-ins,' she added with a hint of sarcasm. 'When are you off?'

'My train is booked for this evening,' Alice replied happily.

'What are you doing here, then? You best get home and pack!' Poppy exclaimed.

'I wanted to say goodbye to you, didn't I?' Alice said coyly while staring down at the ground.

'You silly so-and-so.' Poppy laughed, but she couldn't help but feel touched by the gesture. She suddenly felt bad for assuming Alice had been on the lookout for business. 'Now you've seen me you can go and get ready,' she added gently.

'I also . . . erm . . . I wanted to say goodbye to Reggie, too,' Alice admitted quietly. Reggie was a soldier Poppy had caught in a compromising position with Alice on more than one occasion. He appeared to have become a regular customer of hers since arriving at Gray's Inn. Poppy couldn't stop herself from rolling her eyes – a trait she had picked up from Maggie. It was just like Alice to flatter her to try and distract her from what she was really up to. She felt foolish for having fallen for it, but she had to admire Alice for keeping at it right until the end. Poppy took a quick look around to make sure the coast was clear.

'I'll turn a blind eye, seeing as this will be your last chance to see him.' Alice's face crinkled into a cheeky grin. 'But if you get caught at it then you must promise to keep my name out of it,' Poppy warned her. She would get into serious trouble with the WPS if she was caught letting a prostitute off like this, but she was often softer on the women of the night than her training had taught her to be. She couldn't bring herself to take such a hard line with them, as she understood how desperate they must be to be selling them-selves on the street. No one wanted to do it; they simply had to in order to survive.

'I swear on my mother's life,' Alice said, making the sign of the cross over her chest. Poppy rolled her eyes again; she knew from their previous conversations that Alice's mother was already dead.

'I'll miss you, Alice. It'll certainly be quiet without you,' Poppy called back as she walked off across the gardens. And as she pondered Alice's new life in munitions, she couldn't help but feel jealous of the woman's fresh, exciting start.

2

Poppy met Maggie back at Hunter Street Police Station. They changed out of their uniforms in the cupboard-sized room they had been allocated when they'd first arrived with Annie. The group had received a mixed reaction from the male police officers when they'd originally been stationed in Holborn. They had been the first set of WPS recruits to patrol in the area and many of the men had been convinced they would be more of a burden than a help to them.

Poppy had managed to get a few of the men onside with her cooking. She regularly made big portions of hearty meals in the communal kitchen at the police accommodation and left a note inviting officers to help themselves. Since Annie had single-handedly brought down the trafficking ring, however, the girls had noticed more policemen were showing them a quiet respect instead of simply sneering at them on sight. And, of course, their hard work on the streets had also shown their new colleagues they were capable of a lot more than had been assumed.

The station's chief constable – Chief Constable Green – had been one of the biggest clients of the gang running the slavery ring, so Annie's work had sent shockwaves through the station. Poppy had been worried about a backlash, but it turned out many of the officers had been suspicious of their boss and his constant eagerness to protect certain high-profile characters from prosecution of any kind. None of them had been able to collar him like Annie had, so they'd had no choice but to be impressed by her police work.

Chief Constable Green was rotting in prison now and his replacement, Chief Constable Jackson, was a big hit with everyone. He was a larger-than-life character who always had a smile on his face and a way of keeping everyone in line without having to get too strict. He had been nothing but friendly and accepting of Poppy and Maggie since his arrival, which had been a big relief to them both after spending so long having to prove themselves to their male colleagues.

The girls were just about to leave the station to go and pick up the newborn baby from the Foundling Hospital when Sergeant Turner called out to them from along the corridor. They stopped at the entrance and waited for him to catch them up. Sergeant Turner had always been an ally of the girls. They had helped him gather up the injured following a zeppelin raid during one of their very first Holborn patrols and it had been enough to immediately prove their worth to him.

'I've just had your boss on the blower,' he said.

'Frosty?' Maggie asked. Sergeant Turner looked confused.

'She means Sub-Commandant Frost,' Poppy offered, feeling embarrassed. She loved Maggie but little things like that really showed up the age difference between them. Poppy prided herself on her professionalism and although she was happy to go along with the 'Frosty' nickname when she was talking with her friends, she would never use it in front of other officers.

'Yes, that's right.' Sergeant Turner smiled. 'She wants to see you first thing in the morning.' Poppy's heart skipped a beat. Maybe they were going to be transferred to another patch.

'Thank you,' she replied. 'Does Chief Constable Jackson know we'll be coming in late?'

'Oh, she only wants to see you,' Sergeant Turner explained, holding eye contact with Poppy.

'Me? On my own?' she whispered, her excitement suddenly replaced by panic. 'But . . . but . . . I wonder what she wants? Did she say?'

'No, sorry. Just that she wanted to speak to Constable Davis and that you should make sure you're prompt as she's a busy woman.' He paused, looking serious. 'She's a little scary, ain't she?' he suddenly added with a cheeky grin. 'She made me nervous and she's not even my boss!' He laughed. Maggie giggled along with him, but Poppy couldn't join in the joke. She was too busy fretting about how much trouble she was in. Had somebody seen her allowing Alice to continue touting for business? Surely word couldn't have reached headquarters that fast? But why else would Frosty want to see her on her own?

'That's why we call her Frosty,' Maggie explained. 'She comes across cold as ice, but the irony is that she's actually very caring and kind under her tough exterior. Isn't that right?'

'Erm, yes. Yes, she's firm but fair,' Poppy muttered, hoping their superior would be just that with her in the morning. After bidding farewell to Sergeant Turner, Poppy had to confide in Maggie about her fears. She felt so foolish for breaking the rules for Alice. And now her career could be over because of it.

'I really don't think that can be it,' Maggie assured her after she'd gone over what had happened in the gardens. 'If anybody saw you then they wouldn't have been able to tell Frosty that fast.'

'That's what I thought.' Poppy sighed. 'But I just can't think of anything else I've done wrong.'

'Why does it have to be something bad? Stop putting yourself down. She probably just wants an update on how everything is going over here in Holborn. Or maybe she wants to praise you for doing such a good job.' Poppy smiled gratefully. Then she instantly felt bad for the thoughts she'd just had about Maggie being immature. Her younger friend was being a lot more logical than she was about this. But she still couldn't shake the feeling that something horrible was in store for her.

As soon as Poppy laid eyes on the abandoned baby at the Foundling Hospital, her fears disappeared. It was impossible to feel anxious about anything when dealing with something so fragile and precious. The little boy was beautiful. The innocence of tiny babies like him always made Poppy feel better about the world. He didn't know pain or fear yet, despite what he had already been through. And she knew that with Annie's help and nurturing he would feel as loved as he should have felt from the moment he was born.

'We've called him Joseph,' Sara said as she handed over the Moses basket. 'Our wet nurse has been taken ill, so we've been giving him formula this morning. I assume Annie will be able to feed him, though?'

'Oh yes.' Poppy smiled. 'She's still feeding Charlotte and she's helped out with some of the newborns whose mothers had traumatic births and struggled to feed to begin with.'

'I thought you'd mentioned that. Please let me know how he gets on. I've rather taken to him in the short time he's been here.'

'Of course,' Poppy assured her. Peering into the Moses basket again, it was clear to see why Joseph had had such an effect on Sara. Poppy could have stared at him all day – but they had to get to Hampstead before he needed another feed.

Poppy was delighted when Annie greeted them at the baby home with Charlotte in her arms. The tot's big blue eyes instantly lit up when she saw her two 'aunts', and she treated them both to a huge grin and a gurgle.

'Someone's missed you both,' Annie said with a laugh as Charlotte bopped up and down in her arms in excitement. Poppy couldn't help but notice how tired her friend looked. She always thought life on patrol was hard going but whenever she saw Annie she found herself appreciating what she had. Sure, she was on her feet for up to fifteen hours a day, but at least she was able to enjoy time off, as rare as that was. Poor Annie was on the go day and night with little to no breaks. Not only was she looking after Charlotte, but she was responsible for all the mothers and babies at the home. A lot of the new mums were young and vulnerable, and turned up having no idea how to look after a child, so Annie – not far from being a child herself in Poppy's eyes – would end up mothering both mother and baby.

Frosty sent the occasional WPS recruit along to help out but no one ever stayed long as there was always somewhere else in need of policing. And front-line patrolling took priority as Frosty and the other women at the top of the organisation were desperate to show the police commissioner how good their recruits were at keeping order on the streets. They were hopeful that the more he saw, the more likely he was going to allow them to continue their work when the war was finally over.

'Golly, you look terrible!' Maggie exclaimed as Annie handed Charlotte over to Poppy and took the Moses basket.

'It's always good to see you,' Annie said light-heartedly. Thankfully both Annie and Poppy were used to Maggie's inability to stop herself from speaking the truth, no matter how brutal it might be. And the three of them were so close that they were able to say anything in front of each other, no matter how unforgiving. 'I was just going to put Charlotte down for her afternoon nap and try and get some sleep myself while everyone else here is quiet, but it looks like this little one might need feeding.' Joseph had started making tiny mewing noises.

The girls went through to the sitting room. Nothing had changed since Lady Wright's death and Poppy always felt like she was visiting a rich grandmother when she walked into the room and took in the grand, old-fashioned furniture. There was even a piano in the corner, which Poppy was certain hadn't been used for years. She often stared at it and imagined the lavish parties that had probably taken place at the house before the war, with guests crowded round the piano as it was played. She hoped those happy days would return but she was scared about how long it might take. As Annie nursed Joseph and Poppy rocked Charlotte to sleep in her arms, Maggie explained how Joseph had been abandoned at the Foundling Hospital.

'I don't know what I'll do when my milk dries up,' Annie sighed, staring down at Joseph happily suckling away at her breast. 'I can't see Frosty paying for a wet nurse, and there's no chance they'll agree to cover the cost of formula.'

'There's plenty of mothers working for the WPS,' Poppy said hopefully. 'I know Frosty prefers having as many of us out on the streets and in the factories as possible, but I'm sure they could come up with some sort of rota. And isn't there always somebody here who is managing to breastfeed?'

'There's two women here able to feed at the moment,' Annie explained. 'We'll have to take turns with Joseph as I'm already helping another woman who is finding it hard to keep her supply up. I'm sure we'll muddle through, and I'm not planning on stopping breastfeeding any time soon.'

'I wouldn't worry about your milk drying up, with all the extra feeding you do,' Maggie offered lightly. Annie laughed at the comment.

'I know.' She sighed. 'It's just always a worry when you can't think of an alternative. I see so many women who can't do it.' Poppy was in awe of her friend. She was devoting all her energy to helping these women and children at the same time as bringing up Charlotte all on her own. Poppy often wondered if having a part of Richard with her made things easier for her friend, or harder. She wasn't sure how she would have coped herself if she had been left to bring up John's baby all on her own.

Once Joseph was fed and sleeping contentedly, Annie placed him back in the Moses basket and Poppy laid Charlotte down in her cot to finish her nap.

'We'll leave you to get some rest. You might just be able to get some sleep before one of them wakes up or one of the residents needs you,' Poppy offered.

'Can you stay a while?' Annie asked. Taking in the dark circles under her eyes and her messy hair, which was normally styled into neat, mousey curls, Poppy found she couldn't say no. She had been looking forward to some rest herself this afternoon, but Annie was definitely more deserving.

'Of course,' she said with a smile. 'You go and get your head down and I'll stay here ready to help the first person or baby who needs it.' Annie pulled her in for a hug before disappearing out of the room. As Poppy listened to her footsteps on the stairs she turned to Maggie. 'Don't worry, I know you have plans,' she said. 'Off you go; I can look after things here.'

'Thank you, Poppy,' Maggie said gratefully before heading for the door herself. She had been talking about her impending afternoon tea with her mother for weeks now. Since her abusive father had thrown her out of the family home in Kensington, Maggie had been meeting her mother in secret. Sometimes she also got to see the family cook, Florence, who she had been extremely close to growing up. But it was always difficult to arrange without Mr Smyth finding out and so the clandestine get-togethers were not as regular as Maggie would have liked. Poppy couldn't have her missing one, especially when she knew Maggie had a letter from her brother, Eddie, on the front line to share with her mother. Eddie had stuck up for Maggie after the fallout, going so far as to punch their father during an argument about it, so he couldn't risk sending a letter directly to their mother at the family home.

It wasn't long before one of the residents joined Poppy in the sitting room and as she bustled off to the kitchen to prepare a pot of tea, she couldn't help but feel grateful that Annie had asked her to stay and help. Getting any rest back at the police accommodation would have been most unlikely, she concluded, as she would have spent the afternoon fretting about what Frosty wanted with her in the morning. No, this was a much better way to spend her evening. Keeping busy meant she didn't have time to think about what lay ahead.

3

Sitting outside Frosty's office at the WPS headquarters at St Stephen's House in Westminster, Poppy took a deep breath. She had ended up staying late at the baby home the previous day. She'd helped prepare dinner for the residents as well as putting Charlotte to bed while Annie fed Joseph. Poppy had been so tired when she'd made it back to her room that evening, she'd fallen asleep almost as soon as her head had hit the pillow, despite her fears she had been heading into a restless night.

She had, however, woken at the crack of dawn and been unable to get back to sleep as angst flooded her mind. In the end she'd ventured to the kitchen and cooked up a few pots of porridge for Maggie and the male officers in the other dorms to help themselves to over the course of the morning. She hadn't been able to stomach any herself. Even now her insides were in knots as she worried about how much trouble she was in. Despite Maggie's positive spin, she was convinced Frosty had bad news for her.

'You're early. What a good start.' Poppy hadn't even heard Frosty's door open let alone seen her standing at it looking down at her. Her sub-commandant had an imposing presence at the best of times, but now it was amplified given that Poppy was sitting down and Frosty standing. Despite the light-hearted nature of what she was saying, Frosty's voice carried its usual stern tone. But as Poppy's face broke into a nervous smile, the older woman's serious demeanour softened and, although she didn't smile herself, her face definitely relaxed.

'Good morning, sir,' Poppy said, getting to her feet and saluting her superior. The recruits had to call officers of a higher rank than themselves 'sir' even though they were all female, and they were also required to salute them on sight. Frosty acknowledged Poppy's actions with a slight nod and beckoned for her to enter her office. Sitting down on the chair opposite her boss, Poppy tried to guess from her facial expression what she was there for, but it was useless – this woman never gave anything away.

'There's no need to look so nervous. You're not in any trouble,' Frosty said evenly as she stared directly at Poppy with a serious look on her face. 'I brought you in to tell you about a special job I have lined up for you.' Poppy suddenly left the slouched position she had been sitting in and leaned her body up and forwards towards her sub-commandant, eager to hear more. Relief rushed through her body as she waited to find out what was in store for her.

'Because of your age, widow status and experience, you were the first person I thought of when this posting came up.' Poppy wasn't sure how to take that information, but she patiently waited to find out more. 'It's at a munitions factory.'

Poppy couldn't help but grin at the revelation. Was she going to be stationed at the Woolwich Arsenal? That would be just grand – she would already know Alice and she would be able to take on a fresh challenge without leaving her fellow Bobby Girls! She hoped Chief Constable Jackson would allow her to keep her room at the section house, although surely she'd be able to find accommodation nearer to the factory if not. Actually, maybe that would be better – it was likely to be long hours and the less time she spent travelling the better. Although, if she was at the section house then she was more likely to see Maggie in between shifts—

'You'll be starting work at Gretna next week.' Poppy's rambling, excited thoughts were cut dead by Frosty's interruption.

'Gretna?' Poppy whispered, her heart dropping. 'But that's . . . that's hundreds of miles away.' She'd never even been to Scotland. Frosty locked eyes with her and gave her the glare that meant she shouldn't be questioned. 'I just . . . I wasn't expecting to be transferred quite as far, that's all,' Poppy muttered, staring uncomfortably at her hands in her lap. She had spoken without thinking again, meaning she hadn't taken the time to work on an appropriate reaction. She was beginning to think she was spending so much time with Maggie that she had taken on that characteristic from her friend as well as the involuntary eye-rolls.

'As you know, we've started supplying recruits to munitions factories to help with the female workers. To begin with they asked us for one hundred at Gretna and we immediately obliged. But as the site is growing in size, we are having to increase our staff. The recruits already there are beginning to become spread thin and the need for more is becoming apparent.'

Poppy had heard the factory was one of the biggest in the country supplying munitions. Before the war there were only three national factories producing ammunition, but factories had been springing up all over the country to help get supplies out to soldiers on the front line.

'Construction is still on-going, but cordite production has been taking place since April. There are thousands of female workers to be kept in line, and some of them are complaining about sexual advances from the foremen and other male workers. The policemen who were allocated to the site were not very good at dealing with such issues, as you might well be able to imagine. They, along with the military police who had been stationed at the factory, were withdrawn when our recruits arrived.' Poppy nodded her head in understanding. One of the reasons the WPS was so successful in London and the other towns and cities where they patrolled was because they were better equipped to deal with such sensitive problems, as well as being more respected by prostitutes. 'There are also issues with the women workers bringing in contraband such as hairpins and cigarettes, and it's just not appropriate for the male staff to search them.'

It certainly sounded like the work would be different to what Poppy was used to. And she *had* been keen for a change. But Gretna was so far away. She was London born and bred, and had never travelled out of the capital. She and John had always planned on exploring the world together, but those dreams had been dashed when he'd been killed. Not only that, but if she moved all that way then there was no chance that she'd be able to see Maggie and Annie regularly. She had carved out what she felt was a pretty good life with them, even with Annie moving into the baby home. Of course, it wasn't perfect, as she had lost John and with him her dreams of becoming a mother, but she was finally feeling happy again. She knew Maggie and Annie looked up to her like a mother-figure because of her age and maturity; especially Maggie, given her strained family situation. And Annie herself had told her the way she had coped with John's death had been an inspiration to her when she'd lost Richard last year.

Poppy closed her eyes briefly and thought back to the moment Annie had asked her how she had managed to carry on after being widowed. The truth was that she hadn't been coping very well at all until she had been sent to live and patrol with the two of them. She found that being around her younger colleagues forced her to pull herself together to have a positive influence on them. She felt like she had to stay strong for the two of them. Would she be able to do it without them?

'We've applied for a grant from the Ministry of Munitions and we're hopeful you'll be paid for your efforts in time,' Frosty added.

Poppy pondered the news for a moment. Her WPS role thus far had been on a voluntary basis and she knew the organisation relied on donations to keep going. That's why many of the recruits were from wealthy backgrounds – it was imperative to be able to support yourself, or for your family to pay your way while you were working for nothing. Poppy had her widow's pension coming in, which she used to pay for her room at the section house – as well as Maggie's, seeing as the girl had been cut off financially by her horrible father. And she made sure Maggie always had enough to get by. They had never wanted for anything – they didn't have much free time when they could spend money, after all. Maggie's favourite thing to do on a rare afternoon off was to go for afternoon tea and they occasionally went to the pictures. Poppy didn't need more money. But then, perhaps she could start saving for her future – whatever that might look like.

'Many of the munitions workers are young girls,' Frosty explained now. 'They've left home to do their bit for the war, but they have no one to look up to or to keep them in line. There is no parental guidance. I've seen the influence you've had on your two colleagues and that's one of the reasons I want you to take the role.'

Poppy couldn't help but feel flattered. But at the same time, it reinforced her fear of leaving Maggie and Annie.

'As well as the problems they face from the foremen who are not used to being surrounded by women all day, there are a lot of temptations for young girls at Gretna,' Frosty continued. 'Their work is well paid and they're enjoying a financial freedom they've never experienced as well as having an array of leisure activities on offer to them. These young women having money of their own can drive them to feverish excitements or extravagances and, coupled with their loneliness and anxiety, often to drink. Not to mention the local boys turning their heads.' Poppy wasn't surprised at the news the opposite sex was one of the things distracting the workers. 'Some of them don't bother turning up to work, preferring the attractions of cafés, pubs and cinemas to the long, monotonous hours of factory work. Then, of course, there are the issues with contraband.'

Poppy panicked when she realised Frosty had finished her explanation and was expecting an answer from her. She knew she was expected to jump at the chance to get involved with such an exciting opportunity, and she had to admit that it did sound great. But the pull of Maggie and Annie was holding her back. Maybe she had come to rely on them just as much as she felt they were relying on her. On the other hand, it sounded as though she had the opportunity to help a great deal of young women at Gretna, and surely being called upon to give them guidance would give her the same feelings and drive to keep going? Then there was the danger. She had heard of explosions at munitions factories, and they were prime targets for air raids. Poppy found that she had too many thoughts racing around in her head to be able to think straight.

'Could I take some time to think about it?' Poppy asked cautiously. Frosty's expression hardened – something Poppy hadn't quite thought was possible. She clearly hadn't been expecting her to be reluctant to accept the position.

'You can have until the end of the day,' she replied sternly. As Poppy expressed her thanks and got up to leave, Frosty started talking again. 'This is a brilliant opportunity, Constable Davis. I must advise you to think very carefully before you give me your answer. This is active service with a vengeance, and a post of danger that calls for exceptional qualities of courage, self-control and endurance. Please bear in mind that I wouldn't put just anybody forward for this role.'

'I'll come back and give you my decision as soon as I've taken some time to think it through properly,' Poppy promised before leaving the office. She was so lost in her thoughts about it all that she couldn't remember any of her journey to Hunter Street Police Station when she arrived. Miller, one of the officers who had been friendly to the WPS girls since their arrival in Holborn, was at Reception.

'Maggie's just been back in to check if you'd arrived yet. She asked me to tell you she'll be at King's Cross until lunchtime,' he explained. Poppy's head started spinning. She hadn't even thought about what she was going to tell Maggie about her meeting with Frosty. She needed to decide what she was going to do before she told her friend anything. And she didn't want to lie to her. One thing the Bobby Girls prided themselves on was their honesty with each other – they knew from previous experience how bad things could turn when they kept secrets from each other.

'I don't think I can patrol today. I've had a terrible headache since I woke up,' Poppy said quietly. It wasn't a fib. Her head was in agony from her early morning and all the fretting she'd been doing.

'Sorry to hear that, Poppy,' Miller said, his voice full of concern. 'You get yourself to your dorm and I'll let the chief know you've taken ill. Do you want me to get Maggie to check in on you at lunchtime?'

'No, don't worry. I'm sure I just need some sleep,' she replied, grateful for his understanding. Poppy shuffled out of the station. When she reached her room she collapsed onto her bed fully clothed. There were so many thoughts rushing around in her head that she was struggling to get them all in order. To distract herself from it all, she got up and pulled her memory box out from the bottom of her tiny wardrobe.

Settling back on the bed, she opened the box and felt a sense of calm as soon as she saw John's handwriting staring up at her. All the letters her late husband had written to her during his short stint on the front line were in her memory box and she always turned to it when she needed to clear her mind.

Pulling one of the letters out at random, Poppy pressed the paper to her chest and closed her eyes. She felt instantly calm touching an object she knew John had also been in contact with. The fact he had been thinking about her when his hands had been on it made it feel even more special. After a few minutes thinking about John's handsome face, big smile and the way he chewed on his bottom lip when he wrote letters, Poppy opened the envelope and drank in his words.

Dearest Poppy,

I've had a bad day today, so I just had to write to you to take my mind off things. Whenever I think of you, my love, I'm transported to happier times and I find it hard to be angry about what we are all being forced to go through because of the Kaiser.

I don't want to upset you with details about my life in the trenches – you are far too precious to me to be tainted by such terrible images. So, instead, I will remind you of all the wonderful things we will do together when this wretched war is over! These are the thoughts that keep me going through all of this, after all.

We always wanted to travel, didn't we, Pops? Well, I'm sorry I had to do the first bit without you but at least France wasn't top of our list, hey!

In all seriousness, though, I wanted to experience all the exciting things that come with travelling to a new country for the first time with you. And I will still get to do that. France should be the top of our list now – and when we visit together it will be a journey full of love and fun, not like the journey I'm on right now. Once I'm back home with you we can pretend none of this ever happened and start our travels together. We'll finally make it out of London like we've always dreamed of, Pops. I saw some pretty places on the way here that I can't wait to explore with you.

Poppy smiled as she read on through John's descriptions of all the lovely-sounding French villages and his plans to treat her to the best coffee she had ever tasted. She remembered when she had first read this letter and the hope and excitement it had filled her with. Then she realised with a start that this had been the final letter her husband had written to her. How optimistic he had been feeling, and how full of love despite what he had been going through. As she reached the final paragraph, Poppy had to wipe away tears that had started slowly running down her cheeks.

Remember, Pops, that whatever happens to me, you mustn't forget to live. Take every opportunity that comes your way and live your life to the full. If I don't make it back to you, then you need to get out and see the world without me – FOR me. No matter how many bombs Fritz drops on it, London will always be there. So, make sure you take every chance you can to get out and see more of the world while you still have the chance. You have to promise me, Pops. If the worst happens then you mustn't waste your life grieving for me.

Forever yours, no matter what happens,
John

Tears were streaming down Poppy's face now and she had given up trying to stem the flow. She let out a heavy sob as she thought about all the new, exciting experiences they had been robbed of enjoying together. Dabbing at her eyes with her sleeve, Poppy let out a deep breath.

Of all the letters from John in her memory box, she had picked out the one that encouraged her to get out and see the world. She couldn't dismiss the coincidence. And she certainly couldn't ignore John's pleas. She remembered she had written back straight away and promised to do exactly as he'd said. She didn't know if he'd ever had the chance to read her letter, but she had made the heartfelt vow and now John had managed to remind her of it from beyond the grave.

HM Factory, Gretna certainly wasn't going to be as pretty as France or any of the other foreign countries Poppy and John had planned on visiting, but it was an adventure away from London. It would definitely be more dangerous than patrolling the streets of London, but she would be there to help make it safer for everyone else. Explosions were less likely to happen if the workers were stopped from bringing banned items into the factory, and that's what the WPS were there for. Once Poppy had taken that first step out of London, who knew where it might lead? She suddenly felt like a weight had been lifted from her shoulders and she knew exactly what she had to do, no matter how daunting it felt.

'Thank you, my darling,' she whispered, and she kissed John's handwriting before carefully placing the letter back into her memory box. Before the day was done, she would be going back to St Stephen's House to tell Frosty she was accepting the position at Gretna.

4

Poppy's stomach grumbled aggressively, and she cursed herself for having skipped breakfast. Now she'd made up her mind that she was taking up the post at Gretna she felt anxious but excited about moving away. With the majority of her angst dissipated, her body was reminding her that it needed fuel to get through the rest of the day. Poppy stepped hopefully into the communal kitchen but of course there was nothing left of the porridge she'd prepared that morning. Settling for a dry slice of bread and an apple, she decided to meet Maggie at the police station at the end of her patrol and treat her to an afternoon tea.

Sated but with her stomach not exactly satisfied, Poppy had a wash and changed into one of her nicer dresses. Realising there were still a few hours left of her friend's shift, she decided to head back to WPS headquarters to let Frosty know her decision. She reasoned that it would be a good idea to make everything formal before she had a chance to get too scared to go through with it.

'You're booked on a train to Carlisle tomorrow morning,' Frosty informed Poppy as soon as she stepped into her office and before she'd even had a chance to open her mouth and tell her she had made a decision. 'You'll be met at the train station and escorted to the factory.' Poppy screwed her face up in confusion.

'But . . . how did you know I would say yes?' she asked.

'You'd be foolish to turn down such a brilliant opportunity.

And one thing I know you are not, Constable Davis, is foolish,' Frosty replied evenly, staring right into Poppy's eyes. Poppy shifted uncomfortably in her seat as she suddenly thought of everything she would have to organise before getting on that train. She had to pack up her room, break the news to Maggie and Annie and say goodbye to them both – and Charlotte. She thought it might just be the hardest goodbye she would ever have to say – after the day she saw John off to France, of course.

'You have a lot to get organised,' Frosty said, her voice breaking slightly and her face relaxing a touch. 'I'll let you get on. And don't worry about your room at the section house. If you make sure it's cleared when you leave, I will inform Chief Constable Jackson of your new role so that you have one less person to explain and say goodbye to.'

Poppy smiled gratefully. At least that was one task she didn't have to worry about. Maybe she would ask Maggie to explain her transfer to their male colleagues. She didn't much fancy a string of farewells in such a short space of time. She needed to concentrate on the most important ones. Frosty gave her a parting gift of a pamphlet on factory law and a sheet of paper with instructions on the best way to conduct searches. Poppy slipped them into her pocket, not sure when she would get the time to read them.

Poppy went straight from St Stephen's House to Hunter Street Police Station to wait for Maggie. Nodding hello to a few policemen she recognised in reception she decided she would definitely ask Maggie to explain where she had gone tomorrow. She only had time for the important goodbyes – her Bobby Girls. She didn't want anybody knowing her news before they did. Poppy knew both her friends would be happy for her but as she waited in the WPS room she couldn't help but feel a little nervous. Although Maggie was building a better relationship with her mother since the big fallout with her father, she didn't get to see her very often at all. Poppy and Annie really were the closest 'family' she had at the moment and Annie wasn't around an awful lot.

Maybe this isn't the right decision, Poppy panicked as she heard her friend's cheery voice ringing out from along the hallway. But she quickly brought to mind John's letter, and how certain she had felt on reading his words. She also thought about all the women she would be helping at Gretna. With a renewed sense of confidence, she got to her feet to greet Maggie.

'Oh! Are you feeling better? I was worried about you,' Maggie said, searching Poppy's face. 'You still look rather pale,' she added, full of concern.

'It's nothing an afternoon tea won't fix,' Poppy replied cheerily. Maggie's face lit up.

'Can we go to Ashby's?' she asked excitedly. She jumped in the air and giggled when Poppy nodded her head. She was clearly so excited about the prospect that she forgot to ask Poppy about her meeting with Frosty.

Once Maggie had changed out of her WPS uniform, the two of them made their way straight to Ashby's. Maggie talked animatedly about her morning on patrol, while Poppy half listened and waited for an opportunity to tell her friend her big news. In the end, they had eaten their sandwiches and were about to tuck into some cake before she got a chance.

'I've got something to tell you,' she blurted, just as Maggie had taken a mouthful of cake.

'Mmm?' Maggie replied, raising her eyebrows and chewing on the treat. Poppy dived in, telling Maggie everything before her friend had a chance to swallow her cake and ask any questions.

'That's spiffing!' Maggie exclaimed when Poppy was finished. 'I'd completely forgotten you'd even gone to see

Frosty this morning. You should have stopped my rambling and told me sooner! And there you were worrying you were in some sort of trouble!'

'The only thing I've been worried about is leaving you,' Poppy admitted solemnly.

'You know I can look after myself. I'll be so busy patrolling I won't have time to get lonely.' Maggie took another bite of cake and quickly chewed on it, looking thoughtful, before continuing. 'With us off doing these separate patrols now, I'm used to not seeing you as often, so it won't come as such a big shock.' Poppy breathed a sigh of relief, but she also couldn't help but feel a little slighted that her friend clearly didn't rely on her as much as she thought she did. 'Maybe they'll even send another recruit to keep me company,' Maggie mused. 'And between popping in to help Annie out and meeting up with my mother when I can, I won't have much time for anything else.'

Poppy took a moment to digest her friend's positive outlook.

'I can see you're still worried,' Maggie continued, cutting into her thoughts. 'Honestly, though. This is too good an opportunity for you to miss out on. My, I'm even a little jealous!'

'The factory is huge,' Poppy explained, relaxing now. 'And it sounds as if I'll have a lot of responsibility. I think it will be refreshing to do something a little different.'

'Oh, of course,' Maggie agreed before taking another bite of her cake. Now full of relief, Poppy started on her cake, too. Then she suddenly remembered something important she had meant to reassure Maggie about.

'I'll keep your room going, Mags. And I'll make sure you have enough to get by on. I won't forget about you just because I'm moving away for a short while. And if you ever need anything more, you must write to me and let me know.

Frosty said the post should come with a pay packet soon enough; so you mustn't worry about wanting for anything.'

Maggie broke into a big smile and tears welled in her eyes. 'Thank you. I don't know what I'd do without you looking after me,' she whispered, her voice quivering slightly.

'You're like family. Both you and Annie. Don't ever forget that.'

'Stop now before you make me cry!' Maggie said as she dramatically dabbed at her eyes with her napkin. 'Now, shall we eat up and go and tell Annie your news? She'll be pleased as punch for you, too.'

'That's a great idea,' Poppy replied.

Sure enough, Annie was over the moon when she heard about the transfer. Poppy and Maggie spent the afternoon with her at the baby home before they enjoyed a dinner together with the residents. Getting ready to head back to the section house, Poppy found herself feeling emotional. Giving Charlotte a long cuddle, she breathed in her gorgeous, milky smell and closed her eyes. She wanted to create a strong memory she could think back to in difficult times for comfort. She often thought back to her final embrace with John to raise her spirits. Now she would have another to add to her happiness pot.

'She'll have changed so much by the time I get to see her again. I can't bear it,' Poppy whispered through tears. 'I don't want to miss out on all her milestones.' She suddenly felt anxious about her decision again. Nuzzling her head into Charlotte's neck, Poppy kissed the soft flesh and felt a wave of love as Charlotte giggled and cooed at the sensation.

'Just think about how proud she'll be of her aunty Poppy. You can write to me and tell me everything you're up to so I can tell her all about it. And I will write to you often,' Annie promised. 'Charlotte won't have much of a future if you and

Maggie don't keep on with everything that you're doing to help the war effort. The men in France are relying on us all.'

Poppy knew her friend was right. And she was desperate to fulfil her promise to John. She just hadn't counted on finding it this hard to say goodbye. Handing Charlotte back to Annie, Poppy blew the tot a kiss before pulling her mother in for an embrace.

'The young girls there need you more than we do,' Annie whispered in her ear. 'Maggie and I will look after each other. Go and do us proud.'

'I'll write to you as soon as I arrive,' Poppy pledged.

'You'll be too busy.' Annie laughed. 'Get yourself settled and write to us when you find you have some spare time to yourself, whenever that might be. We're not going anywhere so just focus on learning about your new beat.'

Poppy smiled. She had spent so long feeling like a mother-figure to Annie and Maggie, and now they were acting far more level-headed and parental than she was. She was grateful for the role-reversal, though.

'I'll miss you,' Poppy said firmly before finally turning and leaving, with Maggie following her close behind. Their journey back to the section house was quiet. The two friends linked arms, but they didn't speak to each other. Poppy's head was full of thoughts about what lay ahead for her, and she was sure Maggie was probably thinking about similar things.

Back in Poppy's room, Maggie sat on the bed while Poppy filled up the trunk, which she felt like she had only just unpacked.

'Can I leave some things with you? It seems silly to lug it all to Scotland with me when I won't have much use for most of it.'

'Well, if it makes sure you come back to me, then you certainly can!' Maggie joked. 'But you must take some of your fancy dresses.' Poppy screwed her face up in confusion. She wasn't planning on doing any socialising at Gretna. 'I hear they have huge dance halls over there,' Maggie explained eagerly. 'I know you're not interested in dancing with any young men, but I'm sure you'll make some friends you can go with.' Poppy smiled gratefully before picking out two of her more formal dresses and folding them neatly into the trunk.

Maggie was right. Poppy's WPS work was far too important to her to allow herself to be distracted by a man. And besides, it would have to take somebody pretty damned special to see her move on from her John. No, she wasn't ready for that. But it wouldn't hurt to have a couple of nice outfits with her in case she made some new friends who liked to dance. The opportunity to go to dances had only come up a few times since she had been friends with Maggie and Annie, but she had had such fun with them both.

Walking back to the wardrobe, Poppy crouched down and ran her hand over the memory box she had placed back in earlier that day. She opened it up and took out the letter on the top – the one from John that had made her mind up about Gretna. She slipped it into her pocket. She would keep that with her to read over if she was ever in doubt about what she was doing. The rest, she thought sadly, would be better off staying in London. She didn't want to risk becoming consumed by her grief and running to the box every time she had a bad day. And they would be safe here with Maggie. The letter in her pocket would be enough to pick her up and remind her why she was doing what she was doing. And she knew that before long she would have lots of positive letters from her friends to keep her going.

'Can I leave this with you?' she asked, standing up and offering the box over to Maggie.

'Of course,' her friend replied.

'It's my memory box. But I don't want to get too caught up in it,' Poppy explained.

'I'll keep it safe,' Maggie assured her.

As Poppy packed up the rest of her things, she felt a little lighter knowing all her memories would be safe in London instead of weighing her down in Scotland.

5

After an emotional goodbye with Maggie, Poppy tossed and turned in bed before finally falling into a deep slumber. She rose early the next morning and felt a mixture of fear and excitement as she boarded the train to Carlisle. Finding a quiet carriage to sit alone with her thoughts, Poppy found herself reaching for John's letter. She read it through again before carefully folding it and placing it back in her pocket. With the soothing rhythm of the train bringing her comfort, Poppy ran her index finger over her wedding ring and thought about how proud of her John would be for doing this all on her own.

Trying to imagine what this new life of hers would look like, she found herself gently sliding the ring up and down her finger. She had never taken it off, even during all her training with the energetic and rough suffrajitsu moves, not to mention all the times she had tackled drunken soldiers and prostitutes during her time patrolling on London's streets. But now she toyed with the idea. Did she really want to be known as 'Poppy the widow' for this next chapter of her life? She saw the way people looked at her when they realised her husband was dead.

Tentatively, Poppy slid the ring all the way off her finger. Just to see how it felt. Her heart skipped a beat as she turned the beautiful piece of jewellery around in her fingers. It wasn't the fanciest ring money could buy – John had been a blacksmith of simple means before joining the war effort. But the gold band symbolised her husband's deep love for her and that was what made it so stunning to Poppy. As the single diamond caught the winter sun shining in through the window, John's smiling face flashed into Poppy's mind. Was she betraying his memory by storing the ring away?

No, she told herself. She didn't have any intention of meeting anybody new; that wasn't what was behind this. In all honesty, she still wasn't sure if she would ever be ready for that. How could she possibly find anything as special as what she'd had with John with someone else? This was simply a way of ensuring Gretna would be a fresh start for her, and freeing her from the constant feeling of grief she felt whenever she caught sight of the ring, felt it on her finger or spotted somebody else taking it in. Like the memory box, she wanted to unburden herself of that oppressive feeling once and for all. Being strong for Maggie and Annie had been the thing that had lifted that sensation previously. Now she was leaving them, she felt certain she had to do this to make sure she stayed positive.

Poppy popped the ring into her jacket pocket next to the letter, and she felt a little lighter as she watched the landscape around her changing from bustling towns and cities to sprawling countryside. She took some time to read through the information Frosty had given her, but she found it difficult to concentrate. Hopeful she would be able to learn on the job, she stored the leaflets away again and let her mind wander as she enjoyed the passing scenery. It built up again as the train approached Carlisle, but the surroundings were still sparse compared to the views she had seen as she'd been leaving London.

When the train pulled into the station, Poppy saw two smartly dressed women waiting on the platform. They weren't in WPS uniform, but she couldn't see anybody else who might be able to help her. Stepping off the carriage, she held back as a flurry of young girls flocked past her and approached the women.

'We're the welfare officers, here for the new factory girls,' one of the ladies called out to Poppy. 'Your woman is in the waiting room,' she added, gesturing towards a shelter just along the platform.

Confused, Poppy wondered how they knew she was a WPS recruit. Did they assume she was with the police just because she was older? It was true that the majority of WPS recruits were her age and upwards – Maggie, Annie and Irene were the youngest members of the organisation. And most of the factory workers were young girls, but there were still a number of older women working in munitions. Then she remembered she had worn her uniform for the journey as she'd been unsure about whether she would be expected to start patrolling straight away. She tutted at herself and waved a thank you to the welfare officers before making her way along the platform.

'Constable Davis?' a short, round woman wearing a WPS uniform enquired as Poppy approached her.

'Yes, sir,' Poppy replied. She placed her trunk on the ground and saluted the woman. She was in her fifties, with a harsh look about her, which Poppy was beginning to think was a requirement for higher-ranking WPS officers. Her short dark hair poked out from the bottom of her hat and she looked even shorter than Poppy, who was the smallest of the Bobby Girls.

'I'm Sergeant Ross,' she said curtly. 'I'll take you to the factory and one of my officers will show you around. There's much to take in so I hope you're feeling fresh.' There was a brief pause while she searched Poppy's face with her narrow eyes, her sharp nose twitching slightly. Poppy nodded an acknowledgment. 'Your first shift will be tomorrow morning.'

'Thank you,' Poppy said with more confidence than she

felt. She was doing her best to appear assertive and positive, but inside her nerves were running amok. Sergeant Ross led Poppy to a motor car. On the way, she noticed the new factory workers were all piling into the back of a motorised charabanc and she felt bad for receiving such preferential treatment. Poppy would have happily travelled in the cramped vehicle with its benched seats and open top with everyone else, especially if it meant the workers didn't feel resentful towards her. She had a feeling there would be the same discrepancy in treatment at the factory and she hoped she wouldn't have to work too hard to get the girls onside.

'There's still construction going on at the site,' Sergeant Ross explained as the car started the journey to Gretna. 'Most of the roads are full of mud and there are navvies everywhere. They're hardworking but they like a good drink at the end of the day. They're harmless enough but you'll find yourself directing them back to their lodgings in the dark of the night or trying to keep them away from the female munitions workers during the day.' Poppy smiled knowingly.

'They don't sound too dissimilar to the soldiers in London,' she replied lightly.

'The navvies haven't been through what our men on the front line have experienced. They drink because they like to get drunk, not to forget the terrible things they've seen. It's a *different* kind of drunk.' There was a sudden sharp edge to Sergeant Ross's tone, and Poppy felt like she was a schoolgirl being told off by the headmistress. 'I've patrolled in London and I've been here a month or so now and the men are very simple in comparison to our brave soldiers,' Sergeant Ross continued. 'From what I've heard you did a good job in London, so you won't have any problems here.' Her voice had softened slightly now and Poppy felt less admonished, although she still felt like it was necessary to tread lightly around the sergeant.

'What about the women?' Poppy asked cautiously. She knew she would have no problem dealing with drunken men, no matter the reason for their inebriation. It was the female workers she was worried about. It had always taken such a long time to earn the trust of the prostitutes she had looked out for in London and the thought of fighting to get thousands of women onside at once was just plain exhausting.

'Well, they don't very much like being told what to do, as I'm sure you can imagine. There are always a few silly ones who try to sneak things in and out. But mostly we get on all right. You have to remember they are doing very dangerous work, as are we, and we have to be respectful to each other. A lot of the younger girls act out because they are scared.'

Poppy stared out of the window as the scenery became sparser the closer they got to the factory. She worked best when she was acting the role of mother-figure; it was her way of staying strong. Sitting in silence now with Sergeant Ross, she started feeling more confident that this had been the right move for her. When big buildings loomed in the middle of the countryside, Poppy knew they must have arrived. The car drove through some big gates and then stopped on what looked like the outskirts of the factory.

'The roads are too muddy for the car. The navvies are still putting down the drains. We'll walk from here,' Sergeant Ross announced as she got out and motioned for Poppy to join her. As Poppy clambered out, her boots immediately sank into the mud. She grabbed at the end of her long skirt to try and rescue it from getting dirty. Steadying herself, she heard the rumble of an engine and the sound of tyres slowly sloshing through mud. She looked up and saw the charabanc transporting the women workers driving past. The girls at the back cheered and waved as it squelched through the muddy surface, bopping up and down and flinging them from side to side. Poppy was about to wave back when she noticed Sergeant Ross giving them a civil nod, her expression extremely serious. Poppy nodded to them, too, but couldn't help but smile at their excitement.

'You would do well to remember they are not your friends. You're here to keep them in line.' Poppy flinched at the sudden terseness from her superior. She hoped she wouldn't be patrolling with Sergeant Ross if that was her attitude. She far preferred to build a rapport and get people to behave that way rather than through fear or bossiness. 'They're off to a central waiting room where they will be medically examined and allocated to a particular shift.' Poppy nodded but she hadn't really been listening. She was too busy trying to work out how she was going to get through all the mud without slipping over.

'I wouldn't worry about muck on your clothes,' Sergeant Ross said, staring out at the path of mud stretching ahead of them. 'That's commonplace for all the recruits working here.'

Poppy stopped rubbing at the slimy mark around the hem of her skirt and stood up straight. When Sergeant Ross started talking again, Poppy chanced a glance over at the other woman's uniform and saw that her boots and the bottom of her skirt were caked in a mixture of wet and dried-on mud. She was surprised she hadn't noticed it before.

'I'll send a navvy to pick up your trunk and take it to your accommodation at the township. We'll sort out an extra uniform for you, too,' Sergeant Ross said.

Poppy took some time to take in the enormity of the site. It wasn't one big factory building as she had expected; there were rows and rows of different huts and buildings. There were many quite close together, but she could see more in the distance – some of them looked like they were miles apart. It was like nothing Poppy had ever seen before.

Sergeant Ross explained that they were in the biggest

section of the factory site – named Mossband. 'It takes up more than thirteen-hundred acres. We have a big ether plant here and eight ranges of drying stoves. The western part of the factory at Dornock covers just over twelve-hundred acres and produces nitric and sulphuric acids, nitroglycerine and gun cotton. In the middle is the main township: Gretna. That's where you will be lodging. There's another township near Dornock, at Eastriggs. I hope you were used to getting your miles in when you patrolled in London. You'll need stamina to keep up here, girl.'

Poppy took a deep breath. She had known the factory was huge, but this really was something else. She didn't imagine the walking would be much of a problem for her, but she was nervous about having so many different sections and buildings to get to know.

'Don't worry, it's overwhelming for everybody at first,' Sergeant Ross said kindly, clearly taking in the panic that had engulfed Poppy's face. 'Just think of it like this: in the centre of the factory is Gretna – the chief township and residential quarter. Although the two production areas are Mossband and Dornock, and they're managed as two separate factories each with their own identity, collectively the factory is called after the main township: HM Factory, Gretna.'

Poppy's head was spinning even more now. Would she ever manage to find her way around? Before she had a chance to lose her nerve completely, she realised Sergeant Ross had suddenly bounded on ahead of her. Poppy's feet sank into the soft mud as she struggled to keep up. Her WPS boots had always felt rather cumbersome in London but now they seemed completely useless.

'Is it like this all the time?' she shouted out, desperately trying to keep her balance.

'You'll get used to it, dear,' Sergeant Ross replied stiffly. She stopped and turned around, and Poppy was grateful of the chance to try and catch up with her. 'The mud is constantly ankle deep and you'll return from duty looking like a plough-boy returning from a hard day's work in the fields. Night patrol of the township nearly always includes a thorough drenching. But they are meant to be sending us some better boots soon.' She sighed heavily. 'We've been telling them for months that our boots aren't adequate for all this mud and they did nothing. Then one of the male officers mentioned it in passing and they couldn't wait to send us upgrades.'

'Male officers?' Poppy asked cautiously. She had thought it was only WPS recruits policing the factory.

'There's only two of them – the factory starts in England and goes over the border to Scotland, so there's a super-intendent for each administration. The rest of the police force, and the military, have been withdrawn from the site so we really do have a lot on our plates. But don't worry, the two officers left are not like your London bobbies. They're very accommodating of the WPS, and they can actually be quite helpful.'

Poppy breathed a sigh of relief. At least that was one less battle for her to fight. Sergeant Ross started off again and Poppy did her best to keep up with her, but her feet squished deep into the thick mud and squelched every time she pulled them back out again. She was grateful to her earlier self for tying the laces up tightly, as otherwise she was certain she would have pulled her foot out minus a boot by now. It seemed to take more and more effort with every step. As Poppy put a foot down to go forwards, the other foot would sink backwards, and she felt like she was only getting half as far as she should be. She wondered how long she could keep going without a break, whereas Sergeant Ross appeared to be gliding over the muck despite her plump stature.

As they passed an array of large timber buildings and wooden huts, all spaced out evenly amongst the mud,

Sergeant Ross called back to tell Poppy what was happening in each section. She was able to make out 'boiling house' and 'pipe screwing' but none of it meant anything to her and her superior was too far ahead for her to be able to request more information. Poppy made a silent plea for a detailed guided tour with one of the other WPS officers before she was sent out to negotiate the maze of buildings on her own.

A large horn blasted out, making Poppy jump, and she steadied herself before she slipped over in the mud. As she slowly and carefully turned herself around to see where the noise had come from, she heard the familiar *chug chug chug* of a train and suddenly the air was filled with steam. Panic consumed her until she spotted the train approaching and realised she was nowhere near the track.

'You'll get used to that, too!' Sergeant Ross called back. 'There are railway lines all over the factory. There's more of those than roads at the moment! Just be careful not to wander across one in the dark by mistake!' Poppy couldn't tell if her new boss was joking or not, but she decided to heed the warning, nonetheless.

Finally, Sergeant Ross stopped at a small wooden hut and waited patiently for Poppy to catch up. Another WPS recruit walked out and saluted Sergeant Ross before going on her way. Poppy marvelled at the way the woman stomped through the mud instead of unsteadily picking her way through it like she was.

'This will be your base. You'll clock in and out here and you'll also be able to get your hands on a cup of tea. But don't expect to enjoy much shelter from the wind and the rain. The draught comes in from all sides, so you'll often be warmer out on patrol where you'll be on the move. I'm not sure if they designed it like that on purpose.' Sergeant Ross looked thoughtful and then laughed to herself. 'I'd never thought of that before. Right,' she continued, rubbing her hands together against the cold, 'I'll take you through the list of duties then we'll find someone for you to shadow for the afternoon.'

Sergeant Ross stepped into the hut and Poppy followed closely behind. There were three wooden tables pressed up against the walls and a number of chairs dotted around the small space. Various notepads and pens sat on the tables, unclaimed, and there were two women in WPS uniforms sitting next to a tea-making station, clutching steaming mugs and talking quietly. They both stood and saluted when Sergeant Ross walked in. She gave them a brief nod and gestured for them to sit back down as she carried on past them to the far wall, where a large sheet of paper was tacked up. She waited while Poppy read what was clearly the list of WPS duties.

A. Factory:

1. *Searching women operatives.*
2. *Patrolling danger area.*
3. *Examining passes at main gate and examining passes at search gate.*
4. *Controlling canteen.*
5. *Controlling pay-office queues.*
6. *Receiving reports re. losses of factory and private property and searching for same.*
7. *Reporting any contravention of factory rules.*

B. Township:

1. *Patrolling township and outlying district.*
2. *Receiving complaints, etc., in charge room.*
3. *Meeting and seeing off all factory trains.*
4. *Attending to sick girls on arrival from factory.*
5. *Making investigations and reports in police cases.*
6. *Attending court when necessary.*
7. *Taking charge of women prisoners in cells and escorting them.*

Poppy could feel Sergeant Ross staring at her as she tried to take it all in. She turned to her and smiled nervously when she had finished. She felt like she might be about to be tested on what she had learned.

'The duties read tamely enough in print, but you must remember that we carry these out under the most trying of circumstances, in all weathers, at all hours, in conditions often of utter physical discomfort.' Poppy thought back to the slog through the mud and pictured herself doing that in the pouring rain. Her body gave an involuntary shudder as Sergeant Ross continued. 'We carry out these duties with the full consciousness of the risk of instant death. There is also the heightened danger and terror of air-raids, with the full knowledge that one bomb falling upon a single building would be likely to cause dreadful, fatal havoc.'

Poppy was aware of Sergeant Ross searching her face for a reaction. Was she trying to scare her off? She was certainly making her feel uneasy. She casually reached her hand into her pocket and ran her finger over her wedding ring. Thoughts of John and all his exciting plans for their future ran through her head and she smiled.

'None of that will be a problem,' she said with confidence. Sergeant Ross broke into a huge grin before turning on her heel and making for the door.

'I'll leave you in the safe hands of constables Ruth Lester and Grace Windsor,' she called back. She stopped at the table where the two recruits were once more sitting. 'I trust there is a good reason you're not out on searches or patrol yet?' she asked. They both assured her there was. 'Good. I don't need details. I'll hear from Sergeant Simons if you're not where you should be.' She waved Poppy over before continuing. 'This is Constable Poppy Davis, our newest recruit. Let her shadow one of you this afternoon. I expect a report back on how she gets on.' They bowed their heads in understanding.

'Good luck!' Sergeant Ross bellowed just before the door swung shut behind her on her way back out of the hut. Poppy smiled nervously at her new colleagues and waited to find out what kind of a welcome they were going to give her.

6

The two women stared at Poppy in silence. She fidgeted with the collar on her jacket awkwardly and silently begged them to be friendly. She prided herself on being a confident and independent woman, but after hearing about how hostile one of Irene's new colleagues had been when she was transferred to Grantham, Poppy was only too aware of how awful a nasty recruit could make life for her. *Stay strong. Nobody will warm to you if you're weak*, she told herself and she found herself standing up straighter and pushing her shoulders back in an attempted show of confidence. She breathed easier and had just regained her composure when both women suddenly grinned at her.

'Don't just stand there – come and join us,' the blonde-haired one sang, adding, 'I'm Grace and this is Ruth.' Poppy drew up a chair in between the two of them. They each had their WPS hat hooked over the back of their chair and Poppy took hers off and did the same with it. Her head felt lighter for removing the hat, and she tucked a stray strand of hair behind her ear.

'Cup of tea?' Grace asked.

Poppy nodded keenly. 'I'm parched,' she offered, rubbing her hand over her throat. Grace reached over to the cupboard next to her and collected a mug. As she poured tea from the pot on the table, Poppy took in her soft features. She had a slim face and kind eyes, with a small button nose that looked redder than the rest of her complexion – possibly from the cold. Her hair was pulled back into a low bun but there were a few curly bits hanging loose. At a guess, Poppy would have said she was similar in age to herself, whereas Ruth looked to have at least ten years on her.

'I'm taking over on searches at the cordite press house next and then I've got a patrol round, so she's probably best off with me. What do you think?' Grace asked Ruth.

'That would make sense. I'm on duty at the townships and they're straightforward compared to the factory,' Ruth replied. It was the first time she had spoken, and her voice sounded harsh in tone despite the fact the two women had appeared to be getting along just fine. Ruth picked up her cup and finished the rest of her drink before getting to her feet. 'The newest recruit does the washing up,' she barked at Poppy, slamming her mug down in front of her and making her jump. As Poppy stared up at Ruth in horror and tried to decide the best way to react, she heard laughter coming from next to her.

'She's just having you on,' Grace said with a giggle. Ruth smiled and waved at them both before putting her hat on and stomping out of the hut with purpose.

'You'll get used to her sense of humour,' Grace said just as the door slammed shut behind Ruth.

'She's very . . . loud,' Poppy observed. The walls of the hut seemed to be shaking in the aftermath of her exit. Grace laughed again.

'She likes to throw her weight around – literally sometimes, and she's not one for talking much unless she's snapping orders at someone. It seems to work with the munitions girls. She's as soft as a baby's bum underneath it all, though. She has three sons, all in their early twenties, but all high-ranking officers in the army. I wouldn't expect any less with a mother like that.' Grace drained her mug and stood up. 'You finish your tea and I'll wash all this up,' she offered.

As she worked, Grace explained a little more about the factory. 'I take it you know that cordite is a propellant used in shells and bullets?'

Poppy nodded her head, thinking back to what Frosty had told her about the site. 'But I have to admit that I've no idea about the whole process,' she added sheepishly.

Grace turned back to the little sink before continuing. 'They produce hundreds of tonnes of cordite here every week by mixing nitroglycerine with nitrocotton. The factory is divided into two sections. There's Dornock, at the western end, where they mix the acids, nitrocotton and nitroglycerine. Then we have Mossband, which is where we are. Over here everything is brought together to produce the cordite.'

'It sounds like there's an awful lot going on,' Poppy said, trying not to sound too overwhelmed. Grace turned around to face her again.

'You'll get to know it too once you've spent even just a few days in and out of the various workshops and units. You'll be an expert in no time.'

Poppy inhaled deeply. She was determined to come across as confident, but she was feeling anything but.

'For now, we're headed to the biggest site on the factory grounds, where there are eight ranges of cordite-processing buildings. I'm on search duty at one of them and seven other recruits will be searching workers before they start their shifts inside the rest of them. We have to make sure the women aren't taking in any contraband. Once we're finished there we'll go out on patrol.'

'How long are all the shifts?' Poppy asked. She was wondering why Grace and Ruth had been the only recruits inside the WPS hut when she had arrived.

'Shifts start at 6.30 a.m., 2 p.m. and 10.30 p.m. Myself and Ruth were running late this afternoon as the sergeant in charge of the shift wanted us to go over some paperwork before we set off. Can you believe they refer to this as the office? The rain comes in through the cracks in the wall and we have one tiny lamp to heat it. But at least we have a base, I suppose.'

Poppy thought back to the tiny room that had been allocated to herself, Maggie and Annie when they had started patrolling in Holborn and nodded knowingly. 'We had a cupboard at my last place,' she scoffed.

Grace shook her head, laughing. 'Anyway, the sergeant sent someone over to start my search for me, but we'll need to get over there soon to relieve her. We search the workers before they start their shifts and then we work our way around all the different workshops, magazine stores and danger buildings.'

'Danger buildings?' Poppy asked, her eyes widening in fear.

'We don't go inside them,' Grace quickly assured her. 'We're not allowed. Only those with special clearance can gain access. I don't even know what they do in them but there are rumours new weapons are being developed. There's even been talk recently of German spies trying to get their hands on some of the plans. So it's really important that we ensure there are no shifty characters lurking about who might be trying to get their hands on sensitive information.'

Poppy took another deep breath. This was all sounding a lot riskier than patrolling the streets of London and keeping prostitutes, soldiers and children on the straight and narrow.

'You'll see lots of women in smart dress milling about the site,' Grace continued. 'They're the welfare workers.' Poppy thought back to the women she had seen at the train station and smiled. At least she understood something Grace was telling her. 'There's a big difference between them and us. We're here to make sure everyone remains safe and that nobody is doing anything to jeopardise that. The welfare supervisors are concerned with making sure the girls are working hard enough. They'll step in if somebody's slacking or has wandered away from their workstation without permission. They're also in charge of maintaining discipline in the change rooms and canteens. But you'll sometimes get sent along to a canteen to check meal tickets.' Poppy was concentrating intently on everything Grace was saying, but there was so much to take in.

'It's also down to us to step in if things get out of hand during mealtimes. They don't tend to, though, as the women are too busy eating to replace all the energy they've lost through their hard work.' Poppy was pleased to hear that. She could imagine canteens as being one of the worst places for disorder as all the women gathered without their work to distract them. 'And if there's a problem with wages or someone needs help with uniform then you send them to a welfare supervisor,' Grace added cheerfully. 'Oh, and there are always recruits at the main gates between the townships and the factory, and at the train stations where workers arrive and leave. Everyone is searched on exit, too – you wouldn't believe the number of people who have tried to sneak out bits of cordite as a souvenir.' Grace tutted and closed her eyes briefly.

'It sounds very different to what I'm used to,' Poppy admitted.

'Put simply, we're here to search, patrol and keep order around the factory and the townships. I wish I could fully prepare you for your first patrol but there's far too much to tell you in one go. I'll try and cover the main bits as we go and then the rest is really a case of learning on the job,' Grace explained. Poppy smiled gratefully. She was feeling relieved to have been paired with somebody understanding. 'All the other recruits are really friendly, and you'll always see someone on your travels, so don't hesitate to ask for help if you get stuck,' Grace continued. 'The welfare supervisors are around everywhere, too, and most of the foremen are helpful. You just need to keep an eye out for the handsy ones trying to get too familiar with the girls, but I'll point them out for you.' Poppy regretted leaving her notebook in her trunk. There was going to be a lot more to try and take in over the next few hours.

'It's always better to seek guidance than to get it wrong.' Grace's tone had changed from light-hearted to serious now. 'The workers always know when you slip up, even on the smallest things. They'll pounce on it as soon as they get even a sniff of a mistake.' Poppy couldn't help but look worried. 'They'll mock you and lose a bit of respect is all,' Grace added quickly. Poppy was slowly losing confidence. She liked to be fully equipped before getting started with a job and she felt extremely vulnerable right now.

'It's not the end of the world if it happens, and they're mostly nice girls. It's just that they're risking their lives every day and they take a bit of light relief wherever they can get it.' Grace took Poppy's empty mug and washed it up. 'Catching us out getting something wrong is a bit of fun to them but if they find a nickname for you out of it then it can take you a long time to live it down.' She finished and turned to face Poppy as she dried her hands. 'I was known as "Wash Bucket" by one group of girls for weeks when I first started and all I did was trip over a bucket of suds.'

Poppy stifled a laugh.

'It was harmless enough, but it really undermined my authority. They only stopped when I happened upon one of them out in the township on her own late at night being hassled by an intruder. I stepped in and restrained him before he managed to have his wicked way with her. The lot of them fall over themselves to show me respect now. It's fascinating how fast the tide can turn.'

Poppy wasn't smiling any more. Grace's story was a stark reminder of how young, naive and vulnerable a lot of the workers at the factory were. She felt compelled to look after them and protect them once more, even if they were desperate for her to blunder so that they could poke fun at her. 'Are intruders a common problem?' she asked.

'Not as much as they were before we started patrolling,' Grace said proudly. 'But we still get the odd toerag sneaking in. You'll get a powerful bullseye lamp for night patrols, and they'll equip you with a good, strong truncheon.' She opened up her jacket and pulled a long, black pole out of the waistband of her skirt. Poppy had only ever seen male officers carrying truncheons. 'I've never actually had to use mine, but it's good for peace of mind.'

Poppy wasn't sure she would know what to do with one, but she imagined it would be a nice little backup if her suffrajitsu failed her.

'They had a number of robberies at the hostels in the townships before we arrived, and we do still get undesirable characters loitering around – like the one I told you about. And, of course, we need to be on the lookout for any undercover Germans, too. It's quite easy to climb a fence and gain access to the grounds. We have to patrol all night and latecomers have to be interviewed, escorted to their block and the doors unlocked and relocked to make sure no stragglers make their way in. That's also why searching the workers before they go into any of the factory buildings is so important. If you're on searching duty, then you really need to have your wits about you.'

Poppy nodded.

'The workers get into their uniform in change rooms and then the searching takes place in sheds and workshops before they enter the main work area,' Grace explained as they left the WPS hut. 'They've set up what they can next to each work building, but you'll get used to how it all works before long.' She grabbed a clock from a mount on the wall and put it in her pocket. There were a few other clocks hanging up still, and spaces where it appeared more had been previously. 'I'll show you how this works as we go,' she added.

'I really wish I'd kept my notebook with me,' Poppy muttered as she stepped out of the hut and her boots sank deep into the mud once more.

'Here, take mine,' Grace offered. She reached into her pocket and pulled out a little pad, along with a pencil. Poppy took it gratefully. 'Don't worry,' her new colleague assured her. 'As long as you're looking out for the girls and making sure they're out of harm's way and not getting up to any mischief then the rest will come with time. A lot of it is common sense if I'm honest. The main thing is keeping everyone safe.'

Poppy felt happy with that and made sure to hold her head high and push her shoulders back as they entered the search shed. She may have been feeling more nervous than she had ever felt in her life, but she couldn't let even a glimmer of that anxiety show in front of these brave women.

7

Inside the searching shed, Poppy watched as a constant stream of women were patted down by a WPS officer before being ushered into the work building. All the workers wore a khaki tunic made of cotton trimmed with a red yoke piece. They also had on khaki trousers, khaki-and-red mop caps and rubber wellingtons. Some of them were wearing khaki cloaks with red hoods. They all chatted amongst themselves as they waited. It was noisier than Poppy had expected, and she was struck by the range of dialects she could make out.

When the recruit searching the workers looked over and saw Poppy and Grace, she put her hand up into the air and the line of women stopped still. Grace walked over and swapped places with the officer, who gave her a nod before slipping out of the building. Poppy stood just to the side of Grace so she could see how she conducted the searches.

Immediately, the worker who had been next in line before the change over stepped forward and handed over her pass for Grace to examine. Once Grace handed it back, the woman put her arms out to the side so that Grace could search her. Grace patted her down then tapped her shoulder and sent her on her way. It had all been seamless and Poppy was impressed. As she made her way through the rest of the line, Grace explained that the cordite press house was one of the final stages of production.

'We'll take a walk through so you can see the girls in action once I've searched the rest of this shift,' Grace added before swiftly pulling a hairpin out of her current searchee's hair.

'Ouch!' the woman yelled, putting her hand up to the side of her head and screwing her face up in pain.

'You know the rules, Glenda,' Grace said evenly, placing the hairpin into a tray next to her and putting her palm out in front of her expectantly.

'But my ends are such a mess,' Glenda groaned.

'You can take the rest out yourself or I can rip them out,' Grace offered, holding eye contact. Glenda let out a big sigh, took off her hat and started peeling hairpins out.

'Christ, Glenda, did you want to send us all up in flames today?' a voice called out from the back of the line.

'Oh, shush!' she shouted back, tutting as she continued searching for pins.

'We can't have them in any of the work sheds. You know that,' Grace said sternly. Poppy made a note in her pad. 'We're also looking out for matches, cigarettes, pins, penknives – anything which really shouldn't be in the neighbourhood of explosives,' she added in an aside to Poppy as Glenda carried on with her task. 'One stray hairpin could cause a fatal spark and send the whole factory heavenwards. Would you believe that I've even found some old dear trying to sneak in knitting needles? The cheek of it!' Poppy laughed along with her.

'Careless workers seem to enjoy carrying them despite the frightful risk,' Grace added pointedly, staring Glenda in the face as the disgruntled worker huffed dramatically. 'It doesn't matter at what point of the production line we're at – none of it is allowed. We search them on the way in and then – as I mentioned earlier – again on the way out of the factory site. They're as likely to take away with them keepsakes such as cordite or unexploded shells.'

Poppy nodded but inside she could feel a rising sense of

panic. She was suddenly aware of how many lives were in her hands. One simple mistake, like missing a stray hairpin, could see the whole factory explode and hundreds of people losing their lives.

'Of course, there's the added danger of spies entering as munitions workers,' Grace said, cutting into Poppy's thoughts. Now she couldn't hide the fear from her face despite the fact she wanted the room full of women to think she had everything under control. There would be thousands of workers to keep track of – all of whom she had never seen before. How was she supposed to know if somebody shouldn't be there? Glenda finished rooting around in her hair and Grace gave her a pat down before sending her on. She looked across at Poppy before searching the next woman.

'You'll soon get to know the faces who should be here, and they all know each other, too. The time to get concerned is when a loner comes in who isn't chatting to anybody else in the line.' Poppy looked again at the queue of women. They all seemed to know each other and there was nobody stood on her own. 'You also need to bear that in mind when you're patrolling the townships – but in those situations it's really hard to prove anything. A voyeur could actually be a German spy disguising his actions, but they can only be charged if they're caught obtaining sensitive information or found in an off-limits area.'

'Like the danger buildings you told me about?' Poppy asked.

'Exactly. That's why we have to be extra vigilant when we're patrolling those areas, especially at night.' Grace finally waved Glenda through and moved on to the next munitionette.

'It's also a good idea to look out for illness on their way in,' she said as she took a moment to look the woman in front of her up and down. 'Anyone who appears to be a bit drunk might actually be poorly. That's particularly true at the nitric-acid stores and the glycerine distillery. They get drunk on the fumes and can be subject to fits so they need to be sent to sleep it off. They can also get sick with fumes from the cordite. You would think it would take a few hours of being around the fumes for it to kick in, but sometimes the build-up from the previous day catches up with them and they're wobbly before they even get started. It's better to catch it before they enter the work sheds because passing out around any of the manufacturing equipment could be very dangerous.'

Poppy's heart raced and she made yet more notes. She watched on for the next ten minutes as more and more workers filed through. Grace reprimanded a few of them for not having their hair tidied away properly under their caps. She was just getting to the end of the influx of workers starting the current shift when she paused on a young girl with a red raw nose and streaming eyes. She wondered for a moment if the girl was suffering from the effects of working closely with cordite that Grace had mentioned, but then her colleague pulled up the worker's tunic to reveal a tight bodice.

'It's a new bodice me mam sent me to keep the cold out. I can't shift these sniffles,' the girl croaked. Her eyes were wide and bright despite her obvious illness and the water pooled in them. Poppy was drawn in by them. Her mesmerising eyes didn't manage to distract Grace, though, who sighed and reached over to the table holding the tray of hairpins and other confiscated items. She picked up a pair of scissors.

'Please, miss,' the girl begged. 'It's so terribly cold.' As if on cue, her teeth seemed to involuntarily chatter briefly, causing her pale but round cheeks to wobble slightly.

'What would happen if one of these metal buttons came loose during the course of your work?' Grace asked firmly. Without another word, she cut off each and every button.

'Come on, that's not fair!' the woman behind shouted.

'You all know the rules are there to protect you,' Grace replied sternly. The woman shook her head but said no more. Poppy watched her closely as she glared angrily at Grace. She was tall and her broad shoulders along with her height made her appear strong and imposing, particularly when she was standing close to somebody as short as Poppy. Poppy couldn't help but think that she appeared to be exactly the type of woman you wouldn't want to run into in a dark alley – even if you did have suffrajitsu on your side.

'Next time you'll be fined sixpence,' Grace warned the younger girl, who still looked like she was about to cry. Poppy felt terrible for her. She must have only been around eighteen years old. She thought about how scary it must be to be away from home doing such important and terrifying work, and being poorly to boot. She gave the girl a sympathetic smile, but she looked away and scurried into the unit and into the arms of an older woman who had gone in just ahead of her. The older woman scowled at Poppy and led the girl inside.

'You should be ashamed. Poor lamb is only trying to get herself better, is all,' the stocky woman who had protested previously snarled as Grace searched her. She was looking straight at Poppy and directing her comments at her. Poppy couldn't help but feel affronted. She wasn't the one who had upset the young lass and, anyway, she felt that Grace had been right to cut off the buttons. It was an innocent present from the girl's mother, but it had posed an unnecessary risk to so many people. In fact, the more Poppy thought it over, the more she felt that Grace had actually gone easy on the worker by letting her off without a fine.

'It's all very well her getting better, but she'll be no good to anybody blown to pieces, will she?' Poppy blurted out just as Grace finished searching the woman. The words had left her lips before she'd had a chance to think about whether it was the right thing to do. Maggie's face suddenly appeared in her mind and she felt annoyed with herself for picking up her friend's trait of speaking before thinking.

The woman narrowed her eyes but even through her sudden bout of self-doubt, Poppy stood firm. After what felt like an eternity, during which time Poppy decided she might need to use her suffrajitsu before she'd even started her first shift, the woman broke eye contact, huffed loudly and skulked into the work shed without another word. Poppy hoped she hadn't overstepped the mark. She was only meant to be shadowing Grace, after all. Would her colleague be annoyed that she'd stepped in? Grace looked round at her and smiled.

'You handled that outburst well,' Grace said once the final worker had been searched and sent into the unit. Poppy was flushed with relief. She felt like she might be getting the hang of this already. But the run-in and the subsequent reaction from the other munitions workers were a stark reminder to her that she wasn't at Gretna to make friends. As much as she would prefer to get on with the girls working here, she was here to protect them and save lives, and that had to take priority over everything else.

8

When they walked into the cordite press house, Poppy was overwhelmed by the huge machinery and all the activity taking place. Although there was a constant hum of general chitter chatter ringing out around the huge workshop, gone were the easy-going smiles from out in the searching area. Each and every girl was focused on the task in hand, but they did talk quietly amongst themselves, and every now and then a round of jolly singing started up.

Poppy was surprised to find the workers so laid-back, given the enormity of what they were doing. There were huge mixers churning and giving off heat and noise, as well as a massive steel cylinder. Just to the left and through big, open wooden doors, Poppy could see the top of a train and she was reminded of the locomotive she'd spotted when she'd arrived with Sergeant Ross.

'The whole process starts over at Dornock,' Grace explained now.

'There's our new lady officer! Don't she look smart!' a voice from afar shouted, and a whoop of cries rang out around the factory. Poppy suppressed a smile. She wasn't sure if they were trying to intimidate her or make her feel welcome, but she enjoyed the glee the sudden outburst had put on all their faces. This was the kind of cheeky camaraderie she had enjoyed with prostitutes like Alice back in London. Her spirits rose to think she would be able to carry that on at Gretna.

'That's enough! You've important work to concentrate on,' Grace bellowed. The atmosphere immediately shifted. All at once the general background chatter was back and all the women had their heads down. Poppy's heart sank and she was reminded once again of the importance of her role and the need to put safety before trying to form any friendships with the workforce.

'Don't bother with her, she'll only side with her boss there and snipe at you when you try to protect a friend,' a voice full of venom hissed from behind one of the mixers as Poppy and Grace approached it. Poppy recognised the voice straight away. It belonged to the woman in the search queue who had tried to stick up for the young girl with the buttoned bodice. Poppy craned her head to the side and, sure enough, there she was, handling a bag of paste and muttering under her breath.

Now she was standing next to a row of other workers, Poppy could see just how imposing the woman's presence was. Her height and width meant she stood out from all of her colleagues.

'Take no notice,' Grace said lightly. 'They don't like being told what to do, and they especially don't like being in the wrong. That's Edith, by the way. She'll be upset that you put her straight for a day or so but then something, or someone, else will annoy her and she'll forget she ever had a problem with you in the first place.'

Poppy looked over again as they continued walking through the work shed. She noticed that Edith was standing next to the girl who the poorly worker had scurried to after Grace had cut her buttons off. As Poppy caught her eye, the worker stopped what she was doing and glared at her as if she had just offended not only her but her whole family.

'I think I've upset her friend, too,' Poppy muttered uncomfortably.

'Who? Oh, you mean Marie? The girl with the buttons – Bessie – is Marie's younger sister.'

'Ah. No wonder she's staring at me like she wants to push me into the mixer,' Poppy joked.

Grace laughed. 'She'll get over it, too. Bessie is young. I'm certain she lied about her age so she could come and work here with her big sister, actually. But they would never kick her out even if they could prove it, as they need the extra hands too much. The sisters got close to Edith as soon as they arrived and the three of them are always looking out for each other. And, being older, Marie and Edith are very protective of Bessie. Edith is protective of the two sisters as a pair, too. I mean, just look at her – you wouldn't choose to fall out with her, would you? It's nice, really, but if you cross one of them then you cross all three of them.'

'I wish I'd known that before I snapped at Edith,' Poppy groaned. 'Trust me to pick a fight with the biggest woman in here.'

'No, you did the right thing. You need to assert your authority with them otherwise they'll only pick on you to make entertainment for themselves and the others. You need to stand your ground with them and maintain order at all times. If you do that, then, even if something drastic is taking place, the excitement will soon die down. You can't let anyone or anything fluster you.'

Poppy looked back at the group now and she could see Marie had the same strawberry-blonde-coloured hair sticking out from the back of her cap as her younger sister. She looked to be in her early twenties, whereas she would have said Edith was at least thirty years of age. She could see a very blonde stray curl poking out at the back of her cap. Poppy's attention was brought back to the present when Grace pointed at the train Poppy had spotted when they'd first walked in.

'The cordite paste is made at Dornock and transported over here by rail. The factory is connected to three main railways: the Caledonian, the Glasgow and South Western, and the North British. But there's also a factory railway, which goes from Dornock to Mossband. There's a load of private lines within the factory, too.'

'Are the train lines just for the cordite materials?' Poppy asked.

'There's a mixture of passenger and produce trains. There are eleven special trains that carry in thousands of workers from south-west Scotland, Cumberland and Eastriggs. If you are asked to cover the trains on your patrol, then you're to make sure that the women-only compartments are free of men. And because the trains and the stations here are deemed to be private property, we're authorised to stop and interrogate anyone found on them. So, if you come across a couple talking for any length of time on a station platform then you're to move them on, just as you would within either of the townships.'

'That seems a little heavy-handed,' Poppy commented. Grace looked shocked and Poppy realised she had spoken without thinking again. She was so used to patrolling with Maggie and Annie and feeling comfortable enough to speak her mind without fear of judgement. She kept forgetting she was somewhere new and that she was desperate to make a good impression and show her new colleagues how professional she was. 'I mean, in London we would stop couples if we thought there was something untoward going on or about to take place. But if they were man and wife—'

'That's the difference,' Grace cut in. 'Everyone is here to work and they must stay focused. Yes, some of the male workers have their families here but they spend time with their wives and children at home. Not at the factory or on factory grounds when their minds should be on the task at hand. We are supposed to discourage fraternisation between the sexes or larking about because of the dangers involved in the chemical processes carried out here. The workers can't afford to have any distractions.'

'Of course,' Poppy replied, feeling a little foolish.

'On a normal factory patrol like we're doing today, you'll walk the whole way,' Grace continued. Poppy was glad she had changed the subject, but she couldn't help but widen her eyes in shock.

'But . . . I thought the site was nine miles long,' she gasped.

'You can do double that some shifts,' Grace replied coolly. Poppy watched her face for a hint of a grin, hoping she was teasing her. But she felt deflated when she understood Grace was serious.

'Goodness.' Poppy sighed.

'You walked a lot in London, didn't you?'

'Yes, but not in these conditions. It's just treacherous. I'm tired already from walking through that mud just to get here.' Poppy didn't want to say it aloud, but she was worried about how she was going to cope.

'Your body will soon adjust. Just as it did when you started doing all those extra miles when you first started patrolling.' Poppy smiled weakly. She appreciated Grace's optimism. 'Anyway, I was telling you about what goes on in here,' Grace added brightly.

'Yes, back to the guided tour,' Poppy replied, trying to sound – and feel – more upbeat than she actually did.

'So I told you that they make the cordite paste at Dornock and it travels here by rail.' As they started walking again, Poppy could see girls unloading large bags of paste and pouring it into the big mechanical mixers. They walked past rows of women piling what looked like crumbly dough into bags, and then Poppy saw it being pushed into a steel cylinder. 'We don't need to know the technical ins and outs, just that they end up with strings of cordite at the end, which they cut to length,' Grace said as they continued on their way through the building. 'The strips of cordite are stored on wooden trays and then those poor lasses transfer them to trucks, which they have to push a mile or so to the stoves at the drying section.'

'They *push* the trucks?' Poppy asked, astounded.

'They certainly do. It's the best way to avoid any sparks. I'm not sure I'd be able to do it myself. I wouldn't believe you if you told me, but I've seen them do it enough times. It's an awful job, especially on a night shift. There's cold rain and it's dark and lonely but they keep on going, using all their strength to move those trucks along – even when there are rats running around their feet.' Poppy shuddered at the thought. 'They just roll their sleeves up and get on with it. I don't think anyone realises just how extraordinary these women are.' No wonder they didn't much like being told what to do the rest of the time, Poppy thought.

'The strips are left in the drying stoves for six days before being shipped off to the Woolwich Arsenal, where final firing testing is carried out on each batch. We'll make our way over to Dornock next and you can learn how they make the paste.'

Before leaving, Grace stopped by the door and took hold of a key that was hanging from a hook next to it. She then took the clock out of her pocket and pushed the key into a slot on it. 'This is how they know you've been to every work shed on your rounds. We have to clock on at every point,' she explained.

They trudged through the mud for miles, passing various working buildings as they went. The sludge wasn't as deep and thick in some places and Poppy enjoyed the short reprieves. Grace stopped at each building and explained what went on inside as they walked through. She clocked on at every single one. They also passed some rail stations and the canteen. Poppy was amazed by how many trains chugged around the site. Every now and then they would come across a group of Irish navvies who were busy working on sections of the road.

'Lady Police – God bless 'em,' they chanted every time they spotted Grace and Poppy, stopping to tip their hats and give them a wink.

'They get worse when they've had a beer or two,' Grace groaned as she politely waved at the men. 'I wish they would work a little faster on these roads. They're practically non-existent. Of course, the rail lines and the work buildings took priority and they got them sorted quick enough. The work on laying down the railway lines tore the roads in every direction, which is why we're left with all of this mud to traverse daily. But now all they seem to do is put down drains during the day and fill up the canteen in the evenings during the limited hours when beer is allowed to be sold. You'll often find yourself standing near the rough ground at the entrance to the canteen of an evening lighting the way for the silly drunken fools. It's easy to take pity on them and try to keep them safe even when there is so much else to do.'

'The list of duties *is* rather long,' Poppy commented.

'That's just the routine official work. You'll find yourself carrying out untold forms of consultation on your rounds as well as doing all of that – from settling family quarrels to giving advice in affairs of the heart. You just have to do what you can to keep the factory running.' Poppy thought back to Bessie, Marie and Edith. The three of them appeared extremely close but she could imagine the fallout if they had a disagreement amongst themselves.

'Then there are the problems that come with men and women from so very different backgrounds being thrown together and being expected to spend so many hours in close proximity carrying out high-pressure tasks,' Grace added.

'The workers here come from every grade of society. Indeed, the daughter of a duke might find herself working alongside a former scullery maid or a street pedlar from the slums. There are naturally wild and uncontrollable spirits but, on the whole, everyone comes together to work in peace, connected by the sheer importance of their task. You'd do well to remember all the differing backgrounds we're dealing with here, though.'

Just as Poppy thought Grace was finished, she started talking again.

'You also need to be on the lookout for larking. Remember, we're here to discourage immorality as well as everything else we do. Although the majority of the workers are women, there are a fair number of male labourers, too. It's mostly men in the electrical departments and the laboratories, and there are a good number of boys employed throughout the rest of the factory. Men are also on site to help with maintenance. Then, of course, there are the navvies.' Poppy had given up making notes now. She found she couldn't keep up with all the new information.

The pair of them passed by two WPS recruits as they continued on their way. Grace gave them a wave and a serious-looking nod, which the women returned, but there were no pleasantries exchanged.

'Those two have been sworn in as special constables of the City of Carlisle and the Counties of Cumberland and Dumfries,' she explained. 'They'll be on their way into town now. A lot of the girls and women from the factory head that way for entertainment. I don't know how they manage to keep up with it all but somehow they do.'

Despite her long and growing list of new responsibilities, Poppy suddenly felt relieved that she'd been stationed at the factory instead of being tasked with rounding up the workers across the nearby towns. At least here it seemed they spent most of their time with their heads down getting on with their jobs. Once they were out in Carlisle with extra money to spend and mischief to get up to, then she could be safe in the knowledge that someone else would have to deal with them. She suddenly heard John's voice in her head, praising her for looking at the positives in an impossibly overwhelming situation. She smiled to herself.

Poppy was exhausted by the time they reached Dornock. The walk would have been tiring on a normal road, but the mud made it so much more of a slog. She was looking forward to a rest as they approached a small shed just ahead of the sprawling workshops and buildings.

'Is there time for another cup of tea before we carry on the tour?' she asked hopefully as Grace led her into the room. She noticed immediately that it was in stark contrast to the WPS hut at Mossband. There, the cold air had whistled through the gaps in the wood, but this room felt warm and cosy.

'Well, if you're offering to make it, a cuppa would be most refreshing,' a deep voice called out from the other side of the room, making Poppy jump. Confused, she looked past Grace to find the distinct outline of a policeman in the shadows. She couldn't make out his face, but she hoped the cheeriness in his voice had been genuine and not sarcastic.

'This is the police hut. I brought you in to introduce you to the superintendents,' Grace hissed forcefully, raising her eyebrows at Poppy.

'Oh, I do apologise,' Poppy said, feeling sheepish and rather embarrassed. She was aware that most policemen were convinced the WPS sat around drinking tea all day, and felt ashamed of herself for having helped enforce the misconception. Grace's reaction to her overheard innocent question made her cheeks flush with even more shame.

'No apology necessary. I trust you've walked all the way

over from Mossband in the mud. In fact, I can see that you have from all the muck on your boots and skirt. A cup of tea is the minimum I would expect is needed to recover from that,' the officer replied. As he walked out of the shadows at the edge of the hut, his face became clearer. Poppy was relieved to see he was smiling at her – a smile that spread right across his face and seemed to light up his large, brown, glistening eyes. She took in his soft features and kind face, as well as the slight wrinkles that were showing at the side of his eyes as he grinned. The policeman was a foot or so taller than Poppy, and his broad shoulders made it feel as if he was looming over her, although she didn't feel in the least bit threatened because his presence was so reassuring. 'I'm Superintendent Lawrence Baker,' he said, holding out his hand.

As Poppy shook the officer's hand, he held eye contact with her, and she felt a flutter in the pit of her stomach. Quickly looking away, she put the strange sensation down to the day's exertion.

'Welcome to Gretna,' Superintendent Baker said warmly. Poppy looked at him again as he took his hand away and stepped back. As their eyes met once more, she came over all funny again. Superintendent Baker started boiling some water and instructed Poppy and Grace to sit down and rest while he did so. Poppy forced herself to look away when she felt his gaze on her as Grace introduced her. She wasn't sure what was going on, but she was unsettled by the effect this man was having on her.

9

Grace told Superintendent Baker all about the run-in with Bessie and Edith while Poppy took a moment to try and gather her thoughts. Was she *attracted* to the policeman? It was the type of feeling that she hadn't experienced for so long that she wasn't quite sure. She hadn't looked at another man properly for years. She wasn't sure she even remembered how to do such a thing. She decided that maybe she was just in desperate need of a cup of tea after wading through all the mud.

'Isn't that right, Poppy?' At the mention of her name, Poppy's head flew up and she found Grace looking at her expectantly. She bobbed her head and grinned at her colleague, hoping that was the desired reaction to whatever Grace had been saying. Just then, the door flew open. Another male officer bounded in with such energy that they all swung their heads around to look at him. Poppy silently thanked him for rescuing her from an awkward situation – and distracting her from her own confused thoughts.

'Ah, Superintendent Butcher, you're just in time to meet the new lady officer,' Superintendent Baker announced as an extremely tall, older man with red-flushed cheeks and a larger-than-average nose walked into the room. 'This is Constable Davis,' he added. Superintendent Butcher held out his hand and Poppy got to her feet to shake it. She looked between the two men with a quizzical expression on her face.

'Good to meet you, Constable. I'm Superintendent Jim Butcher and, yes, we are Butcher and Baker. I'm afraid there's no candlestick maker – not that we know of, anyway. Feel free to get any jokes that spring to mind out of the way now, won't you?' His mouth broke into a huge grin and Poppy giggled in relief. She looked round to find Superintendent Baker and Grace laughing along with her. 'I implore you to come up with something the workers haven't already thrown at us,' Superintendent Butcher said brightly as he sat down across from Poppy and poured himself a cup of tea. His tone was friendly and his voice was so loud it seemed to fill the whole room.

'I'll get myself a fresh mug, then, will I?' Superintendent Baker asked jokingly.

'You mean this isn't all laid out for me?' his colleague teased. His voice was louder now, and it seemed to boom and then bounce off the wooden walls as he spoke. To add to that, his height meant he towered over all of them even from a sitting position. He had the kind of presence that demanded all of the attention in the room. Poppy was glad she had an excuse to focus on him and divert her thoughts away from Superintendent Baker and whatever it was that she was feeling about him.

Both men had taken their hats off and Poppy and Grace did the same as they all sat down together. Poppy filled the group in on her background and told them about her WPS journey, leaving out the fact she had been widowed soon after finishing her training. She felt a pang of guilt for the omission but reminded herself that she didn't want to be defined by her widow status any longer.

As she talked, she relaxed, and Poppy was surprised at how at ease she felt with both the male officers so soon after meeting them, given how much effort it had taken to get some of the London policemen onside. She wondered if they were so accepting of female police because they were in the unique situation of being outnumbered by them, but she didn't dare share her musings out loud.

The men explained that they stored a set of keys to all the factory buildings and workshops in their base during the day and then they handed them over to the WPS sergeant in charge of night duty when they clocked off.

'We work twenty-four seven while these two get to have the evenings off,' Grace chipped in, rolling her eyes playfully. 'If you need assistance with anything during the day then, unless it's an emergency where you call on the nearest foreman for backup, you should come here and ask Butcher or Baker for help.'

'What about the candlestick maker?' Poppy asked quietly, uncertain whether she was being too cheeky. She flushed with relief when both men burst into laughter. When she looked up at Superintendent Baker, she noticed he held her gaze for slightly longer than seemed necessary. She liked the way his thick dark hair looked ruffled after having had a hat on top of it all morning, and she found that she didn't want to look away, but she forced herself to do so when Superintendent Butcher started talking. Even as she listened to the older man, she could feel his colleague's eyes on her.

It turned out that the two policemen dealt mainly with any issues arising with the factory foremen and the young boys working on the site while the WPS stuck to looking out for the girls and women. But both men were keen to stress that they would happily step in and help a WPS officer if she found herself in need of assistance. Poppy found it refreshing to hear such offers of support from her male superiors.

During the rest of the conversation, Poppy learned that Superintendent Butcher lived in the Gretna township with his wife. Forty houses had been purpose-built for factory foremen and their families, while another one hundred and fifty had been constructed to house factory officials.

'Yet they still haven't got around to building our barracks,' Grace muttered.

'You mean you're not comfy in your little wooden bungalows?' Superintendent Butcher boomed sarcastically.

'Very funny.' Grace sighed. 'They keep promising us a proper WPS barracks, but we're stuck in rough wooden huts until they get around to building us anything better.' It was clear to Poppy that although the men and women in charge at Gretna seemed to get along better than anywhere she had patrolled previously, there was still a harsh distinction between the way they were treated in general.

Superintendent Butcher quickly started talking about himself again, explaining that he and his wife had four grown-up children and two grandchildren. Poppy had supposed from his grey-speckled hair that he was in his fifties, but she was surprised to learn that he was a grandfather. She smiled to herself when she thought about all the fun those children must have with such a larger-than-life character as their grandfather.

Risking a glance over at Superintendent Baker as his colleague continued his monologue, Poppy found herself wondering whether he was married. Surely somebody with such a kind smile and handsome face had found someone to share their life with, she pondered, before chastising herself. Why should she be bothered whether he was married or not? It would make no difference to her. When he looked over and caught her eye, she grinned nervously before turning her attention back to Superintendent Butcher. She had been just about to chance a glance at his ring finger and was glad she hadn't been caught in the act.

'I've a meeting with a foreman so I'll leave you ladies to your tour,' Superintendent Baker announced abruptly at the exact moment Superintendent Butcher paused for breath during a story he was telling about one of his grandchildren. Grace, who had been mindlessly playing with a strand of her hair as the officer talked, suddenly snapped to attention and put her hat on. She gestured wildly at Poppy to do the same. Poppy smiled when she realised Grace was taking advantage of the pause in the conversation to get away. She thought Superintendent Baker had probably been waiting for an opportune moment to leave and she was grateful to him for helping herself and Grace slip away at the same time. She wondered how often they got caught listening to the older man waffle on. Superintendent Butcher seemed lovely enough, but he certainly wasn't any good at reading the room.

'It was a pleasure to meet you, Constable Davis,' Superintendent Baker said. He put his hat back on and tipped it at her, flashing her a wide grin. Poppy felt her stomach flip again as she found herself smiling back at him. It was only once the door swung shut behind him that she realised she hadn't said anything back to him, but had just stared at him, dumbstruck. She quickly looked over at Grace and Superintendent Butcher but thankfully they were both busy clearing away the tea things and didn't seem to have noticed.

'I should have warned you that Butcher likes to talk. A *lot*,' Grace murmured as they made their way back out across more mud. Poppy quickly searched around for Superintendent Baker, but she couldn't see him. 'I once got caught listening to him drone on about his son's wedding for a whole tortuous hour,' Grace added slowly, shaking her head.

Following Grace to the next workshop, Poppy tried to make sense of what had happened in the room. It was like a fire had been lit inside her when she'd laid eyes on Lawrence Baker, and she didn't know how to put it out. Even now, she couldn't stop thinking about his handsome face and the way the light seemed to glisten off his eyes when he smiled. Poppy's hand instinctively reached for the ring and letter in her pocket as guilt engulfed her. There was no denying it; she felt a definite attraction to Superintendent Baker. And, she couldn't be sure, but she had a feeling from the way he had been looking at her that he felt the same.

The comprehension sent shockwaves through her body as well as a sudden rush of shame. She hadn't so much as looked at another man since losing John – in fact, she had never done such a thing since the moment she had met her late husband. And now she was all aquiver from just one meeting with Lawrence Baker. She couldn't help but feel like she was betraying her one true love. She may have stopped wearing her wedding ring, but she still felt joined in eternal matrimony to the memory of John.

Rubbing her wedding band gently, Poppy decided she must push the feelings away. They were sure to be fleeting, anyway. Nobody had ever managed to compare to her darling John – in life as well as death, so there was no question of that happening now. She quickened her pace as much as she could without falling face-first into the mud. With a sudden renewed sense of purpose, Poppy resolved to push all thoughts of Lawrence Baker aside so she could do the best job possible in her new role.

IO

Grace took Poppy straight to the nitric-acid stores. Poppy's mouth dropped open when she walked in and saw what looked like huge mounds of snow piled up at the back. In parts it was easily two women high. On closer inspection, she could see it wasn't snow being kept in the huge shed but tiny white crystals – it looked almost like salt. Suddenly, one of the women who had been standing at the bottom of one of the piles started clambering her way to the top of it. Once there, she steadied herself and one of the girls below handed a shovel up to her. The woman used the heavy tool to load the crystals into a big trolley on wheels on the ground. The workers at the bottom also heaped shovelfuls into the container and once it was full it was wheeled past Poppy and Grace with apparent ease. Poppy hadn't expected any of the work at the factory to be quite so physical. This was the kind of labour she really would have expected the men on site to be responsible for.

'That's white crystalline nitre,' Grace explained. She motioned for Poppy to follow her as she walked behind the trolley, which was now being pushed out of the storage shed by one of the workers. They followed the trolley as the worker pushed it along outside. The road had been laid here so walking wasn't such a struggle. Poppy could under-stand why the navvies had prioritised this stretch ahead of the rest of the factory roads when she saw how far away the next shed was.

'Most of the roads here at Dornock are in a better state. They had to do them early on because the materials are mainly pushed by hand between the sheds, and the sheds are sometimes more than a mile apart.' Looking ahead, Poppy could see just how spread out all the factory buildings were over at this end of the site.

'Do they keep them far apart in case there are explosions?' Poppy asked.

'Exactly,' Grace replied. 'If one goes up it's bad enough. Just imagine if they were all next to each other. It would be like a big game of dominoes except the sheds wouldn't just topple over, they would all explode, one after the other. We'd lose everything and everyone. It would be a complete disaster.' Poppy decided the miles and miles of walking she was facing every day weren't too bad, after all. As they lumbered along, despite her own tiredness, she was desperate to help the poor girl pushing the trolley full of nitre. She wondered how many times a day she had to make that difficult journey.

When they finally entered the next work shed, Poppy's eyes were drawn to a line of women loading the nitre into a big machine. The machine took over the room as it whirred and hummed along. Just like in the press house, it was a slick production line with every woman focused on the job in hand. Every now and again, someone would pause to say something to the person next to her or shout to someone further down the line, but the process kept churning along steadily.

Poppy followed Grace outside. After around twenty minutes of walking, she could see the next shed in the distance. As they made their way past it, they could hear men's deep voices and coarse language.

'That's one of the men's work sheds,' Grace explained. 'We needn't bother going in – the foremen and Butcher and Baker keep an eye on that one.' Another twenty minutes of walking later they were at the nitrocotton section. Rows and rows of girls used hooks and lifting tackle to take huge bales out of stores. The bales were loaded onto a runway and pushed into another big machine, which looked like a large, round oven. Poppy turned her head to Grace and waited for an explanation.

'Those are twenty-feet-high bales of compressed cotton. Each one weighs nearly five hundred pounds.' Poppy could understand why there wasn't much chatter in here. The women were saving all their breath for the heavy lifting – another task Poppy would have expected the men to be carrying out. Poppy watched on as the women by the machines used what looked like large tin openers to cut the steel bands holding the bales together. They then ripped out handfuls of the compressed cotton and threw it into the shredding machine. Despite the chilly weather, all the women had their sleeves rolled up and their faces were glistening with sweat. Poppy felt warm just watching them.

'Once the cotton is shredded it can be nitrated,' Grace continued as she led Poppy to the other side of the shed and out of the door. On their way to the next building, Poppy could see two workers on the path ahead of them.

'We'll have to see what they're up to. There's not another shift change due for at least a couple of hours so there shouldn't be any workers out and about between the work sheds,' Grace said. The couple were walking towards them and kept on coming when they spotted Grace and Poppy. Poppy felt the fact they weren't running away from them or trying to hide from them was a good sign.

'What are you doing out?' Grace asked when they came within hearing distance.

'Please, ma'am, we're not skiving off. It's just that she's had a funny turn. I don't think she's yet used to all this exertion,' the older of the two girls said. Her voice was full of concern, and she placed her arm protectively around her companion's shoulder. 'The foreman said to take her to the sick bay, but I should think she just needs some peace and quiet. Can I take her to her dorm over at Gretna?' The younger girl was staring at the ground and hadn't uttered a word.

'Do you feel poorly?' Grace asked her kindly. The girl turned bright red and moved her gaze down to her groin area. 'Ah. I think I know what the problem is,' Grace said softly, staring pointedly at a patch of blood on the girl's trousers. When she saw it herself, Poppy felt overcome with affection for the poor lass. Before she could stop herself, she had reached out and taken both the girl's hands in her own.

'Have you bled before, my dear?' she asked softly. The girl looked quickly from side to side before bursting into tears. 'It's all right, my love. It's perfectly natural. Did your mother not tell you about it before you came here?'

'She's an orphan, miss,' her friend explained as Poppy pulled the girl into an embrace and allowed her to weep into her bosom. 'She was in domestic service before but she's only young so I didn't think it could be that. I didn't see the blood. No wonder the foreman was so desperate to get her out of the workshop,' she added, shaking her head.

'See that you take her straight to her hostel. The matron will have everything she needs,' Grace advised. Poppy pulled away and ran her hand gently along the girl's cheek.

'Your friend and the matron will look after you,' Poppy said gently, and her heart almost broke when the girl started crying again. 'You've nothing to be ashamed of,' Poppy stressed just before the pair continued on their way.

'I'm sorry. I got rather caught up in the moment there,' Poppy said hurriedly as she and Grace started to walk again. She hoped she wouldn't get into trouble for being unprofessional. 'I couldn't help myself. I just had to comfort her, the poor thing. Imagine not having a mother to explain that to you.' She hung her head sadly.

'Don't worry. I've been known to get carried away myself in certain situations, so I'm not one to judge. It's difficult to switch off and be tough when you're surrounded by all these young and vulnerable girls. But we need to be careful. We're not here to comfort them or get too familiar – that's what the welfare workers and the matrons are for. We're here to keep them safe and it's better to leave emotion out of it so you can focus on the right things.'

Poppy felt suitably scolded, but she understood where Grace was coming from. If she started letting her feelings get in the way, then she was more at risk of slipping up or missing something that could put everyone at risk. One small mistake could be so catastrophic, it just wasn't worth it.

'I'll make sure I direct anyone who's upset to a welfare worker or their matron,' she said.

Grace nodded her approval. 'The WPS officer on patrol at the township will also check in on her. They go round all the hostels to make sure everything is in order, so the matron will be able to tell her what has happened so it can be reported back to her supervisor at the factory.'

'Can you tell me about the sick bay?' Poppy asked, keen for a change in subject. Grace explained that the factory had its own hospital with eighteen beds.

'There are two male and three female doctors, a dental surgeon and an outpatients department with four nurses, a matron and three ambulances.' Poppy's eyes widened.

'I'd been expecting a wooden hut with a couple of nurses on duty. I've heard of other factories offering little more than basic first aid.'

'Oh no. They're very serious here about keeping everyone in good health. There are so many hazards they just have to be prepared for everything that could go wrong. We've had fingers chopped off, burns from the acids, burns from fires – and then, of course, there is always the risk of explosions. We have to be able to treat those kinds of injuries as soon as we possibly can. There are also resting rooms and dressing stations positioned throughout the factory and qualified nurses stationed at each of them.'

'At least the workers must feel a little reassured,' Poppy sighed. She still thought they were all so brave for carrying out such dangerous work every day. Sure, it was nothing compared to the soldiers putting themselves in the line of fire on the front line, but it still took a brave woman to put herself at such risk continually.

'Baker told me it's more out of concern for the production line,' Grace whispered, raising her eyebrows.

'How do you mean?'

'Well, taking time off for medical examination means production slows down. They want to keep workers in place for as long as possible, so they make sure they're offering the best medical care – and it's on site so there's no time wasted travelling into Carlisle for help.'

Poppy thought about the fact the factory officials seemed to be more concerned about production than the workers' welfare as they made their way to the nitrating house. Inside, it was filled with huge stoneware basins and all the workers were wearing masks covering their mouths and noses. Grace grabbed two from a pile by the door and handed one to Poppy. They both put their masks on and stood back as women threw handfuls of the broken-up cotton into the basins.

'They're mixing the cotton with acids to nitrate it,' Grace explained as they walked swiftly through the room. 'The masks are to give protection from the acid fumes. The masks along with the fumes mean these women don't tend to mess around much.'

'It does seem rather quiet compared to the other work-shops,' Poppy commented.

'It's one of the quietest workshops the factory has. They leave all their quarrels at the door. The only problem with that is that they're quick to pick them back up again when they clock off. These girls are the ones to watch after hours because if they start work annoyed at somebody then they spend the whole shift stewing on it and explode when they leave. I'm not sure what's more frightening – one of these lot exploding or the cordite.'

Poppy laughed at the comparison, but she secretly crossed her fingers and hoped that she never ran into any of these women while they had a bee in their bonnet about anything. 'Is the acid harmful?' she asked. She knew the munitions work was dangerous for the obvious reasons, but she hadn't counted on the workers facing such a hazard.

'The fumes can irritate your throat and eyes, but it's not poisonous. The masks give enough protection but there's always one or two who don't wear them properly or pull them down to chat and get poorly as a consequence. They normally develop an irritating cough, which can lead to total collapse within just a few hours. The main thing to look out for in this work shed is anybody not wearing their mask correctly. The welfare supervisors and foremen are always on the lookout, too. Not surprisingly, there's a high turnover of workers in this section.'

'How do you mean?'

'Girls sent to work here normally only stay for a few months before either transferring to another section or leaving the factory altogether.' Poppy had to admit that she wouldn't very much enjoy working in this part of the factory for long. She could understand why the workers didn't tend to stick around. 'Like I said, there's not much larking around in here so we generally do a quick check and then go on our way.

But there's always a foreman on hand if the workers need any help.' Grace pointed to a man sitting by the door. He was dressed in brown overalls and he was wearing a mask.

'Afternoon, Grace,' the man said, pulling off his mask and giving them both a smile and a wink. Poppy winced at the removal of his mask, considering everything Grace had just told her.

'This is Geoffrey,' Grace said. 'The most relaxed foreman you ever shall meet,' she added, laughing lightly. Poppy noticed that although Geoffrey had removed his mask, Grace had kept hers on, and so she happily did the same. 'Geoffrey, this is our newest WPS recruit, Poppy.'

Geoffrey got to his feet and offered his hand out to Poppy. His shaggy blonde hair looked in need of a good cut and Poppy thought the stubble around his chin looked uncomfortable and itchy. Once he was standing, Poppy could see he was really rather short. He was about the same height as her and she was used to always being the shortest person in the room. She thought back to Superintendent Baker's powerful presence before quickly forcing herself to focus back on Geoffrey.

'It's a pleasure to meet you, miss,' Geoffrey said firmly in a strong Scottish accent. Poppy went to shake his hand, but he took it and gently turned it palm down and kissed the back of it. She tried not to wince as the rough stubble scraped her skin. The move seemed a little unprofessional given the setting and their roles, and Poppy found herself smiling awkwardly as she pulled her hand back. Then she realised he wouldn't be able to tell she was smiling as her mask was covering her mouth and she felt grateful to have it on despite how uncomfortable it felt.

'Don't worry, Geoffrey's just a charmer,' Grace said with a sigh. As if on cue, he gave Poppy another cheeky wink, then replaced his mask and picked up his clipboard. Poppy wondered if he went out of his way to try and be alluring with women in an attempt to distract them from his short stature. She smiled politely and tried not to giggle at her internal dialogue. It wasn't like her to be mean, but she found she couldn't stop the thoughts coming. His efforts just seemed over the top to her.

'Duty calls, ladies. I'll see you both around,' Geoffrey announced cheerfully before striding off in the opposite direction.

'Some of the foremen can be a bit handsy with the girls but Geoffrey isn't one to worry about,' Grace explained as Poppy watched him make his way around the women working at the basins. He stopped to make a comment to each worker and seemed to get a positive response back from all of them. They all seemed happy enough to be in his company.

'He certainly seems full of confidence,' Poppy observed carefully.

'Geoffrey's ever the charmer but that's where it stops. He's actually very useful in a stressful situation. He once jumped in to help when I was breaking up a fight and one of the girls turned on me. Not many other foremen would do that for fear of getting attacked by an angry mob of women.'

'Oh dear, were you both all right?' Poppy asked.

'We were both fine. So were the girls, once they had calmed down. Geoffrey gets on with them all so well that nobody jumped on him for intervening.' Poppy was beginning to feel nervous again. 'I was glad I was here when it happened and not at one of the other workshops where the foremen are less liked. It's always best to call on them for backup, though. No matter what the girls think of them, you're better off with an extra pair of hands on your side than not.' Poppy hoped it wouldn't ever come to that, but it was reassuring to know that aid would always be nearby if she got into a tricky state of affairs.

'However,' Grace started as they made their way out of the nitrating house. 'Just keep an eye out for foremen being over-familiar with the girls – especially the younger ones. Although they're useful for stepping in when we need help, they're not used to being surrounded by young, impression-able girls all day and night, and some of the workers are too naive or scared to tell them to just leave them be.' Poppy remembered Frosty mentioning something along the same lines and nodded her head knowledgeably.

After another long walk, Poppy was ready for more tea, but, instead, she found herself in the boiling house surrounded by women working over rows of round metal vats. After a quick walk around, they were just about to leave when they heard raised voices coming from the entrance. It was in such stark contrast to the constant drone of chatter and machine noise that it made Poppy jump. She looked straight to Grace and followed suit when she charged back towards the boiling vats.

A loud scream pierced the air and Poppy felt her pace naturally quicken despite the fact that she was exhausted. Shouting started up before another scream rang out, and, now fully aware of all the dangers associated with munitions work, Poppy found herself terrified of what they might discover when they got to the source of the noise.

11

Poppy could see a group of workers had gathered around the metal vat closest to the entrance. As the cotton bubbled away, two women scrapped dangerously close to the hot drums. Nobody was stepping in to help either of them. Poppy imagined they were all too frightened of getting knocked into the boiling water. But they were all shouting and egging the pair on from the sidelines.

'Show 'er what for!' one shouted, waving her fist in the air.

'Can't let her get away with talking to you like that. I don't care how important her father is!' another yelled angrily.

Grace pushed her way through the small crowd with Poppy following close behind. As soon as the workers saw their uniform they stopped yelling and gesticulating, and scattered back to their stations, leaving the women to their fight. But as they drew closer, Poppy saw the fight was actually more of an attack. One of the women was trying desperately to defend herself as the other came at her relentlessly. The aggressor was so engrossed in grabbing and kicking at her victim that she didn't realise the crowd had dispersed, let alone that two WPS officers were about to grab hold of the two of them. The lack of audience seemed to give the victim a glimmer of confidence, because she suddenly reared up and started hitting back at her aggressor.

Poppy saw Grace reach for the attacker and so she instinctively grabbed the one who was now fighting back. They wrenched the women apart at the same time. Both were so shocked at being hauled back so suddenly that they didn't have a chance to put up a fight, making things a lot easier than they could have been for Poppy and Grace. The pair of them swiftly used suffrajitsu to incapacitate the warring workers, holding their arms firmly behind their backs. Poppy was relieved when neither of the women wriggled against the grips holding them in place and nobody tried to go to their rescue. The way the rest of the workers had scurried away when she and Grace had turned up reassured her that, although some of the women may not be very happy being policed by them, the WPS name was well respected as an authority by the majority. There was a deafening silence as both women took a few moments to catch their breath.

'Let's go outside for a talk, shall we?' Grace suggested as the normal background chitter-chatter and work noises resumed around them.

'Good idea,' Poppy agreed. Neither woman said a word. Poppy and Grace each led their worker out into the cold air. Poppy kept a firm grip on the arm of the woman she was guiding. She couldn't risk letting her guard down and be caught unawares by the worker suddenly deciding to fight back like she had done on the factory floor. Poppy would never live it down. Relief washed over her when the bitter wind rushed across her whole body. All the steam from the boiling vats, as well as the hot air between the two workers, had left Poppy feeling rather flushed. She was impressed at Grace's idea to take the enemies outside to try and resolve their differences. There would be less chance of anybody else piping up or one of them trying to show off in front of their friends this way.

'Has everybody calmed down enough now to be freed?' Grace asked firmly but cautiously.

Both women nodded their heads and avoided eye contact

with each other. The one Grace had tackled had a strong look of defiance on her face. When Poppy let go of the woman she had been holding on to and stood next to her, she noticed she looked meek and slightly ashamed of her actions. Grace and her worker stood side by side, facing Poppy and hers. 'We'll start with names,' Grace continued slowly, looking between them both expectantly.

'My name is Virginia,' the woman beside Poppy whispered, staring at the ground. Poppy noticed she looked rather pale, and her cap was wonky. She also had a big scratch running down her left cheek. The bright red blood emerging from it told Poppy that it was definitely a fresh wound.

'Lady Virginia,' the woman next to Grace remarked sarcastically. Poppy turned her attention to the owner of the voice and saw her face was full of disgust as she eyed Virginia up and down. 'Just who does she think she is, coming in here and pretending to be one of us when all along she's been hiding the fact that her father's a duke! A duke! Can you ruddy well believe it? I don't know what she's up to but I'm not having any of it!' The woman had gone red in the face and she was clearly getting riled up again now. Poppy felt herself switching to defensive mode. Her hands tensed and she was ready to act the moment the woman might make another lunge for Virginia.

'What does it matter if she's a lady?' Grace asked.

'I did not mean to deceive anyone,' Virginia said in a formal but shaky voice. 'I just . . . I just wanted to do my bit like everybody else.' She paused to take a handkerchief out of her pocket. As her hand took the material to her nose it brushed her scratched cheek and she winced in pain. 'I didn't think anybody here would talk to me if I told them my title.' She sniffed. 'I'm sorry, Frances. I just want to help the war effort like everyone else here. I don't wish to make an enemy of you. I don't wish to make an enemy of anybody, for that matter.' Frances tutted and threw her hands up in the air. Poppy was on tenterhooks now. One step forward from Frances and she was ready to incapacitate her.

'You must think yourself terribly hard done by, having to slum it here with all of us penniless farm girls,' Frances spat back in response. 'Did you not think we would realise your ruse as soon as you opened that fancy little mouth of yours?' There was silence as Frances waited for an answer. When none was forthcoming, she carried on. 'Listen to yourself, Lady Virginia! Do you not hear the posh in your own voice? You stick out here like a whore at a dinner party! I'll bet you've been writing to your stuck-up friends to tell them how awful we all are. Is that why you're here? To make fun of us all?'

Virginia flinched and looked visibly distressed by her colleague's words. She closed her eyes for a moment, as if preparing herself to reply. 'I don't think any of you awful. To the contrary, I think you're all quite wonderful. I've never met women as honest and genuine as you all are in there. It's really quite something to be around.' She paused for a moment to finally look Frances in the eye. 'At least I *did* think you were wonderful before you were so terribly mean to me,' she added before almost shrinking in on herself.

Frances cackled at Virginia's words and Poppy had to stop herself from reaching forward and giving her a clip round the ear. She might have looked older than herself and Grace, but she was certainly acting like a child.

'That's enough now,' Poppy said firmly. She looked quickly over at Grace. She had stepped in again before thinking. She kept forgetting that she was only meant to be shadowing her new colleague. But Grace gave her a subtle smile that told her she was happy for her to take the reins on this. Reassured, she continued.

'Frances, you're being unnecessarily nasty to this poor girl. You must remember that you're all here with the same common goal – to help our lads and make sure we win this war. It makes no odds where you both came from when you're here to do the same job. I'm sure Virginia thinks herself no better than you when she's here getting her hands dirty alongside you. If she thought herself any grander then she would surely have stayed at home being a lady and leaving you and your friends to do all the hard work.' Poppy finished and was quite pleased with herself. As she had been talking she had noticed Frances' cocky demeanour shrivelling as she seemingly took in everything she was saying.

'My father didn't even want me to come here,' Virginia said now. Her voice was a little louder than it had been previously, and she was standing slightly taller. Frances raised her eyebrows.

'You don't say? I don't suppose a duke would want his precious daughter getting close to *the help*,' she said mockingly.

'Let her finish,' Poppy snapped. Frances huffed and folded her arms, but she kept her mouth shut to allow Virginia to continue.

'I can assure you that I do not have the same outdated views as my father. In fact, none of my siblings do. My brothers signed up to fight without telling him and I told him I was going to stay with my aunt in Scotland before coming here instead. I'm afraid he'd rather lose his rag if he discovered what I was really up to. But I don't care a jot. You see, I can't just sit around at home and let everybody else help our lads on the front line – especially not when two of them are my very own flesh and blood.'

Frances smirked as she learned of Virginia's defiance. 'A lady with a bit of a spark. Maybe you're not so bad after all,' she said, unfolding her arms and placing her hands on her hips. 'I reckon we could start again now I know you're not too stuck up.' Virginia's face flushed with relief.

'Maybe next time you should get to know someone before judging them,' Poppy suggested. She couldn't believe how quickly Frances had changed her mind about Virginia, having been so passionately against her co-worker just minutes before.

'It's all right,' Virginia cut in before Frances could respond. 'I would have been suspicious of somebody who had lied about where they came from, too. I should have just been honest from the start. But I was scared. I've never been in the company of such confident women before and I'm afraid to say that I panicked.'

'Come on, let's get back to work before the others think we've got ourselves arrested,' Frances joked as she linked arms with Virginia and led her back into the boiling house. Poppy and Grace followed behind.

'They'll be friends for life after that,' Grace commented cheerfully. Despite the rocky start, Poppy had to agree.

'Sometimes the best friendships start out with a fight,' she replied lightly. The run-in had made her think of Maggie, who she knew had fallen out with a fellow WPS recruit during training. The two girls had ended up being good friends after they'd realised it had all been a big misunderstanding. She had also seen a bit of Maggie in Virginia, with her act of insubordination against her father. Although she was certain her friend would have fought back against Frances with all her might if she had found herself in Virginia's position. Poppy smiled as she thought about her young, feisty friend. She wondered how Maggie and Annie were getting on without her. Poppy's musings were interrupted by a sudden roar of cheers when she walked back into the boiling house with Grace. On seeing Virginia and Frances return arm-in-arm ahead of them, the other workers had stopped what they were doing to whoop and applaud them.

'Show's over! Back to work!' Grace bellowed over the noise.

The raucous behaviour stopped instantly, and everyone returned to what they had been doing in the blink of an eye. Out of the blue, a foreman rushed over. 'Nothing to worry about. There won't be any more trouble,' Grace explained. 'You might want to send that one to get her cheek looked at when she finishes her shift. It can wait until then,' she added, pointing after Virginia. The foreman thanked her and wandered off again. 'It's all been sorted with no thanks to you, you useless lump,' Grace whispered under her breath.

'That was a lot easier to deal with than I'd anticipated when I first saw them fighting,' Poppy remarked. They had made their way through the boiling house now and were on their way to the drying areas.

'We were lucky it was an unfair fight. If there had been two women of Frances' calibre going at it then we might have struggled to pull them apart. Especially with the foreman nowhere to be found despite the noise. And there would have been more chance that the other workers would have piled in on us in that situation. But, as it was, they were probably happy to see us coming to poor Virginia's rescue.'

'But they were egging Frances on.'

'Of course they were. They love a bit of drama, and nobody here is silly enough to stand up to a woman like Frances. Thanks for helping, by the way. I wasn't sure if you'd get stuck in or not.'

'Oh, I couldn't have left you to deal with it alone, even with only one woman fighting back. But, it does make me worry about what happens when you come across such quarrels when you're patrolling by yourself? Surely it would be safer if we were always in pairs?' Poppy couldn't help but feel panicked when she thought about trying to separate two squabbling workers amid a baying crowd on her own.

'If only it were that simple. Ideally, we would never patrol alone, but we just don't have enough recruits at the moment.

That's why the foremen are so important. If I'd have been on my own back there then I would have chased down that foreman before pulling the women apart. Poor Virginia might have suffered a few more bruises before I managed to get to her aid, but I'd rather that than risk getting turned on with no-one to back me up. We didn't know the fight was so one-sided until we were in the middle of it. But don't worry too much. Scraps like that are few and far between. The rough lots here may be mouthy, but they tend to be more mouth than action thankfully. It rarely escalates like that.'

Poppy knew she would have to try hard to think before acting when she was patrolling single-handedly. Her instincts always led her to jump in and help before thinking of any consequences for herself. She couldn't imagine leaving women to hurt each other while she rushed off to find some-body to give her assistance. But she would have to from now on. She crossed her fingers behind her back and prayed for no more fights on her watch.

12

They walked in silence to the drying section. Poppy was thinking about how she had grown used to patrolling alone since she and Maggie had started focusing on different targets. She was trying to reassure herself that she would be able to cope patrolling on her own at Gretna. But, no matter how hard she tried, she still felt nervous. It seemed safer in Holborn because she knew the area. There was also the small fact that she didn't risk killing thousands of people and losing precious ammunition destined for British troops with just one small slip-up. Just before they reached the drying section, Poppy decided that she would have to put her fears to one side and get on with the job at hand. Worrying was only going to lead to mistakes, and mistakes could be deadly here at Gretna.

Grace stopped at the entrance but didn't go inside. 'We check in with the foremen here and we clock on, but we don't enter unless there's an emergency. The drying areas are the highest danger zones because of the potential for the nitrocotton to ignite, so it's important to keep the number of people traipsing through to a minimum. Plus, the workers and the foremen here wear special rubber gumboots because nails in ordinary shoes can produce sparks.'

Grace banged heavily on the door three times. A few moments later it swung open, and they were met by a grinning man in brown foreman overalls. Poppy noticed a pool of water at his feet. When she looked behind him, she could see a female worker directing a hose to the ground and spraying a constant stream of water around the floor. The warmth from the room hit her, and she also took in the now familiar noise of women at work interspersed with their voices and different dialects talking in the background.

'Hello, love. You'll be pleased to know that everything is running like clockwork here today. I thought I might have to send one young 'un down to the sick bay, but she perked up after some fresh air. I think the heat just got a bit too much for her. I've got her on hose duty now.' Grace smiled and introduced Poppy. 'Hopefully I won't see too much of you, love,' he said, still grinning. 'We prefer to keep things quiet and trouble free in here.'

'I'm glad to hear it,' Poppy replied happily. Once he had gone back inside and closed the door, Poppy asked about the water on the floor.

'They keep the floors constantly wet as a safety precaution,' Grace explained. 'There's a women's fire brigade unit in the factory and they recommended it after a fire broke out early on. One of the stoves caught light and killed a man and injured six other workers. Then, a few weeks later, the cotton in one of the drying machines went up in flames. The fire spread so quickly they thought they would lose the whole work shed. It was full of smoke. Honestly, I don't know what I would have done in that situation. One of the firewomen climbed a ladder beside the machine, which was about twenty feet high, and cut away the burning cotton to prevent the flames from spreading further. As she did that, the others operated the steam and water sprinklers to put out the blaze. It was thanks to their quick thinking that the whole section didn't go up.'

Poppy couldn't imagine acting so quickly and calmly in such a dangerous situation. She felt quite content to stay out of the drying section after hearing that story. When they passed two lorries parked up outside, Grace explained that once the nitrocotton had been dried out it was packed into rubber bags and transferred to the nitroglycerine section on the vehicles.

At the nitroglycerine section, the building was full of floor-to-ceiling copper machines, which looked like they belonged in a distillery. They walked past all the machines and stopped at a workstation where a group of women were slowly and carefully kneading liquid and cotton together. None of the workers spoke. Nobody even looked up when Poppy and Grace approached. They were concentrating so intently on their work that Poppy thought she could have run naked through the building without being noticed.

'What are they doing?' she asked quietly, afraid of disturbing them.

'They're kneading together the nitrocotton and nitroglycerine. The smallest generation of heat could cause an explosion, so they have to be particularly careful while they do it. They call it "stirring the devil's porridge".'

'Why do they call it that?'

'Sir Arthur Conan Doyle – you know the author who wrote the Sherlock Holmes stories?'

Poppy nodded her head eagerly. The stories had been some of John's favourites and she had loved listening to him talk about them when he'd been reading them. He would often stop halfway through a tale, so excited was he about what was happening in it that he just had to share it with her. 'Sir Arthur visited a few months ago and then he wrote an article about the factory for the *Annandale Observer*. One of the more local girls brought the paper in one day – I think the page is still stuck up on the wall in one of the canteens. He saw the girls kneading the nitrocotton and nitroglycerine together, and he understood how dangerous it was. He wrote in the article that it was as if they were stirring the devil's porridge and of course the description stuck. The girls in this section were rather pleased with themselves, as you can imagine.'

Poppy couldn't help but wish she had been here when Sir Arthur had visited. Would being in the presence of one of John's heroes have helped her feel closer to him? She would have to make do with walking in the author's footsteps – which she thought was still rather a lovely thing. She wondered if this was another sign that this role was something that John would have wanted for her. But it also broke her heart that John wasn't here so she could tell him the exciting news. Poppy was still thinking of John when a scream pierced the air.

'We need help over here!' a voice bellowed out through the silence that had immediately fallen over the room. Poppy followed Grace back through the workshop towards a crowd of workers near the entrance. A woman was splayed out on the floor, groaning as if she was drunk, while another woman desperately fanned her hand over her face.

'That won't do her any good.' Grace tutted as she pushed past the workers who had gathered to watch and gently nudged the worker kneeling over the casualty to one side. She grabbed the casualty under one armpit and motioned for Poppy to take the other side. Poppy did as she was told and the pair of them hauled the worker to the entrance, her legs dragging along the floor. 'As always, no foreman in sight,' Grace muttered under her breath. Once in the cold, fresh air, they gently laid the woman down on the floor on her back.

'Whatever is the matter with her?' Poppy asked as Grace held the woman's hand and stroked her head reassuringly.

'It's just the fumes. She needs to sleep it off. She'll be all right in an hour or so,' Grace said matter-of-factly. The woman's groans became quieter and less frequent until she eventually fell asleep. 'You'll often see women splayed out on the floor outside the work sheds mid-shift. If they start being sick then you need to get them to a nurse, but otherwise the fresh air and rest will sort them out. We'll find a welfare worker on our way back through and make sure she comes out to check on her regularly.'

With that, Grace was back on her feet and heading back into the work shed. Poppy hesitated before following Grace in. She stopped by the door to take another look at the worker. She couldn't believe they were just going to leave her there. She had seemed so poorly.

'Honestly, she'll be all right,' Grace assured her. 'But it's another thing to look out for on your searches. As I told you before, sometimes the fumes from the day before catch up with them and they can be a little unsteady on their feet before they even clock on. Anyone who seems a bit tipsy when you search them needs to be sent outside for some fresh air.'

Inside the next work shed they found a line of girls working paste – the result of the nitroglycerine being absorbed into the nitrocotton – by hand through leather sieves and into bags.

'From here it's loaded onto the paste train and transported to the cordite section – back where we started.' Grace let out a big sigh. 'Now we've covered the whole process and the main factory buildings, are you suitably exhausted?' she added with a smile.

'It's a rather long process,' Poppy replied wearily. 'And there was a lot of walking involved. But the main thing is that I know where all the relevant buildings are so I can find my way around when I'm on duty tomorrow.' She didn't admit that she had drawn herself a little map as they had walked around. Grace had pointed out more magazine stores and 'danger buildings' that needed clocking in at, as well as more train stations, which Poppy had marked down. She

understood that she wasn't to enter any of the smaller huts
– especially the ones where explosives were being worked on
in isolation – but she was still responsible for making sure
there were no shifty characters lurking who might be trying
to get their hands on sensitive information.

'Finding your way around is probably the most important
thing for now. And if you get into any bother then you just
need to look for another WPS recruit or a foreman. Remember
you can call on welfare workers for advice, too. They know
all the girls really well so they can be very useful. I do think
you'll get the hang of it in no time, though.'

Poppy hoped Grace was right. They made their way back
to Gretna so Poppy could get settled into her new room.

Once they entered the Gretna township, Poppy was
shocked at how much like a town the place was. She had
expected rows of huts with some hostels thrown in, but there
was so much more than that. She felt like she was stepping
into a real community, and it gave her a feeling of warmth
despite the extra chill in the air now the evening was drawing
in. Poppy felt like she had been walking for hours, and she
probably had been, but she had no way of knowing as she
had lost track of all time since arriving in Carlisle.

They walked alongside a rail track as they passed the first
row of houses in the township. Poppy jumped as a train slowly
approached behind them. Instinctively, she went to leap out
of the way, but Grace pulled her back in. Poppy shuddered
as the huge carriages chugged past them. She was terrified of
being so close to something so big and powerful. It felt like
the ground was moving beneath her feet and she could feel
the heat coming off the carriages as they moved past her. She
looked over at Grace and could see that she was saying something to her but she couldn't hear her over all the noise. Finally,
the train overtook them and disappeared into the distance.

'I was trying to tell you that as long as you stay off the

tracks then you'll be all right.' Grace laughed as Poppy tried to compose herself. She realised she was shaking from the fright she had just experienced.

'I don't think I've ever been so close to a moving train in all my life,' she gasped.

'You'll get used to it. There are so many here that you don't have much of a choice. Soon enough it will be just the same as seeing motor cars to you.' They passed by a row of big brick buildings that looked like huge houses. There was merely a thin path separating them and the railway line. They stepped onto the path and Poppy felt like she was walking on air after having dragged herself through the miles of mud at the factory grounds.

'Do the trains run all day and all night?' Poppy asked. Grace nodded. 'How does anybody get any sleep? Oh. Wait. Let me guess. They get used to it?'

'They do indeed. You're getting the hang of this rather quickly,' Grace said with a giggle. Poppy hoped her room wasn't right next to the track. She was used to a certain amount of noise living in London, but the trains were passing by so close to the houses here that she was certain they must make the windows shake. 'These houses were built for the chemists, administrators and factory officials who brought their families with them. All of the other workers are in wooden huts or bungalows like us. Most people call it Timber Town for that reason.' They passed through to a row of large wooden bungalows.

'These are hostels for the workers,' Grace explained. 'There are long dormitories inside. It's a little bit like a barracks, I suppose. They have recreation and resting rooms, dining and sitting rooms, kitchens, sculleries and toilet and washing facilities. Each hostel also has a matron who cooks for the girls outside of the canteen hours and looks out for their welfare.'

Poppy thought back to the bleeding girl and how Grace had assured her that her hostel matron would help her with her problem. Up ahead, Poppy could see a group of young girls talking outside a large hall.

'That's the Border Hall where they hold dances for the workers,' Grace said. 'You'll find the women in particular like to take advantage of their new-found freedom and high wages. Although the work is tough and they work extremely long hours, there is a lot on offer to help them blow off steam.' She approached the group of girls outside the dance hall and introduced Poppy. 'I hope you'll all be behaving yourselves tonight,' she added warmly.

'Oh, but of course,' one of the women replied with a wink.

'We wouldn't dream of causing any trouble, miss,' another chimed in cheekily. Poppy looked to Grace and saw she was smiling along with the girls. They all said goodbye and Grace and Poppy continued on their way while the girls went into the hall.

'They like to tease but the most trouble that lot will get into will be too much liquor and a fumble on the playing fields with one of the male workers or a local boy,' Grace said lightly. 'Or they might stay out ten minutes past the 10 p.m. curfew. They're not too difficult to keep in line.' Poppy thought it sounded a lot easier than trying to keep London's prostitutes on the straight and narrow when they were surrounded by all the temptations soldiers brought with them. 'A lot of the girls who work here are single and childless. They're not used to being paid so well and they only have themselves to spend their wages on. We try to encourage them to join the Girl Guides or go along to gymnastics classes but you can imagine how attractive those things sound to them compared to dances and cinema showings. They even let boys from Carlisle in to go to the dances at the weekends. I think it's to try and discourage the workers from travelling into town with all the extra temptations there. There's also no risk of them being distracted by the local boys when they're at work in the factory.'

'That's one blessing,' Poppy mused.

'Despite all of that on offer in their free time, some of the women still prefer to skive off work and sit in the cafés instead. Butcher thinks they need education on how to spend their money wisely, but I think they just need a little reminder now and then of why they're here. It's as if the extra money goes to their heads and they forget sometimes. It takes away all their focus and patriotism.'

'How much money are you talking about?' Poppy asked. She was intrigued. She had always thought the pay would have to be high to tempt women like Alice off the streets, but she realised now that she had no idea how much these women were being compensated for risking their lives every day. Grace suddenly stopped a pair of girls heading towards them.

'Off to the dance hall?' she asked.

'Yes, miss. We've finished work for the day,' one of them replied nervously.

'Oh, I'm not looking to pull you up on anything. My colleague here is new and she's trying to understand what brought you all here. Would you mind telling her your story?'

'Of course not, miss,' the girl replied. She seemed to have relaxed now and she smiled at Poppy before going on. 'I'd heard about the munitions factories and, like everyone else, I wanted to help our boys however I could. But I didn't know how to go about it and these factories seemed rather dangerous and scary if you don't mind me saying so.'

'Our mother told us we could do anything but go into munitions,' her companion added.

'This is my little sister – we came here together. Munitions wouldn't have been what we chose but a lady came to our town and gave a lecture about it. She made it sound so good that we signed up there and then. Our mother wasn't happy when we told her we were coming here but we've two younger brothers and she's been struggling to feed them since we lost our father.'

'She couldn't say no when we told her what we'd be getting paid,' her sister added.

'It's good pay, isn't it?' Grace replied.

'Oh yes, miss,' the younger of the two sisters said eagerly. 'Before the war we were working as servants. We got paid six shillings a week for working sixty hours. Now we get twenty-two shillings and sixpence every week – each. They take off twelve shillings for board and food but even after that we're so much better off. And if we work on a Sunday or take on overtime then we can get paid double that. It really is something, aint it, miss?'

Poppy smiled and nodded her agreement. It certainly sounded a wonderful deal. But she couldn't help but wonder how much these young girls' safety was worth. She knew that if she had a daughter then she would much rather she worked as a servant and brought home less money. She would prefer that to her offspring putting her life in danger every day for better pay. But then, of course, working in munitions and doing your bit for the men on the front line was something to be proud of. Poppy decided that, for once, she was grateful she wasn't a mother having to watch her children make these sacrifices for the country. She hoped Annie would never have to watch on as Charlotte did anything similar. Grace and Poppy said goodbye to the sisters and continued on their way to the WPS accommodation.

'The women come from all over the country to work here, but a lot of them already live nearby and catch the train in every day. Lots of local businesses have lost workers as they just can't compete with the wages. There's a lot of resentment.

One café owner even took a boy to court for breach of contract.'

'What happened?'

'The magistrates fined the lad. He'd been working as an errand boy for five shillings a week at the café and he was offered work here as a labourers' mate, heating navvies' food tins, for four times that amount. You can't blame him for leaving the café job. I don't suppose he was bothered about the fine what with all the extra cash he was getting paid every week.' They continued walking and Grace pointed out a cinema, a reading room, shops, bakeries, banks, a gymnasium, a billiard hall and the hospital along the way. There were even tennis courts and a primary school for the children of workers who had brought their families with them.

'There's certainly enough to keep us busy,' Poppy commented. 'Do you ever get a chance to rest?' Grace laughed, which made Poppy uneasy.

'I've found that since I got here, it's better to just keep going. You have to learn to power through. It's only when you stop that you realise how completely exhausted you are. But don't worry—'

'I'll get used to it?' Poppy cut in. Grace smiled and Poppy grinned back, but the weariness behind her new colleague's eyes made her feel anxious. 'I do hope you're right,' Poppy replied quietly as she found herself reaching for the wedding ring in her pocket for comfort.

13

When they reached the WPS hostel, Poppy couldn't help but feel a little disappointed. The long, one-storey wooden hut looked just the same as the workers' accommodation from the outside. Poppy prided herself on the fact she didn't see herself as being superior to the women she looked out for in her police role, but she had to admit that she had expected a slightly comfier living space.

'It looks much the same from the outside, but we do have a few more home comforts than the munitionettes,' Grace assured her. Poppy was certain that she hadn't voiced her disappointment, but then she realised she was pulling a face that revealed it very clearly. She smiled uncomfortably, hoping Grace wasn't thinking that she was stuck up. 'Our hostel is actually a lot better than the hostels the workers live in. Our bathing and cleaning facilities are more elaborate, and we have separate bedrooms with hot water pipes in every room.' Poppy smiled now. She was relieved that, unlike the workers, she was going to have more than a thin curtain to separate her from her sleeping colleagues. And a hot-water supply to her room was going to be a blessing in this cold weather. 'Also, remember that the navvies are going to be building us a most comfortable barracks. Once they've finished the damn roads.'

Poppy's room wasn't much to write home about, but it did feel quite spacious compared to her digs back in Holborn and she felt glad to be surrounded by rooms occupied by lots of other women rather than snoring policemen. She had walked and walked with Grace past row upon row of hostels and huts built for the workers until finally reaching the WPS hostel. Her trunk had been waiting on the small but comfy-looking bed in her room, and she had quickly unpacked her clothes into the slimline wardrobe. Then she had taken great pleasure in kicking off her boots and putting on a thick pair of socks before diving under the bedclothes to try and warm up. Poppy read back through the notes she had made in Grace's pad to try and refresh her mind, before setting it to one side to write a letter to Annie and Maggie to let them know she had arrived safely and that she was excited – if not a little daunted – about getting started in the morning.

When her stomach growled, Poppy realised she hadn't eaten since that morning. It was nearly ten o'clock in the evening. Looking around the sparse room, she wondered how she was going to satisfy her hunger before the morning. She knew from Grace that the factory operated all day and all night, so she thought there must be food available some-where. Then she remembered Grace mentioning something about the canteens offering meals to the workers on shift. Racking her brains, she tried to bring to mind what Grace had said but there was so much new information trying to settle in her head that she just couldn't do it. She couldn't quite believe that she hadn't thought to ask her what the WPS recruits did about eating, and she felt rather silly for the oversight.

Poppy's legs were heavy with tiredness, but her stomach won the battle and she dragged herself off the bed, put her boots back on and made her way outside. The rooms next to Poppy's were in complete darkness but she could see a slight light coming from one a few doors down, so she headed towards it. She tapped lightly on the door, worried about waking one of her new colleagues. Standing back, Poppy heard shuffling from inside and she was happy to be met with a smile when the occupant opened the door to her.

'Are you the new recruit?' the woman asked in an Irish accent. She was tall and slim, and looked to be in her late sixties. Her mid-length greying hair was hanging loose but it had kinks in it like it had recently been let down after a long time tied back. She stood sideways to the door and the light from inside her room reflected off her glasses.

Poppy nodded and introduced herself, and the woman smiled. 'I'm Jean. I saw you patrolling with Grace earlier. Are you settling in all right?'

'I am, thank you. But I'm afraid I'm rather hungry after all the walking today. Is there somewhere I can get something to eat?'

'They'll be serving tea and biscuits to the night shifters at the canteen soon. There's always enough for us to have some if we're around, too. And the welfare workers and the foremen will pop in for something if they're around. I was just getting ready to go over there myself for a cuppa before my night patrol. I'll get my jacket and walk you over.'

'Thank you so much,' Poppy replied gratefully. She had tried to concentrate as Grace had led her through the township but there had been so much to see and she had been so tired that she wasn't confident she would have been able to make it back to the factory canteen by herself – especially in the dark.

Jean stepped back into her room and put on her jacket and cap, and then they left the hostel together. As they neared the end of the road a slight murmur of noise started travelling towards them. It grew louder and louder until they turned onto the next row of wooden buildings and joined a flow of women all headed in the same direction. Chatter and laughter filled the air as the women walked through the township on their way to the factory to start the next shift. Poppy thought they seemed to be in such good spirits that you could mistake them for groups of friends heading out to socialise rather than women from all sorts of backgrounds thrown together and expected to risk their lives for their country day in and day out. As they neared the dance hall and cinema, Poppy noticed there were also women fighting back against the crowd to go the other way. She assumed that they must have got caught up in the work crowd while on their way back to their hostels for the 10 p.m. curfew.

'Watch out! It's the lady coppers!' a voice shouted in Poppy and Jean's direction.

'Heads down, girls! Best behaviour!' another woman bellowed from behind them. The remarks were harmless enough but something about their tone made Poppy feel uncomfortable. It didn't feel as if they were being said in jest and she didn't get the sense that the workers were being welcoming or friendly.

'You're not so special! I bet your husband's at home having it off with your sister while you're throwing your weight around here!' someone screeched from the crowd.

'And her mother!' another hollered from further away. Poppy was astonished by the last comments. She had heard some insults during her time working with London's prostitutes but that was just downright mean. And there didn't seem to be any reason for it; they weren't disciplining the women or searching them for contraband. They weren't doing anything that could warrant such a dramatic reaction – they were simply walking through the township alongside them. Unsure of the best way to respond, Poppy looked over to Jean who continued staring straight ahead, seemingly unaffected. Poppy wondered if Jean had heard the horrible remarks.

'They tend to get worse if you react,' Jean said in a hushed voice. 'I like to give a small acknowledgement and then carry on with whatever I'm doing when they're in big groups like this. As long as they're not doing anything to risk their safety or the safety of others then it's best to leave them to it. If mouthing off to us keeps them happy then so be it.'

'I've already learned that they don't much like answering to authority,' Poppy muttered.

'Indeed. Lots of them are full of coarse language and some of the recruits will go out of their way to pick them up on it but they end up getting into silly squabbles and it can escalate rather quickly in this kind of environment. I tend to pick my battles. I don't much care if they are turning the air blue so long as they're not putting anybody in danger.'

Poppy took a moment to mull over Jean's words. She decided that her new neighbour had a very good attitude when it came to the workers. 'I think I shall try and think like you do in these situations,' she said, feeling positive. But she knew that she would have to work on stopping herself from jumping in and reacting before she'd had a chance to think through her response. Just then, a group of girls rushed past them making siren sounds and giggling.

'The more of them there are, the more confident and cheeky they become,' Jean commented, laughing at the group's antics. 'It's mostly harmless fun. I've been threatened a few times, but no one has ever followed through.'

'What happened?' Poppy asked.

'Oh, it's always just someone showing off in front of their friends and workmates. But the majority of them would never act on anything they say. That's why it's best to just let them have their fun – like we're doing tonight. Their childish comments aren't doing any harm so there's no point in challenging them. The last thing you want to do is encourage any bawdy behaviour.'

The chugging noise of a train started in the distance. As it drew closer, Poppy heard whooping and shouting. Girls in the crowd of workers stopped to wave at the women hanging out of the train window and shouted at them as the train roared slowly past. Steam filled the air and as it slowly faded away, so too did the excitement and the noise from the workers.

'That's the women coming in from out of the township for the night shift,' Jean explained. 'The Ministry took over one of the big hotels in Carlisle so workers could stay there. They also turned the skating rink and riding school into a hostel – there's another four hundred workers or so in there. Lots of workers are lodging with local families but it often means four girls being put up in three-bedroomed houses with a family already living there.'

'Golly. I think I know where I would prefer to be living,' Poppy said in wonderment. She couldn't believe hundreds of workers had lucked out and been placed in a fancy hotel while thousands of others were slumming it in wooden huts or lodging with big families in small houses.

'Yes, those girls certainly got the best deal.' Jean laughed. 'You'll need to keep an eye on them as they come in if you're patrolling at any of the stations when they arrive. They've started a new game where they compete to be the first out of the railway station. They jump off the train before it's stopped and run across the railway line. I've seen one of them trip as she darted across in front of the train. Thankfully it was going slowly as it was coming to a stop, but she only just managed to scramble out of the way in time. My heart was in my mouth, I can tell you!'

'Are we supposed to try and stop them if we see them doing it?' Poppy asked. She was feeling nervous about trying to intervene in such a risky competition. She didn't like the thought of somebody going under the wheels of a train one bit – especially not if she was supposed to be responsible for preventing it from happening.

'There's not a lot we can do to stop them playing their silly little game. They get so excited and unruly when they pull in that I think they get carried away with it all and encourage each other. But we're all exasperated by it. They seem to get worse when they see us. It's like they're taunting us. Some of the recruits are planning on talking to Sergeant Ross about it to see if we can start prosecuting them for it.'

It seemed like a harsh punishment for a bit of fun, Poppy thought. But then, it was a very dangerous game to play. Maybe it would act as a good deterrent if the women were punished. 'How will I know if I'm to start prosecuting people for doing it?' she asked.

'Don't worry, you'll get word of it. Make sure you check the noticeboard in the WPS room – you've been in there, I assume?' Poppy nodded that she had. 'They'll put something up in there to let us know and no doubt they'll put a notice up in the canteen and at the stations to make the workers aware. There's sure to be a bit of uproar about it so I wouldn't worry yourself about missing it.'

As they got nearer to the factory site, Poppy could see swarms of workers starting to file in through the big entrance gates. There was a big queue outside the canteen, but she followed Jean past all the workers, to howls of protest and grotesque language. Remembering Jean's advice, she held her head high and kept walking, ignoring all the foul words in the air directed at her.

'Sit here and I'll get us some tea and biscuits,' Jean said, pointing to a table at the very front of the canteen. It was right next to the serving hatch and a few other WPS recruits were already seated there. There were rows and rows of long wooden benches neatly lined up. When the canteen was full up it would surely seat hundreds of workers, Poppy thought, feeling relieved that it was up to the welfare workers to keep order in here and not the WPS. Poppy noticed that the benches at the other end of the canteen were filling up fast, but ones closest to the one where the WPS recruits were sitting were empty.

'They'll sit as far away from us as possible,' one of her new colleagues informed her from across the bench. Suddenly Poppy felt something brush past her and looked round to find Grace seating herself beside her.

'I went back to your room when I realised that I hadn't told you where you can get something for dinner,' she said, sounding apologetic. 'I'm so glad you found your way here.'

'Jean brought me over,' Poppy explained as Jean placed a cup of tea and a plate of biscuits down in front of her and took a seat next to Grace.

'It's not much but if you get to know the hostel matrons and keep their girls out of trouble then they're always happy to put a proper dinner aside for you,' Grace said. Poppy hoped she would be able to find a friendly matron soon because a plate of biscuits every evening certainly wasn't going to keep her going for long. 'Have you got my notepad with you?' Grace asked. Poppy got it out, hoping she wasn't going to ask for it back before she'd had a chance to copy all the notes across to her own. 'You can pick up meals at the canteen too. I would have normally stopped for something during my patrol this afternoon but I'm afraid I got too carried away trying to show you as much of the factory as possible.'

Smiling, Poppy scribbled down all the shifts and meal information as Grace went over it with her. She wasn't going to fade away, after all. Each hostel or bungalow was allocated to one of the three work shifts and all the meals were communal and served up at either their lodgings or the canteen, depending on the time of day.

'There's nearly always a shift getting fed, so even if you're patrolling through the night you can get something to keep you going. You didn't think they'd leave you to go hungry, did you?'

Poppy looked at Grace and had to laugh. 'I was beginning to panic,' she admitted.

'I wish I'd remembered to say something.' Grace sighed. 'I don't think any of us would make it through the hours and hours of walking without some sustenance. And I do believe many of the workers here are enjoying a diet much more substantial to what they were used to before the war. But it's important to keep their energy up when they're doing such difficult and important work.'

Poppy nodded her head eagerly. She couldn't have agreed more. She looked back over the page of notes. There was ample opportunity for refuelling during her shifts. She felt a little more relaxed now she had that information to hand.

'I'll tell you what, I'll go and see if they have anything left over from the afternoon shift's supper. You look like you could do with a little more than a few measly biscuits,' Grace offered.

While she waited, Poppy got talking to some of the other WPS recruits. It became harder and harder to hear them as the room filled with workers and their animated chatter, but she was pleasantly surprised to find her new colleagues at the table were friendly and welcoming. Some of them wore a tough exterior similar to Ruth's but they seemed to soften once they got talking. Ruth herself even joined the table and asked Poppy how she had enjoyed her afternoon shadowing Grace on patrol around the factory.

When Grace returned with a bowl of soup and a chunk of bread, Poppy was so grateful that she felt like jumping up and giving her a big hug. But she managed to hold herself back and opted for a warm smile. She devoured the relative feast and, sitting back with a full belly and a contented feeling inside, she was struck again by the sheer volume of different accents and dialects bouncing around the room. Never before had she seen so many women from such different backgrounds come together for one identical cause. Poppy found herself thinking about her Bobby Girls back in London and how they had become firm friends despite being thrown together in the most peculiar circumstances. She wasn't sure she would ever have crossed paths with Annie and Maggie if it wasn't for the WPS. Her heart ached when she started thinking about what her friends might be up to right now. Looking round the room again to distract herself, Poppy realised that she already felt as though she fitted in here. Smiling again, she found she felt proud to be joining these women as they risked life and limb to get vital ammunition to the soldiers on the front line.

14

Poppy slept well and was surprised to hear a light tap on her door as she was getting dressed the following day. She wasn't due to be at the WPS hut to check in for her first shift – the afternoon shift – until two o'clock, and she had no idea who would be calling for her.

'I didn't think you'd get time to search out food before you started, so I brought you over this,' Grace said, holding out a sandwich. 'One of the matrons put it aside for me but I had already been fed by one of the others.' She grinned.

'Well, you really meant it when you said it was worth getting to know the hostel matrons.' Poppy laughed. She was thankful to her new friend for thinking of her because she had certainly slept in due to her previous busy day and late night, which had left her no time to go to the canteen before clocking in at the WPS hut. When Poppy presented herself for duty she felt refreshed and positive despite having just waded through a sea of mud to get there. She found a group of recruits huddled by the noticeboard. Peering through between their heads she couldn't see any new announcements pinned up, but she took the chance to re-read the duty list and remind herself of everything she was going to be on the lookout for during her patrol. Grace had told her to keep hold of her notebook and she had spent twenty minutes going over the little map she had drawn up to remind herself of the factory layout. But she planned to simply walk from section to section keeping her duties in mind, as Grace had suggested.

'Have you heard what happened last night?' one of the women turned around and asked Poppy. Poppy's brow furrowed and she shook her head. 'One of the night shift saw someone hanging around by one of the danger buildings. She gave chase but whoever it was, they were too quick. Everyone's saying there's a German spy on site trying to get hold of sensitive information.'

Poppy's heart started racing but before she had a chance to ask for any more details, Sergeant Ross walked into the room and everybody fell silent. She was carrying a clipboard from which she read out names and allocated duties. Most of the recruits were sent off to carry out searches of the workers before they entered their workshops. Sergeant Ross directed them to make their way around the factory on patrol once the relevant shifts had been cleared. Two of the women were sent to spend the shift patrolling the separate townships. It meant there would be a constant stream of recruits making their way around the site. Each woman collected a clock when her name was called and left the hut. Poppy waited patiently to hear her name and started growing nervous once all the other women had left. Standing alone with her new boss, she waited nervously to find out what she wanted.

'How did you get on yesterday?' Sergeant Ross asked, her narrow eyes constricting further as she seemed to search Poppy's face for an answer.

'I found it quite overwhelming,' Poppy replied honestly. Then she kicked herself for speaking before thinking yet again. She didn't want Sergeant Ross, or anyone else for that matter, knowing about any of her weaknesses. The look on the older woman's face grew serious. 'But it's nothing I can't handle and I'm ready to get started. None of the workers will be getting any contraband past me or acting out in my presence,' Poppy quickly added. Although it felt completely unnatural to her, she met Sergeant Ross's stern expression with one of her own. They held eye contact like that for a few moments until Sergeant Ross's face softened slightly. Poppy instinctively went to break into a big grin and let out a small, nervous laugh, but she stopped herself just in time. Instead, she relaxed her face a touch and turned the corners of her mouth up ever so slightly. It wasn't quite a smile, but it was enough to show she had also relaxed a little.

'Quite right,' Sergeant Ross replied. She walked over to the rack of clocks, pulled one down and handed it to Poppy. 'I'm sure Grace told you all about clocking in.'

Poppy nodded. 'Yes, sir.'

'I want you to start with a search at the cordite press houses. You'll go to the first searching shed. Then make your way around the rest of the two sites on patrol and make sure you clock in at each main workstation. If you have any issues, I'm sure Grace explained the best people to go to. If you find yourself in a real muddle you should always be able to find myself or another sergeant here.'

Poppy placed the clock in her pocket and accepted the truncheon that Sergeant Ross offered her.

'I trust you have heard about last night's activities?' her boss asked. Poppy nodded her head confidently, grateful to her new colleague for filling her in just in time. 'You need to be extra vigilant for suspicious behaviour. If there is a spy then it could be somebody working undercover.'

Poppy nodded again, then she saluted Sergeant Ross before making her way out of the WPS shed. On her way over to the searching shed, Poppy cursed herself for slipping up in front of Sergeant Ross and admitting to finding her first day overwhelming. She felt as if she had managed to save the situation, but she wished she could insert a filter into her brain that would stop her from saying things – or carrying out actions – before thinking them through. She was so accustomed to speaking her mind in front of Maggie and Annie that this new way of behaving was going to take some getting used to. She was also in the habit of jumping in to help in risky situations, because she knew her fellow Bobby Girls and their way of patrolling and thinking so well, and vice versa. It all came so naturally that it was going to be hard to change.

Poppy realised that jumping in before thinking could have catastrophic consequences at Gretna, especially while she was still getting to know the factory, the workers and the biggest risks. At the same time, though, quick reactions could mean the difference between life and death here. Poppy resolved to take a breath and think of John before reacting or answering any questions that would lead to judgement about her. She hoped that that would remind her to be certain of her responses and reactions before speaking or acting.

Thinking about her work in London made Poppy home-sick. She was startled by the feeling because she hadn't grown up in Holborn, she had simply transferred there for WPS work. She quickly realised it wasn't the thought of Holborn itself that was making her homesick but the thought of her friends. Maggie and Annie had become like 'home' to her. They were her family. She could be herself with them both, with no worries or fears about what they would think – perhaps she'd been foolish to leave them behind.

When the searching shed drew closer, Poppy could see a line of workers already queued up outside in their uniforms waiting to go in. She stopped, took a deep breath, brought John to mind and reminded herself why she was at Gretna. Feeling motivated and confident once more, she trudged on through the mud and past the waiting women.

'Come on, love, we've important work to do!' someone called out from the line.

'We'll be stuck fast in this mud if you don't get a move on,' another one cried in disgust. Poppy held her head high and thought of John instead of shouting back as she was so desperate to do. She let herself into the shed without reacting or responding. There was a loud drone of grumbles and moaning as she got herself into position and made sure her tray for confiscated items was to hand, but she ignored it all. She felt intimidated by the women, but she knew the worst thing she could do was show that. As soon as she was ready, Poppy made sure her face was neutral and calm before she waved forward the first worker. The women seemed thrown by the fact she hadn't reacted to their remarks and each one stepped forward in silence. Some of them looked almost confused.

Poppy longed to smile at the women and throw in some fun conversation while she carried out the monotonous task of searching them all, but she reminded herself that she wasn't here to make friends. And if they were going to take her seriously as an authority figure, then she would have to act differently to how she had done in London. It had worked in her favour to build a rapport with the prostitutes, but she could see now that this was a very different type of policing and there was a lot more on the line.

Once she had searched the first few women, the rest of the ladies in the queue started talking amongst themselves and the sound of chatter slowly started to fill the air, making Poppy relax into her role. She made sure to keep a straight and neutral face as she patted down each worker and checked their passes. Some of them tried to antagonise her with sarcastic or caustic comments but she bit her tongue and thought back to her last milky cuddle with Charlotte to keep her calm and focused.

There were a few women trying to get away with wearing hairpins and one woman even had a penknife tucked into her waistband. Poppy dreaded to think what she'd had planned. Thankfully, everybody accepted it without argument when Poppy took the items off them and placed them on her tray. When a woman in her twenties stepped forward with a defiant look on her face, Poppy knew she was about to find some contraband. Her blue eyes pierced into Poppy's and she looked like she wanted to be challenged. Poppy considered just waving her through to see how she would react, but she decided that tactic was far too risky. Who knew what she might have hidden away and what she might do with it if she got it near the cordite – especially since she now knew that some of these women liked to carry knives? The woman handed over her pass for inspection and then lifted her arms up and Poppy set to work patting her down. She was just beginning to think her assumptions had been incorrect when she felt a small lump on the woman's shoulder.

'Are you going to take it out or will I have to lift up your tunic in front of everybody?' Poppy asked firmly as the worker's face changed from defiant to defeated. Poppy was impressed with how authoritative she sounded despite the nerves jangling in her belly. She was used to confrontation while out on patrol but that had never been in front of a big group of women – all of whom were sure to be on the other person's side. Poppy thought of John to keep her calm as she waited for the woman to respond.

'Oh, come on, love, it's for after me shift,' she grumbled, placing her hand palm-down on her shoulder as if to protect the item. 'The others always let me in with one.'

Poppy raised her eyebrows. She was certain that wasn't the case but how could she be sure? She quickly decided that, even if she was telling the truth, she wasn't going to let a worker in carrying contraband just because her colleagues had let her get away with it. Determined not to get pulled into an argument about it, Poppy simply held out her hand palm-up and fixed the woman with a steely glare.

'What's the hold up?'

'I need to get clocked in!'

'Just hand it over!' a trio of voices called out from the back of the line. Relieved that nobody was jumping to the woman's defence, Poppy held eye contact with her to show her that she wasn't going to back down.

'I'm not gonna light it up in there, am I? I'm not stupid. What's the harm? Just let me have something to look forward to at the end of this godawful day, will you?'

'Last chance,' Poppy said without averting her gaze despite the protests growing louder and louder from behind them. She really didn't want to have to manhandle somebody during her first shift, but she was beginning to think that she might have to. As they stared into each other's eyes, Poppy willed her to back down before she was forced to get physical. She remembered what Sergeant Ross had said about the younger women acting out through fear and she wondered if that was what was happening here.

'Oh, all right,' the woman huffed. She pulled her tunic to the side and yanked a cigarette out from under the strap on her corset. Poppy was still staring at her hard and she still had her hand held out. She allowed herself to feel slightly victorious, but she still wasn't sure what the woman was going to do next, so she didn't feel able to fully relax. If she had matches tucked away somewhere and tried to get them out and light the cigarette right here in front of her then Poppy was going to have to restrain her. She had checked the woman's hair for pins and patted her down all over, finishing with her shoulders. What if she had missed a set of matches while she'd carried out the rest of the search? Could she have failed to unearth something so rigid when she had spotted the soft, small cigarette straight away? The worker turned the cigarette around between her fingers with a look of mischievousness on her face. She looked as though she was plotting something, which made Poppy start to doubt herself even more.

'You jumped-up officers always think you can tell us what to do,' she said slowly, looking from the cigarette to Poppy's face and back again.

Poppy was tempted to restrain the woman before she could do whatever it was that she was thinking of doing. But she took a deep breath and reminded herself of her new mindset. If she jumped in before the woman had actually done anything wrong then she risked causing uproar amongst the other workers. 'Well, when it comes to items that could put you and your fellow workers in danger, then, yes, I can tell you what to do. And I'm afraid you have no choice but to do as I tell you. Now, if you argue with me any further then I shall mark you down for a fine.'

Poppy tried to keep a straight face as a chorus of whoops and gasps echoed out from the women waiting behind them. After a tense few moments the woman finally relented. She scrunched the cigarette up in her hand and then slammed it down on the tray next to Poppy, ignoring the fact that she was still holding out her hand ready to take it from her.

'If I can't have it then I'm not having you sneaking off and smoking it when you're done here,' she spat before storming off into the cordite section.

The next woman to step forward was an older-looking woman – Poppy thought she must have been in her sixties. She was tall and broad, and had been surrounded by a group of younger women as they had waited for Poppy to deal with the cigarette smuggler. The woman looked back at her friends and a big smirk spread across her face. They giggled amongst themselves as she turned back to Poppy and looked at her expectantly. Poppy's heart dropped. She really didn't want to have to deal with another confrontation. Especially not with somebody twice her age. It felt more natural to assert authority with women who were younger than her. Disciplining women in their sixties just didn't sit right with her. Apart from anything, she thought they were old enough to know better. Poppy braced herself and put on her most neutral expression as the woman handed over her pass.

'This one don't take no nonsense – take heed, girls!' the woman shouted back as she threw her arms up into the air to allow Poppy to search her. There was laughter from the line as well as a few other comments that Poppy struggled to make out. She wasn't interested in what the other workers were saying; she was too relieved that this stocky woman who clearly had a big following in the workforce had decided not to give her any trouble. The last thing she needed was to come up against the shift's matriarch. 'That one tries to sneak a cigarette into every shift,' she said quietly as Poppy searched her. 'She's not managed it once, despite what she told you. There's always a few like that – will try and give you grief just for the sake of it. I think she does it for a bit of excitement. You'd think the risk of getting blown to bits every day would be excitement enough, but, alas. I'm not sure she's right in the head if I'm honest with you.'

Poppy tried not to grin. 'I'll bear that in mind,' she said, keeping a straight face and waving the woman into the cordite section.

'Well done for standing up to her. The women police who don't back down are the ones who get our respect,' the woman added before going on her way. Poppy made sure she didn't react to the praise. She didn't want the workers knowing how desperate she was for their approval and to keep them onside.

The rest of the queue moved through without any drama and Poppy felt proud of herself for the way she had handled the earlier confrontation. It hadn't been in her nature to be so stern with the cigarette woman, but it had clearly worked in her favour as nobody else tried to argue with her when she found forbidden items on them. Poppy felt sad that she wasn't going to be able to befriend any of the workers. But she reminded herself that she wasn't here to have fun, she was here to help keep everyone safe, and if that meant staying firm and serious then that was the way it was going to have to be.

15

Once Poppy had finished searching the workers from the afternoon shift, she set off on her patrol. She was surprised at how quickly she felt at ease with making her way around the factory. She simply trudged through the mud from building to building, making sure to take in the magazines and danger sheds in between. When she got to a proper path, she felt like she was walking on air. She pulled Grace's notepad out a few times to check which section she was at because she still hadn't managed to get her head around the cordite-making process. But she hadn't needed it to guide her around the factory site itself and for that she felt rather pleased with herself.

The workers were mostly engrossed in their work, and Poppy found the background murmurs of their chatter and singing quite comforting. She was also enjoying the feeling of a renewed sense of confidence after her run-in with the cigarette smuggler. Because of that, she felt positive that a firm approach was going to be the best way forward for her at Gretna. With that in mind, she made sure to hold her head high when she walked through the different work sections, hopeful that her strong poise would show the women that she wasn't a WPS recruit to mess with. Even though she felt anxious when she entered the press house where Bessie, Marie and Edith were working, she made an extra effort to look as bullish and unstoppable as she could. She definitely heard Edith making a loud remark as she passed through, but there was so much background noise from the other workers and the machines that she couldn't quite make it out and she decided the best course of action was to ignore the antagonistic behaviour. She felt optimistic that Edith wouldn't continue with her silly little vendetta once she realised that she wasn't going to get a reaction from her.

When it came time to head across to Dornock, Poppy wondered if she should stop by the police hut and search out superintendents Butcher and Baker. Grace had only taken her there the previous day to introduce her to the officers and she knew it wasn't strictly part of the WPS rounds, but she felt a strange pull towards it. She wondered if it was because she wanted to see Superintendent Baker again. She hadn't thought about him since realising she might be attracted to him but now, heading in his direction, she found her stomach flipping uncontrollably.

Quickly deciding that she was actually just hungry, Poppy veered off track to double back to the Mossband canteen where Jean had taken her last night. She had been on patrol for a few hours now. She knew she had missed the chance to join the workers for tea as she had been talking to some of the navvies when the bell had rung and the rest of the workers had downed tools to trek to the canteen. Now she was thinking of food, her belly rumbled, and she wondered if she might be in time to sit down for some supper. But when she walked into the canteen it was empty save for a welfare worker hovering by the door.

'Am I too early for supper?' Poppy asked.

'I'm afraid so, dear,' the woman replied in a broad Scottish accent. 'There's sure to be some bits hanging around from the tea they served the afternoon shift, though. The kitchen staff will see you right,' she added, pointing to a door next to the serving hatch. Sure enough, Poppy was presented with a bowl of stew almost as soon as she popped her head around the door into the kitchen. She didn't even need to ask – as soon as the women clearing up spotted her, one of them grabbed a ladle and the other went for a bowl.

Poppy was mopping up the last of the stew with a piece of bread when she heard the canteen door swing open. Chewing contently, she looked up to see Superintendent Baker talking to the welfare worker who had just helped her. Her heart skipped a beat and then started racing in her chest. Suddenly, she was desperate to rush over and talk to him before he left. But she still had some food left, and she was still so hungry. Poppy scraped her bowl urgently with her last piece of bread before stuffing it in her mouth and chewing it as fast as she could. She dabbed around her mouth with her handkerchief as she got up from the bench, and she quickly patted down the hair sticking out from under her hat as she walked as casually as she could over to Superintendent Baker and the welfare worker, with butterflies fluttering around in her stomach. She wondered in that moment what on earth had come over her, but she couldn't seem to stop herself from making her way towards the police officer. It was all she could do to stop herself from running at him.

'Ah, Miss Davis. I trust you are here to refuel before heading out on patrol again. May I join you?' Superintendent Baker's smile lit up his whole face again, and Poppy found herself lost in his eyes. It occurred to her to go along with his assumption and sit down to another meal with him. She could certainly do with another helping of that stew. But she could feel the welfare worker staring at her. She knew that Poppy had already eaten her share. Was she going to point that out and embarrass her? Superintendent Baker probably wouldn't begrudge her a second helping, but Poppy didn't want him to think her greedy. She contemplated telling the truth but offering to keep him company while he ate, but then decided that would be a little too forward and it wouldn't look very becoming of her. There was also the issue that she didn't want to get caught clocking on late on her very first patrol.

'I'm afraid I was just on my way out,' Poppy eventually replied. She was kicking herself now for finishing up her meal so quickly. If she had just stayed seated then he would have come and joined her with his food. But her body and feet had just seemed to move towards him without her consent, as if something invisible had been pulling her to him.

'That's a shame. I hope to bump into you again soon. Have a good day.' He tipped his hat before heading straight to the door next to the serving hatch.

Flustered, Poppy set off for Dornock again. She was grateful to have other things to focus on when she reached the work sheds. As Poppy walked through the nitrating house, she made sure to give Geoffrey a wave, and she spotted Frances and Virginia as soon as she entered the boiling house. She instinctively wanted to smile and say hello when she saw them both, as it was so refreshing to see faces that she recognised, but she stopped herself just in time. Poppy made an effort to keep her expression neutral as she gave them both a brief nod on her way through, reminding herself that she wasn't there to make friends. She seemed to already be getting the respect she needed by keeping things strictly professional and that was making it a little easier for her to act firmer than she was comfortable doing.

Over the next week, Poppy settled into the searches and factory patrols well. She was kept on the afternoon shift to give her a chance to find her bearings before being sent out and expected to find her way around in the dark. She found she was looking forward to being sent out to patrol the townships – mostly so she could find a hostel matron to squirrel away food for her, but also because she hadn't had a chance to explore the Gretna township since arriving and she felt as if having a proper wander around would remind her of London.

The factory patrols were so different to what she was used to that she was starting to miss the familiarity of bumping into people as she walked the streets, and popping in and out of shops and pubs and dance halls. Nobody stopped to chat at the factory – for obvious reasons – and so Poppy was craving the regular interactions she had become used to on her London patrols. Not to mention her Bobby Girls. She had seen Grace a few times since that second morning when she had brought her the sandwich, but it was always in passing and there was never enough time to talk properly. And, although Poppy had been to the canteen for regular meals, she never had the time to stop long enough to get to know any of her fellow WPS recruits. Everybody – including herself – was always in such a rush to either get back out on patrol or drag themselves exhausted into bed. She had been hopeful when she had first arrived that she might be able to strike up bonds with her colleagues, but she realised now that wasn't going to be possible.

She had also kept an eager eye out for Superintendent Baker, but she hadn't managed to bump into him again. She wondered if that was for the best. He had a strange effect on her and it would do her no good to have that kind of distraction from a role as important as this.

As the week drew to a close, she noticed that Edith had stopped making snide remarks when she walked through the cordite press house where she was working with Marie and Bessie. Happy that her tactic of ignoring the nasty behaviour seemed to have worked, she felt a sense of vigour that boosted her spirits. On her final afternoon shift at the factory before a much-needed day off, Poppy walked through their section as usual after having done her searches at another workshop. She didn't even brace herself as she approached the work area where Edith was based. She smiled to herself, happy with the fact that she could finally relax on this part of her patrol instead of feeling on edge as she had done before.

'Miss! Miss! I've a crime to report!' a voice suddenly bellowed from next to the mixer. Poppy's ears pricked up and she started walking in the direction of the shouting. Her heart dropped when Edith raced past her, heading for the same spot. There was a handful of women crowded around Bessie. Poppy couldn't help but tut out loud. She thought it was just typical that there would be trouble surrounding Edith when she was patrolling through the section.

'Get yer hands off her!' Edith yelled, pulling Bessie so hard that she was yanked free of the grip of the older woman, who had seemingly apprehended her.

'We just wanna keep her here until the lady officer arrives,' Poppy heard the woman saying. 'Little thief might try and get away. Or offload her stash onto *somebody else*,' she added, looking Edith up and down suspiciously. The women on the surrounding workstations had downed tools to watch the drama unfold and there was a collective gasp of shock as the woman hurled her accusation at Edith.

Anxious to calm the situation down before too many people got involved, Poppy decided to step in before Edith could react. This was definitely a situation where she could justify not taking a moment to think things through first. She stepped right into the middle of the threesome just as Edith was opening her mouth to defend herself.

'Enough!' she shouted. 'Bessie, Edith – get back over that side,' she ordered as harshly as she could manage, directing them to stand to her left. 'You,' she added, pointing at the other woman. 'Step back that way.' The older woman looked at her in shock for a moment before doing as she was told.

'The rest of you get back to work!' Poppy bellowed. She was rather delighted with herself when the women who had stopped to watch immediately turned back to their workstations. Even Edith had complied with her orders, although the scowl on her face told her that she wasn't happy about it.

Remembering how Grace had dealt with Frances and Virginia, Poppy was torn between getting the causes of the drama away from the rest of the workers before anything got out of hand and dealing with the situation as quickly and as calmly as possible. They weren't scrapping – yet. But they were right in the middle of the cordite press house, so she risked causing more of a scene if she tried to escort them all out of sight and anybody resisted. Somebody like Edith was sure to put up a fight. She decided she was better off dealing with the situation where they were.

Glad that she had taken a moment to think through the best course of action now she had the women at safe distances, instead of leaping in and trying to haul them all off to the privacy of the searching shed, Poppy felt ready to get to the bottom of the ruckus. Before she could get down to business, Marie appeared out of nowhere to stand protectively on the other side of her sister. Poppy sighed but she didn't think it was worth trying to sort this out with just Bessie and her accuser. She already knew from experience that Edith, Marie and Bessie stood together no matter what.

'Now. Would somebody like to tell me what all this is about?' Poppy asked firmly, hoping she was going to be able to keep in control of the situation.

'What's the point? You'll only side with Sue,' Edith spat. Poppy didn't want to get drawn into a fresh argument, so she ignored the remark and looked to Sue for an explanation.

'That little scallywag has nicked me photo,' she growled, pointing at Bessie. Bessie flinched at the accusation. Poppy scrunched her face up in confusion.

Edith groaned. 'She keeps a photo of her son in her pocket. Gets it out every five minutes to talk to it. Holds production up no end.'

'Keeps me spirits up,' Sue retorted defensively.

'My sister is no thief,' Marie said with confidence. She was standing straight as a rod and had placed her arm around Bessie's shoulder.

'Oh really?' Sue laughed.

'What would she want with a tatty old picture of your son, anyway?' Edith replied incredulously.

'Don't you go giving me your lip, young lady. You ought to respect your elders. I'm fed up with you young 'uns round here talking down to me when I'm old enough to be your mother. That one shouldn't even be here. I've a mind to check her age and report her!'

'That's it, I've had enough of this, Sue,' Edith yelled as she lunged towards her. Poppy instinctively stepped forward to block Edith, but Marie and Bessie both pulled Edith back before Poppy had to make any contact with her. There was clanging as more workers stopped what they were doing to watch, and some jeers started up around them.

'That's enough!' Poppy cried out. She had to get this sorted before it escalated any further. When the rest of the workers fell silent, she realised how angry she had sounded when she'd shouted. Now she had the full attention of the workshop floor. 'I'm afraid I'm going to have to search you, Bessie.' The young girl nodded her head solemnly and stepped forward.

'I didn't take nothing,' she muttered, sniffing quietly. Just as she held her arms out to the side so that Poppy could pat her down, Edith stepped forward.

'Hang on, you're gonna take that old hag's word over Bessie? You do know she's notorious for causing trouble, don't you?' Edith raged.

'She accused Sal of punching her last week only she didn't know that Sal was off sick that day,' Marie joined in. 'And, like I told you, my sister is no thief.'

'The best way to prove her innocence is to show Sue she has nothing of hers on her,' Poppy replied. She didn't want this to turn into an argument between herself, Edith and Marie. Despite her rocky start with the threesome, she no sooner believed Bessie was a thief than she believed the sky was green, but now an accusation had been made she would have to search the teen or else she would be accused of favouritism.

'I might have known you'd side with her,' Edith said angrily, but to Poppy's relief she stood aside and allowed her to search Bessie. Poppy felt terrible – her maternal side wanted to draw the young girl in for a cuddle, not pat her down like a common criminal in front of all her work colleagues. The poor thing was clearly distressed by the confrontation. Poppy forced herself to keep a professional front on, despite the fact that she was desperate to whisper some words of comfort to Bessie. When, as she had suspected would happen, she found nothing on the youngster, Edith threw her hands up in the air.

'I hope you're happy now!' she roared at both Sue and Poppy. Marie shook her head in disgust at Poppy as she guided her little sister away. Poppy felt like Marie's reaction stung the most.

'She must have hidden it somewhere before you came over. You were far too slow,' Sue muttered.

Poppy couldn't believe the cheek of her. 'Waste my time again with fibs and I'll put you down for a fine,' she said sternly. Then she turned on her heel and walked away before Sue had a chance to react. She was so angry that the woman's little stunt had meant she had to put Bessie through such a humiliating experience. Even more so because she had just been feeling so relieved that she seemed to have slipped off Edith's hit list and now she was surely going to be back right at the top of it.

'Watch out for this one! She'll take any chance to assert her authority,' Edith jeered as Poppy made her way past her and Marie, who were both comforting a now crying Bessie. Poppy felt sick to the stomach that she had contributed to the girl's upset. She didn't feel she'd had a choice, though. She couldn't just ignore an accusation of theft, no matter how unfounded she felt it was. She wasn't here to take sides, no matter what Edith thought about her. In any other circumstance if Poppy had seen a worker weeping, she would have gone straight over to see if she could help. But there was no way she could even contemplate that. Instead of continuing with her patrol she searched out a welfare worker and quickly explained what had happened and asked her to go and check if Bessie was all right. Even though she knew the three of them probably now hated her, she couldn't move on with her patrol until she was certain that somebody was looking after them.

16

Poppy spent the rest of her shift fantasising about her impending day off in order to take her mind off the fact that Edith's vendetta against her had now surely been reignited. She was desperate to explore the township on her first day of freedom since arriving but, in reality, she knew that she would end up sleeping in, writing to Maggie and Annie, and then spending some time in the living area of the WPS hostel to try and strike up friendships with her new colleagues. She was certain that she would never form bonds like she had with her Bobby Girls with anybody here, but she really felt like she needed companions to talk to after her long and lonely shifts.

When Poppy finally clocked off for the evening, she sat with some other WPS recruits in the canteen while she ate her dinner. She talked briefly to a couple of them, but they were finishing up just as she sat down. Then, when three more joined her table, they were too engrossed in their own conversation to include her. She walked back to the hostel alone and feeling deflated. Her first week of patrolling had gone so well and she was so proud of herself, but she had nobody to talk to about it. She also felt exhausted. She took herself straight to bed, hopeful that she would feel less forlorn in the morning.

The following day, Poppy enjoyed the long lie-in that she had been thinking about all week. She could almost feel her body recharging as she lounged in bed, relishing the fact that she had nothing to get up for. A light knock on the door made her jump and she scrambled around trying to find something suitable to wear in order to answer it.

'It's just me. Don't worry if you're in your nightdress,' Grace called from the corridor. Laughing to herself, Poppy pulled on a cardigan and opened the door.

'Sorry if I disturbed you. I knew it was your first day off, so I thought I'd bring you a sandwich to save you having to get dressed too soon. I know how tiring the first week can be. It looks like I was right – have you not long been awake?'

'No, and I feel like I could sleep for another week!' Poppy exclaimed.

Grace laughed. 'Once you stop, your body realises how much you've pushed it. You should take it easy today. Here, take this and eat it in bed, then make sure you get some more sleep.'

Poppy took the plate gratefully. 'Do you want to have a cuppa in the living area?' she asked hopefully.

'I'm just off to get ready for my shift. But maybe another time.'

Poppy nodded but she could tell from Grace's tone that it would probably never happen. Nobody seemed to have the time to stop for even the briefest conversation here. She had always moaned about Maggie's incessant talking back in London but, now she was stuck with only her own thoughts for company day in and day out, she realised how much she loved listening to her young friend spout on about anything and everything. This constant solitary patrolling was getting to her already and she had only been at it for one week. The realisation made her ache for her two best friends so much that she immediately got out her writing kit and penned her first letter to them.

Poppy felt drained by the time she had finished the letter. Once the pen had touched the paper, she had just let her inner thoughts roll. Writing to Maggie and Annie had made her feel like she was talking to them, and she had enjoyed the feeling so much that she hadn't wanted to stop. She had loved feeling close to them again and now that she was finished, she felt a little empty inside. When she laid it all out she was shocked to see that she had written seven pages of ramblings. Keen to get it all to them as soon as possible to ensure a reply reached her quickly, she threw on some clothes and set off in search of the post office, which she was certain she had spotted near the dance hall when Grace had shown her around.

Sure enough, as Poppy rounded the corner to approach the hall, she saw the post office come into view. She got her letter safely sent off and decided to explore the township after all. Her legs felt like they needed to be stretched out after such a long sleep, and she reasoned that she would need a little fresh air in order to help her drift off to sleep in the evening. She was also starting to feel hungry again and she knew she couldn't spend all day alone in her room, no matter how tired she might be. Just as she was making her way along a row of shops and cafés, she spotted a familiar-looking official uniform. She stopped dead in her tracks when her heart skipped a beat. Why was she so excited to see him? Before she realised what she was doing, she had called out after him.

'Superintendent Baker!' she shouted, before wincing at the embarrassing outburst. She had done so well, over the last week, to think of John to stop herself from acting before thinking. What had happened there? There had been no thoughts of John in her mind, let alone any that had made her think through her actions as they usually did. Poppy reasoned that she was just so excited to see a friendly face she knew – somebody to talk to – that she had forgotten herself. That must have been behind the funny feeling she had felt when she'd spotted him, too. Just like when she had seen him in the canteen. There was definitely nothing more to it. Thankfully, Superintendent Baker didn't seem to mind. He turned around when he heard his name and as soon as he laid eyes on Poppy he started walking back towards her.

'I'm sorry – I didn't mean to hold you up,' she said, feeling flustered as she made her way towards him. 'It was just so nice to see a familiar face.' There she went again. That wasn't the kind of thing she should be saying to him and yet she had just blurted it out. He smiled warmly and all her angst disappeared.

'It's easy to feel a little swallowed up by this place. How do you think I feel? Of course, there are male workers and foremen here, but the majority of the population is female and I'm one of the most senior men on the site.' He looked from side to side and, on finding nobody else within earshot, he whispered, 'It's a little intimidating to say the least. But don't tell anybody I told you that.'

He grinned mischievously and Poppy felt a flutter in her stomach. Why was he being so open with her? Did he feel as instantly comfortable around her as she felt around him?

'Anyway, you must call me Lawrence.'

Poppy narrowed her eyes. She wasn't sure about that. She had always been told to call superior officers by their proper titles back in London.

'That's an order,' he added, smiling, and she found herself shrugging her shoulders and smiling back.

'Well, I'm not one to defy orders, *Lawrence*,' she said jokingly. She couldn't believe she was being so cheery and cheeky with him. They had only met twice before, and she didn't know him at all. But she felt so comfortable and at ease around him that this light-hearted chatter seemed to flow naturally.

'I've just had lunch at my favourite café,' he said, pointing to a small building called Hardy's. 'I take it you have the day off?' Poppy nodded. 'You should try the food in there as soon as you can. I promise you won't be disappointed.'

Poppy's stomach suddenly grumbled, and she realised she could probably do with something to eat. 'I might give it a go right now.'

'I was rather hoping to have some company on my walk back to the police hut,' Lawrence replied, looking at her with a hope in his eyes that made her feel happy. It was the first time somebody had wanted to spend any time with her since she had arrived at Gretna. She was desperate to form a friendship with one of her WPS colleagues, but none of them seemed interested in getting to know her. They were all pleasant enough to her – especially Grace – but they were always so busy. Lawrence was kind and friendly, and here he was, asking to spend some time with her. How could she refuse? She found it impossible to say no, even though her stomach was roaring at her.

'That sounds wonderful,' she said with a smile, and they fell into a gentle pace next to each other. Poppy couldn't believe she was opting to take a walk with this man rather than filling her belly. She must have been feeling more desperate for company than she had appreciated. 'The township is so impressive. I really wasn't expecting anything as grand as this when I was sent here,' Poppy mused as they made their way through the streets, passing groups of workers as they went. 'There's so much for everyone to do in their spare time. It's like a mini London.'

'They learned from the navvies.' Lawrence laughed.

'How do you mean?'

'When the construction workers first arrived to start building the factory, thousands of them would pour into Carlisle and Dumfries every evening in search of pubs and ways to keep themselves entertained. The locals didn't like all the drunken antics that came with it and it caused a bit of uproar. It was all quite chaotic.' He smiled and rubbed his chin before continuing on. 'The landlords, of course, were quite happy to welcome them into the town. They would have their drinks ready in advance on a Saturday night. Some of them would have four or five hundred whiskies poured ready for the onslaught. One of the pubs is known for its "night of the thousand whiskies". But all of that whisky inevitably led to a lot of drunken tomfoolery.'

'I don't need a wild imagination to envisage how that ended up. No wonder the locals want to keep everyone away,' Poppy said. 'Were you here from the start, then?' she asked.

'I grew up around here. Can you not tell by my accent?'

Now Poppy thought about it, she could hear a slight Scottish lilt in Lawrence's voice. But it didn't seem as strong as some of the accents that she had heard ringing out around the workshops. 'I'm struggling to decipher all the different accents,' she said quickly, worrying that she might have upset him.

'It's all right. There are so many different dialects here that I'm not surprised mine doesn't stand out. But don't worry, I'm used to fading into the background.' Lawrence was smiling while he talked, and Poppy liked the fact he wasn't taking offence and could laugh at himself. Lawrence was coming across as quite laid back, which she found refreshing given his status at the factory. 'Once you've worked with somebody like Butcher for a few months you get used to being the quiet one.' Poppy let out an involuntary giggle. 'You don't need to be polite. He's my friend as well as a colleague, but, my goodness, he likes to monopolise the conversation.'

'I can't say I'd noticed,' Poppy replied sarcastically. She felt a rush when their eyes met and they laughed together.

'Anyway, enough about me and Butcher; as I was saying,

the townships were built with the local towns in mind. The Ministry wanted to have enough on offer here to keep the workers from straying outside the area too much. When the workers are flocking to the pubs and cinemas in Carlisle, it's a lot harder to supervise them. It's easier for them to misbehave when they're out of sight. They prefer to keep them here where the surroundings are more desirable and where they are subject to the kindly supervision and restraining influence of the welfare department and the women police.'

'I know they hold dances and I've seen the cinema. What else do they offer to try and keep the workers in line?'

'Oh, they have everything you could wish for!' Lawrence exclaimed with a tongue-in-cheek enthusiasm. 'There's a whole host of sports activities on offer, orchestral recitals, instructional classes and lectures. But, as I'm sure you can imagine, the cinema and the dances are the most popular. However, there are always those who prefer the attractions in Carlisle. And that's not helped by the fact that there are pubs there.'

As they made their way out of the township towards the factory site, Poppy pulled her shawl tighter around her and shivered a little. She had only planned on popping out briefly and would have wrapped up warmer for a long walk like this. She thought about turning around and heading back, but found that she was having such a nice time that she didn't want to. Putting up with the cold seemed like a small price to pay. She had really missed having somebody to talk to. Lawrence pointed out his accommodation. He was lucky enough to be living in one of the brick houses that Grace had shown Poppy when she had first walked her through the township. With a jolt, she distinctly remembered Grace saying the homes were for officials with families. The comprehension made Poppy feel instantly deflated.

'I rattle around in there, that's for sure. Everyone else on the row has families and then there's me tacked on at the end all on my own. I told them it was silly to give me all that room when they could get at least ten workers living in the house. I was quite happy staying with my parents down the road in Annan, but they insisted on having me on site.'

'That makes sense to me,' Poppy replied. He was talking again now but she wasn't listening because she was trying to understand why she felt so relieved to learn that Lawrence was single. John's face flashed into her mind and she was filled with a sense of guilt. But she pushed it aside. Just because she found another man attractive it didn't mean that she was moving on from her husband. She was just glad to have found a friend at a time when she was missing her Bobby Girls so much. She wouldn't read too much into these feelings – apart from anything else, she didn't have the time or the energy for that.

'Do you have family back in London?' Lawrence asked. His interest in her pulled her back to the present and she found herself telling him all about Maggie, Annie and Charlotte.

'They're not my actual family, of course, but they feel like it,' she said with a smile. Before she knew it, she was opening up about John and how she had lost him. Poppy wasn't quite sure why she was telling him so much, but she felt so comfortable and at ease with him, and talking to him about John made her feel less like she was betraying her husband by spending time with another man, even if they were only going for a walk. She went on to tell Lawrence about her parents and how they had died when she was only young, meaning John had been her only family. Lawrence listened sympathetically before opening up about his own family.

'My brother died when we were children, and my parents

were never the same again. They both fell ill some years ago and my younger sister, Sophie, took on most of the responsibility for looking after them. I was so busy with police work that nobody expected it of me. When the war broke out, I wanted to sign up, but Sophie begged me not to. I hadn't realised how much of a burden caring for my parents had put on her, and she was terrified she would never be able to start her own life and build a family if I was killed in action. So, I agreed to stay, and I promised to look after our parents to allow her to start finally living when this is all over.'

'It must have been a difficult decision to come to,' Poppy remarked.

'Not really. Sophie spent all those years caring for my parents and I didn't give it a second thought. And I'm not sacrificing nearly as much as all the men fighting for our country. I feel inadequate compared to them. Compared to people like your husband.'

'You're doing your bit,' Poppy said firmly. She hated the fact that so many men were being made to feel inferior for not signing up when they were so badly needed at home. As they talked more, she learned that so many officers from Lawrence's station joined the army that he was promoted to superintendent at a much younger age than would normally have happened. And that was how he had come to be in such an important position at the factory when he was only in his late thirties.

When they passed by a group of female workers getting searched on their way into the main factory site, Poppy suddenly felt uncomfortable about the fact she was happily enjoying talking to a man on her own when she would have been expected to admonish one of them for doing the same. She wondered whether she should cut their walk short but found again that she just didn't want to. When they made it to the police hut, Lawrence rushed inside ahead of her.

'Wait there!' he called back to her as she stood in the mud feeling confused. Seconds later he emerged carrying a thick blanket which he draped around Poppy's shoulders. 'I noticed you shivering earlier and I feel bad for dragging you all the way out here when you're not properly dressed for the cold.'

Poppy was so deeply touched by the gesture that she didn't know what to say. 'It's my fault for coming out so lightly dressed,' she stuttered, avoiding eye contact with him.

'Well, I really enjoyed talking to you. Thank you for your company.'

'I enjoyed it too,' she responded, still staring bashfully at the floor.

'I know how lonely it can become here, even though you're surrounded by thousands of people.' Poppy looked straight up and met Lawrence's eyes. She could see raw emotion behind them and knew that he genuinely cared.

'I don't know how you could ever feel lonely when you share a base with Butcher,' she joked, purposefully trying to deflect what could turn into an affectionate moment.

'You can always come to me if you need someone to talk to. I see how hard the women police work. There doesn't seem to be much time for anything else and good friends are hard to come by around here.' He had obviously seen straight through the fact she had made the jokey comment in order to avoid admitting to her need for companionship.

'Thank you. And thank you for the blanket,' Poppy replied as she pulled it tighter around her body and started the long walk back to her hostel.

17

Poppy was still thinking about her walk with Lawrence on her afternoon patrol the next day. It was a welcome distraction from her angst about how Edith was going to react to her when she spotted her on her rounds. But once Poppy had finished up on her searches, she forced herself to take a deep breath and walk into Edith's workshop with her head held high, despite her desire to skip the section altogether and face the wrath of Sergeant Ross instead. Once inside, Poppy was sorely tempted to skirt her way around the edges of the workshop so that Edith, Marie and Bessie wouldn't catch sight of her. She lingered just in front of the big door, taking in the busy hustle and bustle of the workers and the machines while contemplating her next move. She felt anxious about a run-in with Edith, but she was finding the mix of different accents, talking and singing along with the whirring of the machinery, strangely comforting.

'You all right, miss?' a sweet-looking girl enquired, turning her back on her work to face Poppy. The distraction startled Poppy and she jumped to attention, ashamed of herself for taking her eye off the ball.

'Yes. Yes, I was . . . I was just doing a head count,' she lied, making sure to look out over the factory floor as if she was still making a note of numbers. 'On with your work, now.' The girl smiled and turned back to her workstation. Poppy was angry with herself. First of all, she had let Edith get to her so much that she had stalled and created a distraction for one of the workers. If that poor girl had been handling something sensitive when Poppy had disturbed her, then she could have ended up being responsible for a horrible accident. Secondly, she had considered doing something that would make her look weak, which would cause no end of problems for her going forward from here.

Poppy held her head high and stomped straight through the middle of the factory with purpose, thinking back to the advice Grace had given her on her first day. She needed to stand her ground – as she had done by searching Bessie despite her sister and her friend's protests. She had to stay strong and follow that through now, and show them that she wouldn't be flustered by them. She wasn't going to walk quietly past Edith's workstation and pretend not to hear the remarks directed at her, she decided now. She was going to confront her in front of everybody and show her that she was the one in charge. She had just caught sight of Edith, who was busy lining up rows of cordite, when another worker stopped her in her tracks.

'I tripped and caught my top. Would you look at that,' the woman said glumly, holding the end of her ripped tunic up to show Poppy. 'I can't very well carry on with my top split in two.' The worker sighed.

'You're right. But that's not something I can help with. You need to speak to one of the welfare workers. Show me where you're working, and I'll go and find one of them and send them over.' The woman smiled gratefully and led Poppy back to her bench. 'I'll send someone over as soon as I can,' she assured her before heading off in search of a welfare worker. By the time Poppy had informed the relevant person of the woman with the ripped uniform, she realised she must have been backwards and forwards past Edith on a number of occasions but she had been too preoccupied to notice if she had glared at her or made any nasty comments.

Poppy headed for the door, pleased that she hadn't let her new enemy get to her in the end. Then, just as she was about to clock off from the workshop, she spotted Bessie sitting on the end of a bench working on some cordite. She was well aware that she should just leave the girl alone and get on with her patrol. She was about to leave the workshop having avoided any kind of confrontation, and approaching Bessie would risk causing another scene with her two bodyguards; but she was desperate to make amends with her and assure her that her actions during their previous encounter hadn't been malicious. As she made her way towards Bessie, Poppy was certain that she could feel Edith's eyes boring into her back. She resisted the urge to turn around and check. She just wanted to get to the girl and say her piece before anybody jumped in to try and derail her explanation. But just before Poppy got to the bench, one of the older foremen walked up and put his hand on Bessie's shoulder. Poppy thought he must be checking on her work, but Bessie visibly shuddered when she looked up and saw who it was standing over her.

Poppy slowed down. Her instincts were telling her to rush over and step in between the pair of them. Bessie looked uncomfortable and she wanted to protect her. But she took a deep breath and brought John to mind to give her a moment to think this through and see what played out between them. She didn't know Bessie, so she could be completely misreading her reaction. If she launched in and caused a scene when they were having a friendly word about work, then she would just give Edith more reason to hate her. Happy that she had resisted the urge to act before knowing the full situation, Poppy held back further and watched as the foreman pulled up a chair next to Bessie at the bench. He was well built and looked about twice the size of Bessie now he was sitting down beside her. Poppy recognised him from seeing him around the factory, but she hadn't spoken to him before. As he smiled at Bessie now, the teenager froze, and Poppy knew for certain that she felt uncomfortable. Nobody else sitting at the bench seemed to be concerned; they hadn't even acknowledged the foreman and they were so engrossed in their work that they didn't seem to notice Bessie as she desperately looked around her. Poppy knew she must be searching for her sister or Edith to come to her rescue. Neither of them appeared, as they always seemed to when Bessie was in need.

The foreman inched his chair closer to Bessie, who flinched at the movement, and, with Grace's warning about handsy foremen ringing in her ears, Poppy decided it was time to intervene before things went too far. As she got closer, Poppy could see the foreman's lips moving and tears welling in Bessie's eyes as she shook her head. Poppy picked up her pace just as the foreman suddenly grabbed Bessie's hand and pulled it under the table towards his crotch. Bessie tried to pull her hand away, but he was too strong. She opened her mouth and Poppy could see she was saying 'no' but the workshop was so noisy that she might as well have been whispering.

Poppy was running at full speed now and the girls on the other side of the bench finally looked up just as she reached the bench. With fury racing through her body, she grabbed hold of the chair at both sides and pulled backwards with all her force. She had wanted to throw her arm around his neck and yank him back off his seat, but she was worried about his feet flying up in the air and knocking the table and all its contents over. Once she had slid him and his chair clear of the bench, Poppy hooked her right arm around his neck and pulled him backwards before jumping clear. She watched on, briefly satisfied, as he flew backwards with confusion and panic engulfing his face and his arms flailing around him. There was a loud thud as he and the chair hit the ground at the same time. Startled, he groaned and rolled over onto his side, but Poppy was straight onto him. She lunged to the floor and pinned him down while he was still disorientated and unable to fight back. Cheers rang out around the workshop.

'Nothing to see here!' Poppy yelled, not breaking eye contact with the foreman, who had started trying to wriggle free. Poppy nudged her knee into his stomach and he cried out in pain.

'Try anything and my knee will move about a foot further down,' she snarled at him, briefly moving her eyes down to his crotch area before staring into his eyes menacingly again. She had all her weight on top of him and she felt a sense of reassurance when she became aware of her truncheon digging into her thigh. She had forgotten all about it when she'd gone in to tackle him, but it was good to know she had some backup if he tried anything silly. She was going to have to get used to having a weapon to hand.

'What do you think you're doing?' the foreman demanded, anger suddenly taking over.

'What do you think *you're* doing, more like! I saw what you did to that young girl, you dirty, pathetic excuse for a man.'

'What? Bessie? We're friends! I've been helping her with her work!' Doubt suddenly swept over Poppy. Everything was quiet except for the whirring of the machines. Poppy could hear Edith's voice asking what was going on and she panicked. Had she misunderstood what had happened? What if they *were* friends and they were just messing around but she had jumped in before establishing the facts first? She'd been so desperate to help Bessie, but had she actually just caused her a whole load of hassle and upset? The last thing she needed was for Edith to have another reason to take issue with her.

'Has he been harassing my sister again?' Poppy looked over at the sound of Marie's voice and saw her rushing over to Edith to help comfort Bessie. Relieved, Poppy's confidence grew again.

'I saw what you did, and I saw you continue to do it after she told you no,' she said through gritted teeth. Just then, Poppy became aware of movement around her. Keeping all her weight on the foreman, she looked up and saw the workers who had come over to watch were moving to the side to let Geoffrey through. As he marched towards them, Poppy braced herself, certain that he was going to stick up for his colleague and undermine her in front of the room full of workers. She was just getting ready to justify her actions when he stopped next to them, bent down and held his hand out to her. Still unsure whose side he was on, Poppy cautiously took his hand and let him help her to her feet. At least she knew the other foreman wouldn't try anything with Geoffrey here.

'Don't worry, I'll take it from here. I'll see that he's disciplined for whatever it is he did wrong,' Geoffrey said as Poppy straightened out her skirt and jacket, and tucked some loose hair under her hat. The foreman was slowly struggling to his feet now.

'Hold up, how do you know it was me who was in the wrong?' he asked. He rubbed his lower back and winced. Poppy wished she had used even more force to pull his chair over. She was just about to defend her actions when Geoffrey spoke again.

'The lady police don't floor foremen for no good reason, Bill. If this one's had to pin you to the ground, then I'm confident she had a good motive for her actions.' He looked over pointedly at Bessie, who was now crying into Marie's shoulder, while Edith glared across at Bill. Then Geoffrey looked back at Bill. 'I don't think I even need to ask this officer what happened, judging by this scene. I think you'd better come with me and let these women get back to their work,' he said before turning and walking towards the door. Bill was just about to follow him when Poppy was overtaken by an urge. She grabbed his arm and went on her tiptoes to put her mouth to his ear.

'Touch her again and you'll have more than a sore back to worry about,' she hissed before shoving his arm away and turning to pick up the chair, which was still lying on the floor. She wasn't sure what had come over her, but she had just felt so angry at him for targeting such a young and vulnerable girl. And the fact that he had done it in a crowded workshop made it all the worse. If he thought that he could get away with it here, then she was terrified to think of what he might do if he managed to get one of the women on their own.

As Poppy pushed the chair back under the bench, the other workers were filing back to their places. She looked over to Bessie and the young girl smiled shyly when she caught her eye and mouthed *thank you*. Poppy knew better than to approach her while she was with Edith and Marie so she simply smiled and gave her a friendly nod. She could feel Edith's eyes on her and, when she chanced a glance at her, was surprised to find the other woman looking at her in what seemed to be an approving way. She wasn't quite smiling, but she certainly wasn't glaring hard at her like she normally did. Poppy gave her a curt nod and continued on her way to clock out of the workshop. She had some time to make up for after that disturbance.

18

Over the next few hours, Poppy went over and over what had happened with Bessie and Bill in her head as she continued on with her patrol. She was proud of herself for dealing with the situation so swiftly and also for holding back just long enough to make sure she was certain of what was going on before stepping in and taking action. She kept putting her hand into her pocket to run her fingers over her wedding ring. She knew that John would be proud of her, too. She found herself wishing that she was on patrol with another WPS recruit more than ever, though. It was after events like this that she missed the companionship and having somebody to talk through it all with. She decided she would write another letter to Maggie and Annie that evening to tell them all about it.

The rest of her patrol was relatively quiet compared to the eventful start. She found a girl skiving off her shift near one of the danger buildings. She ended up marching her back to her workshop because she was convinced that she would simply run off and hide somewhere else once she was out of sight. Poppy also came across a group of workers quarrelling over money. Thankfully Poppy stepped in before the row escalated and she managed to calm everybody down enough that she felt confident they were focused on their work again when she left them to carry on with her rounds.

When Poppy made it to the nitrating house, she was surprised to see Geoffrey wandering up and down between the stoneware basins. She had assumed he would still be off dealing with Bill. She hoped it hadn't all been a show and he'd not let him off with a slap on the wrist once they had left the cordite section. Poppy put a mask on and made her way over to him. His eyes seemed to brighten when he saw her, and he waved her over.

'I didn't expect to see you so soon. I thought you'd be off dealing with Bill.' Poppy was suddenly aware of the fact that most of the workers were now staring over at the two of them. She hadn't stopped in this section to talk since Grace had shown her around, and she had forgotten how quiet it was compared to all the other workshops. Geoffrey looked around them both cautiously.

'Shall we talk outside?' he offered. Poppy nodded. She wasn't keen on going outside on her own with him, as she was feeling wary of him again given that he seemed to have let Bill off the hook. How could the handsy foreman have been appropriately reprimanded in such a short space of time? Maybe Grace had been wrong about Geoffrey, and Poppy had been correct in her initial assumption that he was one of the foremen to be concerned about. But they couldn't very well discuss the fracas in front of all the workers, so she followed him to an exit. She kept her hand resting firmly on her truncheon as they passed through a side door into a big, empty yard. They both pulled off their masks and Poppy took a deep breath of fresh air while she waited for Geoffrey to tell her what he had done to punish Bill for his actions. She hoped he wouldn't kiss her hand again now they were maskless.

'Well done back there. You really showed Bill what for. I doubt he'll be hassling any of the girls again.'

'Well, he probably will if I'm not around,' Poppy said firmly. 'What happens when he abuses the next girl and there's no policewoman there to help?' She wasn't going to permit Geoffrey to charm her into getting away with letting such a predator off scot-free.

'Oh, I wouldn't worry about that,' Geoffrey said, winking at her and grinning.

Poppy raised her eyebrows at him. She was becoming agitated now. She wasn't interested in being enchanted by this man – she just wanted to know that Bill had been dealt with so that she didn't have to worry about him harassing the female workers any more. Geoffrey must have noticed the annoyance on her face, as the smile faded from his own and he turned sombre all of a sudden.

'Sorry, love. I know it's a serious matter. I tend to make light of situations when they make me feel uncomfortable.'

'How do you think poor Bessie felt when Bill thrust her hand upon his—'

'All right, all right, I got the gist of what happened. I don't need all the details.'

'Oh, I think you do. You need to take this seriously and make sure he keeps his hands to himself in the future. I was tempted to thrust his hand into the machinery to make sure he couldn't do what he did again. I didn't because I thought you would be dealing with him.'

'That's what I was trying to tell you. He's been transferred to one of the workshops that is full of men, and he'll have to stay there for the foreseeable. You don't need to worry about him touching up any more of the female workers.'

Poppy relaxed. It seemed Grace had been right about Geoffrey being one of the good ones after all, she thought to herself. They got talking and Poppy learned that a number of women had complained about Bill hassling them in the past, but nothing had been done because nobody had ever managed to catch him in the act. It was always his word against theirs. And, as Poppy had seen for herself, Bill was very good at acting all innocent.

'He seemed to be very good at keeping it discreet. The other girls on the bench were oblivious to what was happening right in front of their eyes. It was only because I was waiting to speak to Bessie that I saw the whole thing unfold. I'm so glad I did. I hate to think what else he's got away with.'

'You'll be a hero over there now,' Geoffrey said, winking again. Poppy was beginning to think the gesture was more of a habit than his way of trying to charm women.

'I shouldn't think so,' she said with a laugh as Edith and Marie's disapproving faces flashed into her head. 'Anyway, what were you doing over that way? I must say, it was perfect timing. I'm not sure how long I would have been able to keep things under control on my own. And, like I said, Bill might well have ended up with a hand missing if you hadn't shown up when you did.'

'You looked like you had a good handle on everything. I was really impressed.' He ran his fingers through his hair and Poppy found herself blushing at the compliment. 'I'd been running an errand before my shift and I was walking past the workshop when I heard all the cheering. I know most of the other foremen down that bit and they're all a bit nervous around the women. They tend to hover back until the female police arrive if anything big erupts, so I thought I'd better pop in and check.'

'It was a good job you did. Thanks for having my back.'

'Don't mention it,' he replied warmly before giving her another wink. Poppy was getting used to his cheeky winks now and she was surprised to find they were starting to make her smile instead of roll her eyes.

Geoffrey asked how she was settling into factory life and, as Poppy confessed that she was missing her friends and the companionship of patrolling in a pair, he listened intently and nodded along as if he understood what she was going through.

'I feel the same a lot of the time. I know they work damn hard and they're risking a lot to do so, but the workers here tend to really pull together through it all. The women in particular form such strong bonds. A lot of the girls do their whole shift together and then spend all their free time together, too. And then there are the supervisors like you and me who spend hours on end on our own. I think you have it harder. I like to wander around in there and check on the workers now and then. But you've got so many work-shops to get around, I imagine you hardly ever have time to stop.' He paused and frowned. 'Oh dear, I've probably held you up something rotten. I'm sorry, love. You should be getting on,' he said, and he ruffled his hair nervously.

'Please, don't worry. It's been nice to have someone to talk to. I'll walk a little quicker for the rest of the patrol to make up for it.'

A smile spread across Geoffrey's face. 'That's my girl,' he said, patting her on the shoulder and winking.

As Poppy smiled back at him, she felt warm inside. He was actually a very sweet man and she felt bad for how wrongly she had judged him when they had first met. And just moments before. Looking into his eyes now, she felt a slight flutter in her stomach. She had been so turned off by how she had wrongly perceived him on that first day that she hadn't taken the time to look at his face properly. She hadn't been able to see past the winking and what she had thought was smarmy behaviour. But now she could see that he was quite handsome. And he had an attractive personality, too. He was caring, understanding and empathetic. All the traits that drew her to a man.

'I'd better get back to it,' she said quickly. She was suddenly aware that she had been staring into his eyes for longer than was necessary while her mind tried to work out how she felt about him. Snapping out of her apparent trance, she hurried back into the nitrating house and felt so flustered by what had happened that she almost forgot to put her mask back on. Geoffrey laughed behind her.

'Duty calls! Stop by for a natter any time,' he said cheerfully.

Making her way to the next workshop with a quicker pace and a bit of a spring in her step, Poppy thought again about just how wrong she had been about Geoffrey. She also pondered the flutter she had felt in her stomach while talking to him. Did she like him?

Poppy struggled to concentrate for the rest of her shift as thoughts of John, Lawrence and Geoffrey swam around in her head. Was she really finding yet another man attractive? First Lawrence and now Geoffrey? Or was it just the fact that these two men were the only people to show her any sign of potential true friendship since she had arrived? No matter what it was, it didn't matter, she decided. She was still married in her heart to her darling John, and she wasn't ready to replace him. Putting her hand in her pocket once more, she slipped her wedding ring on and off her finger, feeling the comfort it brought. So what if she found Lawrence and Geoffrey attractive? She might start taking some time to enjoy their company to get her through a lonely experience, but that was all it would ever be. Neither of them was probably interested in a romance with her anyway and, besides, John was her one true love.

Giving her head a shake, Poppy tried to free all thoughts of men from her mind. She had something more important to deal with and she needed to stay focused. After her shift she was going to track down Bessie to her hostel and make sure she was all right after the afternoon's trauma. Her bodyguards were sure to be with her, so Poppy needed to be ready to stand her ground.

19

It didn't take Poppy long to find Bessie's hostel. All the women on the afternoon shift lived in hostels on the same row, and the matron at the second one that she tried smiled warmly and invited her in as soon as she mentioned Bessie, Marie and Edith.

'I understand there was a bit of commotion on their shift today,' the matron said as she showed Poppy through to the kitchen. She started preparing a pot of tea and put together a plate of food without even asking Poppy if she was hungry. Poppy smiled to herself. This would be the matron she befriended, she decided, as a pile of food was placed in front of her. She didn't care if it meant having to deal with Edith and her vendetta more than was necessary. With a full stomach, she could cope with anything. She tucked into the meal as the matron – who was called Eileen Gilbert – explained that all the girls had still been reeling from the incident when they'd returned to the hostel for their supper following their shift.

'They think a lot of you,' she said as she took a seat across from Poppy at the table and poured them both a cup of tea. 'Bessie is still a little shaken up, but her sister is looking after her.'

'What about Edith?'

'Oh, she's ready to hunt down that foreman and chop off his . . . how do I say it?' Mrs Gilbert leaned forward and whispered, '*Nether regions*. Not that I can blame her, mind.'

'I was close myself,' Poppy admitted, and they both laughed. No matter how she and Edith felt about each other, they definitely felt the same way about handsy foremen. Mrs Gilbert explained that Bessie, Marie and Edith were out enjoying a showing at the township cinema.

'You're more than welcome to stay and keep me company until they return.'

'That would be lovely.' It was the perfect opportunity to get Mrs Gilbert onside so she could turn to her for food when the canteen fell short. Also, she was convinced that none of her WPS colleagues would be interested in spending time with her back at her hostel, so she was grateful once more to have somebody friendly to keep her company. And the food Mrs Gilbert had served up would save Poppy a trip back to the factory canteen for dinner. As they talked, Poppy discovered that Mrs Gilbert was a widow in her seventies who had signed up to become a matron when she'd heard about the townships. She hadn't needed the work; she was simply a little lonely at home since losing her husband and she hated the thought of so many young girls spending so much time away from their families at such a scary time.

'I just had to help. I couldn't bear the thought of them all away from home. But you'd be surprised at how well they stick together and look out for each other. You'd think some of them had grown up together, their bond is so strong already. You would think Edith was Marie and Bessie's other sister, but they only met her when they arrived here.'

'Are you enjoying being here?' Poppy asked.

Mrs Gilbert nodded, and her big, brown eyes beamed with happiness. She adjusted her short, dark hair, which looked as if it had been styled by a professional, before answering.

'I'm so glad I came. There's myself and my assistant at the hostel, as well as cooks and maids. And we have more than sixty workers to look after. We're like substitute mothers to some of these girls; we train, we correct, and we advise. I also make sure they keep up to date with their sewing and cooking skills as their own mothers would do if they were at home. And they bring all their joys and their sorrows to me. That's why I knew about today's drama so quickly. It makes it feel like we're a bit of a family. A big and dysfunctional family but a happy one nonetheless!'

Poppy smiled. It was clear that Mrs Gilbert was perfect for her role. She thought the girls in her hostel were lucky to have her looking out for them. When Mrs Gilbert got up to clear Poppy's plate away, she noticed that the matron was tiny – even shorter than herself.

'A lot of my girls eat better here than they did at home,' she explained as she put more food on the plate and brought it back over. Poppy's eyes widened at the offering. It would definitely be worth putting up with more of Edith if this was the treatment she received every time she popped in to see Mrs Gilbert. 'It makes me happy to know we can relieve them of those worries. And we enforce a minimum of rules. It's so strict over at the factory that I feel they need to be able to relax when they're here.' Poppy nodded her agreement as she tackled her second plate of food. 'The only thing I put my foot down about is the curfew. I need to know they're all safe in their beds before I can rest myself. I've got one girl who's always coming back late, though. Well, she was. I gave her such a talking to the last time I had to let her in after 10 p.m. that she's started staying out all night now.'

'Wherever does she go?' Poppy asked. She could see the strain on Mrs Gilbert's face now that she was talking about this girl. Poppy suddenly thought back to the mysterious figure that had been spotted on the factory grounds on her first night, and the rumours of a German spy being on the site. She hadn't heard anything about it all since then but now a sudden flash of suspicion struck her. Could it be possible that this girl was sneaking around after curfew because she was working for the Germans? Poppy had to admit that it was a little far-fetched, but now she knew about this activity she would definitely need to investigate.

'I wish I knew. Worrying and fretting about her is exhausting me but she won't tell me anything. I think I'm probably a little soft on them, to be honest. There are girls who wouldn't dream of doing such a thing because they're too scared of their matron. But I don't want to be like that. They have enough to be frightened of at Gretna.'

'I suppose that's why you haven't reported her to the WPS?'

'They need to be able to trust me. But I just can't get through to her. I don't know what to do.'

'I could always talk to her,' Poppy offered. Mrs Gilbert's face fell. 'I'll go easy on her. It won't be a telling off. Will you let me do that for you? I'm sure once she understands how much her actions are upsetting you then she'll think again. And if not, well, we can think of something together.'

Mrs Gilbert looked deep in thought for a moment before looking to Poppy again and nodding her head. 'Thank you.'

'We can't have you losing sleep over this.'

Mrs Gilbert smiled gratefully and sighed before revealing the girl's name was Jenny Campbell. Poppy wrote it down in Grace's old notepad. Once Poppy had finished eating, Mrs Gilbert checked the clock and, on seeing that the evening showing at the cinema would now be over, she went to Bessie's dorm to fetch her. Poppy took a deep breath to prepare herself when she heard footsteps coming back along the corridor towards her. There were more than two sets approaching. She wasn't surprised – she'd known Bessie's two bodyguards wouldn't have let her meet her without them. She stood up to ensure she was at the same level as all of them when she greeted them – her training had taught her to avoid being in a vulnerable situation during a confrontation. She would still feel in a weak position with Edith towering over her, but at least she wouldn't be sitting down. Poppy braced herself, but she was shocked when Edith walked in first and smiled sweetly at her.

'Thank you for rescuing our Bess,' she gushed. She leaned down and threw her arms around Poppy, who was too taken aback to do anything but stand frozen to the spot. 'Sorry, I forgot myself there,' Edith said awkwardly, taking a step back and staring at the floor. Poppy was struck by the mane of blonde curls that was dancing around her head. She had only ever seen the girls with their hair tucked under their hats. 'I wanted to thank you at the factory, but everything happened so quickly. And I was so angry at myself for not spotting what was happening and dealing with that filthy man myself.' Poppy was still lost for words as Edith went on as if she hadn't spent the past week or so with a vendetta against her. 'The way you floored him. It was a sight to behold and no less than he deserved! You're the talk of our shift, you know.'

Poppy smiled and gestured for everybody to sit down. It was a little unnerving to have Edith gushing over her like this given their only previous interactions had been so hostile. She remembered what Grace had said about how quickly the tide could turn with the munitionettes. She'd been right about that, too. They all sat down together, and Mrs Gilbert went about preparing more tea and started cutting up some cake.

'I just wanted to make sure you were all right, Bessie,' Poppy said. She was being careful not to seem grateful for Edith's turnaround in attitude. She didn't want them to know how desperate for friendship and acceptance she was.

'I'm fine, thanks to you,' the teenager answered timidly while staring down at the table.

'I want to thank you, too,' Marie piped up now. 'I take such great care to look after my little sister and it terrifies me to think what might have happened if you hadn't stepped in when you did.'

'That's what I'm there for.' Poppy shrugged. 'I'm here to protect all of you and look out for you – like I did today. Despite what you might think,' she added pointedly, staring over at Edith.

'I'll be the first to admit I was wrong about you,' Edith admitted quietly. She had been talking animatedly when they had first walked in, but now she was coming across as meekly as Bessie always did.

'You're not the only one guilty of making a wrong assumption about somebody,' Poppy said as Geoffrey's face popped into her head. In her mind, he gave a cheeky wink. She smiled slightly before catching herself and feeling silly.

'I'm just so protective of Bessie. When you stood up for your friend who cut those buttons off her bodice, I wanted to string you up, too,' Edith said.

Poppy inwardly groaned. *Here we go*, she thought. How could she have been so naive as to think Edith would let her grudge go so easily? 'That's all well and good, but you have to understand that we couldn't let her into the factory wearing those buttons, it was—'

'Stop.' Marie laughed. Poppy looked across at her, confused. 'We've talked about this today and what Edith's *trying* to say is that while she's protective of my sister, she understands why you both did what you did that day.' Poppy looked across to Edith now and found that she was nodding in agreement.

'Oh,' Poppy replied. She was lost for words again. She'd got herself riled up and ready to defend herself and now she wasn't sure what to say.

Edith shrugged. 'Sorry. I'm not very good at explaining myself in these situations. And people are so used to me being harsh about everything that it's difficult to realise when I'm trying to be nice.'

'Bessie's the quiet one and Edith's the snappy, brash one. So, I tend to get stuck in the middle – talking for Bessie and calming Edith down,' Marie explained.

'Your main task is to try and catch us out slacking on the job, talking to men, or to tell us off for being out and about after hours,' said Edith. 'I couldn't envisage what kind of a woman would take on such a role.' Poppy opened her mouth to defend herself, but Edith started to talk again before she had the chance. 'But you coming to Bessie's aid like that has changed my mind. I can see that you *do* care after all and you're not just here to chastise us. You want to look after us, too.'

'That's *all* I want to do: make sure you're all safe.' Poppy sighed. 'The same goes for my colleagues. And yes, that might mean telling you off for talking to one of the male workers for too long but that's not because we want to stop you having fun. We don't want you so distracted that you put yourself or anybody else at risk.'

'I understand that now. And I understand why you had to search Bessie the other day.'

'I honestly didn't think she had stolen anything.'

'I know. I'm sorry for making things harder for you.'

'Shall we start again? All four of us?'

'That sounds like a good idea,' Bessie said. It was the loudest that Poppy had ever heard her speaking. Everybody, including Mrs Gilbert, turned to look at the teen. It seemed they were all as shocked as Poppy was at the fact that she had spoken up. 'I like her. I don't want you to be mean about her any more,' Bessie added in a quieter voice. Poppy could well imagine all the nasty things Edith had been saying about her since their two run-ins, but she wasn't one to hold on to things like that.

'Well, if you've won over our Bess, then you can't be that bad, after all,' Edith said happily.

Poppy looked over to Bessie and smiled. She thought it was no wonder the youngster was always so quiet when she had such a loud and outspoken companion. But no matter what had happened between them thus far, one thing was clear: Edith wanted to keep Bessie safe, and Poppy couldn't fault her for that.

20

Poppy was relieved to have straightened things out with Edith, and she came away from the girls' hostel feeling a little lighter. Not only did she no longer have to worry about doing anything to antagonise Edith, but Mrs Gilbert had instructed her to visit whenever she was in need of sustenance. The fact that meant no more concern about where her next meal was coming from, as well as having somebody to spend some of her limited free time with, made her feel happy. Mrs Gilbert might have been forty-odd years older than her, but Poppy had a mature head on her shoulders – Maggie was always telling her that – and she found her new friend easy to talk to.

Now that she had a full belly she was ready to get into bed earlier than usual and she couldn't wait for sleep to reach her. Once under the covers, Poppy thought about how quickly her friendship fortunes had changed. Just days before she had been feeling so low about not having anyone to turn to for a bit of company, and now she had Mrs Gilbert, Lawrence and Geoffrey. She felt like she might also be on the way to being able to call Bessie, Marie and Edith friends too. That was certainly a turnaround!

Poppy knew that she wasn't supposed to strike up friendships with the workers, but things had gone so well with the two sisters and Edith that she had a feeling they would probably start joining her and Mrs Gilbert on some of the occasions when she visited the hostel. She was keen to get to know them a bit better and she thought it would be nice to be able to stop and have a brief chat with each of them on her rounds. She'd have to be discreet, of course, and make up the time later on, but she felt like it would be worth it if it eased her loneliness.

Thinking about her new friendships with the women brought to mind Lawrence and Geoffrey, too. Poppy's heart fluttered when she pictured the pair of them. In her room, with nobody else around to intrude on her thoughts, she decided that she had to accept that she liked them both a little more than she had been willing to admit so far. Not that it mattered – they were both strictly friends and nothing more. But, she thought cheekily . . . if there was to be more to it, then who would she like the most? She convinced herself that there was no harm in thinking it through. They were both so different, from what she knew about them so far. Geoffrey was charming and funny, and always trying to make people smile; whereas Lawrence, although quite laid-back and friendly, had a serious side to him that she admired.

Poppy drifted off to sleep, deep in thought about the two new men in her life. When she woke up the next morning, she felt a little embarrassed about where her mind had wandered to the previous evening. Once she was dressed for patrol, she pulled her wedding ring out of her jacket pocket and stared at it as she turned it around in her fingers. It felt wrong to be spending time with Geoffrey and Lawrence and daydreaming about them while the ring and John's final letter were in her pocket. She had originally put them there as a way of having an instant connection to her husband, and their presence had been bringing her comfort while she found her way at Gretna. But, now she had settled in, she wondered if it might be best to store them both safely in her room. Some people might see it as moving on from John but that wasn't what it was, she assured herself. She felt as if she was betraying his memory by getting to know Geoffrey and Lawrence while those items were on her person. It was like she was carrying a piece of him with her and while that had been a comfort when she had first arrived, it was probably time to let go now.

She might not be ready to move on from John, but maybe she was ready to take a tentative first step. John wouldn't have wanted her to waste her remaining years grieving for him and, the more she thought about it, the more she realised that a future without love and a family wasn't what she wanted. Thinking back to Charlotte, she remembered their last cuddle back at the baby home. She closed her eyes and could almost smell the fresh, milky scent that she had drunk in during that final embrace. That was what she wanted. That was what John would have wanted for her. And, as terrifying as the thought of being with a man other than John was, she couldn't do it all alone. And she couldn't start working her way towards the possibility of building a family unless she started to at least try and let go of the past. With a heavy heart, Poppy took the items out of her pocket and carefully placed them in the top drawer of her dresser. Holding her palm down on top of them, she closed her eyes and brought John's face to mind.

'I don't need these to have you with me,' she whispered, and then she slowly pulled her hand away and closed the drawer.

Out on patrol, Poppy found that the usual dread she had become accustomed to feeling on her way to the cordite sections had lifted. She started off by doing her searches and she had another run-in with the woman who had tried to sneak in a cigarette during her first solo patrol.

'Did you really think I wouldn't check down here?' Poppy asked as she pulled the offending item out from the woman's sock. Thankfully, the worker just tutted and made her way into the workshop without causing a scene. When she walked into Bessie, Edith and Marie's workshop, Poppy definitely felt lighter than she had done on entering the area previously. And when Edith waved her over she was glad. She had official business to discuss so she didn't need to worry about being reported to a senior WPS officer for slacking on the job. Mrs Gilbert had banished Poppy's food woes and so now helping the generous matron was at the front of her mind.

'How are you getting on today? Is the new foreman all right?'

'He's just fine. They sent over Barry. He's the gentle giant of the factory – wouldn't harm a fly and really takes care of us all. I'm so glad he's here now instead of that dirty rotter, Bill.'

Poppy smiled. Edith was obviously still angry about what had happened. She hoped that Bill realised how lucky he was that it was Poppy who had caught him in the act and not Edith. She wasn't sure he would have made it out of the factory in one piece. 'I'm glad to hear it. Now, listen, do you know where I can find Jenny Campbell?'

'Little Jen? Yes, sure. She'll be unloading over at the train. Do you want me to walk you over and point her out?' Poppy nodded gratefully and they started making their way towards the back of the workshop. 'Is she in trouble? What's the little minx been up to?' Edith asked excitedly.

'Never you mind,' Poppy said lightly. She grinned at Edith to let her know that she was being playful with her. 'I just need a quick word with her, that's all.' Poppy already felt very loyal to Mrs Gilbert, and she knew it was important that none of the workers discovered that she had spoken to her about her problems with Jenny. They waved at Bessie and Marie as they passed by them and then Edith pointed out a girl who couldn't have been much older than Bessie. She was hauling huge packages down from the train.

'Everything all right?' Edith asked. Poppy realised her confusion must have been showing on her face. She had just assumed that Jenny was an older woman when Mrs Gilbert had told her about her. She was wondering now what on earth a girl so young was getting up to when she stayed out all night long. No wonder Mrs Gilbert was worried about her.

'Oh, I just expected her to be a little older, that's all.'

'Jenny can't be much older than our Bess. Wisp of a girl, too. Tiny, isn't she?'

Poppy nodded her agreement. Jenny was the shortest worker in the room by far and her uniform looked to be hanging off her scrawny frame. Poppy really hoped this youngster hadn't got herself caught up in anything nasty. And she would be shocked to the core if it turned out she was spying for the Germans.

'So, what's she been up to, then?' Edith pushed. She was definitely one for a good gossip.

'You can get back to work now,' Poppy said firmly before making her way towards Jenny. '*Now*,' she stressed, turning around when she could sense Edith staring after her. Edith pulled a face and walked away. Poppy had a feeling she would be getting a lot of questions the next time they met. But for now, she had to focus on Jenny and getting her the help she needed. All the women working around the train stopped what they were doing and stared at Poppy when she got closer. She had wanted to be as discreet as possible, but she should have known that would be impossible here.

'Ooh, who's been up to no good?' someone commented through the silence.

'You come back to floor another foreman?' somebody else pitched in, to a chorus of laughter and jeers.

'Back to work, you lot. I just need a quick word with Jenny here. It's about her pay,' Poppy lied. She knew the welfare workers were responsible for any queries with the workers' pay but she felt confident that nobody would pull her up on the discrepancy. Looking disappointed, the other women sighed collectively before getting back to what they had been doing. 'Follow me outside,' Poppy said quietly to Jenny. The teen followed her without a word of protest and Poppy was grateful she hadn't made a fuss like some of her colleagues – including Edith – might have done in the same situation.

'What's going on with my pay?' Jenny demanded as soon as they stepped outside. Poppy was surprised. Jenny was short and slim with small features. She hadn't expected her to speak with such force and confidence to somebody in authority. She was beginning to understand why Mrs Gilbert hadn't managed to get any answers out of her.

'There's nothing going on with your pay. I just wanted to get you outside so I could talk to you about your all-night stop-outs without anybody listening in.'

'Oh, well, in that case,' Jenny huffed. She went to step back into the workshop, but Poppy quickly jumped forward and blocked her path.

'Not so fast,' Poppy said, holding up her palm to stop Jenny trying to get around her.

'What do you think you're doing? It's got nothing to do with you what I get up to of an evening. Let me get back to work before they dock my pay and then there will be an issue with it!'

'Mrs Gilbert might be too nice to stand up to you about it but if my superiors hear about it, or one of the factory officials, then you'll be out on your ear. Then you'll have no pay.'

Jenny snapped her mouth shut and took a step back. 'Did she tell on me?' she hissed suddenly.

Poppy couldn't believe somebody so tiny could be so ferocious, but she got the feeling that it was more of a defence mechanism. 'She's worried about you. She doesn't want you to get into trouble, which is why she came to me.' Jenny raised her eyebrows in disbelief. 'She could have reported you for missing your curfew so many times, but she let it go. And she said nothing when you started staying out all night. You would be thrown out if she reported you for not sleeping at the hostel, but here we are. So, no – she doesn't want to get you into trouble. But you *will* be in trouble if you don't start telling me the truth.'

Jenny sighed, leaned her back up against the wall and folded her arms. 'If I tell you it will make things worse.' She dropped her arms to her side and her defensive demeanour disappeared. She was coming across like the quiet and friendly teenager she appeared to be.

'I can't help you if I don't know what's going on. At the moment your options are to tell me or to get thrown out when you inevitably get caught away from your hostel in the middle of the night. So, I would say that confiding in me is probably your best choice.' Jenny still didn't look very sure. 'Surely whatever I do can't make things any worse than they would be if you lost your job?' Poppy pushed. Her maternal instincts were kicking in as fear crept across Jenny's face and she found she felt desperate to help her. 'I just want to make sure you're safe. I can't bear the thought of any young girl out on the streets on her own all night.'

'I'm not out on the streets. I'm paying to lodge in Carlisle with one of the other girls whenever I can afford it. I'm perfectly safe. In fact, I'm safer there than I am at the hostel!' Jenny scoffed slightly before looking away and folding her arms again.

'I don't understand. The money for your board at the hostel is taken from your wages and you can get into trouble for missing the curfew. Why would you pay extra to sleep somewhere else? And what's so bad about Mrs Gilbert's hostel? I couldn't find any fault with it when I visited.'

'There's nothing wrong with her hostel. It's the other girls. There's a few in my dorm have taken a dislike to me. It started with a bit of teasing and name-calling here and there. I don't think they expected me to fight back, because of how small I am. Maybe I should have kept my mouth shut but that doesn't come naturally to me. When you're this small you get used to having to stand up for yourself.'

Poppy nodded sympathetically. She might not have been as tiny as Jenny, but she was certainly short and slim, and she knew what it was like to have people assume that they could just walk all over you because they were bigger than you. It's why she had felt so much more confident after completing her suffrajitsu training. 'What happened when you fought back?' she asked.

'What do you think? As soon as I stood up for myself, they got physical. Well, one girl did, anyway. All her little cheerleaders just sat back and watched and then patted her on the back while I nursed my bleeding nose. From then on it was relentless. And it wasn't like I could just hide myself away in my room – we're all in one big room with just curtains separating our beds and belongings. How can I protect myself living like that?' Poppy had been unimpressed with the WPS hostel when she had arrived, but, hearing this, she was grateful that she at least had a room to herself and her privacy. 'That's why I started staying out late. I thought if I could just sneak into bed once they were all asleep then I could get by without being bothered by them.'

Poppy felt terrible for her. How awful to feel so unwelcome in what was supposed to be your home. 'Why didn't you tell Mrs Gilbert that was why you had been staying out after the curfew?'

'And have her stepping in and making things worse? Don't be so silly. Anyway, staying out late only worked for a little while. Once they realised what I was doing, they started waiting up for me. They threw freezing water over me in the middle of the night. I ended up sleeping in one of the bathtubs using my wet towel as a blanket . . .' Jenny closed her eyes and visibly shuddered at the memory. 'That was it for me. From that moment on I started spending as many nights lodging with my friend as I could afford. When I have to stay at the hostel, I stay awake most of the night to make sure I'm not vulnerable to attack.'

'Oh, you poor love.' Poppy sighed.

'You don't have to feel sorry for me. I'm getting by just fine,' Jenny barked.

Looking at her properly, Poppy could see the exhaustion on her face. And, now that she thought about it, it was also evident from her snappy and defensive manner. 'But you must be so tired.'

'Better that than beaten to a pulp.' Jenny shrugged.

'No. This is no good. Apart from anything you could end up having an accident at the factory if you're working here on next to no sleep.'

'I won't tell you their names. I'd rather risk injury here than at their hands.'

'I don't need their names.' Jenny looked up at Poppy with confusion on her face. 'Don't get me wrong – there's nothing I would like more than to have their details so I can see that they're dealt with appropriately. But I understand your fears. This isn't the kind of place where disciplining them for what they've done to you would work so well. You all have to live and work together; and you're right: they would just take it out on you.'

'So, what are you going to do?' Jenny had started to look hopeful and Poppy felt a rush knowing she could make things better for her.

'I'm going to rescue you.' She smiled confidently. Jenny looked sceptical but she gave Poppy a small smile. 'Leave it with me,' Poppy sang as she headed back into the workshop. She opened the door and let Jenny go through in front of her. 'I'll come and find you at the hostel this evening and explain everything.'

'I'm staying with my friend. I can't possibly go another night without a proper rest.'

Poppy paused to think. 'That might actually be for the best,' she replied. 'I'll get everything sorted and then I'll find you here again tomorrow and confirm the details.'

Jenny appeared to be a little bit taller as she walked back towards the train and Poppy felt a rush of adrenaline. *This* was the reason she was here. This was the type of work that she thrived on. She didn't care what Sergeant Ross had to say about not getting too close to the workers. She was going to be able to help Jenny out of a desperate situation precisely because she *had* started getting to know some of them. She was looking forward to heading back to Mrs Gilbert's hostel after her shift to put her plan into action. And she might just enjoy a nice plate of food while she was at it.

21

Poppy felt like she had a spring in her step for the rest of her patrol. When she stopped by the nitrating house and saw Geoffrey, she motioned for him to follow her out into the yard so they could talk. She was desperate to share her plan with somebody and she was surprised at how happy she was to be able to tell him about it.

'Good for you,' he replied once she was finished. Poppy noticed that his face had brightened as she had been talking and, as he spoke now, she got the sense that he was almost proud of her. 'Nobody should be too frightened to sleep. That poor girl.' Geoffrey shook his head sadly. 'It's good to know there are officers like you who are looking out for the workers.' Poppy was so used to his cheeky demeanour that it threw her to see such a serious side to him. 'I don't know, first Bessie and now this Jenny girl. You'll be like the munitionettes' hero before too long. We should get you a cape,' he added, before grinning and giving her his signature wink.

Poppy couldn't help but laugh bashfully. She realised that she enjoyed it when he was playful like this with her. 'And to think that for a moment there, I thought she might be the famous factory spy,' she added lightly as Geoffrey laughed along with her.

When her shift was over, Poppy headed straight to Mrs Gilbert's hostel. She wanted to let her know what had been going on with Jenny and clear her plan with her before bringing Edith, Marie and Bessie in on it. Poppy told Mrs Gilbert all about Jenny's problems while the matron served her up some vegetable stew. Thankfully, she was keen on Poppy's proposal. She went to fetch the three girls while Poppy helped herself to another portion of the stew.

'Can't get enough of us, hey?' Edith joked when they walked back in with Mrs Gilbert and joined Poppy at the kitchen table. Her hair was still pulled back from her shift, but some big ringlets hung down at the side of her face.

'I think she's just back for the food,' Marie joked, pointing to Poppy's empty bowl.

Poppy smiled but inside she felt guilty that she'd originally had an ulterior motive in getting to know Mrs Gilbert. Once they had told their matron all about the new foreman and how much happier they felt in his care, Poppy explained what had been happening to Jenny at the hands of the bullies in her dorm.

'Why, those rotten apples!' Edith cried. 'Just tell me who it is and I'll go straight to their dorm and give them a taste of their own medicine. Fancy terrorising the poor girl so much that she can't even sleep in her own bed! They ought to be kicked out for what they're doing!'

'Edith,' Marie said sternly. 'Calm down a minute and let Poppy finish. I'm sure she has something figured out.'

All three of them looked over at Poppy expectantly. She smiled at the roles Marie had explained previously coming into play. And it seemed that it wasn't just Bessie who Edith was fiercely protective of. This was just what she had been counting on. She was somebody who couldn't stand for anybody being picked on, no matter who they were or how well she knew them. Edith was just the kind of overzealous bodyguard who Jenny could do with right now. And Marie was kind and caring, while Bessie could probably do with a quiet, less overpowering friend her own age to help her come out of her shell a little.

'There's too many of them – the factory bosses won't want to lose so many in one go. And I don't want to make things worse for Jenny by taking any action against them. She would benefit most from having some proper friends to look out for her at the moment.' Now it was Poppy's turn to look at the threesome expectantly.

'We'll look after her,' Edith barked without missing a beat. 'I can't guarantee that I won't accidentally hurt someone, trying to protect Jenny,' she added with a mischievous grin.

'I don't think it will come to that,' Poppy said cautiously. The last thing she wanted to do was to start a battle between the two groups of women. 'I'm confident these bullies won't dare mess with Jenny if she's part of your group,' she added.

Edith sat up straight and looked pleased with herself. 'But, hang on. How are we going to look out for her overnight? It's all very well us keeping her close when we're not at the factory, but, surely they'll all just pounce on her once she's in bed? Isn't that the reason she's been staying elsewhere up until now?'

'My maids are going to move her into your dorm tomorrow while you're all on your shift,' Mrs Gilbert explained. 'When they come back, her cubicle will be empty and there'll be no fuss made.'

'I don't imagine they'll question it with anybody as they won't want to draw attention to what drove her out,' Poppy said. 'She's staying with her friend tonight, so I'll pull her to one side during her shift again tomorrow and explain what's happening. Then I'd like you three to wait for her when your shift is over and help her settle into your dorm.' They all nodded eagerly. Poppy got the impression they were going to relish taking on this challenge together. 'I'd like you to keep an extra eye on her at the factory for the first few days just in case the bullies try to get at her for an explanation. I don't think they'd be silly enough to but—'

'I bet it's Martha and her stupid gang of witches. If they come anywhere near her, I'll show them what for,' Edith interrupted, sitting back in her chair and rubbing her hands together.

'We don't want to make *more* trouble. Let's just keep her close so that whoever it is leaves her alone,' Marie said firmly. Poppy breathed a sigh of relief that she was going to be able to rely on Marie to keep Edith in check through this.

'I'll stick with Jenny. She seems nice.' Poppy had to stop herself from looking startled when she heard Bessie's voice piping up from the other side of the table. She still wasn't used to the teen speaking and it had come out as almost a whisper.

'That's decided, then.' Mrs Gilbert smiled. 'Now, how about some cake?' Poppy didn't have anything to rush back to her hostel for, so she decided to stay a little longer and get to know everyone better before going back for some precious sleep. As they started talking, she found herself opening up about Maggie and Annie back in London and how much she missed them.

'Do you have any children?' Mrs Gilbert asked suddenly. 'It's just that you seem very maternal.'

Poppy blushed. She tended to sound like she was talking about her own children when she spoke about Maggie and Annie, such was her bond with them and the dynamics of their relationships. 'I don't have any children of my own,' she said, and a wave of sadness swept over her as she told them about what had happened to John. She went on to talk about her strong bond with Charlotte, and then she found herself admitting that she longed for a family of her own one day. It was the first time she had said it out loud and she was surprised to be confiding in near strangers about it rather than her best friends.

'You're still young. You have time,' Mrs Gilbert said kindly.

'Once this war's over you'll be free to focus on building a new life and a family for yourself,' Marie added, and Poppy smiled. She still felt guilty for even contemplating moving on from John, but she liked how Marie had worded that. She wasn't betraying her husband, she assured herself – she was simply building her family the only way she was able to now he was gone. And John would always be a part of her family because he would live on forever in her heart.

'Maybe she doesn't have to wait until after the war. There's a few half-decent men here,' Edith said, giving Poppy a cheeky look. 'Of course, we're not allowed to get ourselves into any relationships with the opposite sex, but I don't suppose it's against the rules for you?'

Poppy wasn't sure if Edith was making a dig, but one look at her face told her that she was being playful. It didn't stop her feeling bad for the fact that she was enjoying getting to know two new men while it was in her job description to stop these women from enjoying any time with a man.

'Yes, I've seen you speaking to one of the superintendents . . . what's his name?' Marie pitched in. 'The younger one, not that loud giant.'

Poppy felt her cheeks flushing crimson and she laughed nervously. 'Superintendent Baker. I must admit, he is rather pleasing on the eye. But we're strictly friends. He's been very kind to me.'

'I'll bet he has,' Edith roared.

Poppy couldn't help but join in when they all erupted into laughter. It felt good to talk about these things with other women rather than agonising over it in her head all the time. Their laid-back reaction was making her feel less guilty for her feelings of lust. Especially as, like Edith had pointed out, the workers weren't allowed to get too close to the men at the factory. Poppy wondered if she should mention Geoffrey, too, but she was worried that she might come across as a bit of a harlot if she admitted that she had taken a liking to more than one man since arriving at Gretna. Deciding to keep that to herself for now, she changed the subject.

'How are you all finding factory life? It must be hard, being away from home.'

'Well, we're pretty well looked after at the hostel – we get our food and board, and we never want for anything,' Marie said, giving Mrs Gilbert a grateful smile. 'It's hard work at the factory, but once we step outside those gates, we don't have any responsibilities.'

'I was working in a shop full time before I came here,' Edith explained. 'Then, when I got home, I would have to help my mother with all the housework. And you can bet that there was always one of my brothers or sisters to tidy up after or chase around after because they were out after bedtime'. It made sense to Poppy that Edith was responsible for younger siblings at home. No wonder she had taken on the role she had done when she had met Marie and Bessie.

'Being fed and looked after – it's a kind of lady's life in a way,' Bessie quietly remarked.

'Apart from the daily risk of getting blown up,' Edith scoffed, rolling her eyes. Bessie looked embarrassed and Poppy felt for her. She knew Edith looked out for her and she was protective about anybody else being mean to her, but she wondered if she realised that comments like that probably hurt Bessie's feelings. Edith was just having fun and she meant well but, even from the limited contact they'd had so far, Poppy could tell that Bessie was very sensitive.

'Our Bessie's a bit of a dreamer.' There went Marie again, thought Poppy – jumping in to save the situation after Edith got carried away. 'She likes to romanticise all of this, although, like I said, we are treated pretty well.' Bessie gave a small smile. 'We send most of our wages home to our mother. She couldn't get by without them. But we keep a little back to use for cinema trips and soft drinks at dances,' she added.

As the evening wore on, Poppy got to know the group better and she even learned more about the township and what was on offer for the workers out of their factory hours. The threesome had started going to Gretna Institute soon after their arrival in hopes of being able to spend some time in the company of men without getting into trouble for it, but they had been disappointed to discover the building was sexually segregated.

'You can imagine our faces when we were walked past all the rooms filled with men on the ground floor and were escorted straight to the upper floor which was filled with ladies!' Edith exclaimed merrily.

'Now we're signed up to all these different classes that we have absolutely no interest in but can't get out of,' added Marie, laughing. 'And, of course, the men get a room for playing chess and draughts while we get one full of sewing machines. You would think that with the men's work we do here they would at least let us have a games room, but no, we're expected to spend our free time sewing.'

'Do you think they'll let women stay in the police force after all of this is over?' Edith asked.

'I do hope so,' Poppy replied. 'That's what my bosses want, and I think we're doing a pretty good job of convincing the commissioner that we can handle things rather well.'

'Would you stay on?' Bessie asked.

'I think I would. I think Maggie and Annie would, too.'

'But what about your plan for a family?' Marie asked.

'I think I can do both. Annie's managing it quite well, and there are many women in the WPS who have families. In fact, the majority of them are mothers and even grandmothers. If you look at what they're doing while their men are away at war, then just imagine what we could all achieve once they're all home and life isn't quite so tricky.' All the girls smiled and Poppy felt a rush of positivity. She hadn't much thought about her future with the WPS past the end of the war but now that she had started to explore the possibilities with her new friends, she was feeling excited about it.

As Edith started talking animatedly about the dances held at the Border Hall in the township and how boys from Carlisle were allowed in for them at the weekends, Poppy's mind started to drift. She was really beginning to feel hopeful about achieving a happy future. She put her hand into her pocket to reach for her wedding ring and the letter from John, and started when her fingers failed to find them. Her heart jolted as she patted around and panicked as she tried to locate them.

'Are you all right? You've gone ashen,' Mrs Gilbert whispered, leaning into Poppy as Edith babbled on, oblivious. A sense of calm drifted over Poppy as she remembered that she had left the items safely in her room that morning.

'I'm really good,' she replied, breaking into a big grin and tuning back into Edith's animated chatter. And it was the truth.

22

The next few weeks passed in a blur for Poppy and she was shocked to see they were nearly at the end of October when she spotted a calendar on the wall of the WPS hut for the first time. She had been so busy with her patrols that she hadn't even noticed the weeks passing by. How was it possible that she had been at Gretna for a whole month already? In that time, a number of other WPS recruits had been transferred to a different factory and so Poppy had been kept on the afternoon shift to avoid any confusion. She had also missed out on any more days off while replacements were sought. But she didn't mind because she was really enjoying the routine she had fallen into at the factory now that she had friends to see along the way to break up her patrols. She wasn't keen to be allocated a morning or night shift as she would miss the familiarity of the workers on the afternoon shift.

Poppy clocked on at two o'clock, did her searches and then patrolled the cordite sections. There, she stopped to catch up with Bessie, Edith, Marie and Jenny before breaking into a half run, half walk to get across to Dornock and make up for the time lost to talking. At the nitrating house, she always stopped to say hello to Geoffrey. They spent time talking in the yard away from prying eyes – none of the workers were allowed out there and he told her that the only other people who had permission to go out there were foremen and Butcher and Baker – who sometimes dropped by to report on issues with male workers at the section.

Doing the rounds every day for weeks on end had started to feel a little monotonous, but Poppy found that Geoffrey's smile and laid-back attitude broke up the tedium of this part of her patrol, and she had been shocked when she had been left feeling empty on the days when she turned up to find him absent. Geoffrey had confided that he'd signed up to join the army soon after war had been declared, but a training accident meant he had never made it out of the country. He hadn't gone into detail and Poppy hadn't wanted to push, although she was desperate to know what had happened.

From the nitrating house, Poppy completed the final part of her patrol with a quicker pace again so that she wasn't pulled up for dawdling or slacking. She had taken to going to see Mrs Gilbert at least every other evening following her shift. She stayed in her uniform so that she wouldn't be questioned if Sergeant Ross or any other of her superiors ran into her over by the workers' hostels. She had decided that she would lie and say she was checking in on a worker who had come over poorly during their shift if she was ever caught out. Mrs Gilbert fed her well and told her that she was welcome every day, but Poppy didn't want to take advantage of the kind matron's good nature. So, she made do with the canteen food on the other days, where she did her best to try and forge friendships with her fellow WPS recruits.

Bessie, Edith, Marie and Jenny sometimes joined Poppy and Mrs Gilbert for extra food and company, but they tended to go out together to dance or watch a film at the cinema most evenings. Jenny had slipped into their friendship group without a hint of a problem and the bullies from her dorm had backed off as soon as they had seen her with Edith. According to Edith, the women had visibly shuddered when they had spotted Jenny in her company, and Poppy wished she had been there to see their reactions. The important thing, though, was that Jenny hadn't had any trouble from them at all since moving dorms.

Every time Poppy passed the police hut, she glanced over, hopeful that she might catch a glimpse of Lawrence inside. She hadn't bumped into him since they'd taken a walk together on her day off, and she had found herself longing to see him again. She had plucked up the courage to knock on the door once, but she had instantly regretted it and hadn't ventured that way again since. Instead of Lawrence's handsome face, she had been met by a grinning Superintendent Butcher. She'd listened to him rambling on for almost an hour while she kept an eye on the door, yearning for Lawrence to walk in and brighten her day. That afternoon she had been forced to lie to Sergeant Ross, making up a tale about a skiving worker to account for her lateness clocking on at the rest of the workshops because she had failed to make up the time on the remainder of her patrol. Following that disaster, she had steered clear of the police hut despite the pull she felt every time she walked past it on her way to the Dornock workshops.

When Poppy was finally granted a day off, she planned to lounge in bed all day. But she found herself awake at the usual time and feeling unable to relax. She was just about to get up when a letter was pushed under her door. Excited, she jumped out of bed and grabbed at the envelope. She knew instantly that it would be from Maggie and Annie, and she felt her belly flip as she took in the familiar handwriting. Reading through it greedily, she almost yelped when she got to the end. They were hosting Christmas Day at the baby home again this year, and they had permission from Frosty to invite her along. Maggie's part of the letter read:

Frosty wasn't sure at first, due to the fact the workers at your factory will all keep going during the festivities. It seems that it's business as usual at Gretna – but not for you, dear Poppy! We told her you simply had to be with us for Christmas again and, well, you know she seems to have a soft spot for me, so I might have played on that a little bit. But the upshot is that she put in a formal request for your leave, and it's been approved. You have two days either side for travelling and the whole of Christmas Day with us. I believe you should get the paperwork any day now. We absolutely can't wait to see you and hear all about your new adventures. That is, if you want to come and spend Christmas with us?

Poppy couldn't believe that Maggie could even question it. Her heart was racing with excitement just thinking about seeing her Bobby Girls again. And Charlotte! According to Annie's part of the letter, she was crawling around already. Poppy hadn't even thought about Christmas – it wasn't even quite November yet, after all. But she was so grateful to Annie and Maggie for planning ahead and organising the time off for her.

She wrote a letter straight back to them to tell them how excited she was at the prospect of being reunited, even if there was nearly two months to wait for the moment. She made sure to tell them all about her new friends, although she left out her romantic feelings towards Geoffrey and Lawrence. She had been enjoying her daily talks with Geoffrey and she definitely felt keen to spend more time with Lawrence, but she still wasn't sure she would ever act on the fancies. She was feeling content to simply get to know them both without feeling the terrible guilt she had experienced in the beginning when she realised that might mean she could be ready to move on from John. It was all a bit much to try and explain in a letter, and she was wary of her words being taken the wrong way. Annie's own loss was still very fresh, and Poppy didn't want to upset her with talk of her desires for new men. She didn't have long to wait until she would be able to see her Bobby Girls again so she decided she would explain everything face to face. Everything was always easier that way.

Keen to post her letter straight away, Poppy jumped out of bed, threw on some clothes and made a dash to the post office. Once the envelope was safely on its journey to London, she stepped outside and felt a strange sense of déjà vu. As the cold breeze hit her and she wrapped her shawl tighter around her body, she smiled to herself. This was how her previous day off had started. Thoughts of her subsequent walk with Lawrence and his kind gesture with the blanket to keep her warm flashed into her mind and before she knew what she was doing, she was walking in the direction of Hardy's. Glancing up at the big clock on the side of the dance hall, she saw that it was lunchtime and Lawrence was bound to be at his favourite café enjoying some food. She wondered if she should turn back and leave Lawrence to eat his lunch alone. But then she reminded herself that she was just enjoying getting to know him and Geoffrey, and that there was no harm in that.

Walking into Hardy's, Poppy felt a rush of pleasure when she saw Lawrence sitting at a table on his own. When he looked up and spotted her, a big smile spread across his face and Poppy was filled with relief. He looked just as pleased to see her as she felt to see him. He waved her over and she happily took a seat across from him, and ordered herself a sandwich and a cup of tea.

'I've been wondering when I would bump into you again,' he said cheerfully.

Poppy could feel herself blushing. If only he knew how desperate she had been to see him over the last few weeks. She had even been tempted to use the blanket he had loaned her as a ruse to visit the police hut when she was off duty.

But it would have meant skipping breakfast or lunch at the canteen to fit in a trip before her shift and she hadn't wanted to risk getting stuck with Superintendent Butcher again. She wouldn't have minded missing a meal to spend some time with Lawrence, but skipping food to listen to Superintendent Butcher drone on just wasn't something that she was willing to do.

'This is my first day off since I last saw you. I had hoped to see you around on site, though.'

'I had to take some time off at the last minute, I'm afraid. Otherwise, I'm sure our paths would have crossed.' Lawrence looked sad now and Poppy wanted to reach her hand out to comfort him. She stopped herself though, aware that the move would be too overfamiliar for somebody she hardly knew. She felt so comfortable around him that she had to remind herself they had only met a handful of times. 'Maybe now I'm back we can see more of each other.'

Poppy could feel her palms starting to sweat as Lawrence's words sank in and she saw the bright smile return to his face. 'That would be most pleasant. What was it that took you away?' She immediately felt bad for prying. He didn't owe her an explanation – he barely knew her. 'I'm sorry. Ignore my question,' she quickly added, feeling flustered and embarrassed.

'I'll do no such thing,' he replied kindly. 'It's nice to know somebody cares about what has kept me away.'

Poppy tried to keep a level head as he held eye contact with her. She felt giddy when he stared into her eyes like that.

'Do you remember what I told you about my parents being ill?'

Her heart lurched as she realised what was coming next. She nodded her head solemnly and waited for Lawrence to elaborate.

'My mother's gone,' he whispered.

Before she could stop herself, Poppy had reached out and grabbed his hand. To her relief, he didn't flinch at the gesture but instead gave a small smile as he squeezed her hand gently. As Lawrence explained how his mother had finally succumbed to the illness that had been blighting her life for years, Poppy could feel the eyes of the workers sat around the café on them. She knew they would be judging her for grasping Lawrence's hand as she was, but she didn't care. She was comforting a grieving man and that was all there was to it.

'How is your father doing?'

'I'm sorry to say that I don't think he'll be far behind her.' Tears welled in his eyes and Poppy longed to walk round the table and embrace him. She made do with rubbing his hand comfortingly. 'I always thought he would be the first to go. Mother's always been so much stronger than him. But she took a turn for the worse and she just gave up. I think her fight has been fading as she's got older.' He sighed and looked up into Poppy's eyes again. 'She was the one keeping him going, so I'm bracing myself.'

'You poor thing. It must have been such a difficult time for you.'

'And to think, I passed up the chance to help defend our country so I could look after them and save my sister that burden. I've failed at that now. How many people will think it was just a coward's excuse once they have both gone?'

'Nobody will think that,' Poppy replied fiercely. 'You couldn't have foreseen this happening and, besides, you are helping defend our country. Every day. And I won't hear another word about it.' She released her grip slightly on his hand when she saw it going white. She had become so impassioned while talking that she had squeezed it tight without realising.

'Sorry about that,' she said sheepishly, staring at Lawrence's hand.

'Not at all. How wonderful to have somebody so strongly on my side.'

'It's not about sides. Anybody with any sense can see you wanted to join the ranks, but you had a responsibility at home. And you haven't shirked away from protecting this country.' It felt like an appropriate moment to gently release his hand altogether. She looked up at him awkwardly as she did so, and he smiled at her gratefully.

'So, you missed me, then?' he asked playfully as Poppy finally took a sip of her tea. She almost spat out the mouthful while laughing at his comment. She was still getting used to the fact that he had a bit of a spirited side to him. With Geoffrey, it was obvious as soon as you looked at him – even more so because of his incessant winking and joking around. But Lawrence came across as straightforward and serious, so Poppy found that the glimmers of cheekiness were sometimes unexpected.

'I actually stopped by the hut once to try and see you,' she confided. Lawrence raised his eyebrows quizzically. 'Yes, you guessed it. I got stuck with Butcher for a whole hour! I never risked it again!' They both burst into laughter and Poppy felt glad she had managed to cheer Lawrence up after the tough time he'd been going through.

'I shall have to enhance my presence around the factory so that you don't feel the need to put yourself in danger like that again,' he said so solemnly that it made Poppy giggle even more. They spent the next thirty minutes talking and laughing, and then Poppy agreed to walk back to the police hut with him.

'You're such a good policewoman, escorting me back to work,' Lawrence joked as they wandered through the township.

'I take my duties very seriously,' she replied with a straight face.

'On a serious note, though, I do have a great admiration for you and your fellow WPS recruits and everything you're doing.' Poppy tried to bat the comment away. 'I mean it. It can't have been easy – it probably still isn't easy. I can only imagine what you had to come up against in London.'

'We're a tough lot. You can't scare us off very easily.'

'The whole poacher-turned-gamekeeper aspect of it is fascinating to me,' Lawrence admitted. 'One minute you're all part of the suffragette movement and you're fighting the police tooth and nail, and the next you're working alongside them with a common goal. It's quite the turnaround.'

'Oh, I never got involved with the suffragette movement, although I agreed with it all wholeheartedly. I was married at the time but I'm not sure it would have been for me anyway. It was a bit too extreme. Plenty of the women I trained with were heavily into it, though. My sub-commandant was even force-fed in Holloway because of her suffragette actions.'

'And now she's helping run the country's first female police force. It's just so unexpected but I think it's brilliant!' Lawrence was talking really animatedly now. Poppy wasn't sure she had ever met a man who was so enthused about the WPS. She had come across men who showed their support, of course, but Lawrence seemed to really understand what was at the core of the organisation. 'You're all doing so well to prove that women can do men's jobs with equal skill and competency,' he added. 'I'm rooting for you to be able to continue on with the roles once the war is over.'

'It's so refreshing to hear that from a man. Especially one who is so high up in the police force himself,' Poppy replied.

Their conversation didn't halt until they arrived back at the police hut. Once Poppy had bid Lawrence farewell, she found herself on a train to Carlisle. On a whim, she had decided to explore the town. On the short train journey, she thought back over her lunch and walk with Lawrence. She'd had so much fun with him, and she had felt as if she'd known him for years. She also loved how open he was about his support for the WPS. As her mind started wandering on to Geoffrey, she realised that she was now in a bit of a pickle – which of the two men did she like best? Staring out of the window as the buildings of Carlisle came into view, she laughed at herself. What did it matter who she liked the most? They were both friends and no more, so nothing was going to come of her desires anyway. That didn't stop her feeling happy that she was going to be seeing more of Lawrence around the factory from now on, though. Between him and Geoffrey, Poppy's long, cold and dark days on patrol were certainly going to start feeling a little brighter.

23

Before she knew it, Poppy was packing her overnight bag ready to head to the baby home to spend Christmas with her Bobby Girls. The weeks since she had received the letter from her friends with the news of her festive leave had passed in what seemed like the blink of an eye. Not only had she been enjoying the company of Geoffrey every time she had stopped by the nitrating house when he was on shift, but she had been regularly bumping into Lawrence on her patrols. She seemed to come across him at least once every couple of days, and she found herself looking out for him as she made her way around the factory. She had even stopped by Hardy's to enjoy lunch with him on her days off on a few occasions.

'I can't believe you won't be here for Christmas Day,' Edith huffed a few days before Poppy's departure. She had stopped by Mrs Gilbert's hostel for some dinner and Edith, Marie, Jenny and Bessie had all come into the kitchen to join her and their matron. Edith had been trying for weeks to convince Poppy to cancel her trip to London and instead share a festive dinner with them all. While she was flattered after having worked so hard to make friends at Gretna, Poppy was too desperate to see Maggie, Annie and Charlotte to accept the kind invitation.

'She'll be back the day after Boxing Day,' Marie said with a laugh. Poppy couldn't help but smile. A few months before, Edith had hated the sight of her and now it seemed as though she couldn't stand to be away from her.

'It just won't be the same, is all.' Edith sighed. 'I know everything will be normal here, so we'll hardly notice that it's Christmas Day, but I've grown used to seeing you every day – even if it's only for a few minutes. I look forward to seeing you walking through our section.'

Poppy felt bad that Christmas Day would be business as usual for the workers, apart from a slightly fancier dinner, while she was allowed to go home and see her 'family', even if it would be a flying visit. 'I'm sure they're holding some extra special dances to mark the occasion,' she offered hopefully.

'They're letting boys from Carlisle in for some dances,' Jenny piped up excitedly.

Poppy was so glad that Jenny was able to enjoy factory life now that she had Edith looking out for her and she was safely away from her bullies. She had never taken things further with the women who had been behind the cruel behaviour that had seen Jenny too frightened to sleep in her own bed. She had been worried at first that they might turn their attentions to another victim, but Edith had made it clear that she had her beady eye on them. Poppy was confident that Edith wouldn't let them get away with any more bullying. 'There you go. What fun that will be.' Poppy smiled, but Edith just rolled her eyes dramatically and groaned.

'Yes, how lovely. More creeps to protect our Bessie from.' Bessie's face flushed red and she looked away uncomfortably.

'I'm sure we'll all have a wonderful time celebrating. And I might even have some special gifts for everyone,' Marie said eagerly, pulling the attention away from her little sister. She rubbed her hands together and looked around the table at everyone.

Poppy smiled with them all, but she felt confused. She distinctly remembered Marie telling her that she and Bessie sent most of their wages home to help their mother, who was struggling financially. Maybe she had skipped a few cinema trips to afford presents for her friends, she thought to herself. And they were probably only small gifts, anyway. She caught herself and scolded herself for the thoughts. It really wasn't any of her business what money Marie had or how she spent it. She laughed to herself at how detective work was coming to her so naturally now.

On her shift the following day, Poppy stopped off to see Geoffrey as usual and they popped into the yard next to the nitrating house for a quick talk.

'I bet you can't wait to see your Bobby Girls,' he said, giving her a big grin and an overzealous wink. Poppy was impressed that he'd remembered she was on her final shift before heading back to London. She had mentioned it weeks before, but they hadn't talked about it since. She also loved the fact that Geoffrey referred to Maggie and Annie as her Bobby Girls. It almost made it feel as if he knew them both, too. And, somehow, that made them feel closer even though they were hundreds of miles away.

'Will you be seeing any family at Christmas?' she asked him. Although they spoke most days, Geoffrey hadn't revealed much about his background. Now she thought about it, Poppy realised that she didn't know very much about him at all. She had told him an awful lot about herself and her friends, but he always started laughing and joking when the conversation was ready to naturally turn to being about him. He was so good at it that she didn't normally notice it was happening, and it was only when she thought back on their interactions that she recognised what he had done. Poppy wondered if Geoffrey didn't talk about his homelife because it wasn't a very happy one. She still didn't even know what training accident had stopped his quest to serve in the army.

'I'll be here making sure no one blows the place up. Duty

calls, as always!' He laughed and winked. 'I bet little Charlotte is going to be overjoyed to see you again,' he added as he swept his hair off his forehead. Poppy's heart swelled when she thought of the tot. Then she realised he had done it again – made a joke and then turned the conversation back to her to deflect away from him and anything personal. She wasn't going to push him, though. Despite the fact he seemed reluctant to open up to her, Poppy still felt sweet on Geoffrey. There was just something about his fun nature and charm that made her feel happy when she was around him or when she thought about him.

At the end of her shift, Poppy found herself feeling glum at the fact she hadn't seen Lawrence to bid him farewell. She had looked out for him throughout her patrol but hadn't managed to spot him. She knew she was only going to be away for a matter of days, but she had been looking forward to seeing him one last time before she left. Turning into the road of the WPS hostel for an early night ahead of her long journey, her breath caught in her throat when she looked up and saw Lawrence bounding towards her. His warm smile instantly soothed her against the cold winter air, and she stopped to take in the friendliness behind his eyes as he greeted her.

'I wanted to wish you a merry Christmas before you took your leave,' he said cheerfully.

'Merry Christmas to you, too,' she replied, feeling giddy at the thought that he had tracked her down specially to say goodbye to her. She knew that he was going to be working through Christmas but had a special dinner planned with his father and his sister. He was also going to be having a meal at Superintendent Butcher's home on Boxing Day. 'I hope your ears don't get too sore from listening to all the stories from Butcher,' she said lightly.

'He's not actually quite as bad when he's with Mrs Butcher,

would you believe it? She never lets him harp on for too long. I think that's why he's such a chatterbox when he's away from her.' They both laughed and then Poppy suddenly shivered from the cold.

'I'm sorry, I shouldn't be making you stand around in the freezing cold.' Lawrence's voice was full of concern. Poppy's heart sank and she felt annoyed with herself. She didn't care a jot that her hands felt like icicles – she would stand and talk to him all night even if it meant she turned into an ice sculpture. 'Make sure you don't complain to an officer that you're feeling cold,' Lawrence added, suddenly coming over all serious.

'Why ever not?'

'They'll say that you should be being kept warm by the thought you are working for your king and country,' Lawrence replied, smiling.

'I'm sure they would.' Poppy sighed. 'I just wish they had made our uniforms a little warmer, is all.'

'Yes, it's ironic that the clothes made for women police are useless in the cold and wet weather.' As he spoke, Lawrence ran his hand quickly up and down the sleeve of Poppy's jacket in a gesture to try and warm her up. She started at the intimacy of the move and then she felt her legs going weak at his touch. 'You get going and get yourself warm. I hope you still have that blanket?' Poppy smiled and nodded. She was too flustered to say a proper goodbye, so she just gave him a small wave before walking away.

Later, as Poppy wrapped herself up in the blanket in her room, she realised how conflicted she still felt about the two men. Her heart was still with John, so it didn't really matter – but she wondered if a few days away from them both might clear her mind. Thinking of her husband reminded her to retrieve her wedding ring and his final letter from the drawer. She felt comfortable not wearing her wedding ring any longer, but she didn't feel ready to leave her connection to John hundreds of miles away. She popped them into her overnight bag and settled into bed to try and get some sleep. She had an exciting few days ahead of her and she needed her rest.

24

Standing on the doorstep of the baby home, Poppy took a moment to prepare herself. She could hear lots of different voices as well as a mixture of laughing and crying coming from inside the house. It took her a minute to understand why she was hesitating: she'd grown to like the monotony and relative calmness of factory life over the last few months and spending time at the baby home was going to feel like a bit of a shock to the system. Of course, at Gretna there was the odd fallout between the workers to deal with here and there but, on the whole, everybody was focused on the job and keeping safe. As soon as she had stepped off the train in the city, she had felt the difference in her surroundings. Everybody was rushing about in London, and she already missed the quiet of the countryside. Did her future lie in Scotland?

Poppy knew that her reluctance didn't mean that she wasn't overjoyed to be seeing her friends again – just that she needed to take some time to adjust to the difference in atmosphere. She was beginning to mull over whether she was ready to leave London behind as well as possibly moving on from John when her thoughts were interrupted by the door swinging open. Looking up, she was met with Maggie's smiling face. Her friend reached out and practically pulled Poppy in over the threshold. After wrapping her arms around Poppy, Maggie swayed from side to side while holding her in the embrace. Finally, she let go and took a step back.

'I've been watching out for you all morning. What were you doing standing on the doorstep for so long? It's freezing! You were looking so deep in thought, too! You're supposed to knock, you know.' She giggled.

'Sorry, I was just thinking about the last time I was here and how much has changed,' Poppy lied. She didn't want to upset Maggie by revealing her desires to possibly start afresh somewhere new. But maybe that was what she needed. Perhaps she was beginning to feel like the life she had longed for, with a husband and children, was possible because she had spent so much time away from London – and the connection she felt between the city and John. She didn't have time to think it over further because Annie came to greet her and when Charlotte reached out her arms to Poppy, she couldn't think of anything else but her love for the child.

'You're crying! Are you all right?' Annie asked, full of concern.

'I've missed her so much,' Poppy said as Charlotte pulled at her hair and grabbed at her nose while giggling. It was true – she had missed her. But she was actually getting so emotional because she suddenly understood that she needed to be out of London to fully get over John and move on with her life. And that would mean leaving behind this little cherub – and her Bobby Girls. Poppy quickly pushed the thoughts from her head. She was here to enjoy Christmas with her friends, and she needed to make the most of the limited time they had together.

'Irene and Jack couldn't make it in the end,' Maggie explained sadly as they made their way to the big dining room. Poppy smiled when she saw Annie's mother and father sat at the table, with Annie's friend Bert sat opposite them. Bert had let Annie use his home as a lookout when she had been keeping tabs on the slavery ring that she had uncovered the previous year. The two had remained friends despite their age difference and Poppy had enjoyed getting to know the old man last Christmas. She pulled up a chair beside him and he started asking her questions about Gretna straight away.

Before Poppy knew it, the Christmas dinner was over, and all the guests had gone home. There were two new mums staying at the baby home who had joined them for the meal, but they had both gone to bed, leaving Poppy and her Bobby Girls to finally talk without interruption. While Annie slipped upstairs to check on a sleeping Charlotte, Maggie scooted up close to Poppy on the sofa.

'I've been waiting all day to ask you, but I didn't want to bring it up in front of anybody else, especially not Annie,' she whispered as she took hold of Poppy's left hand and ran her finger over the space where her wedding ring used to sit. Of course Maggie had spotted it straight away, Poppy thought to herself. She was impressed that her friend hadn't blurted anything out at the dinner table.

'Thank you for not mentioning it,' she replied quietly.

'So, have you met somebody?' Maggie asked excitedly. 'Oh, you must tell me! Please! I need some happy news in my life!' Maggie had revealed over dinner that her brother Eddie had been injured on the battlefield. The family didn't have much information at the moment, so it was just a waiting game to find out his fate. The news had taken Poppy straight back to the day she had received the telegram about John, and it had hit her square in the gut, rendering her unable to finish her food. She had placed her hand protectively over her ring finger at that point and prayed that Annie hadn't noticed.

'I haven't exactly met somebody, no,' Poppy whispered. She couldn't help but grin at the twinkle in Maggie's eyes as they lit up with joy. And the thought of being completely honest with somebody about her feelings for Lawrence and Geoffrey had her feeling quite giddy.

'You have!' Maggie cried, jumping up and down in her seat.

'Charlotte's just gone back to sleep,' Annie hissed from the doorway. 'What are you shouting about, anyway?'

Poppy's heart dropped. She hadn't heard Annie coming back down the stairs. She'd been hoping to explain everything to Annie on her own, in a sensitive manner. She didn't want to risk upsetting her. Annie sat down opposite them and looked directly at Maggie's hand, which was still placed on top of Poppy's left hand. Maggie drew it away sheepishly.

'It's all right, I noticed as soon as you sat down for dinner.' Annie sighed. 'You don't have to keep things from me to protect my feelings. I may have lost my fiancé, but I do understand that life goes on and I would never wish for anybody to feel a widow's grief forever – especially not one of my best friends.'

Poppy breathed a big sigh of relief. Annie had been a shell of herself after losing Richard and had put herself in so much danger bringing down the slavery ring on her own to distract herself from her immense sadness. Poppy knew she had come out of the other side stronger – having a baby to look after often did that to a woman – but she hadn't counted on her friend being quite this resilient and she suddenly felt bad for underestimating her.

'Nothing has happened,' Poppy explained carefully. 'But I've taken rather a fancy to a couple of the chaps at Gretna and, well, I took my ring off before I even got there so that hasn't anything to do with them. I just . . .' She knew that she was rambling, but she couldn't find the words to explain all of her feelings on the matter adequately. She wasn't even sure she understood what was going on in her head. It was all such a muddle of feelings and fancies. She took a deep breath while her friends sat waiting patiently. 'I decided on the way to Gretna that I didn't want to be weighed down by my grief any longer or defined by my widow status,' she explained finally.

'We didn't think you were.' Maggie shrugged.

'Because that's the front I put on for you. But there is only so long you can keep that kind of thing up for, and it felt like Gretna was a good time to make a fresh start.' They both nodded their understanding. 'Don't get me wrong – I didn't go there with the aim of meeting a man and getting married and starting a family but, well, I've realised over the last few months that that is what I want one day. I had thought that possibility had been taken away from me when John was taken away from me, but I'm beginning to see that isn't true. I think I might be ready to move on, and taking the ring off was the first step to getting to this point. Does that make any sense at all?'

'It doesn't have to,' Annie said kindly. 'All that matters is that you're happy. Wedding ring or not, moving on or not – we just want to see this beautiful smile more. I don't think I've ever seen you looking as radiant as you have done today!'

Poppy blushed. She *was* feeling happier.

'You said you hadn't *exactly* met somebody?' Maggie asked leadingly.

Poppy had to laugh. She might have known that Maggie wouldn't have let that go. She felt herself grinning like a child again as she told them all about Geoffrey and Lawrence and her attraction to them both.

'None of it matters a jot, though. They're just friends and nothing more. I don't even think either of them like me in that way. But I must admit that it makes the patrols pass by a little easier when I get to spend some time with them both,' she added. 'This whole thing may have made me feel like I'm ready to move on from John but I'm not sure I'm quite there yet.'

'Oh, I think you are!' Maggie cried happily.

'I'm sorry but I have to agree with Maggie.' Annie laughed. 'Just watching how you light up when you talk about them both. And, from what you've told us, neither of them would be turning you down if you admitted your feelings, so—'

'It sounds like you have a decision to make,' Maggie cut in.

'Well, if I were to choose,' Poppy sang playfully, twisting her head to the side and closing her eyes, looking deep in thought. 'And this is only hypothetical, you understand . . . Oh, goodness, I just can't pick,' she giggled.

'What do you like about each of them?' Maggie pushed.

'Well, Geoffrey is always laughing and joking, and just looking at him lifts my spirits. He's never revealed much about himself, though, whereas I feel like I know Lawrence on a deeper level. And he is certainly easy on the eye.'

'You'll know soon enough,' Annie said gently. 'And until that time, you should just continue enjoying getting to know them both. There's no harm in that. And it might turn out that neither of them is right for you – and that's all right, too. Perhaps you just needed to meet them both to realise that you're ready to start the rest of your life.'

'Those are very wise words,' Poppy replied gratefully. She was so glad now that she had confided in her friends. She felt better about everything already.

'I'm glad you told us,' Annie added quietly. 'You've given me hope that I might one day find happiness after Richard.'

Poppy had been so worried that her news would upset Annie, so she was overjoyed that it had actually given her hope of a happier future for herself. Tears welled in Poppy's eyes as she saw a stream of them suddenly running down Annie's cheeks. Poppy got up and went over to sit next to Annie, and Maggie sat down on the other side of Annie. They each put an arm around her and leaned into her together. The three of them sat like that for quite a while, content in their silent companionship. Poppy thought about how much had changed over the course of a year. Last Christmas, Annie had realised she was pregnant and now Charlotte was here crawling about and filling them all with love. And Poppy would have laughed back then if somebody had told her she would be seriously contemplating moving to the other end of the country to start afresh within the year.

When they finally separated and went to bed – Poppy was sharing one of the spare bedrooms with Maggie – Poppy found that she was sad to be leaving them again in the morning. But at the same time, she was desperate to get back to Gretna. Drifting off to sleep, she wondered when she would next see her best friends. She had promised to write to them as soon as there was any update on Lawrence or Geoffrey – but she wasn't confident that there would be anything exciting happening with either of them any time soon. And she was happy with that. Poppy was content to get back to Gretna and her patrols and just enjoy spending time with them both. She didn't desire any more excitement than that right now.

25

When Poppy returned to Gretna, she was placed on night shifts, much to her disappointment. The routine she had so enjoyed was thrown right out of kilter as none of her friends were working by the time that she had clocked on for patrol at half past ten in the evening. She had been so looking forward to walking into the cordite section and seeing Bessie, Edith, Marie and Jenny, but of course there was a different group of women entirely manning all the stations when she entered after searching the workers at the previous section. And Geoffrey had long since clocked off by the time she made it to the nitrating house each night. As for Lawrence, well, she knew that he would be tucked up in bed at that late hour – so there was no hope of bumping into him on her rounds, either.

The change in working hours knocked Poppy for six. She had been used to working through the night back in London, but she hadn't done so for months now. She felt positively exhausted, and it took her a few days to adjust. Once she was into the swing of it, though, she popped by Mrs Gilbert's hostel a couple of hours before her shift was due to begin on the day before New Year's Eve.

'Oh, the girls will be so happy to see you,' Mrs Gilbert exclaimed when she opened the door to Poppy. 'They've been ever so worried about you – they were expecting you back a few days ago.'

'I *was* back a few days ago. Only they put me on night shifts,' Poppy groaned.

'Well, I will go and fetch them, and we can all have some tea together. And I'll make you up some dinner. You'll need your strength if you're to be walking around that factory all night long.'

Poppy smiled gratefully as Mrs Gilbert pottered off. She knew that she had really struck gold when she had met her. As expected, the girls were all overjoyed to see Poppy.

'We were worried you'd realised how much you missed London and decided not to come back,' Marie said as they settled down at the kitchen table together.

'Quite the opposite, actually,' Poppy admitted. 'But don't tell my friends in London that.' She immediately felt a pang of guilt but then reminded herself of Annie and Maggie's desire for her to be happy. She knew they would be sad if she left London for good, but they would understand. Anyway, it was just an idea at this point, so it wasn't worth getting in a muddle over. She told them all about her dinner at the baby home and then listened intently as they filled her in on the gossip from the past week; there had been a scrap over one of the local boys at the Christmas dance (involving women on another shift, thankfully), two new girls had started on their shift but they hadn't been any bother so far, and one of the girls from over at Eastriggs had been caught trying to sneak one of the male workers into her dorm in the dead of the night.

'And what about the special gifts you had planned?' Poppy asked Marie. She had noticed beautiful blue earrings dangling from Edith's ears. The colour complimented her eyes, but the expensive jewellery looked rather out of place in the current setting. And Bessie had walked in clutching a rather fancy handbag, which Poppy definitely hadn't seen before. She looked to Jenny now and, oh yes, there was a particularly lovely-looking bracelet hanging daintily from her wrist.

'See for yourself.' Marie grinned, gesturing around the

table. Each girl gave her new item a loving rub and smiled across at their friend:

'You really have been generous,' Poppy said admiringly. She had no idea how someone like Marie could afford all of it – even if she wasn't sending any of her earnings home. But she reminded herself that it was none of her business and bit her tongue.

'I even treated myself to a fur coat,' Marie added, beaming from ear to ear. Poppy gasped.

'It really is quite the thing,' Jenny said admiringly.

'What did you and your friends get for each other?' Edith asked Poppy.

'Oh, we don't do gifts,' Poppy said quietly. She felt a little embarrassed now in light of all this grandeur. 'I'm not sure when I would have had the time for shopping, anyway,' she added. The truth was that they had all been so happy to see each other again that they hadn't needed to exchange presents. But for some reason she felt a little silly admitting that to her new friends. As the conversation turned to New Year's Eve, Poppy found herself feeling envious of the group's plans to attend a special dance in the township. She had never been one for toasting the start of a new year but, with all the new beginnings she was feeling ready to embrace, it felt like this year might be the time to make an exception.

'Why don't you come along tomorrow night?' Bessie suggested shyly. She had started gaining confidence since Jenny had joined their group, but she still wasn't nearly as outspoken as her sister and Edith.

'I had Christmas Day off, so I can't imagine I'd be lucky enough to be off duty on New Year's Eve, too. Unless they put me on duty at the dance,' Poppy replied hopefully. She'd already been moved from the afternoon shift to the night shift – maybe they would put her on a township patrol tomorrow?

'I don't think so. They never have WPS on for the dances. They pop their heads in as part of their patrols, but it's the welfare workers who supervise us in the hall. That's why so many girls get away with fraternising with the boys,' said Jenny, giggling, and Poppy's final bit of hope was dashed.

'I guess I'll be traipsing around the factory in the cold while everyone is toasting the start of 1917,' she said glumly.

'I expect they'll down tools at midnight and say a few words wherever you are on your patrol, dear,' Mrs Gilbert said kindly.

'And if you're not on duty then you can always come along and celebrate with us,' Marie suggested.

'As much as I would love that, I don't think it would be appropriate. I'm not meant to be friendly with the workers, remember. I'd get in trouble if my bosses found out I came and spent time with you all here, let alone turning up at one of your dances. I think they'd dismiss me on the spot.' They all looked deflated. 'I was lucky enough to go home for Christmas,' Poppy said, with forced positivity. 'I can't complain if I have to work for New Year's Eve.'

However, when Poppy turned up to clock on for her night shift later that evening, she was surprised to discover that she was marked down to have the following day off.

'Is this correct?' she asked Sergeant Ross, pointing to the list of recruits on the wall. Sergeant Ross nodded her head, but she didn't smile.

'Only, I was off on Christmas Day.' Poppy knew she should probably keep quiet and enjoy her day off, but she couldn't bear the thought of any of her fellow recruits resenting her for getting yet another special day off while they were working their way through the festive season.

'We've had an influx of new recruits, so you'll be enjoying more days off from now on. You've done well keeping up these last few months and you deserve a break.' Sergeant

Ross still had a stern expression despite the kind words she was speaking.

Poppy smiled gratefully before picking up a truncheon and clock, and heading out on patrol. She wondered if she had been moved to night patrols to facilitate the new recruits taking on the day shifts while they got used to working at the factory – as she had done previously. Things like that were never explained to her; she was just expected to go along with whatever they told her to do. Not that she was complaining, because it had certainly paid off now. It didn't matter that Poppy didn't have any friends to stop and speak to on her night patrol, because she spent the whole shift planning what she was going to do with her precious day off. One of many more to come! First off, she would sleep all morning. Then she would pop along to Hardy's and finally see Lawrence again. Oh, how she had missed him! She dared herself to wonder whether he had missed her, then scolded herself for getting carried away. He probably hadn't even noticed that she hadn't been around during the day as usual!

She longed to see Geoffrey, too, but she knew it wouldn't do to go along to the factory while she was off duty. Otherwise, she would have popped in to see him and the girls over the last week. She would just have to wait – and hope that now there were more WPS recruits on site that her shifts would start switching between day and night as they had done in London. She really did despise the night shift. The workers were pleasant enough, but she hadn't been able to get to know any of them like she knew Jenny, Bessie, Marie, Edith and Geoffrey. Her rounds at night were just dull compared to the afternoons.

After lunch with Lawrence, Poppy would probably head back to her room for some rest and to write to Maggie and Annie. She knew that they would be so excited to hear about her time spent with Lawrence. She wished that she could spend the evening at the dance with her worker friends, but it was strictly out of the question. She decided she would knock for Grace or Jean and find out if the other off-duty WPS recruits were planning anything to mark the start of the new year. She had only seen them both in passing a few times over the last few months, but they were the closest she had to friends at the hostel and with any luck at least one of them would also be off duty and happy to spend the evening with her.

Before she knew it, Poppy's night shift was over without a hint of any trouble. She used her lantern to find her way back to the hostel through the pitch-black township, and she fell into a deep slumber as soon as she got into her bed. She slept so soundly that it was well into the afternoon when she woke up – and way past lunchtime. Poppy was shocked at how upset she was to have missed 'bumping' into Lawrence for lunch. She toyed with the idea of taking a walk around the factory site on the off-chance that she might bump into him or Geoffrey, but she knew she was likely to be spotted by one of her colleagues and if word got back to their supervisors then she would be in bother. It would also risk making her look rather desperate, she decided. Even if nobody else realised what she was up to, she couldn't let herself resort to such pathetic measures.

Poppy wrote her letter to Maggie and Annie, wishing she had more exciting news to share about Geoffrey or Lawrence. Then she went for a walk around the township before settling down on the sofa in the communal room at the WPS hostel. A few other recruits popped in and out, but nobody seemed interested in talking at length to Poppy, as hard as she tried. Now she remembered why she had given up on attempting to forge friendships with her colleagues before. She was just about to give up when Jean walked in wearing casual clothes.

'I haven't seen you properly in a long while,' Jean said kindly, sitting down next to Poppy. It was nice to see a friendly face. She asked how Poppy had been getting on and they started exchanging notes on afternoon and night shifts. Jean actually preferred the night shifts, although her favourite place to patrol was the township because 'the girls get up to more bother, so it keeps things more exciting.' It made Poppy think of her London patrols and she found she didn't miss all the running around after ladies of the night or couples cavorting where they shouldn't be. The factory felt safer to her, despite its obvious dangers.

'Will you be joining in the celebrations this evening?' Jean asked.

'What celebrations?'

'Oh, it's nothing fancy – just a few drinks in the canteen at midnight. It's all the girls here have been talking about for weeks; I don't understand how you didn't know about it.'

'I don't really spend much time here. Everyone seems to know each other so well and I've tried to join in but, well, we're all so busy and tired, aren't we? I take most of my meals at one of the worker's hostels but when I frequent the canteen everyone seems to be talking amongst themselves.' She made sure not to mention her friendship with the workers.

'It's hard to get involved when everyone's here, there and everywhere all the time,' Jean agreed. 'But to be honest, Grace and I thought you were a bit of a recluse as we hardly ever saw you after the first week or so. I didn't realise you felt left out. I feel terrible now.'

'Please don't. I think maybe I didn't try hard enough,' Poppy admitted. Looking back, maybe she shouldn't have expected to be accepted in instantly without making more of an effort. Her colleagues weren't unfriendly after all – they were just tired and busy.

'Well, come along this evening and I'll make sure to introduce you to some more of the girls. The more faces you get to know, the easier it will be.'

Poppy was excited to have plans for New Year's Eve after all. She put on one of the dresses that Maggie had encouraged her to bring along and silently thanked her friend for having done so. She allowed herself to wonder whether Geoffrey or Lawrence might be at the get-together. Jean had said that the off-duty WPS recruits, along with some of the other supervisors, would be gathering in the canteen for an hour or so to have a toast to the new year starting. The workers on duty would all be stopping what they were doing for a little sing-song and celebration, so the canteen would be free until the next meal was served at two in the morning. Jean and Grace knocked for Poppy and they all made their way to the canteen together.

Poppy found she enjoyed talking to women more her age, and it made her realise that she tended to befriend younger girls. Maggie and Annie were both younger than she was and, of course, Edith and her group were all years behind her. She laughed to herself. There was her maternal side showing itself again.

The canteen was bustling with women and men, and Poppy scanned the room intently for the two faces she longed to see. Her heart dropped when she failed to spot either of them in the crowd, but Jean and Grace made good on the promise to ingratiate her with more of their colleagues, and the introductions and conversations served as a welcome distraction from her disappointment. Around ten minutes before midnight, the canteen staff started walking round and offering small glasses of beer to everybody. Poppy laughed as she took one from a tray.

'It's what we've got in for the navvies. Better than a glass of water!' the lady who had offered it to her exclaimed haughtily.

'Oh, I'm not complaining. It's very welcome,' Poppy replied.

'Don't go upsetting the kitchen staff, love, or else you'll be going hungry from now on,' a deep Scottish voice whispered in her ear. Poppy recognised it instantly and her heart did a somersault as she spun around to be greeted by Geoffrey's cheeky face. He rubbed the stubble on his chin as he took her in. Poppy found herself desperate to throw her arms around him for a hug, but she just about managed to stop herself, knowing that it wouldn't look very becoming of her, as well as the fact it would be downright inappropriate.

'It's so good to see you!' She settled for a smile instead, as he winked and grinned back at her.

'I take it they slung you on the night shift on your return from the city?'

'Yes, for my sins! It's so dull. I really do miss our little meet-ups.' What was she doing? She couldn't even blame her loose lips on the beer as she hadn't taken but a sip yet. She just felt so excited to see him; it was like she was high on the feeling it gave her. Did that mean she liked Geoffrey the most? They talked a little and he said hello to Grace and Jean. As the countdown to midnight began, though, Poppy found herself searching around for Lawrence. She felt ever so greedy for feeling so desperate to see him when Geoffrey was standing right next to her. All too soon, someone rang a bell and the room erupted into cheers and cries of 'Happy New Year.' Geoffrey grabbed Poppy's hand and kissed it, and she found herself flushing crimson as he gave her yet another cheeky wink.

Jean suddenly pulled Poppy in for a hug and, as she looked over her shoulder, she saw the unmistakable outline of Superintendent Butcher at the other end of the room, next to the serving hatch. He was so tall that he towered above everyone around him and stuck out clearly to her. If Lawrence was here, surely he would be nearby. Before she knew what she was doing, Poppy had pulled away from Jean and started pushing her way through the crowd of people hugging and dancing and singing to try and get to Superintendent Butcher. The need to see Lawrence again was all-consuming. As she drew nearer, the man next to Superintendent Butcher turned around and her knees went weak when she saw that it was Lawrence. On seeing her, his eyes lit up and he opened his arms. Without thinking, Poppy threw herself into them. She closed her eyes as she took in the feel of his strong body next to hers and she drank in every detail of how he felt against her before realising what she was doing and quickly drawing herself back. Lawrence was looking down at her and laughing with a shocked look on his face.

'It's good to see you too!' he exclaimed.

'I'm so sorry, I don't know what came over me,' Poppy gasped, but as she looked around relief swept over her; everybody was hugging and embracing still. Nobody seemed to be staring at them so she would be able to put this inappropriate display of affection down to a friendly gesture to mark the tolling of the new year. Even if it had meant a lot more to her than that.

'I'm not complaining,' Lawrence said, holding eye contact with her. Now Poppy really was in a muddle. She had hoped that a week away from Lawrence and Geoffrey would help her determine who she liked the most, but now she had been reunited with both men she was just as confused as ever.

26

As January passed into February, Poppy's confusion about the two new men in her life only grew. To her relief, she was put on a regular rota, which saw her working three night shifts followed by three afternoon shifts. She then enjoyed a day off before going back to the same routine again. She didn't get to see her cordite friends as much as she had grown accustomed to before Christmas, but she was happy in the knowledge that she would be greeted by them during her rounds on three days in a row every week, and she found convenient times to stop by the hostel to spend time with Mrs Gilbert, and sometimes Edith and her friends joined them.

The new shift pattern also meant three days when she was certain to bump into Lawrence around the factory site at some point, and, of course, she was able to stop and have her conversations with Geoffrey on those days, too. It became routine for her to visit Hardy's for lunch on her days off, and before long it became a sort of unofficial date between her and Lawrence – so much so that once Lawrence was used to her shift patterns, he took to ordering her sandwich for her before she had even arrived. She was still enjoying the company of both men so much that she really couldn't decide who she liked the most. But, as Maggie and Annie explained in their letters, as long as things were still friendly between them, then it didn't matter. So, for now, she was just delighting in spending time with each of them whenever she could. She had even allowed herself to accept that maybe one day things could go further with one of them, and she hadn't felt nearly as guilty about John as she had done previously.

Along with the change in her shifts came a change in Poppy's fortunes. It seemed that the WPS had finally proven themselves to the Ministry of Munitions because Poppy started receiving twenty-four shillings a week for her patrols. The move finally opened up the WPS to women who were not from wealthy backgrounds and brought with it another influx of fresh recruits.

Poppy found that she quite enjoyed the peace and quiet of her night patrols as she made her way between factory buildings. There had been no mention of the rumoured spy for months, so she felt quite safe despite the fact she was alone. However, she still kept a keen eye out for anybody lurking in the shadows.

Poppy's time spent getting from section to section during the day was also mostly done without seeing anybody other than the navvies, because workers were only allowed on the site when they were coming and going from shifts. But there was something about finding her way through the darkness with her bullseye lamp and the light from the moon that brought her a strange kind of comfort. The work buildings were so bright and noisy with chatter, singing and machinery that she found the contrast of the dark, silent strolls between them all quite soothing.

For that very reason, she was surprised to spot a familiar figure ambling towards the nitrating house near the end of one of her night patrols. Uncertain whether it definitely was who she thought it was – it was long after his shift had finished and she couldn't think of a reason for him to return to the factory after hours – she picked up her pace to try and get a closer look. As the figure turned a corner, she caught a glimpse of his face in the moonlight and, sure enough, it was Geoffrey! Excited, Poppy was just about to shout out to her friend when an unexpected and unexplained instinct kicked in, which warned her to keep quiet. Was there something in his demeanour that suggested he didn't want to be seen? He certainly wasn't walking with the same casual swagger that she had become accustomed to, and he kept looking around him almost . . . shiftily.

Poppy couldn't for the life of her imagine that he was up to anything he shouldn't be, and she was certain that there would be an innocent explanation for his out-of-character behaviour and presence on site so late. So, she decided it would be fun to follow him and give him a bit of a surprise. They could have a giggle about how good her police skills were if she managed to follow him for a while without him realising and then leap out in the darkness and make him jump! Then he would be able to explain whatever innocuous activity he was up to. He had probably forgotten something after his shift and popped back to pick it up. She imagined he was feeling nervous about being told off for returning when he was off duty.

Poppy switched off her lamp and slowed down her pace to avoid Geoffrey realising she was on his tail. Laughing quietly to herself as her eyes adjusted to the darkness, she pictured his face when she finally revealed herself. She couldn't wait to see his reaction! But Geoffrey didn't go into the nitrating house as Poppy had expected. Instead, he walked straight past it and on to the dirt track that led to the next section. Intrigued, Poppy held back before following him further – he was in wide open space now so she would be easier to spot even though she had the cover of darkness. She was glad she had switched her lamp off now. Once Geoffrey was far enough ahead that Poppy could only just make out his silhouette, she slowly followed in his footsteps. She thanked her lucky stars that the last few days had been dry so that she wasn't having to noisily squelch her way through mud. As Geoffrey finally neared the next section, he suddenly turned around to look behind him. Poppy held her breath and stood dead still, stifling a giggle. She was certain the game was up, and she was just about to shout out 'You got me!' when he turned back around and started walking again. Congratulating herself on staying far enough back that he hadn't been able to make her out in the darkness, Poppy shuffled along a little quicker to make sure she didn't lose him amongst the next lot of buildings.

Just as Geoffrey reached the first building in sight, Poppy noticed his pace pick up. She did the same but by the time she made it around the side of the building he had disappeared. There was no entrance on this side so she didn't understand where he could have gone.

'Goodness me,' she whispered under her breath. Now she would have to walk back to the previous section to clock on and patrol, and make up the time lost when she hadn't even managed to play her trick on Geoffrey. Although, wasn't there a danger building around here? Without her lamp on she had almost missed it. *Of course there is!* She rejoiced cheerfully in her head. Geoffrey had probably spotted her ages ago and decided to turn the tables on her. Smiling, she quickly made her way along the work building and then turned down an alley next to it that led to the danger building. But when she got there, there was no sign of him. Deflated, Poppy started walking slowly back towards the work building. She had thought her night shift might have been a tiny bit exciting for once tonight, but now she was back to her usual uneventful patrol – and she was behind on her route to boot. She came out of the alley and BUMP! She'd walked straight into Geoffrey. Poppy smiled and was just about to claim she was the winner in their secret game of cat and mouse when she noticed Geoffrey was frowning. Confused, she closed her mouth and took a step back to study his face. Yes – he was looking at her accusingly and he wore an expression she had never once seen before on his usually fun and happy-go-lucky face.

'Were you . . . following me?' he asked with a slightly uncomfortable laugh at the end of the sentence. There was no wink and none of his usual playfulness. Poppy suddenly felt embarrassed. She had been convinced he would really enjoy the surprise when she jumped out on him, but this uncharacteristic seriousness was leaving her feeling extremely foolish. 'Well, what the devil were you up to?' he pressed.

'I was just playing around,' Poppy muttered, looking away from him. 'I thought it would be funny to jump out at you.' Now she had spoken the words out loud, she felt extremely juvenile and silly. But when she looked up, Geoffrey's face was softening. He slowly broke into a smile. Flooded with relief, she smiled back as the Geoffrey she knew reappeared. They both laughed awkwardly.

'You daft so-and-so,' Geoffrey said, running his hand through his hair and winking at her. But although he was acting himself again, it seemed a little forced to Poppy. 'You seem busy, so I'll leave you to your patrol – I don't want to get you in trouble with your bosses,' he added, speaking a lot quicker than was usual for him. He stepped aside and held out his arm to signal that she should walk off first.

'Oh, erm . . . all right,' Poppy said. She was feeling flustered by his strange attitude. He wasn't normally bothered about keeping her from her work. In fact, it was often she who had to insist on getting back to her patrol while he pleaded with her to stay and talk for longer in the yard at the nitrating house. But he was behaving so oddly that she didn't really feel like she had any option but to head back to the previous work building and pick up her rounds again. She blustered past him and, unsure how to bid him farewell, she gave him an awkward half wave. She waited for Geoffrey to say something as she walked away but he stayed silent.

After taking a few steps she turned around to see if he had walked back down the alley, but he was still standing in the same spot, staring intently after her.

Poppy was distracted for the rest of her patrol. She didn't know quite what to think about her peculiar run-in with Geoffrey. What had started out as something fun had turned into something a little worrying and she hadn't the foggiest idea what to do about it. *Should* she be worried about it? What *could* he have been up to? She racked her brains, but she just couldn't figure it out. And he had acted so shiftily. When she thought about Geoffrey asking her what the devil she was up to, she grew angry. She was the one who should have been demanding that of him! She was the police officer and now she felt naive for having been so confused by her friend's behaviour that she had let him off for wandering around the factory out of hours. What if she got into trouble for the indiscretion? Now she was disappointed with herself as well as Geoffrey.

The more she thought about it, though, the more Poppy became convinced that she knew Geoffrey too well to have missed the fact that he could be up to something sinister at the factory. But then, that had always been the problem, hadn't it? She had even confessed as much to Annie and Maggie. Poppy knew Lawrence inside and out. But while she loved spending time with Geoffrey, and he made her laugh and made her happy, she didn't actually know an awful lot about him. Not really. Did she know him well enough to know that he definitely hadn't been up to anything suspicious?

But, then, if he hadn't been up to no good, what had he been doing at the factory late at night? If there had been an innocent explanation, then, surely, he would have just offered it up to her? Instead, he had acted oddly, and he had gone out of his way to get rid of her as soon as possible. It was just all so strange. They had been near a work building, but those sections kept going all day and night so he wouldn't have been able to do anything in there undetected. So, that only left the danger building, where weapons were being built. They were always locked and bolted overnight because only specialist personnel were allowed in, and those people were too important to work through the night. Obviously, building weapons had to be done with a clear, well-rested head. They couldn't just be churned out twenty-four seven like the cordite was. But what could Geoffrey have possibly wanted with plans for weapons? Anyone else would have suspected him of being the rumoured spy, but Poppy couldn't bring herself to think that of him. She had to admit, though, that none of it seemed to make any sense.

Shaking her head, Poppy pushed the doubts about Geoffrey from her mind. She felt guilty for thinking badly of him. Of course she knew him too well to think he had been up to anything bad. Yes – she didn't *know* him know him, as in know everything about him. But she knew about his personality and good nature, and that was reassurance enough that he wouldn't creep around getting up to anything that might jeopardise the safety of the factory or the country's war effort. That was a big accusation to make about somebody and she wasn't ready to think that about somebody she had grown to really like and trust.

However much she trusted Geoffrey, though, Poppy still desperately needed to get to the bottom of his actions. She decided that she would act normally with him the next time she stopped by the nitrating house for a quick break during her afternoon patrol. She would let him believe that she had forgotten all about this evening, but she would be paying close attention to his movements until she discovered what was going on. Certain that she was going to be able to laugh with him about how silly it had all been once she knew the truth, she clocked off from her shift feeling a little lighter.

27

Poppy was back to afternoon shifts the following day and she practically leapt out of bed despite her exhaustion from the previous trio of night shifts. The start of her run of afternoon shifts signalled the beginning of her regular contact with her friends and that always held such excitement and promise. And, at the end of these day shifts, she had her day off and her much anticipated lunch with Lawrence. Poppy didn't want the situation with Geoffrey to taint her feelings about the upcoming few days, but she couldn't help but feel a little niggle about it all as she made her way to carry out her searches on the women starting their shifts at the cordite section. She was keen to get everything cleared up between them so they could go back to their usual fun, laughter-filled friendship. She didn't like that she felt slightly suspicious of him, no matter how hard she tried to block the sensation.

When she got to her friends' cordite section following her searches, Poppy decided to do some investigating with the girls. She casually asked Bessie and Jenny if they often saw foremen wandering around the factory and away from their allocated work buildings. As soon as she asked the question, an alarm bell sounded in her head. Geoffrey had been 'passing by' the day his colleague got handsy with Bessie. How had she forgotten about that? She had been so grateful for his help at the time that she hadn't questioned it but, now she thought about it, surely that should have been a cause for concern. Why exactly had he been away from his post? She could vaguely recall an excuse about running errands, but all workers – supervisors or not – were meant to stay at their sections until their shift was over.

'We always see the same faces,' Bessie said quietly. Jenny nodded her head in agreement. Marie had the same answer when Poppy asked her, but of course Edith wanted to talk at length about why she was bringing it up.

'Has another one of them been up to no good?' she asked, her eyes lighting up at the prospect of a scandal and some gossip.

'No, no, nothing like that,' Poppy said, trying to laugh the suggestion off. She hoped she was telling the truth. 'I was just thinking about the day Bessie had her run-in, that's all. That foreman who came to help – Geoffrey – he was from the nitrating house and—'

'Yes, well, I wouldn't be surprised if he was up to something,' Edith cut in. She had frowned at just the mention of his name, which Poppy hadn't expected given the fact that he had leapt in to help deal with Bill.

'What do you mean?' Poppy was trying to make her question sound casual and hoped the angst and desperation hadn't come through in her voice. Was there something more to what had happened the previous night? She crossed her fingers behind her back and prayed for this to be some kind of misunderstanding.

'I just wouldn't trust that man, is all. I know he helped with Bess, and I appreciate that but, well, there's just something about him that I don't like. Some people you just get a bad feeling about. Do you know what I mean?'

Poppy shrugged and smiled in response. So, it was just one of Edith's snap judgements; she didn't have anything to back it up with. Continuing on her rounds, Poppy wondered what it was about Geoffrey that made Edith so distrustful of him. She had certainly made the same judgement about him when they first met, but he had won her round with his charm and humour. Was she naive to have fallen for all that, or was it just that Edith didn't know Geoffrey well enough to ascertain that he was a decent man? No matter what the answer, Poppy certainly wasn't going to be admitting to her fancy for him to her new friends any time soon. She had been toying with admitting to spending time with him and Lawrence to the group, but she had feared they might think badly of her. She would definitely keep it between herself and her Bobby Girls for now. She needed to get to the bottom of Geoffrey's strange behaviour before admitting to anybody at the factory that she had taken a shine to him. She didn't want to end up looking silly.

Poppy's heart was racing when she walked into the nitrating house. She felt anxious about how Geoffrey might behave following their run-in the night before. But when she spotted him standing next to the door leading to the yard, he waved his hand in the air frantically and beckoned her over. Even through his mask, she could see that he was grinning from ear to ear. She followed him into the yard and they both removed their masks.

'How are you, love?' he asked, as though nothing had happened. Before she had a chance to answer, he launched into a long-winded story about two of the workers who had been fighting over a man earlier in the afternoon. 'One of your lot hauled them both out and they've not been back since,' he added, whistling and shaking his head dramatically. 'We're not used to all the excitement over here — everyone's normally so well behaved because of the heat and the masks.'

'I've certainly never come across any trouble over here,' Poppy commented. She was glad to have missed it.

'I prefer it when they take their quarrels back to the hostel with them and have it out over there,' Geoffrey added, before laughing and giving her a wink.

Poppy couldn't help but chuckle along with him. She was beginning to feel bad for doubting him. Surely it had just been a one-off that they could forget about and move on from? Just because he might have an innocent explanation, didn't mean that she had to demand it. It wasn't within her authority to discipline foremen – she was there to take care of the female workers. If it had been another foreman wandering around the factory off duty then she probably would have just sent him on his way, no harm done. And if she really had felt cause for concern then she would have reported him to his superiors – as had happened in the end with handsy Bill. She definitely didn't want to get Geoffrey into any sort of trouble, but she would still keep a close eye on him for now, just in case. She was confident that she had been worrying over nothing, though.

Geoffrey seemed to have forgotten all about their strange late-night encounter. He was his usual self over the next few days when Poppy stopped by for her regular catch-ups. She doubled back to the nitrating house a few times and waited out of sight next to one of the nearby buildings. She wanted to see if Geoffrey would sneak away from his post at any point. But she was never able to keep watch for long as she had rounds to complete and clocking on to do. She knew it wouldn't do to sneak back on to the site when she was off duty to try and keep tabs on him. She would end up looking just as suspicious as him!

On her day off, Poppy enjoyed another lunch with Lawrence. She felt tempted at one point to ask him if there had ever been any problems with workers – or foremen in particular – going back to the factory outside of their shifts. But she decided against it. She needed to get to the bottom of this herself or let it go. She didn't want to risk getting Geoffrey into trouble without justification.

Once she was back on night shifts, Poppy kept a beady

eye out for anybody lurking in the shadows when she made her way through the darkness between sections. She started regularly turning her lamp off to avoid giving anybody who shouldn't be there notice that she was on her way. She lingered near the place where she had first spotted Geoffrey after hours, and she searched around the alley where he had surprised her. But she failed to find anything that incriminated Geoffrey. After a few weeks of her extra surveillance, Poppy had come up with nothing to make her doubt Geoffrey, and he was still acting as if nothing had happened. His acting so normally afterwards, along with her failure to uncover any further suspicious activity, left her wondering whether she had imagined the whole encounter. So, she decided to cast any doubts she had left to the side and forget all about it. It was time to move on.

During her first night shift without doing her extra surveillance, Poppy found herself at a bit of a loss. She quickly realised that the added excitement had been helping get her through the long, dark and cold hours that she dreaded so much. Giggling to herself as she switched off her lamp, she decided to pretend she was hunting down a suspect who was running around the factory grounds trying to evade capture. The silly game made her shift pass by so much more quickly that she played it again the following evening. She was just passing by the nitrating house and thinking about how she was going to tell Maggie and Annie all about it in her next letter – she knew Maggie would find it really funny – when she heard heavy footsteps coming towards her. At first, she froze, but then she remembered that her lamp was switched off so whoever it was wouldn't be able to see her.

With her blood now pumping around her body at what felt like four times the normal rate, Poppy ducked behind a pile of wooden crates and waited for the footsteps to draw closer. She held her breath as she heard them getting nearer and nearer. She was desperate to poke her head out and try and catch a glimpse of whoever it was, but she didn't want to risk being spotted even in the pitch black. As she waited, she told herself it was probably just the next WPS recruit. The next woman on the shift sometimes caught up with her if she spent too long talking to friends on her rounds and didn't manage to make up the time, or if she had to stop to deal with anything. And she had been slower than usual this evening due to her little game. Now she had relaxed, Poppy felt a bit silly for getting so het up about it. But maybe she could pretend her colleague was an intruder, or maybe even a spy, and see if she could stay on her tail without being spotted for the rest of the shift. If the shift in their clocking-on pattern was raised then she would simply say she had been delayed dealing with a rowdy worker.

Poppy waited for the light from the WPS recruit's lamp to come into view as the footsteps made their way past her hiding spot. The footsteps continued, but there was no lamp-light as they passed by her. She put her hand over her mouth to stop any noise from escaping as a figure swept past. Her blood was pumping fast again while she tried to decide what to do next. This had all turned into a game for her but now it seemed like it might be about to become horribly real. It definitely hadn't been a WPS recruit. She would have seen the outline of the hat and skirt even in the darkness. It looked like it had been a man, but she couldn't be certain. Who would be creeping around in the dark during a shift?

Poppy edged out from behind the crates, taking extra care not to knock any of them or make any sound as she went. The run-in with Geoffrey had been the first time she had ever come across anybody on the factory grounds who wasn't supposed to be there in the middle of the night. She had known it was him straight away, so she hadn't been scared of his intentions when she'd followed him – even if he had acted oddly in the end. Now that Poppy was pursuing an unknown person she was feeling alarmed, especially after all the previous rumours about a spy, but she knew that she had to keep them in sight. The figure walked straight to the path linking the nitrating house to the next section, which gave Poppy a chance to get a little closer with the darkness cloaking her. She fell into the same step rhythm as her assailant but took longer strides to get nearer. She could see now that it was definitely a man, and that he was short – about the same height as she was. Something started niggling at her. There was one man at this factory who she knew was exactly the same height as her. And now she was closer she could see the person ahead of her had a certain swagger to their walk. Feeling nervous as the next section drew into sight, she placed a hand over her truncheon. She wondered if it would get its first use this evening. Poppy felt her breathing getting quicker and tried her best to steady her nerves.

When they got to the next section, the man turned down the same alley that Geoffrey had done previously, and in a flicker of moonlight Poppy saw his face. She felt relief wash over her when she saw Geoffrey's familiar face. She had been so worried about coming face to face with a violent intruder! But Poppy's relief was quickly followed by a cold shiver of realisation – what if Geoffrey was up to no good after all? She had been so convinced she'd been wrong about him previously that she had forced herself to rule out the prospect of it being her friend this time! She had to cover her mouth to stop herself from shouting out at him in anger. She was furious that after so long doubting herself and feeling guilty for thinking badly of him, Geoffrey would saunter back to the factory grounds off duty in the early hours of the morning again. Just what was he up to? She was going to make damned sure that she found out this time!

She held back at the top of the alley and watched as he walked towards the danger building. Poppy was too far back to see properly so she very carefully edged her way along the alley, taking extra care not to get spotted by him this time. When she realised that she was shaking she was surprised – she didn't feel frightened of Geoffrey, did she? Then it dawned on her: she wasn't shaking through fear but through rage.

Poppy held back again when Geoffrey reached the door to the danger building. She knew that only top-level personnel were allowed inside and that it was locked and bolted overnight, so just what was Geoffrey doing here? Her heart sank in her chest as she came to the conclusion that she had been completely wrong about her new friend. She didn't want to risk Geoffrey using his charm to talk his way out of anything this time, so she decided to stay put and wait for him to pick the lock before presenting herself and hauling him to the work building to seek backup. She needed to catch him in the act breaking into the off-limits building before she struck.

Poppy's jaw dropped when she saw Geoffrey pull out a set of keys from his pocket. How on earth did a foreman get hold of keys to a top-secret danger building – where weapons were being worked on – and what was he doing sneaking in in the dead of the night? She knew that Butcher and Baker handed over their full set of factory keys to the WPS sergeant in charge of the night shift, but she didn't know who else had access to keys to the danger buildings. She always assumed only the top-level personnel who oversaw the work in them were able to lock and unlock the buildings.

Very carefully, Poppy tiptoed her way to the door just after Geoffrey had entered. He had left it slightly ajar and so she could see him standing just in front of her. He took something out of his pocket and then turned on a small torch and started reading. Poppy didn't know if she should follow him inside and confront him. She was desperate to see what he was up to and to potentially stop any criminal activity taking place. What was that piece of paper in his hand? But what if he was really dangerous? She couldn't think of any other way that he would have a set of keys other than stealing them. Had he left a victim – the owner of his keys – injured in his wake? Poppy suddenly didn't feel brave enough to take on Geoffrey on her own. This had all turned very sinister very quickly.

Would she be better off running back to the work building and dragging a foreman down here to help her? That would make her look pathetic, of course, but it would be a hell of a lot safer. And surely people would understand why she had done it. It would give Geoffrey more time to do whatever it was he was planning on doing. She might be too late. But she would be able to go after him and prove she had seen him entering the building. The piece of paper in his hand had to be incriminating. Poppy had just decided that she was going to run for backup when the door creaked in the wind. She stood frozen to the spot, eyes wide open in the torchlight, as Geoffrey spun around and locked eyes with her.

28

Geoffrey's face didn't break into its usual cheeky expression when he saw Poppy standing in the doorway. He seemed to be just as shocked as she was. The pair of them stood staring at each other for what felt like minutes before Poppy let out an involuntary squeak, whipped around and ran full pelt back down the alley. She could feel her heart beating out of her chest as Geoffrey's heavy footsteps followed behind her. She just had to make it to the work building where they would be surrounded by other people and she would be able to raise the alarm and he wouldn't be able to hurt her. Panting with exertion and fear, she could hear his footsteps getting closer. She was going as fast as she could, but it was no good. He would be on her before she reached safety.

Poppy slowed down and braced herself. When she heard Geoffrey's footsteps just behind her she suddenly spun round and launched herself at him, grabbing hold of his arms and throwing all her weight into pushing him back against the wall. He clearly hadn't been expecting the move and his face grimaced in shock as he flew backwards. He didn't even have time to try and fight back before his shoulder blades struck the wall and he yelped as his head followed suit. Poppy winced at the sound his head made against the brick, but she didn't have time to feel bad for hurting him – his arms had come up in the air ready to fight back. She grabbed hold of one of them and swiftly twisted it behind his back, pushing his body round so that she was able to hold him against the wall with his arm pinned behind his back.

Poppy held Geoffrey there for a moment while she caught her breath and tried desperately to gather herself, all the while panicking about what her next move should be. This man had been her friend and now she was restraining him – for what? She didn't know if he was a spy or up to something else, but she felt certain she was in some kind of danger, so she held firm. Geoffrey let out a small rasp. Poppy realised that she had her other hand firmly on the back of his head and that she was pushing it into the wall. Easing off slightly, she silently marvelled at how well she had taken to suffrajitsu – she had incapacitated him without even reaching for her truncheon – when her former friend's indignant voice interrupted her thoughts.

'What the devil are you doing?' Geoffrey demanded fiercely. There wasn't even a hint of his normal friendly tone. This was a voice she had never heard before despite how close they had become. Poppy couldn't help but let out a gasp of outrage at his question.

'What the devil am *I* doing?' she almost shrieked. 'I should rather be asking *you* the very same thing! I might have brushed it off and let you get away with it last time, but you won't be able to charm your way out of this one. I've caught you red-handed this time!'

'Red-handed doing what exactly?' Geoffrey growled, suddenly trying to wriggle free of Poppy's grip. Furious, she pushed his head into the wall again and twisted his arm further back. He groaned into the bricks and she felt an odd sensation of satisfaction. She had him collared and there was no way that he was getting out of this.

'Don't act all innocent with me,' Poppy hissed into his ear. 'All this time I trusted you. I thought we were *friends*! I didn't even say anything when I ran into you last time as I was certain there would be some innocent explanation, but you took me for a fool. All this time you were just pretending to like me so that I wouldn't suspect you of . . . of . . . oh, of whatever it is you were doing back there!' Poppy couldn't bring herself to say the word 'spying'. She felt herself flushing red and she was glad that Geoffrey couldn't see her face. She had been doing so well then, but her dressing down had fallen flat. The truth was that she still had no idea what he had been up to in that danger building. Would his superiors even take her seriously if she reported him? He'd been in possession of keys, after all. Poppy heard some muffled sound and released her grip on Geoffrey's head once more so that he could talk.

'It's not what you think it is, I promise. But I can't tell you the truth,' he whispered now.

Poppy scoffed. 'You're a liar!' she cried.

'I'm not. Why do you think I had keys?'

'You could have stolen them from somebody with authority to hold them. How do I know you haven't left some poor soul for dead in order to get your hands on something in that building?'

'Is that really what you think of me?' Geoffrey demanded. He sounded hurt as well as angry now. But Poppy ignored that. She couldn't let him sweet-talk his way out of this.

'Don't you think the alarm would have been raised by now if I had attacked somebody for those keys?' Geoffrey tried now, beginning to sound a bit more reasonable and calmer.

Poppy paused to think. He had her there. But if he wasn't going to tell her what he had been doing in the danger building, then, surely, she couldn't just let him go? If he had permission to snoop around in there, then his bosses would back him up. She might look a little foolish for reporting him but wasn't it better to be safe than sorry, especially when it came to plans for weapons? Especially when he had been in there in the dead of night and with a flashlight to guide him around? The more she thought about it, the more convinced she became that he was the enemy.

'If you're innocent then you don't have anything to worry about. We can go and see your bosses right now and straighten all of this out,' Poppy suggested brightly.

'You can't tell them,' Geoffrey quickly blustered, starting to fight back against her grip again.

'I *knew* you were lying! I can't believe you would think I would fall for your fibs again!'

'Please, Poppy, I'm not lying.' He was pleading now. 'But you have to trust me. It could be a matter of life or death. An awful lot hinges on me finishing what I started up there and if you hold me here any longer then it could all go to pot.'

Poppy couldn't help but scoff again. He really was taking her for a fool.

'Poppy, you've got to take me seriously!' he shouted. He pushed back against her so hard that she momentarily lost her grip on his arm and he broke free. But as he spun round to face her, she pulled out her truncheon and whacked it across the back of his knee with as much power as she was able to muster. Her first instinct had been to hit him around the head but she hadn't been able to bring herself to do it. Geoffrey let out a wail like an injured animal and dropped straight to the floor. Poppy immediately jumped on top of him and pinned him there. The truncheon had proved to be quite handy, after all. Their faces were inches from each other. Poppy stared down into Geoffrey's eyes and found herself wondering how she could ever have found someone as deceptive as he was attractive. Personality meant so much to her – how could she have missed this? Another time she would have had butterflies having her lips this close to his, but now she just felt rage.

'Poppy, please don't do this,' Geoffrey whispered. 'I can explain . . .'

'I'm not interested,' Poppy replied. She could hear the venom in her voice and it took her by surprise. Maybe she had really felt like she and Geoffrey could have had something. She took a deep breath and then leapt to her feet, truncheon still in hand and ready to whack Geoffrey again if he tried anything. This time she might go for his head. She stood over him, waiting for him to get himself up, but he let out a long sigh and covered his face with his hands.

'You can put it off as long as you like but we'll be visiting your bosses before the sun comes up,' Poppy said firmly. 'And I'm sure secret services would be delighted to speak to the spy caught rummaging around in all the new weapons plans.' There. She had said it. Geoffrey kept his hands over his face as he spoke so that his words came out all muffled, but Poppy understood what he said, and it left her stunned back into silence.

'I'm *with* secret services,' he groaned.

29

Geoffrey slowly staggered to his feet while Poppy tried to digest his revelation. He was *with* secret services? So, he *was* a spy? No . . . he was trying to *catch* a spy? Happy-go-lucky, playful Geoffrey – doing something so important and serious? He didn't fit with her vision of a secret agent – that was one of the reasons she had dismissed him as being a mole when she had first come across him acting strangely. But, then, maybe that was the point? He was meant to blend in and act in a way that meant nobody would ever suspect him. If he was telling the truth, it would mean all the rumours were true and there really was a German spy operating at Gretna. When Poppy looked up, she realised that Geoffrey was now stood in front of her, staring at her, waiting for her to respond. She was still holding her truncheon out in front of her, ready to defend herself. She really wasn't sure whether she could believe him or not.

'I didn't want to tell you that, Poppy, but your thinking that I was up to something dreadful with those weapons plans is the last thing I'd ever want because I really do like you. And it hurts my heart to think that you might doubt my intentions when it comes to our friendship.'

Poppy found that she was still unable to speak. She stood gawping at Geoffrey, her truncheon still raised and ready for action. It was the most serious she had heard him sound the whole time she had known him. What was she supposed to believe?

'I may as well be hanged for a sheep as a lamb,' Geoffrey muttered under his breath, sighing and turning away from her. He ran his hands through his hair and took a step away from Poppy. She was just about to leap into action when he suddenly turned and stepped back towards her. 'Look, I'll tell you everything,' he offered, his eyes suddenly searching the area around them cautiously. 'But you'll have to come to my lodgings.'

An alarm bell immediately rang out in Poppy's head. She still didn't know if she could trust this man, so there was no possibility that she was going to agree to that. 'How about the canteen? It will be dead in there at this hour,' she suggested carefully.

Geoffrey frowned and shook his head slowly. 'It's too risky. We need to do this somewhere safe, where I know that nobody can listen in.' Poppy narrowed her eyes at him and involuntarily strengthened her grip on the truncheon. 'What I'm going to tell you is too top-secret to be discussed anywhere but a completely private place,' he quickly added.

Poppy was desperate to find out more, but she couldn't help feeling that she was being taken for a fool. Was this all just a ruse, or could she trust Geoffrey? What if he had stolen those keys and he was planning on doing to her whatever it was he had done to the owner of them, once he got her alone? Was she going to walk herself straight into a trap? How silly she would look when everyone found out.

As she grappled with all of it, a little voice in her head suddenly cut in. If Geoffrey was telling the truth, she didn't want to rock the boat and get him into trouble or even ruin his mission by exposing him to the factory bosses. And, once he'd told her all about it, maybe he could enlist her help in whatever he was doing. The game she had been playing on her night shifts would come to life and she would get some real excitement to break up the monotony of the long and lonely patrols. And just think, she could end up helping to catch the spy all her colleagues had been speculating about over the last few months. She would be helping her country, to boot!

Poppy looked into Geoffrey's eyes, and she saw the kind and caring man she had come to know over the last few months staring back at her. She had to trust him. And, besides, the curiosity and possibilities were too much for her. If she went with him then at least she would know either way, once and for all. She had done well to defend herself against him once already, so she knew that she would be able to fight him off if she ended up being wrong about all of this – especially if she made sure she stayed on her guard and was prepared.

'Well?' he asked.

'I'll come with you,' Poppy said quietly. Geoffrey looked relieved and gave her a weak smile. 'But I'm due to clock off in the next hour and if I don't do so, they'll send my colleagues looking for me,' she added slowly and firmly. That wiped the smile from Geoffrey's face and Poppy could see he felt hurt by the insinuation. She started to regret saying it but then reminded herself that she still wasn't sure if she could trust him, as much as she wanted to. She had to think about her safety over his feelings. With any luck he would be able to prove her wrong and then she could apologise and they could get back to being friends. That would be the best outcome, she decided.

They started walking in silence. There didn't seem much point in making small talk. Poppy felt anxious about cutting out the last stops on her patrol – she had always been so diligent in making sure she clocked on at every point on time and it would surely show up when Sergeant Ross checked through everything later that morning. Maybe she could tell her that she'd thought she'd seen an intruder and spent her last hour on duty searching the mystery person out, only to discover that she had been mistaken. She could say that it was so near to the end of her shift by the time she had finished her wild goose chase that she simply took herself to clock off as it would have been impossible to make up the time without raising concerns that she hadn't returned to the WPS hut on time. It would sound suspicious, and Sergeant Ross might wonder why Poppy hadn't simply gone for backup, but she would just have to deal with the questions if they arose. She might be lucky and get away with nobody picking up on the fact she had missed her final few stops.

Besides, if it turned out that Geoffrey was lying then she might not be alive to face the interrogation, anyway. The thought made her feel slightly nauseous. On the other hand, she might actually be too busy being rewarded for bringing down a spy to get into trouble with Sergeant Ross! Poppy tried to clear her head of all her wild thoughts. She needed to focus on the task in hand again. The last thing she needed to be was distracted at a time like this.

They made it to the township without coming across another soul. Poppy wasn't sure if that made her feel reassured or unnerved. If she screamed right now, would anybody hear her and run to her aid? Geoffrey's room was in a hostel similar to the WPS hostel, although Poppy immediately noted that his room was a lot bigger than her own. He had ample space for a small table and two chairs, as well as a little stove. There was also a small writing desk tucked into the corner. Poppy felt a pang of jealousy. She wrote extremely long letters to Maggie and Annie, and a desk in her room would make it a much more comfortable experience.

'I'll make us tea,' Geoffrey offered. She was grateful – the brisk walk back to the township hadn't done anything to take the edge off the chill she was feeling from the cold

February air. He pulled out a chair for her before walking over to the stove.

'I'd rather stay standing,' Poppy said as lightly as she could manage, although there was no masking the suspicion behind her words. Geoffrey looked wounded once more. 'Look, if you just tell me what all this is about then maybe I can relax a little,' she snapped. She hated hurting his feelings, but it was his secrecy that was making her do it. She was beginning to feel frustrated as well as a little bit anxious.

'I think we need tea to get through this,' Geoffrey said, smiling kindly. 'I'll put some sugar in yours – you'll probably need it as I think you're in for a shock.' If Poppy had felt apprehensive before then she felt positively angst-ridden now. 'It's just a lot to take in, that's all,' Geoffrey added reassuringly. 'Please, take a seat. It doesn't feel right to have you standing by the door.'

'I'll sit when I feel comfortable to do so,' Poppy said firmly. Geoffrey shrugged and got on with the tea. When he handed Poppy her mug, she couldn't help but laugh to herself about the absurdity of accepting a hot refreshment in the room of an unmarried spy – or indeed an undercover secret agent – in the early hours of the morning. Geoffrey sat down at the table and gestured to the seat opposite him. Now that he was sitting, Poppy felt more comfortable stepping away from the door. She joined him and, finally, he opened up.

'I'm working for a British security service called MI5. My bosses sent me to Gretna to search out a German mole operating here. I've been tasked with finding them before they do untold damage to the war effort.'

Poppy took a deep breath. If Geoffrey was telling the truth then she had stumbled into something way out of her depth. So, why was she already planning on getting involved? And why was the thought of unmasking a traitor making her feel so excited? She exhaled and made herself focus on what Geoffrey said next.

'They have intelligence that the mole is looking for top-secret plans and I've got to stop them before they get hold of them and ruin Britain's chances of winning the war.'

Poppy gulped. This was getting bigger and bigger. 'What kind of plans?' she asked eagerly, leaning across the table towards Geoffrey.

'I don't know exactly,' he admitted, staring into his tea awkwardly.

Poppy scoffed and flung herself back against her chair. He'd almost had her there – it had all sounded so plausible! She felt foolish all over again for believing his tales.

'Honestly, Poppy,' he pleaded. 'I promise I'm telling you the truth. It's just that it's above my security clearance to know any of the details. All I know is that it's something to do with new weapons, but all that stuff is on a need-to-know basis and as far as my bosses are concerned, I don't need to know – I just need to catch the mole before they become in the know and pass that knowledge on.'

Poppy sat up a little straighter again. That did actually make sense. So, there were new weapons being developed in the danger building and they were so impressive the Germans were desperate to get their hands on the plans. 'Go on,' she said, her belly flipping with anticipation now.

'The plans they're trying to get hold of have the capacity to change Britain's fortunes in the war. If the Germans get hold of them, then they will be able to produce their own new weapons. Not only would that mean Britain loses its advantage over the enemy, but the Germans would be able to use the weapons against us.'

'Why don't they just move it all somewhere else?'

'They're halfway through building the prototype and it's imperative they get it finished and ready to deploy as soon as possible. Moving something like that will take far too much time and planning – not to mention risk. As well as that, we're so close to sniffing the mole out. The plans and half-finished prototype have become our bait, in a way. If we take them away, then the mole will fade into the background again and carry on working among us and passing information back to the Germans. It won't be anything as damaging as the weapons plans, but it will still be detrimental to our war efforts. We're so close to catching them that we have to keep dangling the weapons plans until they reach too far for them and we catch them once and for all.'

Poppy let out a long sigh. 'You did warn me it was a lot to take in,' she whispered, taking a big gulp of her tea and silently thanking Geoffrey as the sweet taste of the sugar hit her tongue. 'So, how do they know there's a German spy at the factory?' she asked.

'I can't reveal too much, of course, but there's definite evidence that someone has been passing on information to the enemy already – information that is only held here at Gretna in the danger buildings.'

Poppy paused to think for a moment. She remembered Grace's warning about looking out for loners at the workshops when they had discussed the risk of spies trying to get in – anybody who looked out of place and wasn't chatting to the other women. From what Geoffrey was saying, it sounded as if somebody had infiltrated themselves into factory life and blended into the background to make it easier for them to steal and pass on information unnoticed. This spy hadn't just sneaked in once to snatch some plans. They could be living among them – it could be somebody she knew.

'The prototype is going to be ready to be deployed within the next month,' Geoffrey continued. 'So, we need to keep it secret until then, which is why I was so wary about telling you about it anywhere else but here.'

Poppy nodded her understanding. 'I'm sure you can appreciate the reasons why I was a little apprehensive,' she replied.

Geoffrey smiled. 'I would have been suspicious, too, if I had caught somebody acting the way I've been behaving lately,' he admitted.

The statement sparked a realisation in Poppy and she kicked herself for getting carried away with the excitement and losing focus. 'Why exactly *were* you sneaking around the danger building in the middle of the night, Geoffrey? If you're on our side, then why the need to creep around a classified building after hours?'

'My handlers had intelligence that suggested the mole was going to make their move tonight. I was on my way to try and ambush them when you ambushed me,' he explained. His calm tone had tightened a little and Poppy suddenly felt horrified at her actions.

'Oh, goodness, have I sent it all up the spout?' She panicked. Thoughts of a powerful, deadly weapon in the hands of the enemy and hundreds of fallen British soldiers flashed through her mind as her hands turned clammy. She couldn't live with herself if she had set into motion a chain of events like that. 'You must go back. Right now! You need to spring your trap, Geoffrey. We can't let the Germans get hold of national secrets!'

'It's too late now. I've missed my chance.' Poppy's heart dropped. 'It's all right – we get a lot of intelligence but it's rare it comes to anything. We always have to act on it, though, as you need to be ready to pounce on that one occasion when the intel is on the nose. I've been out to the danger building a few times recently and staked it out with no luck. The mole is obviously getting ready to make their move.'

'So that's what you were doing the night I bumped into you?'

'Yes. I thought you were the mole at first, then I was so

annoyed with myself for getting spotted. I'm much better than that.'

'Maybe I'm just good MI5 material,' Poppy said jokingly. Geoffrey laughed and gave his signature wink, and she knew they were back on track with their friendship. She trusted everything he had told her, and she was going to do everything that she could to help him catch this mole.

'You're not as good as you think you are – I've been back a fair few times since we bumped into each other and you haven't spotted me. You walked straight past me on one occasion. You really should keep your lamp on when you're patrolling in the dark.' Poppy couldn't help but feel deflated. 'Anyway, we'll just have to hope it was another wasted trip and that the intel was wrong again this evening,' Geoffrey added quietly. The playfulness had vanished from his voice. Fallen soldiers flashed into Poppy's mind again and she was flushed with guilt.

'I'm going to make up for ambushing you tonight and interfering with your spy-catching,' she announced, sitting up straight.

'Oh, really? And how are you going to do that?' Geoffrey asked, laughing lightly.

'I'm going to help you catch the mole and bring them to justice. And I won't take no for an answer,' Poppy said proudly.

30

Geoffrey was still laughing to himself as he got up to pour another cup of tea. Poppy fixed him with a stare so cold it could have frozen his drink.

'Oh! You're . . . serious?' he asked cautiously, the grin slipping from his face as he stopped what he was doing and stared at her.

'Why ever would I joke about something so important?'

'Sorry, I just . . . well, you're a policewoman, not an under-cover agent. They're very different things, Poppy.'

'Exactly!' Poppy cried triumphantly. Geoffrey passed her a fresh mug and sat back down opposite her with his drink. He looked confused.

'I can't believe I have to explain this to you. I'm here working for the police force. I get to hear about all the different goings on around the factory and I have access to most of the site at my disposal. I can start keeping an eye out for suspicious activity and watch the workers with more care. If anybody is in a good position to pick up on someone behaving out of the ordinary, then it's me. I've been keeping my eye on you for long enough.' Poppy raised her eyebrows accusingly and Geoffrey narrowed his eyes at her. 'You said yourself that you would have been suspicious of somebody acting the way you had been!'

'All right, that's a fair point,' he conceded. He ran his fingers through his hair and groaned. 'Oh, I just don't know, Poppy. I don't feel comfortable bringing you into something that could put you in danger. And this could be very dangerous. I could never forgive myself if something happened to you.'

'Won't I be in more danger if this spy gets away with the plans? Come to think of it, won't every one of us based here be in more danger? Not to mention the rest of the country and our boys on the battlefields! I can't sit back and let you do this on your own now that I know what's going on. I'm sorry but I'm helping you and that's all there is to it!' Poppy jumped at the sound of a bang and then realised it had been her pounding her fist on the table to help make her point. Geoffrey jerked back in shock.

'I suppose your position within the WPS could come in handy,' he finally replied slowly, sounding thoughtful.

Poppy's heart raced with excitement. 'That's that settled, then!' she cried, standing up and clapping her hands together.

'Hold up, you can't just get up and leave – we've got to talk through how this is going to work. This is a very sensitive operation.'

'I told you, I need to clock off. But you don't need to worry about me. I won't utter a word about this to anyone, and I will keep my investigations discreet.'

'Poppy, I don't want you doing any *investigating*. I just need you to keep an extra eye out for suspicious behaviour; anybody acting out of the ordinary or skulking around the factory between shifts – that sort of thing. If you see somebody acting the way that I was acting, then you let me know as soon as possible. You really can't draw attention to what you're doing – please.'

'Everything you've mentioned is exactly the kind of thing I'm here to do,' she said confidently.

'Please don't start asking questions that might arouse suspicion. If the mole gets even a hint that we're on to them then this could all end terribly.'

'Understood,' she replied sombrely. And she meant it. She had got carried away with her thoughts of poking around and questioning people, but she could see now that she would have to make sure she didn't do anything out of the ordinary. As desperate as she was to start interrogating suspects and getting straight to the bottom of things, she had to remember that this was an MI5 operation and not a police investigation.

She opened the door to leave, before turning back to Geoffrey. 'You can rely on me,' she said firmly.

'I know,' Geoffrey replied, just as firmly, and Poppy felt her heart do a little flip at the fact he had so much faith in her that he was willing to bring her on board for something so important. She felt bad for having had so many doubts about him, but she knew she would be able to put things right by helping him. Despite that feeling of guilt, Poppy felt an overriding sense of excitement. The fact there was a traitor on site passing information to the Germans was terrifying, but at the same time, she couldn't help but feel elated at the prospect of being part of something as vital to the war effort as bringing down a spy! And, to top it all off, things were back on track with Geoffrey, and they were going to be working together as a team on this secret mission. The first thing Poppy wanted to do was to write to Annie and Maggie and tell them all about it. They would be so proud of her. But, of course, that was far too risky. She would have to keep this secret between herself and Geoffrey until they had caught the mole red-handed. Then, how she would revel in relaying it all back to her Bobby Girls. She couldn't wait!

Over the next few weeks, Poppy was overzealous on her patrols. She had a sudden new lease of life and a fresh passion for her rounds now that she had the added quest to find the mole on her list of duties. Her shift rota had been moved around, so she now worked three afternoon shifts followed by three night shifts and then her day off. She spent more time in the factory workshops, observing the workers and keeping a keen eye on anybody who stepped away from their station for even a few seconds. Knowing that a spy wasn't likely to act out while a WPS officer was in the vicinity, she often left a workshop and waited outside for a short time before doubling back and re-entering with the element of surprise. At one point she thought she was on to something when a woman from the glycerine distillery suddenly left her station and wandered outside. But her surveillance came to an abrupt end when the poor worker spun back around and vomited all over Poppy's boots.

'You thought she was a spy, but she'd actually had dodgy eggs for breakfast,' Geoffrey laughed when she told him about it. They had taken to meeting up in the yard at the nitrating house on Poppy's days off to compare notes and exchange any important information, on the understanding that Poppy was to search him out there during his work hours or at his lodgings in the evenings if she unearthed anything that couldn't possibly wait. Not that Poppy had managed to gather anything incriminating on anybody so far, much to her disappointment. She was desperate to help Geoffrey bring down the spy and she was getting frustrated at her lack of progress. She wanted to impress him, but she felt like she was letting him down.

Following their morning meet-up on her day off, Poppy went to join Lawrence for their usual lunch. She had hardly seen him around the factory since taking on her secret mission. She was too busy looking for leads to keep an eye out for him or hover around the police hut on her way past in the hope of bumping into him. Walking into Hardy's, though, her heart skipped a beat when she laid eyes on him waiting at their normal table. She realised she had missed him. So, as well as having no leads on the spy, she had also made no progress on deciding who she liked most out of Lawrence and Geoffrey.

'How have you been? Your rounds must have been busy, as I haven't seen you much,' Lawrence said, sounding downbeat. Poppy suddenly felt bad for casting Lawrence aside in favour of her – so far – failed mission. She wanted to confide in him about it all but knew it wouldn't be wise.

They had a lovely lunch, but Poppy found herself sitting back and letting Lawrence do most of the talking. She understood now how Geoffrey must have felt when they had been getting to know each other. It was really difficult not to open up to Lawrence about all her extra activities and observations around the factory, and it left her with very little else to talk about.

On the way back to her room, Poppy thought once more about how she had never managed to learn very much about Geoffrey and suddenly it all made sense. He hadn't been able to reveal much about his true self because he was at the factory undercover. Had he chosen to be elusive instead of making up a whole new background to tell her about because he liked her too much to lie to her? She found herself wondering if his story about joining the army and having a training accident had been a fib. She hoped she wouldn't have to start lying to Lawrence. The musings made her even more determined to bring down the spy as soon as possible.

The following day, when she was back on her afternoon shift, Poppy found herself feeling even more on guard than usual. She was desperate to spot some suspicious activity so that she could report back to Geoffrey and impress him, but she didn't find anything untoward on her rounds. She started wondering if the workers she had experienced small run-ins with when she had first arrived would be worth looking into, but then she realised that a spy wouldn't go out of their way to draw attention to themselves by kicking up a fuss about being caught trying to smuggle a cigarette into a workshop or accusing another worker of stealing. They would want to blend into the background. Whoever it was, she thought they were doing a mighty good job of covering their tracks.

That evening, Poppy went to Mrs Gilbert's. She wanted to try and switch off from her mission for a few hours and catch up with her friends, who she had neglected as much as Lawrence lately, but instead she found herself scrutinising everything they were saying.

'Have you been to Betty's tea rooms?' Edith asked Poppy as they all tucked into one of Mrs Gilbert's delicious cakes. She had taken to baking one that she put aside for the group every other week. Poppy wondered if she would get into trouble for giving the girls special treatment and using ingredients that were meant for all of the hostel residents, but she wasn't about to say anything to anybody about it.

'I haven't. Is it nice?' Poppy replied. She had thought about suggesting it to Lawrence as an alternative to Hardy's for one of their lunches, but she was worried about coming across too forward. She missed her afternoon teas with Maggie and Annie, but maybe it was best to keep them as a Bobby Girls treat anyway. Something told her that it wouldn't be quite the same tucking into the spread with a man.

'Oh, it's wonderful,' Edith exclaimed. 'Marie took us all there as a treat yesterday and I'm still daydreaming about the sponge cake!' Her face suddenly turned ashen, and she quickly glanced over at Mrs Gilbert. 'It's got nothing on your cake, though, of course,' she added sheepishly. Mrs Gilbert grinned and waved the awkward comment away.

'You paid for everyone?' Poppy asked Marie, who nodded and grinned in response. 'That must have cost a fair amount?' Even as she said it, Poppy felt awful for feeling suspicious of one of the people who she had grown closest to at Gretna.

But she had to admit that Marie's sudden splurging looked dubious to say the least. First of all, the fancy Christmas presents, and now an afternoon tea for four? She hadn't been free and easy with her cash when they had first met, so just where was all this extra money coming from?

'I don't get much opportunity to spoil my friends, so it felt good to do something special for them for once,' Marie replied casually.

She hadn't looked uncomfortable at the questioning, Poppy thought to herself. But surely a good spy wouldn't get flustered under scrutiny? Poppy noted that Marie was very quick to change the subject to something else and, as the conversation turned to what the group were going to watch at the cinema next, Poppy continued to mull over her suspicions about her friend in her head. When Bessie suddenly excused herself to go to bed early, something switched in Poppy's head. Now she thought about it, Bessie was always sloping off before everybody else when they had these little kitchen catch-ups. Was she really going to bed so early, or was she sneaking off to do something sinister? But surely not innocent, quiet, naive Bessie? Poppy had to admit that her persona would be a brilliant cover for a spy. Who would ever have suspected someone so shy and timid of passing top-secret information to the Germans? Just as Geoffrey was the last person she would have expected to be working undercover for MI5, could Bessie be the traitor she was looking for?

Lying in bed that night, Poppy went over it all in her head again. There had to be another explanation for Marie's sudden extra wealth, but she was struggling to come up with one. And was Bessie just one of those people who needed a full eight hours of sleep, or did she use that as a cover to stake out the danger building and try and get hold of the weapons plans? She was certainly tiny enough to slip in and out unnoticed under the cover of darkness. Poppy hated doubting her friends like this, but everything was stacking up against them. Could she trust anybody any more?

After tossing and turning for a little while and failing to get to sleep, Poppy started thinking about the rest of the group in detail. She found herself wondering why Edith had been so negative about Geoffrey when she had mentioned him to her previously. Was it as innocent as Poppy had first assumed or did Edith dislike him so much because she was spying for the Germans and she knew that he was trying to take her down? Then there was Jenny. She had been staying out all night long when Mrs Gilbert had asked Poppy for help reining her in. Had the bullying all been a cover-up? Maybe she hadn't been staying with a friend to avoid the nasty workers in her dorm. Poppy had never confronted the women, after all. What if Jenny had been staying out all night trying to get her hands on the weapons plans? Now she thought about it, Poppy realised that she didn't know much at all about Jenny or where she came from. Was that because Jenny had gone out of her way to avoid talking about her background, or was it because Poppy just hadn't shown an interest?

Her suspicions about her friends weren't enough to report back to Geoffrey with and, besides, she didn't want to put them under further scrutiny from him until she was certain there was something to be concerned about. She hoped she could rule them out and move on to fresh suspects before too long. So, Poppy decided that she should try and do some more digging on all of them over the following days. Next time Bessie went to bed early, Poppy would slip away too and follow her to confirm the fact that she was enjoying an early night and cross her off her suspect list. And she would make an effort to ask Jenny about her background to see what kind of a reaction she received. She might even talk to some of the workers from her old dorm to see if they could back up her claims of bullying. As for Edith, she felt it was worth asking her about Geoffrey again. She could casually throw his name into conversation to see how she responded, and then go from there. And she would keep a close eye on Marie's spending, too.

Poppy felt terrible for doubting her friends' integrity, but she told herself it was all for the greater good. Anybody in her position would be foolish to ignore any of the behaviour she had seen from the four of them, she reassured herself. She hoped she would be able to look back on this and laugh about how suspicious she had been of her innocent friends, but another part of her was so desperate to collar the traitor that she hoped – just a tiny bit – that one of her hunches paid off so that she would at least have something to report back to Geoffrey.

Settling into a light sleep, Poppy felt like she was finally getting somewhere with her secret mission. It felt refreshing to have some leads to work on, even if they were likely to lead to nothing. Maybe she would even have a solid lead to present to Geoffrey on her next day off.

31

Poppy's optimism didn't last long. She spent the whole of the following week focusing on her closest friends and their actions, and all she got out of it was a feeling of having betrayed them as well as a huge sense of failure. Bessie didn't excuse herself for another early night all week, and whenever Poppy tried to drop Geoffrey's name into conversation with the group to gauge Edith's reaction, the subject got changed before Edith had a chance to speak. There was no more splashing out from Marie, and, out of nowhere, Jenny actually started talking about the village she had grown up in and divulging details about her family.

Despite all of this, Poppy couldn't stop her suspicions about her friends from floating around in her head. She found herself being very guarded around them and over-analysing everything they said and did. She could feel herself pushing them all away but there was nothing she could do to stop it.

After meeting with Geoffrey on her next day off and having to admit to still having no leads, she wasn't sure if she was up to meeting Lawrence for lunch afterwards. It had always been the highlight of her week but, on this occasion, she found herself dragging her heels all the way there and pausing for thought by the door when she arrived at Hardy's ten minutes late. She felt so disappointed in herself and unable to bear trying to put on a brave face so that she wouldn't have to lie to Lawrence about why she was so down. Just as she was pondering whether it would be better to stand him up than act miserably throughout their meal and deceive him when he inevitably asked her what was wrong, she spotted him through the window and found herself grinning from ear to ear. That was that settled, then – she absolutely had to go ahead with their lunch because time with Lawrence was clearly what she needed in order to feel better.

Laughing to herself, Poppy was just about to push open the door when she noticed something odd. There was a huge bunch of keys hanging from Lawrence's belt. They were all attached to a metal loop – much like the set of factory keys she had often seen stored at the police hut. But those keys were always kept at the hut during the day for safekeeping – Butcher or Baker were always inside or, if not, the door was locked and an alarm set. So why would Lawrence have them with him on his lunchbreak? Poppy shrugged and went to push open the door again. She was certain there was an innocent explanation. She would ask him once she had greeted him and sat down.

As she opened the door and the bell above it rang, Lawrence looked over at her. He smiled and waved but then an expression of panic swept over his face. A waitress came over to greet Poppy and she desperately tried to watch Lawrence out of the corner of her eye as she explained to the woman that she was here to meet a friend and didn't need a table cleared for her. Poppy saw Lawrence moving but wasn't able to see him clearly enough to establish what he was doing. However, when he stood up to greet her, she subtly glanced at his waist and her heart dropped when she saw that the keys were no longer there. His big winter jacket was hanging over the back of his chair. Had he suddenly remembered they were clipped to his waist when he'd seen her and panicked – because he wasn't supposed to have taken them out of the office? And then had he stowed them away somewhere in his jacket? Poppy wanted to ask him but what could she possibly say?

'How has your day off been so far?' Lawrence asked casually as they both took their seats. Poppy took a deep breath and made up a story about sleeping in and missing the breakfast she'd had planned with Grace and Jean, because she couldn't very well tell him she'd been to see Geoffrey to give him a progress report on their secret mission. Instead of feeling her usual guilt for the fib, she half listened to his response while she turned the key situation over and over in her head. None of the work buildings were locked during the day; it was only danger buildings that were unmanned. And they were locked and unlocked by the officer in charge of whatever was being worked on inside. If Lawrence had been asked to go along and lock or unlock one for some reason then maybe he did so on his way to their lunch date, and so kept hold of the keys to save time instead of trekking back to the police hut and back out again. But if that was the case, why had he hidden them now? Surely Lawrence wasn't the mole she had been trying to collar? Poppy almost spat out her sandwich as she scoffed at the thought.

'Are you all right?' Lawrence asked her, looking concerned.

She nodded, wiping her mouth. 'Sorry, something went down the wrong way,' she muttered before taking a sip of her tea. What a ludicrous thought that had crossed her mind! She tried not to laugh at the very idea of it. But as their lunch continued, a doubt started creeping into Poppy's mind. What if Lawrence was the spy? She had grown really very fond of him. She would be devastated if it turned out that she had fallen for the enemy. She would also feel incredibly foolish. Even more so than when she had thought Geoffrey was the bad guy. But Poppy just couldn't bring herself to think the worst of Lawrence, despite the strange situation with the keys. She was certain there was a reasonable explanation but, try as she might, she just couldn't fathom out what that could be. Suddenly, she was imagining the terrible ways a German spy would be punished once they were captured, and her stomach turned.

'You're very quiet today. Is everything all right?' Lawrence's concerned voice cut into her thoughts.

'I feel rather queasy,' she whispered. Constantly feeling suspicious of the people she was closest to was beginning to really affect her. It was exhausting and upsetting. And now that Poppy had thought about what could happen to Lawrence – or any of her friends, if her niggling fears were proved correct – she felt as though she might bring back up what little of her sandwich she had managed to eat.

'You poor thing. I'll settle up and walk you back to the hostel.'

'No, really, it's fine. You still have a plate of food there. I can get back on my own.' But it was no good – Lawrence had already laid a wad of notes on the table and he was on his feet with his jacket in his hand. She almost retched when she heard the unmistakable sound of keys jangling. She knew there was an innocent reason for him having the keys and hiding them away when he saw her, so why did she feel so sick every time she thought about it?

Before Poppy knew it, Lawrence was guiding her out of the café. Her head was spinning with all the conflicting thoughts and so she let him take charge. Once outside he paused in the street. She thought he was going to put his big jacket on but, instead, he wrapped it around her shoulders. She slumped slightly to the side from the shock of the weight and Lawrence looked horrified.

'I'm so sorry,' he spluttered, reaching into an inside pocket. Poppy's eyes widened in shock as he pulled out the set of factory keys. 'There, that's better,' he said, and he clipped them back on to his waistband. 'I'd forgotten they were in there but they're so damned heavy.' Poppy kept staring at him, trying to work out what was happening. 'The alarm on the police hut is playing up so Butcher and I are taking it in turns to keep the full factory set on our person until it's fixed. I prefer to have them clipped to my belt so I can feel that they're always there – it's such a big responsibility and I'm not afraid to admit that I'm terrified of them falling into the wrong hands. But the problem with having them on my belt is that when I sit down they start digging in after a while and it's rather uncomfortable. I had them on my belt while I was sitting waiting for you, but I had to unclip them and put them in my jacket after a while because they were starting to make me sore.'

So, that explained it. Poppy had her innocent explanation. Lawrence's look when he'd seen her at the door hadn't been one of panic because the keys were on show – it had been one of pain because their rough edges had started digging into his legs. Poppy's own legs went weak when she realised what a wild conclusion she had almost allowed herself to jump to, and what the consequences could have ended up being for such a kind and genuine man. Lawrence caught her just in time as she nearly fell to the floor.

'I'm sorry,' she whispered, looking into his eyes as he swept her up in his arms. She knew she would never be able to bring herself to explain exactly what she was sorry for – how did you explain to somebody you were so close to that you were so consumed by your need to prove yourself that you started suspecting them of one of the worst things possible? She wasn't thinking logically any more.

'Don't be silly, you shouldn't be apologising. I'm the one who kept on talking at you when you were clearly struggling. I should have escorted you back to your hostel long before now.' He gently lowered her to the ground and insisted on walking back to her room with her.

As they strolled in companionable silence, Poppy fought back tears. She had got so carried away with it all that not only had she suspected her closest friends, but she had come close to being ready to throw the book at Lawrence of all people. She clearly wasn't cut out for this undercover lark. Lawrence insisted on escorting Poppy all the way to her room, and he even knocked on Jean's door to ask her to put Poppy to bed and keep an eye on her. The more caring he acted, the worse Poppy felt. She knew that her silence throughout the whole exchange would be put down to her mystery illness and she was thankful. In reality she was just too ashamed to speak to anybody. She stayed in bed for the rest of the afternoon, too mortified to even consider venturing out and seeing anybody else. She couldn't face her afternoon shift the following day so when Jean knocked on her door to check on her, she asked her to inform Sergeant Ross that she was too poorly to patrol. Poppy wallowed in bed for the whole day, wondering how she had come to behave so terribly and make such snap judgements about people who had only ever been kind to her.

When evening rolled around and there was a soft knock on her bedroom door, Poppy groaned to herself. Thinking that it was Jean checking in on her again she decided that she would accompany her to the canteen for some dinner. She was still feeling sorry for herself, but her stomach was growling in anger, and she couldn't put off eating any longer. When Poppy opened her door, however, her jaw nearly dropped to the floor.

'What are you doing here?' she hissed. She poked her head into the corridor and checked in both directions. It was clear. She grabbed hold of Geoffrey's shirt and hauled him into her room before slamming the door shut behind him.

'Well, you certainly appear to be feeling better, love.' He tutted jokingly, flattening down his rumpled top and giving her a wink.

'Have you any idea how people would talk if they saw me entertaining a gentleman in my room?' Poppy exclaimed. 'I'd be the talk of the WPS. I might even get thrown out! This is exactly the type of behaviour I'm here to put a stop to.' She might have spent time at his lodgings but that was completely different – for a start it had been the middle of the night, so they had been unlikely to be spotted, and there had definitely been extenuating circumstances.

'Don't get carried away. I'm here to check on a poorly patient, not sweep you off your feet,' Geoffrey replied, looking serious. Poppy suddenly felt awkward. He probably didn't like her like that anyway. But that wasn't the point – people would still talk, and she would still get into bother! 'Mind you, you did a good job of sweeping me off my feet when you hauled me over the threshold back there. Strong little thing, aren't you?' Geoffrey added cheekily before flashing her another wink.

Poppy couldn't help herself. It was the light relief she needed after her day of self-pity. She bent over double laughing.

'Are you . . . all right?' Geoffrey asked cautiously.

Realising she had got carried away, Poppy stood up straight again and composed herself. 'I'm absolutely fine,' she said, with a big sigh.

'Only, they told me you weren't very well? I was worried when you didn't stop by on your patrol as usual and I asked around. Your colleague seems to think you've been struck down with some mystery ailment.'

'If a crisis of confidence can be classed as an illness, then I suppose I'm pig sick,' Poppy replied dramatically, throwing herself onto the bed. All her worry about acting inappropriately in her bedroom with an unmarried man had gone out of the window along with her enthusiasm for spy hunting.

'Right, well, you're going to have to explain yourself because I'm none the wiser.'

Poppy sat up and looked Geoffrey in the eye. 'I've been doing this for weeks. *Weeks*. And I don't have any leads for you. Not even one tiny crumb. But the whole thing is driving me crazy!' She felt hot tears prickling her eyes and she didn't do anything to try and stop them. 'I feel like I'm going mad! I don't know friend from foe. I've thought the worst of all the people closest to me. I'm an awful person for that. And I've wasted so much time following up hunches and suspicions that have all ended up being down to my imagination. I promised you so much and all I've done is let you down.' Before she knew it, Poppy was blubbing into her hands. Suddenly, she felt Geoffrey's hands on top of hers. He was pulling her up to stand opposite him. She went with it and fell into his arms as he wrapped them around her to comfort her. As soon as her head was buried in his chest her tears flowed faster. They were uncontrollable.

'Hey, it's all right,' Geoffrey said soothingly into her ear as he rubbed her back slowly up and down. 'I've been on this job a lot longer than you have and I'm no further forward than you are. I have no idea who it could be, either.'

Poppy pulled herself back abruptly to look him in the face. 'That's not true!' she cried. She was aware of the fact that her face must be red and blotchy and damp, but she didn't care. 'You nearly had the culprit red-handed until I bustled in and brought the whole operation crashing down. I've made such a mess of everything!'

'We don't know that for a fact,' Geoffrey replied firmly. He was gripping her arms now and their faces were nose to nose. He was staring into her eyes intensely, and she found that she couldn't look away. Despite the huge mix of emotions that she was processing, Poppy suddenly felt a flutter in her heart at being so close to Geoffrey. 'We don't know that the spy was ready to make a move that night,' he whispered softly. He gently brushed a strand of hair off Poppy's face.

'All the intel suggests the spy is still active, so the chances are they were nowhere near the danger building when we had our run-in. So, everything has worked out for the best because I have you on my team now. And I couldn't have wished for a better teammate.'

They stared into each other's eyes and Poppy felt her heart start racing. When Geoffrey leaned in closer, she closed her eyes and waited for his lips to touch hers. When they started kissing, she was so wrapped up in the moment that she didn't hear the light tapping on the door. It was only once the door opened and a breeze ran down her neck from the draft that she realised somebody was in the room with them. She quickly pulled away and spun around to see who the presence she could feel belonged to. Her heart dropped right down to the pit of her stomach when she saw Lawrence, a look of pure hurt etched across his face, staring back at the two of them.

32

As soon as Poppy locked eyes with Lawrence, he turned around and walked out of the room. She pulled further away from Geoffrey without a second thought and ran after Lawrence, a million conflicting thoughts rushing through her head. He had certainly been desperate to get away – he was already out of the building by the time she made it into the corridor. She ran as quickly as she could and felt a dash of relief when she saw Lawrence making his way back along the road towards the main township. She called out to him, but he kept walking, well, stomping to be exact, with his head hanging low.

'Leave him to it,' she heard Geoffrey's voice saying casually behind her. Had there been a hint of contempt in his tone? She ignored the comment and started running again until she finally caught up with Lawrence. Grateful that there was nobody else around to witness whatever happened next, she reached up to touch his shoulder.

'Please,' she begged.

He spun around to face her, jolting her arm off him in the process. 'I was worried about you after yesterday, especially when I didn't see you on your rounds today. But it seems as if you've made quite the recovery.' Lawrence's voice was low and cold. He looked hurt and angry and the realisation that her actions had caused that made Poppy want to bend over double and howl. The sensation shocked her, but she didn't have time to dwell on it; she needed to try and fix this.

'It's really . . . it's not what you think,' she stuttered, but Lawrence wasn't looking at her any more. He was staring past her. Poppy turned around and saw Geoffrey slowly making his way towards them.

'*Him*, I would have expected it of.' Lawrence pointed at Geoffrey in disgust. He turned his stare back to Poppy. 'But you, Poppy,' he said softly now. 'I honestly thought that you were better than this. I can't believe I could be so wrong about somebody I thought of so highly.'

As she watched him storm off again, Poppy felt as though she had been punched in the stomach. Never before had somebody's words had such a devastating effect on her. They had cut her to the core. She felt more tears coming but she was unable to hide herself away because she was frozen to the spot, staring after Lawrence.

'That was a bit much, love. Don't worry about him. He doesn't know what he's talking about,' Geoffrey said lightly, putting a hand on her shoulder. Poppy turned around and when he saw her tears, he looked concerned. 'Let me walk you back to your room,' he offered kindly.

'No.' She shrugged his hand away and then remembered the sense of rejection she had felt when Lawrence had just done the same to her and she instantly felt bad about it. 'Thank you,' she added as she sniffled. 'It's been a long day. I just need to be alone,' she whispered before hurrying back to the hostel.

Poppy got straight into bed and didn't plan on getting out again until the end of the war. She was mortified. Devastated. Confused. Her head was spinning, and she didn't know how to make sense of everything that was going through her mind. Geoffrey had kissed her – and she had kissed him back. Did that mean he was the man she liked the most? But then, she had been so upset at Lawrence's reaction. Was she upset because he thought badly of her? Or was it because he had seen her and Geoffrey kissing, which meant any chance of things progressing further between the two of them had been scuppered? And, what about that kiss? She was so confused that she didn't even know how she felt about it. She had thought that if things had got to that stage with one of the men, it would mean he was the one she preferred – but she still didn't know. Her heart felt heavy when she realised it might not even matter any more – this evening's events would probably mean it was too late to pursue anything with one of them, anyway.

As well as all those conflicting inner ramblings, there was a huge amount of guilt pushing its way into Poppy's mind regarding John. She had been so happy spending time with Lawrence and Geoffrey, and getting involved in the secret mission, that she realised now she had barely thought about John over the last few weeks. She had felt as though she was moving on and she had been almost at peace with it. But kissing another man had really taken that to another level. As if she hadn't felt bad enough about feeling attracted to other men. John would have wanted her to move on and be happy, and that's why she had been so determined to make a start – so why couldn't she rid herself of all the associated shame? She ended up pulling out her wedding ring from the drawer and falling asleep clutching it, feeling utterly miserable.

Poppy woke up feeling just as wretched. She didn't know how to make things right with Lawrence, everything involving Geoffrey and the undercover mission was a mess, and she felt like such a failure that it seemed as if the only thing to do would be to take herself off home. She kept replaying the scene in her head and seeing the hurt on Lawrence's face and hearing the disappointment in his voice. She decided it would be better for everybody if she left Gretna.

Poppy threw on a dress and wrapped a shawl around her.

The spring sunshine was beating down already but she knew from experience there would still be a chill in the air – especially this early in the morning. It wasn't yet seven o'clock but she knew Lawrence opened up the police hut at half past every morning so he could enjoy a cup of tea and prepare for his shift before Butcher turned up at eight o'clock to shatter the peace. She felt like a nervous wreck as she made her way to Dornock, but she just needed to get this over and done with, and then she could tell Sergeant Ross she was too poorly to continue and pack her bags and get back to the comfort of her Bobby Girls. She felt sad to be leaving but it felt like the best option when the alternative was to keep bumping into Lawrence every day and having him look at her the way he had done the night before. She couldn't stand it. And what would she do on her days off? Their lunches had been the highlight of her week. There would just be a big empty space pushing at the wound that losing his friendship – and possibly more – had caused.

'Poppy,' Lawrence said with a curt nod as he walked up to the police hut. She had made it to Dornock just before seven-thirty and had been waiting anxiously for him to arrive. 'Good morning.' His voice was clipped and professional, and Poppy felt another jab to her chest. It was the polar opposite to the warm and friendly welcome she normally received from him. She knew then in that instant that she definitely couldn't bear to stay at Gretna with Lawrence being like this with her. She had ruined everything.

'Good morning,' she replied nervously as he edged past her to unlock the door to the hut. She held back as he turned off the alarm, her guilt overwhelming her as she noted it had now been fixed. She tentatively followed him inside, terrified he would usher her straight back out before she could offer him an apology for her appalling behaviour. He turned around to face her and looked at her impatiently. Poppy cleared her throat and tried to keep her voice as steady as possible when she spoke. 'I would like to apologise for being so unprofessional,' she said firmly. She had wanted to come across softer, but this was the only way she could stop her voice from shaking. 'I think it's probably for the best if I resign from my position,' she added with an unmistakable quiver. Lawrence's expression didn't break and there were a few seconds of terrible, gut-wrenching silence before he finally spoke.

'Don't be silly,' he replied softly. Poppy felt a rush of relief at the change in his tone. 'You're a wonderful policewoman, Poppy, and you're doing great work at Gretna.' He paused for a moment and then stared at his feet as he continued. 'I'm the one who should be apologising.' Poppy's jaw dropped in astonishment. This certainly wasn't playing out the way she had expected. 'I'm so sorry for my behaviour last night.' His eyes flickered up to meet hers again briefly and then he moved his gaze back to the floor uncomfortably. 'I must admit that it was quite the shock for me to see you and Geoffrey together like that. And in your bedroom of all places.' Poppy's cheeks flushed red, and she jumped to try and explain but Lawrence held up his hand to stop her from speaking.

'I'm afraid I spoke quite out of turn and I was somewhat harsher towards you than I should have been. With anybody else I would have left without a word and forgotten all about it but with you I had hoped . . .' he trailed off and Poppy silently willed him to continue. What had he been hoping? Did he like her, too? No – had he liked her? It didn't matter now, did it, because she had put paid to anything he might have felt for her and anything that might have happened between them. When Lawrence spoke again his voice was quiet but firm. 'But never mind. Like I told you once before, I've always been used to fading into the background.' He gave a little cough and looked embarrassed. 'None of this is your fault, Poppy, and I shouldn't have reacted in that way. Clearly, I had been under a misapprehension.'

She wanted to step forward and throw her arms around him and tell him that he hadn't been mistaken and that she was delighted to hear that he felt the same way that she did. But her happiness at his revelation was clouded by the fact she had acted inappropriately with another man, and Lawrence would surely never see past that. Poppy was desperately searching for the right words to say in response to what he had told her when Lawrence started talking again.

'No matter, I'd like for us to be friends still and I would just like to stress again how genuinely sorry I am for the way I spoke to you,' he said formally. Poppy opened her mouth to respond but he hadn't finished. 'Now, if you'll excuse me, I must get my report book in order before Butcher arrives and hauls me over the coals for being behind with it.' Lawrence was already at the door. He held it open for her. Poppy smiled nervously and scurried out without saying a word. She wanted so desperately to explain everything to him but that would mean telling him about the spy and, besides, he had made it clear that their conversation was over.

Poppy walked back to the township in dismay. She was still trying to get her thoughts in order when she reached the hostel. Unable to stand spending any more time in her room after hiding herself away in there for so long, she found herself walking aimlessly around the township until it was time to get ready for her afternoon shift. She was relieved to not be leaving Gretna, but she was mortified to think that Lawrence was under the impression there had been something romantic going on between her and Geoffrey for some time. How foolish he must have been feeling – and how awfully he must think of her!

It was true that she had felt a little uncomfortable spending time getting to know them both so well, but Maggie and Annie had reassured her that there was no harm in it as long as there was no courting taking place. And there hadn't been. But that wasn't what it looked like to Lawrence and now he thought that she was the kind of woman who enjoyed lunches with one man while carrying on inappropriately with another. She walked past Hardy's and felt a pang of pain in her heart. There would be no more long lunches to enjoy on her days off.

Trying to look on the bright side, Poppy told herself that at least her problem of not knowing which man she liked the most had now been solved. There was certainly no chance of things going further than a friendship with Lawrence after everything that had happened. She didn't even know if their friendship could last now that she had tainted it. She would have to push aside all thoughts of Lawrence to protect herself.

Thinking back to the kiss with Geoffrey, Poppy sighed. Their first kiss – my, what a dramatic way for that to happen! Maybe it was better this way, Poppy tried to convince herself. She had never even come close to kissing Lawrence, so the fact that she had so willingly returned Geoffrey's affections could be proof that it was him that she had been gravitating towards all along. Poppy started to perk up a little at the revelation and she started smiling to herself when she replayed the kiss in her head. She supposed that it had felt quite nice. She was so determined to stop herself from feeling hurt by the mess she had made of things with Lawrence that she found herself almost believing that Geoffrey had been her favourite of the two men all along . . .

33

Poppy was exhausted from walking and overthinking by the time she made it back to her room to get changed into her uniform for her afternoon shift. She made the mistake of sitting down on her bed to rest for a moment and it took all of her will to haul herself back up and out of the door. She thought the hours of soul-searching she had just done would have firmed everything up in her head for her, but as she carried out her searches at the cordite section, she found her mind wandering back to everything that had unfolded over the previous twenty-four hours. She patted down worker after worker, but she wasn't her usual focused self. All she could think about was how much faith Geoffrey had seemed to have in her when she had broken down and offered to give up on the secret mission.

'You wanna see me pass or not?' a voice broke into her thoughts to ask. Poppy came to and realised the worker in front of her was holding out her pass expectantly. 'You do realise we're not allowed in until you've checked it over?' the woman added impatiently. Poppy shook her head to snap herself back into the present and she took the pass from the worker and gave it a quick scan.

'All fine,' she said firmly, giving the worker a curt nod and trying to come over with some authority, although it was clear that she now looked like a bumbling fool. The next woman stepped forward and Poppy made herself focus fully on searching her. As more and more workers approached her to be patted down, she found her concentration slipping again. Geoffrey had told her to carry on with the mission, and now she knew that he liked her as more than a friend she felt like she had even more to prove to him. Their kiss was giving her a renewed sense of purpose when it came to catching the spy, and that along with his encouragement had certainly given her confidence the boost it had so desperately needed.

Poppy patted down another worker and gave her pass a cursory glance while she mulled over the best course of action to take next. She still didn't have any solid leads, but there was definitely more she could explore with her friends. She wanted to be careful about suspecting people she cared about, but she also had to make sure she wasn't naive enough to rule people out simply because she knew them. The spy could be absolutely anybody and a good undercover agent would suspect everybody until they had good reason to discount them. If she picked up the threads with Bessie, Edith, Marie and Jenny again, then she was hopeful that her investigations would prove their innocence and turn up more leads at the same time. In all honesty, she didn't have much else to go on and so it seemed like the best place to start.

'I don't think so.' Poppy sighed as her hand brushed over a cigarette-shaped item tucked inside a woman's waistband. The worker – an older woman who Poppy had confiscated cigarettes from previously – huffed and rolled her eyes as Poppy retrieved the offending item and placed it on her tray. Glad that the woman hadn't put up a fight, Poppy waved her in and waited for the next worker to step forward. Poppy felt a rush at the fact that she had turned up the contraband despite the fact her mind hadn't been fully on the task in hand. But she chose to take it as a bit of a wake-up call to concentrate. She could have just as easily missed the cigarette and then been found out – or worse than that, the cordite section could have gone up in flames.

Turning her attention back to the searches, Poppy decided to work on her action plan once she was out on patrol. She could devise her next steps in her head when she was walking from section to section and her focus didn't need to be so sharp. But as she patted down the next few contraband-free women and monotony set in, her mind started to wander again. This time, thoughts of Lawrence were trying to distract her. She kept seeing his face when she'd turned around and spotted him in her bedroom, and all she seemed to be able to hear was the hurt in his voice when he talked about fading into the background, as much as she tried to block it out. She didn't want to think about him and cause herself more upset, so she brought Geoffrey to mind instead.

A young girl stepped forward to be searched as Poppy started thinking about her kiss with Geoffrey. As Poppy ran through their intimate moment in her head, she fleetingly looked into the girl's eyes and noticed that they appeared to be glazed over. Maybe she'd had a bad night's sleep too, Poppy mused as she started her search. She didn't feel as though she had slept much at all, although she knew she must have dozed off at some point. Her mind was wandering to Lawrence again as the girl suddenly swayed to the side. Instinctively, Poppy lunged forwards to steady her. The worker laughed quietly, and Poppy smiled at her as she continued patting her down, wondering if Geoffrey would be put off by her reaction to Lawrence seeing them kiss. The girl started coughing. It sounded like a nasty cough.

'I'm almost done. Go and get some water before you start your work,' Poppy instructed her. Her reaction to Lawrence stumbling upon them kissing couldn't have looked good to Geoffrey, could it, she thought as she finally waved the young girl on and motioned for the next worker to step forward. She decided that if Geoffrey mentioned it then she would say that she had been worried about Lawrence telling other people she had been entertaining him in her bedroom and what they might think of her. Yes, she smiled to herself, that would work nicely. But her smile faded when she looked up and saw the worker in front of her was staring at her accusingly. Poppy's brow furrowed as she tried to come up with a reason for the worker's bad temper, but before she could ask her what the matter was, she had tutted at her and stomped away. Poppy shrugged to herself and went back to her searches. She just wanted to get them finished so she could work on her plan.

Poppy couldn't help it. She started thinking about her next steps as she continued her searches. Her first task would be to drop Geoffrey into the conversation with Edith and then push for more information from her if she reacted negatively again. She was better off doing it at the factory so she could get Edith on her own to avoid input or distraction from anybody else, as had happened the last time she had tried. The four of them were stuck together like glue outside of the factory. Then, she would visit them every evening that she physically was able to. If they were out, she would tell Mrs Gilbert she had something to return to Marie so she would give her access to her dorm and cubicle. She wouldn't have long but she would be able to draw the curtain around Marie's bed and personal possessions, and have a quick root around for – she wasn't sure what. Maybe a big pile of cash she had been given by the Germans in return for her snooping? And if the girls were in then she would wait for Bessie to have another early night and she would follow her to see if she really did go to bed or if she sneaked off to the danger building. As for Jenny's bullies, well, maybe she could seek them out for a talk at the factory soon. They worked at the other end of the workshop so Poppy's friends weren't likely to see her with them and if they did, she could easily make up a reason for their interaction.

When her searches were finally over and all the women were in the section working away, Poppy did a quick sweep through to make sure everything looked as it should before she made her way to her friends' section. She was counting on the WPS recruit behind her being more thorough to make up for her lack of time spent there, and to give her longer to talk to Edith. But if her colleague caught her up then she would simply say Edith was giving her some information on a worker who she suspected of being up to no good.

Poppy was smiling to herself with her hand on the door to leave when suddenly a loud scream brought everything in the workshop to a standstill. Poppy spun around to see a commotion near one of the workbenches. She sprinted back towards the scene where a group of workers were huddled around somebody lying on the floor. Pushing her way through, Poppy heard a voice.

'She's all right – just give her some space. She's drunk from the fumes, is all. I can't believe that policewoman let her in with the state she was in before she even started!'

Poppy stopped still as she took in the woman's words. Had this been her fault? She finally made it to the poorly worker and her heart dropped to the pit of her stomach. Sitting on the floor was the young girl who had swayed as Poppy had searched her. Cradling her was the woman who Poppy had searched next and who had looked angry with her. Poppy felt overwhelmingly hot as everything fell into place and she realised her awful mistake. She had been so distracted that she hadn't even acted, past steadying the girl when she had swayed. She had just assumed she was being clumsy and had lost her footing and taken a stumble. But she had been so poorly from working around the cordite fumes all week that she had collapsed almost as soon as she had made it to her workstation. It was something that Poppy should have picked up on straight away.

'There she is,' the older woman spat, pointing at Poppy. 'Don't you dare come anywhere near her. I'll get her to the sick bay meself and you won't say a word about me leaving my post or else I'll report you for slacking on the job.' Poppy just stared blankly at her. There was no question of her asserting her authority in this awful situation. How could she? She had been completely in the wrong and they both knew it. 'If any of your colleagues ask, I had your permission to take her. Understood?' Poppy nodded and stepped aside as another worker helped the angry woman get her friend to her feet.

As they guided the young girl out of the workshop, Poppy looked around and wished she could make herself disappear as she took in all of the disappointed faces of the workers staring at her. She had let them down and she had most certainly let that young girl down. She was lucky the consequences for the girl hadn't been worse – and that it didn't appear that she herself was going to get into trouble for her mistake. And it had all happened because she had reignited her obsession with the mole and allowed that and her thoughts about Lawrence and Geoffrey to distract her so much that she had put a worker's welfare at risk. Poppy had never felt so ashamed of herself. She cleared her throat loudly.

'Show's over. Everyone back to work,' she announced as firmly as she could manage. But she was well aware of the fact that that she didn't deserve for anybody to obey her. She wouldn't have blamed any of them for ignoring her order and making things difficult for her. Luckily for Poppy, all the workers slunk back to their workstations without a word of protest. With her head hung low, she walked at speed out of the workshop and across to her friends' section. But she didn't stop to talk to Edith as planned. She didn't stop to talk to anybody. She did carry out a thorough check of the workshop, and of all the subsequent sections, without allowing a thought of anything else to creep into her head and cloud her judgement.

Once Poppy was on her way over to the Dornock site, she allowed her mind to unravel everything that had happened. It was clear to her now that she should have stuck to her guns and given up on the secret mission the night before. She had been right – she wasn't cut out for it. And now her obsession with it was affecting her WPS work – one of the most important things in her life. It didn't matter how she felt about Geoffrey romantically; there was absolutely no way she could continue helping him with his undercover work. She was angry with herself for allowing herself to get pulled back into it so easily when she had been so set on giving it up.

Poppy had everything she wanted to say to Geoffrey planned out in her head and she was desperate to get the conversation over with. She walked into the nitrating house with purpose, but she couldn't see Geoffrey anywhere. Confused, she searched around, doing her usual checks of the workers and the site at the same time, but he was nowhere to be found. She even popped her head out into the yard, but it was empty.

'You all right there, dear?' a voice called out from behind her. Poppy jumped and shuffled back into the nitrating house, closing the door to the yard behind her. 'You won't find any workstations out there – the workers aren't allowed back there,' the foreman told her. He was in his sixties and had a streak of white hair cutting across his dark locks. Poppy had seen him around at Dornock before but never in the nitrating house.

'Yes, I'm aware,' Poppy replied awkwardly, hoping he wouldn't ask her why she had been searching out there. 'Is Geoffrey not working this afternoon?' she asked casually.

'He was. Poor sod got sent to his lodgings after he came

over a bit funny. And I thought it was only the girls who couldn't cope with the fumes.' The foreman laughed to himself and shook his head while Poppy stared at him, unimpressed. 'But then, the silly chap is always taking his mask off to chat to the girls,' he added, rolling his eyes.

Poppy smiled. She had to admit, she had often wondered how he had never had a problem with the fumes given the number of times that she had seen him without his mask. She thanked the foreman and went on her way. She was anxious to tell Geoffrey her decision, but she would have to wait until the evening. Their agreement was that if he wasn't on duty, then she searched him out at his lodgings at night with any spy developments, to avoid anybody spotting her hanging around the foreman's hostel. And she was to wear her uniform so that if anybody did see her, they would assume she was on police business. She felt sad that the first time she had to put their plan into action it was because she was giving up and not because she had a super important lead to share with him.

Despite her tiredness, Poppy was extra vigilant for the rest of her shift. When she finally clocked off, she wanted to get her conversation with Geoffrey over and done with so that she could go to bed. But she knew she needed to wait a little while to make sure the night shift had started and any stragglers who had missed the curfew were tucked up in their lodgings. The less risk of people seeing her, the better, even if she was in her uniform.

At Geoffrey's hostel, Poppy let herself into the empty communal area. It was far too late for foremen to be sitting around talking but she edged her way in carefully just in case there was anybody hanging around who might spot her. She peeked carefully down the corridor to make sure there was nobody going in or out of any of the rooms. Once she was certain that the coast was clear, she tiptoed along the hall towards Geoffrey's room. But just as she was about to reach it, she noticed that the door was ever so slightly ajar. A small sliver of light was shining out from the crack. Stopping dead in her tracks, Poppy tried to think of a reason why Geoffrey would have left his door slightly open in the middle of the night. But then she remembered that he was poorly, so maybe he'd made a trip to the bathroom and forgotten to close the door properly on his return? The acid fumes made you feel and act as if you were intoxicated, so it would make sense for him to be a little disorientated on his way back.

Poppy was feeling concerned for Geoffrey's wellbeing now and she was glad she'd had reason to stop by and see him. She hated the thought of him suffering on his own all night, especially when he had rushed round to check on her when he'd thought that she was unwell.

Once she was at the door, Poppy could hear a rustling sound coming from inside the room. Thinking that Geoffrey was awake, she poked her head around the door without knocking, but then she let out a loud gasp. There was no sign of Geoffrey in the room but kneeling on the floor in front of his desk, trying desperately to open one of the drawers, was Edith!

34

There was a clang as Edith jumped up and dropped the tools she had been using to try and pick the lock to Geoffrey's desk. Poppy kicked herself for gasping and giving herself away. It seemed she really wasn't the right woman for the role of secret agent – first she had blundered into the danger building and given the game away when she'd been following Geoffrey, and now this. But it wasn't a time for self-pity – she was standing in front of the mole, and she needed to act quickly. She drew out her truncheon and stepped into the room. She was ready for Edith to put up a fight but instead the other woman held her hands up in surrender.

'Please, Poppy. It's not what you think,' she whispered urgently, looking past her to the door. Poppy wondered if she was checking for Geoffrey returning. Where was he, anyway? He couldn't be far away. Maybe it would be best to keep Edith talking until he got here, then they could apprehend her together. Poppy slowly worked her way into the room and then stopped a few feet in front of Edith.

'Oh, really? Well, what is going on here, then?' she asked, holding eye contact.

'I'm working for MI5,' Edith whispered, peering around Poppy to the door again, looking nervous. 'You've got to believe me. I've been sent in to find an enemy spy.'

Poppy's head started to spin but she kept her expression neutral so as not to give anything away. What was going on?

She'd thought she'd caught the mole red-handed but now Edith was saying . . . was she saying that Geoffrey had been the mole all along? It would explain her attitude towards him. But Poppy had jumped to conclusions too many times before.

'I'm going to need more information than that,' she said quietly and calmly as Edith started tapping her heel on the floor. She was acting rather jittery for somebody who was meant to be an MI5 agent.

'This spy has been making slight but catastrophic adjustments to plans for new weapons and massively hindering the British war effort. And they've been passing the correct versions of the revolutionary new weapons designs to the Germans. I've always believed Geoffrey was the spy, but I need evidence to nail him. I think his copies of the plans are in this desk.'

Poppy had no idea what to believe. Had she been right to suspect Geoffrey all those weeks ago, and had he been lying to her all this time? Or was Edith, one of her closest friends at the factory, the liar and traitor? The only thing she knew for certain was that she wasn't going to be able to answer that question any time soon. And time was of the essence.

'Just get out,' Poppy blurted before she knew what she was doing. Edith looked shocked. 'If you're right, we'll get the evidence you need. But not now. Go, before he comes back,' she added forcefully. Edith scrabbled around on the floor for her lock-picking tools and ran out of the room.

Poppy waited until the sound of her footsteps faded and she heard the door at the end of the hallway closing. What was she going to do now? Had she just let the spy go free, or was she standing in the mole's bedroom waiting for him to return from goodness knows where? She stared hard at the desk. Did she have time to try and break her way into the drawer to see for herself? She laughed quietly to herself. Of course she didn't. She didn't know the first thing about picking locks! She wished she had listened more carefully when Annie had told her about the skills she had picked up when she went undercover at the brothel.

Poppy turned on her heel and ran along the corridor, desperate to get out into the fresh air to try and get her head around what had happened and come up with her next step. But just as she hurried through the door and into the night air, she bumped into Geoffrey, who had flown around the corner at such a speed he'd been unable to stop himself in time. Poppy jolted backwards when their bodies made contact.

'Woah! Are you all right, love? You were really going some there!' he cried light-heartedly.

'So were you,' Poppy blustered, straightening her hat and steadying herself.

'Oh, what's the matter?' Geoffrey said, suddenly full of concern. He placed his hand gently on her arm and searched her face. 'You look like you've seen a ghost.'

Poppy looked into his eyes, hopeful they would somehow tell her whether she could trust him or not. Her heart started racing when she realised that she had no idea who she could trust any more. If Geoffrey was the spy, then she couldn't let him know that Edith was on his tail. But if it was Edith, well, then, surely she should tell Geoffrey what she knew? But who was telling the truth? They could both be lying to her for all she knew!

'Is it to do with the mission?' Geoffrey whispered, looking around them conspicuously. 'Is that why you're at my hostel so late at night?'

Poppy couldn't stand it any longer. 'I know something, but I don't know who to trust and I just need some time to think,' she blurted before setting off on her way again. But she felt a hand clamp down tightly around her arm and pull her backwards. She let out a small yelp – more from shock than anything. Geoffrey pulled her round to face him. She shrugged his hand off her arm. 'What do you think you're doing?' she demanded.

'Come on, you can tell me,' he said, failing to hide the desperation in his voice. 'Poppy, if it's to do with the spy then I need to know. You can't mess around like this with something so important.' Poppy turned to leave but he grabbed her again. Poppy let Geoffrey spin her round to face him again and once she was stood in front of him she swiftly lifted her knee up and pushed it between his legs as hard as she could manage, just like she had been taught in suffrajitsu lessons. He let go of her arm and dropped to the floor on his knees. Poppy fled immediately, relief flooding her as his cries of pain got further and further away.

Poppy kept running until she reached the WPS hostel. She paused only to yank open the main door, her mind firmly fixed on getting to the safety of her bedroom. But once she had her hand on the door handle, she stopped. Her mind started racing. Was her bedroom the refuge she so desperately needed? There were two people who knew she knew something. Both those people knew where her room was. One of those people was a real danger to her. She shook her head and backed away from the door. She had been in such a panic that she hadn't even contemplated the risk of staying in her room on her own overnight. But who could she go to for help? The first name that popped into her head was Lawrence. She knew without a shadow of a doubt that she could trust him. If anybody was willing and able to protect her, it was Lawrence. Well, it had been before their last couple of awkward encounters. She had hurt him so badly now that there was no way she could turn up at his home in the middle of the night and expect him to let her in, let alone help her get out of this terrible mess.

Looking up and down the corridor, Poppy let out a sigh. She knew for a fact that Jean was on a night shift, but Grace had been on the afternoon shift with her. Terrified of some-body creeping in behind her, Poppy threw open her bedroom door, grabbed her bedding and nightclothes and literally jumped back out into the corridor, making sure to pull the door shut tight behind her. She let out a sigh of relief when she saw the hallway was still empty and she made her way to the other end of it to wake up Grace.

Grace was half asleep when she answered the door. Poppy lied that she'd had another funny turn and she was worried about staying on her own in case it happened again during the night. Thankfully Grace was so sleepy that she didn't ask for any more information but just waved her in. She offered up her bed, but Poppy insisted on bedding down on the floor with her covers – she felt bad enough lying to her friend as it was.

Poppy changed into her nightclothes in the dark and tried to get some rest on the floor but she hardly slept a wink. She had never felt so uncomfortable in her life. But she wasn't sure she would have managed sleep, even in a bed fit for a queen, because of all the thoughts running through her mind. She kept replaying all her interactions and conversa-tions with Geoffrey and Edith as she tried to decide who was telling her the truth. But it was no good – even after hours of contemplation she was still no closer to knowing who she could trust. As she watched the sun rise through the window, she felt the most helpless she had ever felt. She longed to see Maggie and Annie and ask for their advice. How she missed having them both to turn to.

When Grace started stirring, Poppy decided to head back to her own room. She would feel safer in daylight, and she didn't want to tell any more lies to her friend. So, she crept out before Grace was fully awake and able to question her about her 'illness'. But as she went to open her bedroom door, her heart lurched. She had definitely closed the door properly after collecting her things the previous night. She could remember pulling it shut behind her, as it had been trickier than normal due to the fact her hands had been full. She knew for a fact that she had closed it properly. Now it was open just a fraction – as Geoffrey's had been when she had turned up the previous evening.

Poppy dropped her bedding and uniform on the floor, and took a cautious step forward. She craned her neck and strained to listen for any noise that might be coming from inside. She couldn't hear anything. She wondered whether she should run and get help before checking inside – but who would she go to and what would she say? No, she needed to investigate on her own. It was a tiny room, and she didn't need to go right inside to see if anybody was in there. She could just poke her head in, and if there was someone on the other side of the door then she would scream and alert the rest of the recruits in the hostel before the person could get hold of her.

Poppy held her breath and leaned forward to tap the door. Her heart pumped faster than she could ever remember feeling it pump as the door swung open an inch. She waited for the noise of an intruder being disturbed inside. But there was nothing. Tentatively, she gave the door another nudge, harder this time, and when there was still no noise from within, she took a couple of shaky steps forward. When Poppy finally peered inside, she gasped – and then decided she had to stop doing that. At least there was nobody in the room to hear the noise this time, she thought to herself. But there *had* been somebody in her room. And they hadn't gone to any effort to conceal the fact. They wanted her to know they had been there. The chair she normally hung her uniform over had been kicked on its side, and the drawer where she kept her wedding ring and final letter from John was . . .

'No!' Poppy cried, lurching forward and grabbing hold of

the drawer handle. Had she been burgled? Maybe this was nothing to do with the spy at all. She pulled the half-open drawer fully open and felt a flush of relief when she saw her ring and the letter staring right back up at her. It hadn't been a burglary, then.

She walked back out into the hallway and surveyed the rest of the doors just to be sure. None of the other rooms looked as though they had been disturbed. So, if it hadn't been someone looking to steal her jewellery, had they been there to steal *her*? Was that how the spy – whoever it was, or whoever they were working with – was going to get away with what they were doing? Silence her before she could reveal their identity?

Poppy's palms felt clammy and she started to panic as she realised how much danger she was in. Whoever the spy was, they now knew for certain that she was on to them, and they were obviously looking to keep her quiet. Had it been Edith in her room or Geoffrey? Or had one of them sent somebody even more cold-blooded to deal with her? Poppy threw on her uniform, grabbed her wedding ring and the letter, and then rounded up some clothes. She only had her trunk, and she didn't want to attract any attention, so she bundled everything up in her sheet and sprinted out of the hostel and into the township.

Once the cold morning air hit her face, Poppy realised that she had no idea where she was running to. But her legs kept moving. She couldn't go to Grace or any of the other WPS recruits. Whoever was after her clearly wasn't afraid to show their face at the hostel and she didn't want to put any of her friends in danger. Racing through the streets, Poppy realised where she was headed. The family quarters. There was only one person who she could trust and although things were less than ideal between them right now, she had no other option.

When she reached Lawrence's house, Poppy tapped lightly on the door. When there was no answer, she banged loudly. A curtain twitched at the house next door and she realised that she was now past caring what anybody thought about her visiting unmarried men. She had no idea what the time was, but she hadn't seen anyone on her journey from the hostel to Lawrence's, which made her think the early shift must be well under way – meaning that Lawrence could well be at the police hut already. On a whim, she tried the door handle and she almost cried with joy when it opened. She praised Lawrence's slack security measures before resolving to have words with him about leaving himself so exposed to burglars.

Poppy checked around the house and the kitchen clock confirmed her fears – it was gone eight o'clock so Lawrence definitely would have started his shift by now. She couldn't very well tell him about the spy at the factory. Besides, she was terrified to venture there in case the spy or their cronies were waiting to swoop in and silence her. Knowing that nobody would think to look for her here – and thanking God that she had played down her relationship with Lawrence to Edith and the others, Poppy decided to wait for him to return. This was unquestionably the safest place for her. She just hoped that he wouldn't be too disgruntled when he came home to find her here. Settling down on Lawrence's comfy sofa, Poppy intended to rest for just a moment before getting to work on a master plan to present to Lawrence on his return. But almost as soon as she closed her eyes, her terrible night tossing and turning on Grace's cold, hard floor caught up with her and she was fast asleep.

35

Poppy dreamt of Lawrence. It was an odd dream; he was kneeling next to her and gently whispering her name as she lay on a sofa. As she started coming to, Poppy smiled to herself as she recalled the dream. Then she slowly opened her eyes and nearly fell on the floor in shock when she saw Lawrence sitting in front of her, smiling. It hadn't been a dream but real life – Lawrence was here right now, and he had been softly coaxing her awake. Rubbing her eyes and looking around in a panic, Poppy sat straight up and then relaxed a little as she took in Lawrence's living room and remembered where she was.

'Sorry, I didn't mean to give you a fright,' Lawrence said. It was clear he was trying to stop himself from laughing and Poppy was glad that her jumpy reaction had broken the ice between the two of them. She was also relieved to find that he didn't seem angry to have found her asleep in his house.

'I'm the one who should be apologising for giving you a fright,' she croaked with a hoarse voice.

'I'll fetch you a glass of water,' he offered, getting to his feet.

Lawrence must have finished his shift. No wonder Poppy's mouth was dry – she must have been asleep for most of the day! She took a big glug of the water when Lawrence returned, and he sat down beside her on the sofa.

'You really should be more careful with your security. Any old waif or stray could have let themselves in while you were out,' Poppy said sternly but giving Lawrence a cheeky look. She couldn't help but break into a grin when he laughed.

'But instead, I got you,' he replied. 'What a lucky man I am. But please don't tell Butcher – I'll never hear the end of it!'

Poppy giggled along with him. They were teasing each other again and she couldn't have been happier about it. But then she remembered why she was in his house in the first place and her heart sank.

'I suppose I'd better explain why I let myself in,' she said in a serious tone now. Lawrence nodded and Poppy took a deep breath before telling him everything, starting with her spotting Geoffrey at the factory in the middle of the night. He listened intently but did raise his eyebrows when she told him about Geoffrey's claim to be an MI5 agent. 'I know. I was shocked, too. But then I thought those top-secret agents are meant to blend into the background, aren't they?' Lawrence took a moment to consider that before shrugging and motioning for her to continue. She left out the bit about how she had suspected Lawrence of being the spy. She couldn't bear to hurt his feelings again, let alone how it would make him feel to know she had feigned illness to cut their lunch short. She reasoned with herself that that part didn't add anything to what Lawrence needed to know in order to help her – and it also made it easier for her to skip out the night when he had walked in on her and Geoffrey in her room. She was desperate for him to know that there hadn't been anything romantic between the two of them before then, and there hadn't been since, but now wasn't the time to bring all that up.

'And that's how I ended up letting myself into your house this morning,' she said with a sigh once she had finished. 'I'm very grateful for your relaxed security but I do think you should start locking the door from now on.'

'I normally do but I was in a rush this morning after sleeping in and it must have slipped my mind. I had a rough night the night before and hardly slept a wink so it caught up with me.' As soon as he'd said it, Lawrence flushed red and looked away, and Poppy felt herself turn crimson too. He had meant the night he'd had the run-in with her and Geoffrey. Poppy was searching for a response when Lawrence switched back to his normal self. 'Maybe that all happened for a reason, though. Because if I hadn't had a rough night the night before last then I would have slept normally last night, I wouldn't have been in a rush this morning, and I probably would have locked up this morning as usual,' he replied with a smile. 'On a serious note, Poppy, I'm so glad you felt you could trust me and that you felt safe here. I hate to think of you in danger with no refuge. I'm so relieved I forgot to lock up this morning.'

Poppy was relieved, too. She wasn't sure what she would have done if she hadn't been able to hide out at Lawrence's. She couldn't think of anywhere else she would have felt as safe.

'I'm really glad you came to me. We're going to get to the bottom of this together,' he added confidently.

'Well, I was meant to be coming up with a plan while I waited for you to finish your shift but . . .'

'You fell asleep on the job,' Lawrence teased, before growing serious again. 'I think I know how we can set a trap to catch the real spy.' Poppy motioned for him to elaborate. 'I'd need to get going soon to make sure Geoffrey and Edith are still at the factory, but what if I make sure they both overhear me talking about how I've got to be at the danger building at two o'clock tomorrow morning to escort a top-secret package to London? Whoever the spy is, they will know I mean the weapon, and they will surely be desperate to get their hands on it one final time before it's gone forever.

The Germans will want details of the finished product. We can stake out the danger building and take them down as soon as they come sniffing around.'

'That could work,' Poppy replied, nodding slowly. 'But who would you talk to about it? It will look odd if you just bound in and start telling munitionettes about an important job you have booked in.'

Lawrence frowned and rubbed his chin as he thought it through. Then his eyes lit up and he was smiling again. 'I know all the foremen at the factory! I'll go to the nitrating house and seek out whoever is on duty with Geoffrey. Then I'll walk around the workshop with them until Geoffrey wanders over to eavesdrop.'

'How can you be certain he will?'

'Because he's always into everybody else's business. I've had to pull him up for slacking countless times. All he's ever doing when I go in there is talking to the workers, and if I ever try and have a conversation with one of his colleagues, he drops everything to come and linger nearby.' Lawrence's distaste for Geoffrey made sense now. 'Whether he's the spy or the MI5 agent, he's not very subtle about it,' he added sniffily. 'Anyway, once he's within earshot then I'll mention how I'd best be off as I need a nap before the early-morning trip.'

Poppy felt a rush of excitement. 'That is perfect,' she beamed. 'But what about Edith? Do you even know who she is?' His face fell and he shook his head. They both sat in silence for a few moments before Lawrence jumped up.

'We have all the workers' records at the police hut!' he cried in victory. 'I'll go straight over there now and pull up her file so I can look at her photo. Then I'll drop into her section—'

'She works at the cordite section – the second unit in,' Poppy cut in.

Lawrence closed his eyes and gave a quick nod as if committing the fact to memory. Poppy went on to detail exactly what bench he would find Edith stationed at.

'I'll find the foreman there and tell him I need to check some of the equipment near Edith's bench. Then while I'm fiddling around, I'll start telling him about how I'm off on a special job in the morning and I'll make sure Edith hears me.'

'I think this will work,' Poppy said positively. 'But, should we be alerting anybody else? I mean, won't you get into trouble with your bosses if you set a trap to catch a German spy without running it past them first? What if something goes wrong?'

'I don't think we have time, Poppy. Whoever it is, they're on to you and you said yourself they had already been to your room. Also, we don't know if they're working with somebody else higher up who might be able to warn them. Time is of the essence here if we're going to keep you safe and, to be honest, keeping you safe is my top priority here.' Lawrence suddenly seemed embarrassed and he looked away from Poppy, as if he hadn't meant to reveal that he cared so much about her. Poppy's heart fluttered and she could feel herself blushing.

'Oh, Lawrence . . .' she started, but he waved her away and started rounding up his things. She longed to tell him that he was the one she had wanted all along. That was clear to her now. Whether Geoffrey was the spy or the MI5 agent made no difference. She'd made a terrible mistake kissing him back and she needed Lawrence to know that, but it was clear that Lawrence wasn't ready to have any kind of conversation about it all. And quite rightly so – they had a spy to catch first.

'I'm off to check Edith's details and make sure both she and Geoffrey hear me talking about accompanying the weapon in the early hours. Then I suggest we go and hide out near the danger building as soon as darkness falls. We only have one chance at this and we don't know how quickly the mole will pounce. If they're panicked, they might turn up soon as the night shift has clocked on and the factory grounds are quiet again.' Lawrence rushed to the door but he stopped just before leaving. 'Help yourself to something to eat from the kitchen,' he called back with his hand on the door handle. 'There's not much there but there's probably enough for a sandwich. And get some more rest – it could be a long night.'

Poppy smiled gratefully but she was worried about when Lawrence was going to get a chance to rest. She felt anxious the whole time he was out. She paced up and down his living room countless times and she made a sandwich, more to pass the time and distract herself than anything. She didn't have the stomach to eat it, not when she was so full of nerves. When Lawrence finally returned a few hours later he was looking pleased with himself.

'I didn't even have to make any small talk with the other foreman on duty before Geoffrey was hanging round just behind us trying to look inconspicuous.' He laughed. 'I chanced a glance over at him once I'd mentioned my special job and he looked ashen. He's definitely taken the bait.'

Poppy wasn't sure if she was relieved or more worried now. Had Geoffrey looked worried because he was the spy and he didn't want the weapon to be taken away before he'd got his hands on the final details? Or had he panicked because he was the MI5 agent and there were plans to move the weapon that he didn't know about, which would also mean he might never catch the mole.

'And Edith?' Poppy asked.

'Hook, line and sinker,' he said with a grin. 'She stopped what she was doing as soon as I walked into the section. I heard someone try and talk to her while I was still speaking to the foreman. I watched her bat them away out of the corner of my eye. She was definitely listening in.'

Poppy had a sudden panic. 'What if whichever one is the MI5 agent tells their handler and they step in, and it all goes pear-shaped?'

'There won't be time for that. That's another reason why we need to act so quickly. We can't give either of them a chance to get anybody else involved. Because if we leave enough time for MI5 to get involved then we're leaving enough time for the Germans to send in more manpower.' Poppy shuddered at the thought.

'Is that for me?' Lawrence asked, spotting the sandwich sitting on the side. Poppy nodded. She could at least make sure he was turning up for action with a full stomach, if there wasn't going to be time for him to get any rest. They didn't have long until the night shift clocked on, so there was no time for sleep. Poppy waited anxiously as Lawrence devoured the measly offering. She wondered when he had last eaten and the thought made her think about her last meal. She couldn't even remember. She was operating on nerves alone right now. Lawrence finished his last mouthful, then put on a dark jacket over the police uniform he hadn't yet changed out of.

'You're probably best off staying in your uniform as it's such a dark colour. Whoever sees us will just think we're on official business.'

'We're leaving . . . now?' Poppy stuttered. Her heart fell straight to the pit of her stomach when Lawrence nodded his head and he started towards the door. 'I thought we might have more time to talk through the plan,' she whispered, holding back.

'What's to discuss? We need to get to the danger building before the spy so we can catch them red-handed and hand them over to the authorities. The afternoon shift will clock off soon so we can blend into the crowds filtering in and out of the factory grounds as they leave and the night shift clock on.' Poppy knew he was right, but she felt terrified all of a sudden. She tried to move but she was frozen to the spot. 'The mole could very well go straight to the danger building after finishing their shift, Poppy. They might use the same cover of the bustle of the shift change as us,' Lawrence added urgently. Then suddenly his demeanour relaxed and he walked back towards her. 'We can do this, Poppy. You and me together. You're the best policewoman I know. Hell, you're better than some of the policemen I know.'

'Even Butcher?' she asked cheekily. She couldn't help it – Lawrence just had a way of making her feel so at ease and he brought the fun side out of her, even in a situation as stressful as the one they were in.

'Especially Butcher,' he said, grinning and holding out his hand. Poppy felt a burst of pride and grabbed her jacket. She might have messed things up on the romantic side with Lawrence, but at least she still had him as a firm friend.

36

Lawrence had been correct – of course. The two of them slipped in amongst the throngs of workers as the afternoon shift changed over with the night shift and they were able to hide in plain sight and make their way to the danger building. Nobody gave the pair of police officers a second glance. They ducked into the alley leading to the danger building – where Poppy had had her scuffle with Geoffrey – and they waited with their backs up against the wall until the last of the workers had trickled past. Once there had been no movement for ten minutes, they tiptoed towards the danger building to check all was as it should be.

'It's still locked up and there's no sign of anybody having entered recently,' Lawrence said as he carried out a check around the outside of the whole building. 'Wait here, I won't be long,' he instructed, turning off his torch and handing it to Poppy. Her eyes widened. 'I'll be a matter of seconds, and anybody headed for the weapon will have to get past me before they get to you, anyway,' he promised.

Poppy didn't move an inch as she watched him run back down the alley. Once his figure had completely disappeared into the darkness, she felt beads of sweat starting to gather on her forehead despite the chill in the air. But just as soon as he had gone, she saw movement headed back towards her. Feeling relieved that he really had been gone for a matter of seconds, she started to relax. Once the figure got close enough for her to make out a little, though, she realised that she couldn't be certain it was Lawrence. She couldn't see who it was because they were carrying a pile of crates, which were blocking out their face. The height and build looked like Lawrence but, as she squinted through the dark, she just couldn't be certain. Poppy felt her heartbeat speed up and she looked around for somewhere to hide. The narrow alley was the only way to get to the danger building and it led straight to the door. If this was the spy, then she would either have to confront them head on, or hide round the side of the building and hope Lawrence would get back in time to help her ambush them inside.

Taking a deep breath, Poppy carefully placed Lawrence's torch on the floor and drew her truncheon. She could do this on her own. She stood braced, ready to pounce as soon as the person behind the crates lowered them and spotted her. Where was Lawrence? She tried to look past the figure for somebody coming up behind them, but she couldn't see anything further down the alley and there was no second set of footsteps. Poppy was a bundle of nerves as the person stopped and lowered the crates. She was doing her best to look menacing with her truncheon raised but she could feel it shaking in her grip. When the figure stood back up, Poppy nearly collapsed on the floor in relief when she saw Lawrence's face from behind the pile.

'What on earth are you doing, Lawrence?' she hissed.

'I should be asking you the same thing,' he replied. 'Should I be concerned?'

Poppy screwed her face up in confusion before looking up and seeing that she still had her truncheon raised. She lowered her arm and put the truncheon back under her jacket sheepishly. 'Well, I couldn't see who was behind all of those,' she explained defensively.

'I'm impressed you were ready to take on the spy alone,' Lawrence said. 'Now, help me arrange these so we can sit behind them.'

Suddenly, everything became clear. They were going to hide behind the crates, so they had a good vantage point when the mole turned up. Nobody would approach the danger building if two figures could be seen waiting in the darkness, and if they hid round the side of the building then they wouldn't be able to see who was coming without revealing themselves and giving the culprit a chance to turn around and run away with a head start. This way they would have the element of surprise and they would be able to catch the culprit before he or she set foot anywhere near the weapon.

Lawrence and Poppy lined the crates up and settled in behind them. Lawrence had left the tiniest gap between the crates so that they could keep an eye on movement in the alley. As soon as they heard footsteps, they would be able to observe the spy walking down the alley, and they could pounce as soon as the culprit was close enough.

Sitting in silence waiting for the mole to appear, Poppy realised she felt happy and safe in Lawrence's company, despite the stress and danger of the situation they found themselves in. They sat behind one crate each, facing each other so that they would both be able to lean forwards and get a view down the alley as soon as they heard any noise coming their way. Now Poppy's eyes had adjusted to the darkness, she could just about make out Lawrence's face.

'Thank you so much for helping me,' she whispered. She knew she shouldn't really be talking but she needed to let him know how grateful she was. They had no idea how dangerous the spy was or what they might do now they were in a desperate situation. She had to set things straight with Lawrence in case anything happened to either of them. She was trying to find the right words to explain how she really felt about him and go some way to clearing up the mess she had made regarding her relationship with Geoffrey, when Lawrence responded.

'I'd do anything for you, Poppy,' he said quietly. 'I meant what I said earlier about keeping you safe. I'd rather lose my job than lose you.' There was real emotion behind his voice, and she could see that he was looking straight at her. His eyes twinkled in the moonlight as she stared into them. 'I knew as soon as I laid eyes on you that I would move heaven and earth for you. I didn't even know you, but something about you just felt like home.'

Poppy was stunned into silence. She thought back to their first meeting in the police hut and how she had felt a pull towards him so strong that she'd had to do her best to not get caught looking at him too much.

'I know it sounds silly and I'm making a fool of myself,' he added defensively, looking away. 'Your heart is clearly with somebody else.'

'No, Lawrence, I—' she started, but he continued talking over her.

'It's my fault for not acting sooner. I just didn't want to come on too strong after everything that happened with your husband. But I've always been a coward when it comes to affairs of the heart, so—'

'Lawrence, stop,' Poppy said quietly but firmly. It was her turn to interrupt him now. He looked at her again and she thought she could make out tears welling in his eyes, although she couldn't be sure. She longed to pull him into her arms and comfort him, but words would have to do for now. 'There's nothing going on between me and Geoffrey. And not just because he may or may not be a German spy. There never *has* been anything between us.' She felt a flash of guilt. She needed to tell him the truth. 'Well, seeing as we're being so open and honest, I must admit that I took a bit of a fancy to him.' Lawrence's face fell. 'I took a shine to both of you,' she added, reaching her hand over and placing it on his arm. 'I know it won't make things any easier for you and I appreciate that it makes me sound terribly dreadful. But, you see, I hadn't had feelings like that for such a long time and it all took me by surprise. I didn't think I was ready to move on from John and I never expected anything to go anywhere with either of you, so I was just enjoying the company of you both – as friends. I never set out to hurt anybody.'

'But you kissed him,' Lawrence said, and she could hear the hurt in his voice again. He pulled back gently, but it was enough to make sure that her hand fell away from his arm.

'He kissed me,' Poppy said, looking down at the floor. 'And, yes, I kissed him back. But I was in a bit of a state about this whole mole situation, and he was comforting me, and I guess I just got carried away with it. When you walked in and I saw your reaction, I knew I'd made a mistake. I tried to convince myself that Geoffrey was the man I'd wanted all along, but I haven't been able to stop longing for you.' Poppy paused for breath and suddenly felt grateful for the darkness as she knew it would be shielding her blushes. 'It's always been you,' she added, risking a glance up at Lawrence, who looked suddenly lighter.

'You don't know how good it makes me feel to hear you say that,' he whispered, leaning forward. Poppy felt butterflies whipping into a frenzy in her stomach as she leant forward too. Their lips were just about to touch when he abruptly pulled back. Poppy felt like she had been punched in the stomach, but she very quickly realised what was going on. Lawrence had twisted his body round and he was staring intently through the gap between the crates. Poppy opened her mouth to speak but Lawrence quickly put his finger up to his own mouth to motion for her to be quiet. And that was when she heard the footsteps. She put her hand over her mouth to stop any noise escaping and she tried to take long, deep breaths. This was it. The spy had taken their bait and they were about to catch someone red-handed attempting to steal top-secret British weapons plans to pass to the Germans.

The footsteps grew louder. Poppy edged her head closer to Lawrence's to try and catch a glimpse of the spy. Despite the seriousness of the situation, she felt the whole of her body tingle as their cheeks touched and she had to remind herself to stay focused on the task in hand. She was about to discover who had been deceiving her all this time and who was a true friend. But when the figure approaching them finally came into focus, Poppy didn't get the answers that she had been hoping for. Whoever it was wore a long, dark jacket and seemed to be hunched over, so that there was no way of knowing from the outline whether it was a man or a woman. To add to her confusion over who it was, the spy's face was also covered by a balaclava. But it didn't matter if it was Geoffrey or Edith – or somebody else altogether. Whoever it was, they just had to be stopped.

Poppy was dying to run out and confront the mole, but Lawrence held his hand out, palm facing her, signalling that he wanted her to stay put. She kept switching her gaze between his hand and the figure as it drew closer, willing for Lawrence to let her pounce. When were they going to reveal themselves? Suddenly, Lawrence pointed one finger in the air and then swiftly pointed it towards the danger building. They were in action! The pair of them darted out from behind the crates just as the spy was reaching the doors of the danger building. The figure jumped at the noise and then quickly turned around at the sight of Lawrence and Poppy hurtling towards them. Lawrence was ahead of Poppy. He reached out and grabbed for the figure. He seemed to have managed to grab hold but then Poppy heard a loud ripping noise and Lawrence stumbled backwards as the spy lurched forwards and continued at a pace. Lawrence had grabbed hold of the mole's jacket, but the figure had sped away so quickly that the fabric had ripped, leaving him holding a big chunk of it in his hands. Lawrence took a moment to regain his composure, but Poppy flew after the figure as it ran down the alley. She wasn't going to let them get away.

As they neared the end of the alleyway, Poppy knew the spy would need to slow down to get round the tight corner without flying into a brick wall. She gave herself a final big push so that she was able to lunge forward just as the figure slowed. Her heart pounded in her chest as she felt the material of the jacket firmly in her grip. The mole jolted and Poppy quickly grabbed a shoulder. She wasn't about to risk being left with a piece of coat in her hand like Lawrence. But as the culprit spun round to face Poppy, she saw a large knife glistening in the moonlight. No sooner had she spotted it than it was being thrust towards her. She had no choice but to let go of the spy and leap back to avoid being stabbed. As she stumbled back, the figure thrust the knife towards her again. She held her arm up defensively and then watched on hopelessly as the figure disappeared around the corner. She flinched when she felt a hand on her shoulder.

'It's me,' Lawrence said. There was concern in his voice and Poppy wondered why he wasn't as angry as she was about the spy getting away. 'Here, let me try and stop the bleeding.' Confused, Poppy looked down at where Lawrence's torch was now shining and saw that her jacket was ripped. Her legs went wobbly when she spotted a pool of blood on the floor underneath her arm. She had been so upset about the spy getting away and so full of adrenalin that she hadn't even registered the pain. But now she could see the dark red liquid, she winced. Lawrence was reaching into his pocket when a yelp made them both look up. The cry was soon followed by the unmistakable sound of flesh being thumped. Poppy and Lawrence immediately darted off in the direction

of the noises – it was coming from the same area the spy
had fled to. Poppy could hear scuffling noises now, but it
was still so dark. She strained to try and make out what was
happening as they drew nearer. Lawrence's flashlight scanned
the scene until it landed on two figures grappling with each
other, and Lawrence and Poppy both stopped dead.

'Who is it?' she whispered. One of the people was the
person who had slashed her arm. Poppy could see the balaclava as the figure tussled with their opponent, and the
realisation made her subconsciously cover the wound up with
her hand. Her whole forearm was feeling numb now. The two
figures were moving too quickly for Poppy to be able to make
out who the second person was. She couldn't even make out
their heights or builds in amongst their grappling and fighting.

'They've got a knife!' she yelled in warning.

'That's it, I'm going in to help,' Lawrence said firmly. He
passed his torch to Poppy and walked towards the fracas.
Poppy reached out her arm to try and stop him. She just
wanted to keep him safe. The spy had already taken a deadly
swipe at her – who knew what they might do once they were
cornered like this? But she had taken hold of the torch in
her good arm and a wave of pain swept over her as she
reached her injured arm out after Lawrence. Poppy stumbled
back in agony. Tears welled in her eyes as she watched on
helplessly while Lawrence approached the warring couple,
now lit up by his flashlight.

The balaclava-clad suspect took a step back and raised
the knife. Poppy could only see the back of Lawrence and
the second figure as they stood next to each other facing the
spy. Lawrence turned his head to the newcomer and they
both nodded in unison. Then, as quick as a flash, they leapt
into action. Poppy held her breath as Lawrence ran at full
speed towards the mole, who lunged towards him with the
knife. Poppy had to stop herself from screaming out. But

instead of getting stabbed, Lawrence stopped and pivoted on one leg while bringing the other one up into the air – and kicking the knife clean out of the spy's hands. The suspect lunged at Lawrence, but the newcomer was already on them; Poppy had been so concerned about Lawrence that she hadn't even spotted the newcomer sneaking up from behind.

The newcomer pulled the spy back and held them firmly in place as Lawrence gathered himself. Poppy waited anxiously for the newcomer's face to come into view. With everybody finally standing still, she smiled as she realised the spy was a lot taller than the person who had apprehended them. When Geoffrey's victorious-looking face popped out from behind the spy, Poppy almost wept with relief. Geoffrey was in the clear, and maybe the spy wasn't Edith, either? Could it be somebody else altogether?

Lawrence and Geoffrey each took hold of one of the struggling mole's arms as the flashlight continued to light up the space around them. Poppy hoped against all hope that there had been a big mix-up and that they would be presented with a stranger instead of one of the people she had spent so much time getting to know over the last few months. Someone she considered a friend. But as Geoffrey pulled the mask off in victory and the tell-tale blonde ringlets shook free, Poppy's heart sank at the sight of Edith's face, a look of pure hatred all over it as she stared straight back at her.

37

'How could you do this to your country?' Poppy asked, holding her forearm tightly to try and stem the flow of blood and attempting to cover the uncontrollable shake in her voice. She hoped that none of them could see the tears pooling in her eyes. As well as the incredible amount of pain in her arm, she felt overcome with emotion. First of all, there was the relief that Geoffrey had been telling the truth all along. Then there was the incredible sense of guilt she was feeling for having doubted him so much. On top of all that, she was battling the huge betrayal she felt from Edith, while her heart was breaking for Bessie and Marie, who had considered Edith another sister.

'My country?' Edith scoffed bitterly. This wasn't the Edith that Poppy knew and loved. This was a different woman all together. 'You mean the same country that murdered my parents?' Edith hissed angrily. Poppy could see the emotion taking over her friend now. What on earth had happened to her parents to make her want to take such drastic action in their memory?

'What do you mean?' Poppy asked quietly. She noticed Lawrence and Geoffrey loosening their grips on Edith and she relaxed a little, too. It was clear that all the fight had left the younger woman.

'I was born in Germany,' Edith announced proudly, straightening her back as a sign of defiance.

Poppy screwed up her face in confusion. 'But your accent. . .'

she began. She had never detected even a hint of a foreign accent in Edith's voice. Was she that good a mimic?

'My parents brought me to Britain when I was so young that it has always felt like my real home,' Edith explained. 'My parents kept their German intonation, but I picked up the accent of everybody else I grew up around.' She paused for a moment and looked deep in thought. 'My friends always used to laugh at the difference between the way I spoke and how my parents sounded. They would joke that my mother and father must have adopted me, but I knew we were related by blood.' She looked emotional again now and her voice was quivering as she talked. 'Sometimes the bond is just undeniable, isn't it?' she asked, looking straight into Poppy's eyes.

Poppy thought about how she had always felt about John – like there was something invisible pulling them together and keeping them interwoven, and then she looked to Lawrence and felt the same flutter in her stomach she had felt when they had first met. How he had told her that she felt like home to him. She looked back to Edith and nodded her agreement. 'So, what happened to them? Your parents?' she asked carefully.

'This country was our home, for all those years. We were accepted despite our obvious differences. We were happy here. I would never have dreamed of betraying Britain.'

'Then the war broke out,' Geoffrey said resolutely.

'As if the Aliens Restriction Act wasn't bad enough – making us register with the police, wiping out all our German newspapers and clubs. My parents had come here for a more liberal life and suddenly they were being controlled by a government again!' Poppy could feel the anger rising in Edith once more. 'Then we were being accused of spying for our Fatherland. The friends I had grown up with turned their backs on me. People spat at my parents in the street. I thought it would all calm down once the war was over, but when the *Lusitania* went down and the riots started, I knew the happy family life we had been leading for so long was doomed.'

Poppy racked her brains. She recognised the name. '*Lusitania*? Wasn't that the passenger liner sunk by a German submarine?'

'That's right,' Geoffrey answered. 'More than a thousand innocent people died.' Edith shot him a look and Poppy suddenly felt nervous.

'The papers were full of it, of course,' Edith continued, turning her attention back to Poppy. 'They were blaming us – the Germans who had lived here all our lives and had always considered ourselves a part of the community.'

Poppy remembered reading about the reaction in the newspaper at the time. 'But, I thought the riots took place in Liverpool – the home port of the ship? You grew up in London, didn't you?'

'The riots started in Liverpool, but they spread to the rest of the country. London was one of the worst-hit cities.' Poppy was slowly recalling the extent of the violence now. 'Not surprising, really, given the amount of hatred towards hundreds of innocent Germans who were living in the capital. We were against the war as much as everybody else there!' Edith paused again before continuing. 'My parents sent me off to stay with a family friend when they heard about the growing unrest and the spreading riots. I begged them to come with me. They thought I was in danger so surely that meant they were in danger, too. But they wanted to stay and protect our home. The home they had worked so hard for since arriving in Britain.' When Edith paused again, Poppy braced herself for whatever was coming next. She knew this wasn't a story with a happy ending. Edith sniffed and Poppy realised she was crying. Part of her – the part that had grown to love Edith as a friend – longed to reach out and comfort her. But the other part of her – the rational part – knew that there was no excuse for betraying Britain as Edith had done and putting so many lives in danger.

'Tell me what happened. Please,' Poppy pressed. She wanted to try and understand what could drive somebody to do what Edith had been doing.

'We lived near a row of shops that were mostly owned by Germans. When the rioters started smashing all the windows, my father rushed out to try and help. He was fiercely loyal. A good man. But the stress was too much for him. When I went back for the funerals, our old neighbour told me that my father confronted some looters before clutching his chest and collapsing in a heap. The neighbours tried to save him, but his heart couldn't cope with it.'

'Edith, I'm so sorry,' Poppy started, but Edith wasn't finished.

'He'd ordered my mother to stay inside to keep her safe, so she had watched it all from the window. She watched him die in the street trying to protect our neighbours' livelihood from the British who were too stupid to understand that we were on their side. She couldn't forgive herself and she couldn't live without him.' She paused and took a deep breath. Then suddenly her voice was full of venom. 'That's why I didn't think twice about betraying my country when somebody from the German government approached me and asked me to help. My parents died because you all thought they were moles. You made me into one!'

'All right, that's enough now,' Geoffrey said firmly as he took hold of Edith's arm again. 'We need to get you processed and make sure those plans are moved somewhere safer.'

Poppy was relieved. It was clear to her what had happened to Edith's mother, but she didn't want to hear the details. She'd heard enough. 'You punished us all for what happened. You're as bad as the rioters,' she whispered.

'You deserved it,' Edith hissed as Geoffrey led her away. Poppy was startled by how easily Edith could switch from the woman who had been her friend to the bitter German traitor.

'My handlers will need to speak to you both. Let's meet at the police hut,' Geoffrey called back over his shoulder.

Lawrence pulled a handkerchief out of his pocket and wrapped it around Poppy's wound. Then he put a protective arm around her and they walked in silence to the police hut. Poppy was lost for words. All she could think about was Edith's poor parents. But she still couldn't find any justification for Edith's terrible actions.

Inside the hut, Lawrence made a pot of tea and sat down next to Poppy. She rested her head on his shoulder and sighed.

'I know,' he whispered, running his fingers through her hair. 'But it's all over now – thanks to you.' Poppy's heart tingled and she smiled as her eyes drifted closed.

She started when the door flew open. Rubbing her eyes and sitting up straight, she realised she must have dozed off. When she looked up, Geoffrey was standing in front of her and Lawrence.

'Well, that was a turn-up for the books!' he exclaimed. Poppy went to drink her tea, but it was cold.

'I'll make a fresh pot,' Lawrence said with a laugh, getting to his feet.

'Actually, my handlers want a word with you now. Just a formality – they need to take a statement. Are you all right to go and see them at the main gates? Seeing as you're the big boss, they'll only need your version of events. They won't need to bother Poppy here.'

Lawrence smiled and nodded. He seemed to have changed his view on Geoffrey after seeing him in action. But he hesitated at the door.

'Don't worry, I'll look after Poppy until you're finished,'

Geoffrey offered as he made his way to the stove. Lawrence looked to Poppy and she smiled to reassure him that she felt safe with Geoffrey now. Lawrence gave her a wave and he was on his way.

'You came through in the end, then.' Geoffrey smiled as he prepared the pot of tea. Poppy squirmed uncomfortably in her seat. Had she detected an edge to his voice? Was he upset with her for suspecting him and keeping him in the dark about her plan with Lawrence? 'I told you that you could do it, didn't I? You should never have doubted yourself,' Geoffrey added cheerily. Relief washed over Poppy as she sat forward in her seat.

'I'm sorry for suspecting you,' she said awkwardly. Geoffrey looked serious as he sat down at the table opposite her and poured two cups of tea. 'It's just that Edith was so convincing and I really didn't know who to trust, so what we did tonight seemed like the best way to—'

'You did what any good agent would have done in the circumstances,' Geoffrey cut in. 'You were right to do what you did, and it worked. I'm proud of you, Poppy.' She couldn't help but beam. She'd been desperate the whole time to prove herself and she had finally done it — with Lawrence's help. 'I'm sorry for getting you involved in the first place. I know it took its toll on you.'

'I didn't give you much choice.' Poppy laughed.

'Well, you unearthed the mole in the end,' he said with a grin, giving her a wink. 'I'd suspected Edith for a while but she was too good to leave me any proof. You saved the day, love. I told you that you'd be the munitionettes' hero before long!'

Poppy felt so happy they were back on friendly, cheeky terms again so soon after she had as good as accused him of being a traitor. It just went to show how strong their friendship was that it could survive so many hurdles. And as she looked into his eyes, she knew that was just what they had – a true friendship. There was no doubt in her mind now that Lawrence was the man for her.

'He's good for you,' Geoffrey said, smiling warmly. Poppy screwed up her face in confusion. 'Lawrence,' he explained. 'I know we had our little moment, but I could tell from your reaction to him disturbing us that your heart was with him. That was my fault and I'm sorry – I shouldn't have kissed you when you were so upset.'

Poppy didn't know what to say. 'I'm sorry too. I shouldn't have kissed you back. I don't want to lose our friendship.' And she meant it. They had grown so close over the last few months. 'I think that because we get on so well, I got confused about whether we should be friends or more.'

'We'll always be friends. And if things don't work out with your man of the law, well, you know I'm not too bad at the old kissing lark.' He gave her another cheeky wink, and Poppy couldn't help but laugh as she waved the mischievous comment away.

Lawrence walked back in and Geoffrey got to his feet. 'I'll leave you two lovebirds to it,' Geoffrey said. 'Thank you for your help today,' he added, shaking Lawrence's hand.

Poppy smiled as Geoffrey left the hut. There was nothing she wanted more than the two main men in her life to get along, and she was thankful to see them on good terms. Lawrence sat down next to Poppy again, but this time he took her hands in his. She winced in pain as she moved her wounded arm.

'We need to go and get that looked at,' Lawrence said, his voice full of concern.

'I need to know what's happened to Edith first,' Poppy said firmly.

'They've taken her away to be questioned. We won't be seeing her again,' he explained.

Poppy's heart sank. She had known that Edith was in a lot of trouble – and rightly so. She wasn't sure what she had been expecting, but part of her had hoped to see her again before she was dealt with. To what end she wasn't sure. Now she just felt empty. 'What will happen to her?'

'I don't know exactly, but it won't be anything good.' Tears filled Poppy's eyes. She couldn't help but feel for her former friend despite what she had done. 'We did the right thing,' Lawrence said tenderly, drawing Poppy into his arms now, being careful not to touch her injured arm. She nuzzled her head into his chest and found that she felt so comforted there that she wasn't sure she ever wanted him to let her go.

She closed her eyes and an image of John flashed into her mind. She prepared herself to feel the familiar pang of guilt and sorrow, but this image of John was smiling at her. Poppy knew in her heart that he approved of Lawrence and that he was happy for her. She squeezed her eyes shut tighter and took a moment to thank John in her head – then the image of him faded again. Poppy thought back to Annie's advice at Christmas, and how she had told her she would know who the right man for her was when the time came. She slowly pulled away from Lawrence so that they were face to face, and she knew Annie had been correct.

'We make a good team, me and you,' Lawrence whispered, and before she knew it his lips were on hers and she was kissing him back – finally.

Epilogue

Poppy watched out of the window as the countryside gave way to buildings, roads and motor cars. When she felt a gentle squeeze on her knee, she turned her head and kissed Lawrence tenderly on the cheek.

'I still can't believe this is happening,' she said excitedly as more London landmarks chugged into view and the train started to slow.

'Let's take another look at the letter,' Lawrence said, grinning at Poppy like an enthusiastic schoolchild. She giggled and pulled it out of her pocket proudly. She couldn't quite believe that when she had left London for Gretna, she had been carrying John's last letter to her and her wedding ring in her pocket. And now she was returning to the city proudly wearing an engagement ring and with a letter from WPS headquarters telling her that she was to be awarded a commendation in recognition of her brave actions in bringing down a German spy. It really had been an eventful time at Gretna!

Poppy rubbed her arm as she thought back to the night Lawrence had proposed. She had ended up needing stitches on the wound Edith had inflicted and Lawrence had gone down on one knee while she was being stitched up at the factory hospital. It had all come as a bit of a shock, but Poppy didn't hesitate in saying yes; facing such danger together had made them both appreciate that time was of the essence – especially with the war still raging on. Lawrence had proposed without a ring, but his sister and father had happily agreed to let him use his mother's engagement ring to make things official. Poppy knew it brought Lawrence comfort to know she would always carry a piece of his mother with her.

And now the large scar on her arm brought her happy memories instead of reminding her of the night she discovered her so-called friend's treachery.

Marie and Bessie had been devastated when they'd discovered what Edith had been up to, but, with help from Jenny and Mrs Gilbert, they seemed to be coping by throwing themselves into working as hard as they could at the factory. Poppy had been astounded to learn that Marie's new-found wealth had actually been down to Edith. She had been giving Marie wads of cash but swearing her to secrecy, claiming she had been left a significant sum of money in a distant family member's will but she didn't want anybody else to know. Poppy wondered if it was her way of showing her friends that she cared about them, or just a way of throwing suspicion onto Marie.

'I think you'll have a letter waiting for you when we get back,' she said, squeezing Lawrence's hand. Poppy had worried that Lawrence might feel slighted that her actions were being rewarded and his had gone seemingly unnoticed – especially when the whole plan had been his idea. But he had taken the news gracefully and if he had felt disgruntled then he had never shown it.

'There is nobody more deserving than you are of this accolade, my dear,' he whispered into her ear. She still tingled all over when he did things like that. The train came to a stop and Lawrence got to his feet and held out his hand to help Poppy up. They had spent every spare moment between their shifts together since their first kiss and Poppy was desperate to introduce him to her Bobby Girls. But Maggie had written to tell her they hadn't managed to get any time off for the ceremony. Poppy had thought it rather mean of Frosty not to invite the two of them along, but then she supposed there was still a war raging on and the WPS was still desperately trying to prove their worth to the police commissioner, so they couldn't very well go dishing out days off willy-nilly.

Lawrence opened the train door and jumped down from the carriage ahead of Poppy. Then he spun round and grabbed her by the waist, lifting her into the air and onto the platform. Poppy held on to her hat and giggled. Straightening herself out, she heard the unmistakable giggle of a baby and felt a pang for Charlotte. It just didn't feel right coming to London and not seeing her best friends. But the noise also gave her a rush of anticipation; now that she had found love again, her hopes for a family of her own were now looking possible once more. Poppy looked up to see where the baby was and there, standing on the other side of the platform, was Annie, with Charlotte in her arms and Maggie by her side. Poppy felt a rush of love and nearly knocked a gentleman over as she ran directly towards them all at speed.

'I do apologise,' she heard Lawrence saying to the man from behind her, but she was just too desperate to hold them all to turn back. Poppy swept the three of them up in her arms and cried with joy as Charlotte babbled and grabbed at her hair.

'Hey, little one. Aunty Poppy needs to look her best; you leave the hair pulling for later,' Annie said playfully as she gently worked Poppy's hair out of the tot's chubby little fingers.

'I didn't think I'd be able to see you all,' Poppy cried as she took Charlotte from Annie and bounced her up and down.

'We wanted to surprise you,' Maggie said.

'I think you just about managed that,' Lawrence announced from behind Poppy.

'Oh, this is—'

'It's a pleasure to meet you, Lawrence,' Maggie said cheerfully. 'Now, let's go and watch our hero here get her commendation.'

'What a wonderful idea,' Lawrence replied. And as they all set off to the WPS headquarters together, Poppy couldn't help but think about how grateful she was feeling to be given this second chance at true happiness with her friends and a man who loved her.

Acknowledgements

I would first like to thank Thorne Ryan – for trusting me with your Bobby Girls and for your constant support and guidance. You've been a dream to work with! And to Olivia Barber: I was anxious about getting a new editor so far into the series, but you have been wonderful, and I can't thank you enough for all your hard work on this latest Bobby Girls tale. Also, massive thanks as ever to my agent, Kate Burke at Blake Friedmann.

I'd like to thank the Devil's Porridge Museum for supplying such great resources about HM Factory Gretna. I was disappointed that lockdown prevented me from visiting the museum, but I found a wealth of fascinating information on their extensive website as well as inside some of the booklets sold in their online shop, including my favourite: 'Lives of Ten Gretna Girls'. If I'm ever up that way I will definitely be paying the museum a visit!

I also discovered a lot of the smaller details about life at Gretna through reading *Gretna's Secret War* by Gordon L Routledge and *Timbertown Girls* by Chris Brader – who also wrote a PhD thesis about Gretna's female munitions workers in World War One.

A big thank you must also go to my family and friends for their patience while I've been busy with my Bobby Girls. And the biggest thank you of all goes to my mum for expanding Nana Daycare this time around to accommodate not only a toddler but a baby – there is no way this book would have seen the light of day without you!

I must also thank Beverley Ann Hopper, Janice Rosser, Deborah Smith and Louise Cannon: my online cheerleaders who have shown me incredible support from the very beginning. I'm so grateful that you are still enjoying my books and sending new readers my way.

And of course, you, reader – thank you for joining the Bobby Girls on their latest adventure.

I love this photo of WPS recruits at HM Factory Gretna.
I assume the gentleman in the middle of them all is one of the
factory's superintendents – looking extremely outnumbered,
just like Butcher and Baker in The Bobby Girls' War.

(Image courtesy of The Devil's Porridge Museum)

A DORNOCK GIRL'S COURAGE.

UNITIONS MEDAL FOR A MUNITION
WORKER.

On her factory tour, Poppy learned of a fire which broke out in one of the units and the heroic actions of one of the workers who prevented the flames from spreading. I based that tale on the brave actions of Maud Bruce. Maud, aged just 23-years-old at the time of the blaze, was later awarded an OBE. She lived to be 100 years old.

(Image courtesy of The Devil's Porridge Museum)

I was so impressed by this photo of the women workers getting stuck in at the nitric acid stores (mentioned in Chapter Ten). Some of the labour they carried out was a lot more physical than I had realised.

(Image courtesy of The Devil's Porridge Museum)

COTTON EXCHANGE

592 28.6.18

Gretna

Another example of how physical the work was for the women at Gretna. I was shocked when I read that some of the workers pushed the carts of materials for at least a mile between worksheds.

(Image courtesy of The Devil's Porridge Museum)

Bookends

When one book ends, another begins...

Bookends is a vibrant new reading community to help you ensure you're never without a good book.

You'll find exclusive previews of the brilliant new books from your favourite authors as well as exciting debuts and past classics. Read our blog, check out our recommendations for your reading group, enter great competitions and much more!

Visit our website to see which great books we're recommending this month.

Join the Bookends community:
www.welcometobookends.co.uk

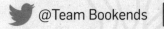 @Team Bookends 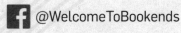 @WelcomeToBookends